BLOODY NIGHTS

BLOODY NIGHTS

LA VEGA VAMPIRE SHOWSTOPPERS, BOOK TWO

by

GINNA MORAN

ISBN 978-1-951314-62-0 (soft cover)
ISBN 978-1-951314-63-7 (hard cover)

Cover design by Silver Starlight Designs
Cover images copyright Depositphotos

For Inquiries Contact:
Sunny Palms Press
9663 Santa Monica Blvd Suite 1158
Beverly Hills, CA 90210, USA
www.sunnypalmspress.com
www.GinnaMoran.com

AUTHOR NOTE

Dear Reader,

All murders and heart punchings that come in this book are done so with love. I never write in my blood enemies as characters. The real people portrayed fictitiously asked to be or had won a contest to be included in the gore-filled Fright Fights madness you're about to endure.

With saying that...

Warning! This book is not for the faint of heart and contains triggering situations such as attempted rape, coercion, abuse, enslavement, human trafficking, self-mutilation for show, violence, gore, humiliation, forced pregnancy for population growth and other nefarious reasons, graphic consensual sex, male groin mutilation, fang removal, and men who go to extreme lengths to punish those who hurt their woman.

If you have a trigger, it could be in this book. Proceed with caution or not at all.

I DIG MY fingernails into the bloody dirt. My whole body screams in pain, my neck throbbing because of the vampire bite. Why won't he just kill me? Why won't he ensure my final donation?

He kicks me, rolling me onto my back. "Get up. Get up and fight."

I don't have it in me. All I can think about is death. I

don't care about life anymore. It was never good for me.

"You're acting as if you are weak. Get up now and show me what you got. If you don't get up, Lawrence will come back. You don't want him to do that. I promise." The rumbly voice of the vampire vibrates over my cheek as he kneels beside me and grumbles in my ear. "Please."

I blink a few times, my vision hazy. I don't understand why he is asking me so politely. He just attacked me, bit my neck, and instead of finishing me off, he's asking me to survive this torture.

"Kill me." My words come out as a breathy whisper, and I draw my attention to the vampire's face for the first time.

He's filthy. Blood and dirt stain his skin, but his eyes no longer flash silver with starvation. Of course not. He sucked my neck, filling himself up with what he needs to get himself in control. I've seen it time and time again in the casino of the Aris.

Doesn't mean anything, though. Just because he's satisfied in this moment doesn't mean he won't take more of my blood.

His mouth twitches, and his nostrils flare. I rip my focus away and stare at his clothes instead. A rip cuts down the center of the front of what I think might have once been a white shirt, showing off his muscular chest. Jagged tattoos mark his pecs, creating some sort of symbol. I don't know exactly what it is because part of his torn shirt covers it. It could be a coven crest, but I highly doubt it. Not if he's here. He looks like an imprisoned Strip dweller. We're not that far from La Vega...at least, I think.

"So, you're just giving up. That's fucking disappointing after what Lawrence told me about you. He thought you would be badass and not some weak, pathetic donor." The vampire clicks his tongue. "You're supposed to be better than that."

My mouth trembles with his words. Me, badass? I can't be. The few times I've tried nearly got me killed. "I'm not. Sex, blood, and bringing in customers. That's all I'm worth. Lawrence was mistaken."

Something dark flickers in his eyes, and they flash with what could be blood hunger or desire. Maybe both. Now I regret even mentioning it, but he needs to lower his expectations. He wants me to fight him, but I don't know how. I'm just a blood donor and dancer.

"Hmm. Of course, you think you are. The La Vega asshole leaders made sure you'd think nothing more of yourself. I'm here to prove them wrong. Now, get up. Get up and fight me. You won't like what happens if you don't." The vampire flashes his fangs, extending them. He bites his wrist and holds it above my face, using his other hand to part my lips until blood pools in my mouth. "You saw the herd out there."

I intake a sharp breath at not only his comment but also at the tingles zinging down my throat to bloom warmth in my stomach. My body loses control, and I snatch his arm and yank it to my mouth, latching my lips to him. His blood tastes unlike anything I've ever experienced.

And damn it.

With his blood, the pain in my body subsides. My stomach roars in hunger, and I moan as the sweet, warm liquid courses through me, healing my wounds and filling me with energy. He's forcing me to live instead of allowing me to beg for death.

He yanks his arm away after another minute, and a surprising guttural growl escapes my lips. I try to grab him again, but he stands up and puts space between us. It takes everything in me not to lunge at him in an attempt to get more.

What is wrong with me? I feel on the verge of...something unexplainable. It's the same feeling I would get before a show, listening to the audience call for blood. But this time, I feel as if I'm the one about to shout for another taste.

"You like that, don't you?" The vampire presses his hand over his puncture wounds, staunching the bleeding.

"If you get up, you can have more. Wouldn't you like that? I can see it in your eyes. Lawrence wasn't kidding about you."

I heave a couple of breaths, my chest rising and falling as I process his words. Lawrence told me unbelievable things during the car ride here, and this guy obviously believes him. But me? I can't. If I believe that I'm the dhampir he claims me to be, it makes this real.

This can't be real.

The vampire wiggles his fingers at me with a teasing smile that digs under my skin. He bites his arm again and taunts me as if I'm some sort of wild animal.

Fuck. This is real.

My stomach screams in pain, the noise loud enough to send the vampire's eyebrows shooting up his forehead.

"What will it be, my showgirl?" he asks, smirking. "Come to me for another taste, and then we'll fight. Doesn't that sound more fun?"

"No, and I'm not your girl," I snap, digging my fingers into the ground again, trying to find the strength to push myself up. It's not that I feel weak anymore, but I'm afraid. I'm terrified. I thought I was going to die, and now that I'm not...this is all so fucked up.

"But you are. You're going to be my perfect performer. Neither of us has a choice. Lawrence said he was bringing you here, and the only way I get out of the fucking herd myself is if I get you in shape for the Fright Fights." The vampire cracks his neck and rolls his shoulders. "Help me and I'll help you. Either do that or face whatever twisted shit Lawrence has as a backup plan if you don't comply."

Tears burn my eyes. I can't do this. I can't be here. I just hope that the Bella Crew manages to find me. Maybe I can hold on a little longer. I know how to survive. I just…I don't want to survive like this. It was one thing being an obedient Gemstone. This is far, far worse. A show called the Fright Fights sounds fucked up. But I must hold on. I need to do it not only for my guys, but I also need to do it for my friends. I need to do it for Mya.

"This is so messed up. I don't even know what you're talking about or what's really going on. I don't belong to Lawrence. He kidnapped me. I know my master will come. A whole lot of vampires paid for a part of a contract for me. Lawrence isn't going to get away with this." I don't know why I say any of this, but it feels as if saying it out loud helps me get my shit together. I thought Alexander was bad. But this situation? It's fucking worse.

The vampire raises an eyebrow. "If you're here, that means he has gotten away with it, my showgirl. Stop dwelling on what you have been through and focus on what is happening now. I'm sure you're starving. Like I said, if you come here, I'll give you some more blood. Wouldn't you like that?"

My stomach growls, proving that despite my mind shouting fuck no, my body craves to experience his blood again. It's the strangest thing to feel as if his blood will satiate me in a way it never has before. This is more than healing me.

"I just need food. I don't want your blood." I rub the back of my hand across my mouth.

"The hell you don't. You're a dhampir. You survive on vampire blood." Biting his arm again, the vampire extends his wrist to me, slowly stepping forward.

Oh, no. I can smell it.

Impossible.

He's wrong. He must be wrong. I can't believe what Lawrence told me and what this guy is telling me now. There's no way Alexander bit my mother while she was pregnant with me, turning me into a half-vampire and half-human. I would've known. Right?

As I think about the words, I think about my life growing up at the Aris Hotel. I try to think of all the times that I've been given blood. And it has always been to help me heal or to make me feel better when I was sick. As a child, I used to get sick often. I never really thought about it because as I hit maturity and as an adult, the stomach pains went away. I always thought it was normal hunger because I went without.

Fuck. It makes sense. I was also getting more blood from Opal and Alexander. Almost every night because of Vampire Nights.

"Come on. Have another taste if you want. Maybe you'll think more clearly and behave for me." He tilts his arm, getting the blood to stream toward his elbow.

It steals my attention away from my thoughts, and I fly forward as if I'm catapulting from the ground during a floor routine. I jump at him with a scream. He spins out of my way, and I nearly eat shit on the ground. My feet slide across the slippery dirt. Locking his hand to the back of my shirt, the vampire hoists me to him and envelops me in his arms.

I scream and buck my body, jerking my head back and smashing it into his face. Pain explodes in the back of my skull, and stars pepper my vision. The force of my move is enough to get him to release me. I don't know how I do it, but I manage to spin on my feet and launch at him. This time, he doesn't have a chance to move. We collide together, and he takes the brunt of our fall, catching me as I land on top of him.

I freeze at our closeness, our faces only inches apart. His startling green eyes flash silver, and his sharp fangs peek out from beneath his plump top lip. The longer I look at him, the more handsome I realize he is. He might be dirty, but he is probably the type to clean up well.

"My showgirl, take what you want. You've earned it." The vampire's voice deepens with his words, and he tilts his head sideways, showing off his throat as if our roles are reversed, and he's the donor while I'm the vampire.

It's enough to knock some sense into me.

Swinging my hand, I slap him across the face and hop to my feet. I rush across the muddy, bloody room and toward the door. I need to get out of here. I need to escape. If I stay in this room, I don't know what will happen. This guy already told me he has a deal with Lawrence. He claims he wants to help me, but I highly doubt that's the case. He's just here for himself.

"Not so fast." Strong hands lock onto my shoulders, and the vampire jerks me away from the door and spins me around.

I don't even have a chance to react as he yanks my hair and bends my head to the side. I gasp as he sinks his fangs into my throat again, sending shooting pain through my body. His bite is far deeper than necessary to draw blood. He is doing it on purpose. He wants to hurt me.

I shriek and step on his bare feet with my shoes, trying everything I can to break away from him. He grunts but doesn't let me go. Thrashing my body, I wiggle so much that he can't lock his lips to his puncture wounds for long. I elbow him in the gut, my sudden movement enough to wind him. I twist around and shove my hands to his chest, knocking him back.

And holy shit.

My push sends him flying off his feet and into the wall, my strength unlike anything I've experienced before. He hits the metal with a clank and drops to the ground. How in the hell did I do that? There's no way.

Shaking his head, the vampire chuckles. "That's what I'm talking about. I knew you had it in you, my showgirl."

Anger rushes through me, the adrenaline helping to ease the pain in my neck and shoulder. "Stop calling me that. My name is Hayley. I'm not your fucking showgirl."

"Hayley is a beautiful name. I like it. Lawrence only ever called you his heir." His comment surprises me, and I'm stunned silent, watching him get to his feet. He rubs his filthy hands on his pants and flashes me a smile.

I'm like a donor on the Strip. I can't get myself to move as he closes the space at vampire speed. Reaching up his hand, he combs my short hair from my face and behind my ear. It feels as if he's going to lock me in his stare and manipulate my mind.

He doesn't. I don't think he can because I consumed

his blood.

"But you're going to need something tougher for the stage. I go by Savage Saint instead of Cooper." He inspects every inch of my face, from my eyes to my nose, and then he studies my lips for an extra-long time. I should step back. I should put a dozen feet of space between us for what he's done to me, but my feet refuse to move. My mind and body shut down on me. I can't help it. It's how I've always survived before. With Alexander, I could never fight. It would end far worse than if I just gave in.

"Savage Saint? You're a performer?" I wish my curiosity would chill out. I shouldn't keep this conversation going.

"A fighter. Does that surprise you?" he asks.

I shrug. Instead of saying what's on my mind, I say, "What about Ruby Vixen? I respond to that name as well." Hearing me call myself Ruby opens an invisible wound inside me. A dozen memories flit through my head about my life at the Aris Hotel. Ruby has gotten me through Hell and back. Maybe that's why I mention it. If Ruby got me through Hell before, Ruby can do it again.

"That won't do. You're supposed to be a new Blood Princess performer and not the stolen possession of Alexander Aris. From now on, you're going to be Violent Violet. Has a nice ring to it, doesn't it?" The vampire, Cooper, smirks with his words.

I tighten my jaw. "I hate it."

"Good. Maybe you won't fall into the act of living that persona then. Some of the other donors and vampires tend to...never mind. I'm sure you'll find out." He finally drops his hand from my face, but the cool sensation of his fingers lingers.

"Tell me. What does that mean?" I need answers. I didn't know how badly I needed them until this moment. Lawrence had mentioned a performance, except it doesn't sound anything like what Alexander has set up.

Jerking me around, Cooper locks his hand across my chest and forces me forward. I try to fight him again, but it's as if my strength vanishes. "That's something you can ask our master. He's coming right now."

I stiffen as the door clinks and rattles, and the lock slides open with a screech. Cooper walks with me, practically pushing me to keep moving. He jerks me to a stop when he thinks we're close enough, and his body molds against mine. I twitch my fingers, considering trying to punch him in the cock. I can feel his hard-on pressing against me. Damn horny and hungry vampires. All they ever want is to suck and be sucked. I'd call him out if my heart didn't pick up in erratic beats.

Fear courses through me as the door cracks open, and Lawrence peeks his head in with a smile wicked enough to stab through me. I tremble at the sight of him. I shouldn't be so afraid of a vampire after everything I've been through, yet here I am on the verge of tears. There is something monstrous about him. I can't put my finger on it, but my human fear rationale classifies him as the bigger predator, even though Cooper attacked me.

"Did you get a good enough taste, Hayley? It looks as if you've already gotten stronger." Lawrence drinks me in from my dirty feet to my bloody face. Cocking his head to the side, he studies the way Cooper grips me from behind but reverts his attention quickly back to me. "That's very pleasing for me to see."

His words snap the fear right out of me, and I manage to throw myself forward and out of Cooper's hold. Lawrence growls and whips his arms up, but all he can do is brace himself for my attack. We hit the concrete floor outside the room, and I link my fingers through his graying hair, pinning him in place. He doesn't try to fight me. All he does is smile.

It pisses me off.

"It would be in your best interest to get her off of me." Lawrence doesn't talk to me, keeping his voice even in tone. "If she bites, you will end up in the herd together. But you would like that, wouldn't you? I see you've encouraged her to drink from you several times."

"I wouldn't have had to if you hadn't starved me before tossing her in the room. She couldn't get up. It was the only way to ensure her good health. I drank a lot. I couldn't help myself." Cool fingers latch under my arms, and Cooper drags me off Lawrence. He restrains me against his chest and returns to the room with me.

"It was important. You know dhampirs need to be threatened a bit to really get them motivated. This one in particular has been sheltered and doesn't know her own capabilities. It's up to us to push her. What better way than to put her in a situation where neither of you was in control." Lawrence dusts off his tailored suit and straightens his back. "If you have a problem with my method—"

"I don't," Cooper says, cutting off Lawrence's oncoming threat. "I was only explaining the circumstances."

Turning his attention to me, Lawrence steps closer and narrows his eyes. "What about you, my dear? Did you enjoy the taste you got? Do you understand what I was talking about on the ride here?"

My stomach twists with his words, and I don't respond.

"Answer his questions, Hayley," Cooper whispers so quietly that I don't think Lawrence heard him. I'm not even sure I should be able to hear him now. Something's different. I can hear more than his whisper. I hear his heart beating.

I slowly shake my head, silencing the noise buzzing around me. "I don't understand any of this."

Lawrence huffs a breath in annoyance, and I tense and prepare for him to smack me for speaking the truth. He doesn't. How am I supposed to wrap my mind around the fact that I'm not who I thought I was my entire life? How am I supposed to understand that he supposedly bit me with his venom to prove I'm not a normal donor? If I was, I would've transformed. Or died.

Stepping back, Cooper puts another foot of space between me and Lawrence. I expect Lawrence to snap at him, but all he does is tighten his fingers into fists and continues to glower.

"She will understand soon. I will teach her," Cooper says, his chiseled body flush against my back. "I just need time."

Lawrence doesn't respond right away, staring at the two of us as if he can read our minds. My breathing quickens under his scrutiny. I want so badly to yell at him, but I know better. I'm lucky he hasn't already beaten the shit out of me. If I ever went after Alexander like this, I'd get the paddle.

"How much exactly? What is your assessment of her?" Lawrence asks, keeping his eyes trained on me. Without having to ask, I know he now regards me as a threat. Something about it satisfies me on a deep-seated level.

"With enough training, she will be an excellent fit as a headliner for the Fright Fights." Cooper breathes a cool breath against my ear.

"I asked you how long." Lawrence leans in the doorway, his frame seemingly bigger within the small entrance to the disgusting cell.

I can't help darting my eyes to look at the weird, twisted room behind him with the stacked beds filled with donors and vampires, taking it in again. The herd. That's what they both called it.

"A couple of weeks if you really want something spectacular." Pushing me forward, Cooper finally releases his grip on me. "Things like this take work. We have to break the habits instilled in her by Alex."

"I want her in a show within the week. Even if it's just the opening act." Lawrence flares his nostrils with his words as if hearing Alexander's name sets him off. "We don't need it to be spectacular. We don't even need a full house. All it will take is a couple of people, and word will get out. We will be able to get this fucking hellhole in shape."

Cooper hums under his breath with his agreement. "Then don't put her among the herd. We will need every hour we can get."

"I suppose that will work. But if she fights or resists..." Lawrence's voice trails off, and he motions behind him by tipping his head back. "Do you understand, Hayley? Give me a good show, and maybe I'll reward you. Resist, and you will regret ever being born."

Except I already do.

This is too much.

How will I ever survive?

Oh, right. These fuckers will make me.

This is now my new fucked up life.

2

SAWYER

CONDITIONS

"I DON'T GIVE a fuck. You can take every goddamn thing I have. We were set up. We know it was you, Aris." Monroe slams his fists on the table separating us from the La Vega Leadership. "You wanted us to break the contract, so you had somebody kidnap Hayley. We were not at fault."

Knox grabs the back of Monroe's jacket and holds him,

ensuring he doesn't jump across the table and start beating the shit out of one of the leaders. I wouldn't put it past him to do so in his state of fury, but there are too many of them and not enough of us to get out of this alive. He would probably only get in a couple of punches before one of the fuckers would take his heart. They're ancient shits—from before the uprising—and rumor has it that they helped start it. It's how they managed to take over Las Vegas and mold it into La Vega under their authority.

And fuck them. I don't want to lose Monroe like that. I would die protecting him. He's like a coven brother to me. A blood brother, even. And if something happened to us, Hayley would...fuck. I can't think about it.

My chest tightens at the thought of her with some strange, sadistic asshole. Who the fuck knows what he's doing to her? He collared her like a pet. There are far too many monsters in our world, and though the leaders are some of the worst, there are others out there that could top everyone. I've seen it for myself. I shudder at the thought.

Aris straightens his back in his chair and laces his fingers together, raising an eyebrow. He ignores Monroe and turns his attention to me. I've always been the face of the Bella Crew, and it's not unlike people to disregard Monroe because he is our fighter and security while I tend to the bigger stuff like our donors and our alliances. He's also younger, which means when it comes to power, I beat him. But I would never rub that in his face. He is as much my equal as Knox is.

"Do you have any proof, Mr. Noble?" Aris asks, showing off the tips of his fangs with his serious expression. "You cannot come in here and accuse me of wanting to break a contract without it. There are more important things to attend to, don't you think? Like where my donor is. That should be the concern, which is why you're here to be held accountable in the first place."

This fucking asshole. He says it as if he cares about Hayley. It digs under my skin, because the only thing he cares about is his power, wealth, and his control over La Vega. He sees the Bella Crew as a threat and would absolutely try to steal our power through breaking a contract without regard as to what happens to Hayley.

"Yes. I know you think that we're stupid and weak for not having a leadership position or qualifying to unite legally as a coven, but we have what it takes despite what you think. I have all the documentation, the surveillance videos of the man stating that Hayley is his heir and it was illegal for you to put her up for auction, and I also have surveillance records from several other crews along the Strip proving it. Don't underestimate me, Aris. You can't take down the Bella Crew that easily." I growl with my words and set my com device on the table before the silent leaders. They all allow Aris to speak, which is a load of shit to begin with. He shouldn't be the one handling this because Hayley is his property. It's a conflict of interest.

Aris darts out his hand, trying to snatch the com device from the table, but the man beside him intervenes and scoops up my tablet. He scours the screen, flicking his finger over the evidence with a smirk softening his stern features.

"Alex, he has substantial evidence." The leader of The Grand smiles wider.

"I'd say so, Starks." Another leader snatches the device. The vampire, Reed, who I have only seen one other time, hands my device over to the other four leaders of the La Vega Leadership. He controls the Golden G and the downtown Frem area. "This is rather interesting, Alex. It seems that Mr. Monroe is indeed telling the truth."

I remain expressionless despite his hesitation in addressing Monroe. Everyone in the Bella Crew refuses to take on any sort of surname until we qualify to come together as a coven under the Noble name and the leadership refuses to admit control over the Bella, so they stumble like dipshits over trying to assign formal titles in this fucked setting. The scared little dicks feel threatened by any sort of alliance outside of their terms, and they should be. If they'd smarten up, things could be different. Now we have to change things by force.

Proving ourselves now is the first step.

Thank the fucking universe for our paranoia and pre-paredness. Without it, Aris would've screwed us.

"The hearsay against them must be discarded," Reed adds, glancing to the rest of the leaders. "Do your due diligence next time, Alex. If you had, we wouldn't have a possible predicament."

Aris grumbles under his breath. "What are you talking about?"

"What seems to be retaliation for your dearly departed coven sister. It looks like Lawrence is up to his old ways again and is taking advantage of your...rash decisions. Now our redistribution of The Whiskey township has gone to waste." Augusta flashes his fangs. The leader of Tru glances between Aris and the tablet before looking at me. He slides it back without allowing Aris to get a look. "Perhaps you shouldn't have executed his blood sister in front of an audience. You deserved to have your best performer taken from you for that behavior."

Aris slides his chair back and stands up, unsheathing a blade from his jacket. "I did what was lawful. Opal had betrayed me. She put the whole foundation of La Vega at risk. You should thank me."

"You want a thank you for something that was your fault to begin with? I think not. You must deal with this on your own. I suggest if you don't want a problem with those who hold your donor's contract, then you need to retrieve her. We will stand by the law regarding this matter. You have toed the line far more often than any of us. Either pay the fees for breaking the contract or work something out. I'm sure you have other donors that could fill her place." The only woman leader, Narcisa of the Tropic Hotel, rubs her lips together, smoothing out her plum-colored lipstick. She turns her attention to Monroe. "How does that sound? You can pick any of the other dancers to fulfill the contract."

Monroe shakes his head with a snarl, his anger rolling through his muscles. I join Knox and restrain Monroe's other arm, stopping him from lunging.

"We paid for Hayley. We want Hayley." Knox steps in front of Monroe, ensuring his safety. He's always been better at smoothing out disagreements. "And if you don't have enough power or backing to get her, we will offer our services to you, Aris. If you provide us with the resources, we will bring her back ourselves. Under a few conditions."

Aris flares his nostrils. He opens and closes his mouth, but whatever he plans to say he ends up keeping to himself.

"That sounds acceptable," the leader of the Palace says.

I think his name might be Biddeford, but I can't be certain. Only the coven names are ever shared among the populace unless you meet one of the leaders directly.

"Acceptable? Far from it. I'm sure their conditions mean that they keep my donor permanently." Aris points his dagger in my direction. "Which will never happen. She is mine. She was born an Aris and will remain one."

"According to your contract, she also belongs to Monroe and five others. It would be in your best interest to comply and prevent any disagreements among those who show interest in power on the Strip. We will not go to war because of your ego. You have done enough damage already." Starks presses his palms together, eyeing Aris and daring him to argue.

"What will it be, Alex? Accept the Bella Crew's offer for help or arrange something with Lawrence yourself. It is quite obvious that if one of the crews stands up and wants your headlining dancer, then surely the others will as well. This is all on you." Augusta gets to his feet and nods at the others of the leadership. "Give us your answer by the end of the day. Meeting adjourned."

Without another word, the five vampires of the leadership vanish, leaving Aris standing in front of us with a glower plastered on his face.

It takes everything in me not to go after him this second. Without the leaders here, it would be so easy. We could destroy him and move on from this mess.

But if we do...I'm not sure we will manage to get Hayley back or possibly get out of here alive. Our power and influence only goes so far and killing him is a death sentence. One of the leadership members mentioned that Lawrence controls The Whiskey, which is in a small town outside of La Vega. It's even wilder than within the walls here. I've never been, and I'm not sure I could ever afford to without giving away most of my donors to do so. It takes a lot to pay for a pass out of the city.

"Last chance to agree with us. Our condition for doing your dirty work is that you will ensure Hayley is not treated as a prostitute or sex slave. You'll ensure that her only duty at the other hotels is to perform her aerial acrobatics show. You will also allow her to pick a couple of her friends to join her for support. And after her contract is up, we want you to approve a coven union for the Bella Crew as Nobles and allow one of us a Blood Vow to Hayley." I cross my arms over my chest and straighten my back to tower over him. There is no one as tall as me in La Vega, and I always use my height as an influencer and way to intimidate. It's kind of hard to terrorize somebody who always looks down at you.

"A Blood Vow? Impossible. Though, I might be able to

arrange a coven contract with some of those on the Bella Crew. That is my offer. I will not be pushed around. You started this mess. Hayley is precious to me despite what you think. She is not like other donors. You must understand who she is and what she is to fully grasp how to handle her." Alexander shifts on his feet and scratches his hands into his hair, his voice lowering. "Lawrence understands this and will use it against all of La Vega. I know him. There is a reason he is not part of the leadership here."

My brows furrow at his words. What the fuck is he talking about? I already know Hayley isn't like other donors, which is why I want forever with her. It's why I will do what it takes to transform her into a vampire.

"We need the Blood Vow. That is our number one condition. Hayley will not be a donor after her time is up as a performer. She will be one of us." Knox cracks his knuckles, his body rigid. We don't care who acquires the legal contract with the leadership as long as she gets recognized as a Bella resident. "We will get her regardless, so make this easy on yourself, asshole."

Aris surprises us by tipping his head back with a laugh. "Stupid, stupid man. You all think you know so much. You have no idea. The leadership has no idea. Hayley will always be a donor. She cannot transform. She was born to serve me. I'm the one who created her."

Monroe breaks away from Knox and jumps over the table, colliding into Aris. He smashes his back into the wall and sucker punches the asshole in the face. Blood squirts from his nose, but Aris doesn't fight back. All he does is laugh harder. If I thought Monroe could get away with it, I'd allow him to take the fucker's fangs. But something about what he says doesn't sit right with me. He said he created Hayley, and I don't think he meant in the way of teaching her the art of aerial acrobatics and performing. It's something different. Something darker.

But what?

"I should fucking cut off your dick and shove it down your throat. How you could be so cruel to the most magnificent woman I have ever met is beyond me. What the fuck is wrong with you?" Monroe snarls and spits in Aris's face. Punching him once more in the gut, he sends Aris bowing forward and steps away to stand beside me.

"You'd be dead before you could even try. There's nothing wrong with me, and you will figure it out soon enough. I will take you up on your offer to bring her back. You will have access to my resources. If you can manage to bring her back alive, then perhaps I will share a secret with you. I will agree to pay for your coven union myself. I will also let you think that you can have a Blood Vow. But be prepared. It is impossible and none of this comes without a price. Hayley is mine and always will be. If you want her, you can serve me beside her." Aris heaves a couple deep breaths, his eyes flashing with his fury.

"Fuck no. We will not fucking serve you." I bare my fangs with my words. "We can continue our agreement."

"If you allow me to acquire part of the Bella." Aris knows we'll agree. The one thing that matters is Hayley. Everything else we'll figure out later.

"Five percent. No donors. Only property," Knox stabs his knife into the table. "Don't try to negotiate anymore. We have the upper hand. If you weren't concerned about whoever the fuck Lawrence is, then you would've denied us already and gone after him. We know you Aris. You don't let people get away with shit without reason."

Aris glances between us. "Do you know how I got into the position of power I'm in? Intelligence. Strategy. I pick my battles carefully, and one with Lawrence is unnecessary. If you want to retrieve Hayley, that's fine. I'll humor you...but I doubt you'll succeed."

This fucker. I will prove him wrong. He underestimates us the same. It's why he's still alive. We pick our battles. Hayley is worth fighting for.

"Say that when I return and shove Lawrence's balls in your damn mouth." Monroe cracks his neck. "Now tell us. Do we have a deal?"

Aris tightens his jaw. "We do as long as you get the others with Hayley's contract to comply and not come after me through the leadership. That is my other condition."

I scowl at him. "Fucking fine. You have a deal."

"You guys can't be fucking serious. You're going to abandon us? For how long? And outside of the city? You need to fucking name who is in charge while you're gone." Walcott stabs his knife into the middle of an old poker table. He keeps his voice low to prevent the others from overhearing our conversation. Apart from him, we only allow Govan and Tatum to really know what's going on. All the others don't need to know our business. They're a part of the Bella Crew because they help with things around here. They're not one of us because of trust.

"You know it's going to be fucking you, Walcott." Monroe shoves him in the side and then punches him in the stomach, sending him flying back a few feet.

Walcott growls and unsheathes a throwing knife. He flicks his wrist, aiming it at Monroe. Knox jerks out his hand and catches the blade by the hilt and throws it toward one of the broken slot machines, sinking it into the side.

"I vote for Tatum. She has more intelligence than both

you and Govan combined." Knox smirks at Tatum. "She'll also keep shit together if we can't make it back. The donors love her. They're who are important."

"You have to fucking take me with you then. I can't stand around and be Tatum's little bitch. You know she loves a good power trip. What do you say, Sawyer? You know I'm good for something. I'll fuck some people up. Watch your back." Walcott scratches his fingers into the sides of his neck. "The trip sounds like fun."

"The three of us going is already risky enough. The Bella Crew needs you. They look up to you." I nod my head and motion to a couple of guys lingering near the front entrance. "You have to keep this place safe. I want somewhere to bring Hayley back to. You got it?"

"Then you better fucking bring me a souvenir or some shit. I've never been outside of this hellhole of the city." Walcott flares his nostrils and slumps his shoulders. "If you don't, I get a free punch to your damn dick. You got it?"

"And you have to get a vagina tattooed over your belly button for me to poke." Tatum wags her eyebrows and winks at me with a laugh. She's so damn twisted. No one compares in creativity.

"Hell no," I say, shaking my head.

"Fine, then you better get me something good. I want a souvenir too. Bring me someone hot. Or maybe just someone's really big cock for my collection. I don't have anything over nine inches yet, and I'm growing disappointed every time we rip a damn pair of pants down to discover lame angry inches. Nub rubs aren't fun. I want to polish some poles."

"Jesus Christ, Tate. Stay the fuck away from me." Walcott covers his groin with his hands protectively. "You are one crazy ass."

Tatum tips her head back and laughs, her musical voice echoing through the air. "Like I said, I want to polish a damn pole. I know you don't have something up to my standards behind that zipper. Unless you've managed to swap with someone I don't know and want to prove me wrong."

Monroe groans and turns his back away. "He can't prove shit. Now just go fuck each other. Maybe you can work together to keep this place going. We gotta head out."

"You're leaving already?" Govan asks, speaking up for the first time. His mind is all over the place since Aris now keeps his girl under lock and key. It's why we negotiated Hayley being able to bring some friends with her when we get her back.

I drape my arm over Govan's shoulders and give him a little squeeze. "We have no time to waste. Apparently, Lawrence is one fucked up son of a bitch. I'm already worried that he's done something unforgivable to Hayley."

"The sooner we leave, the sooner we can get back here. We stayed good on our word to you in the negotiation, Govan. If we get Hayley, we can bring Mya too. Okay?" Knox holds out his fist to Govan. "We always have your back."

"Fuck yeah. We all have each other. It's going to be official too." Monroe bounces on the balls of his feet, curling and uncurling his fingers. When he's like this, he's more reactive to things. He is tougher and stronger with his anxiety. Usually, I try to say something to chill him the hell out, but I need the fucker to be as psycho as possible.

"I can't wait. I swear to fucking hell if you don't get Hayley, I will take all of your cocks for my collection. I'm counting on you. We all are." Tatum throws her arms around me and gives me a hug. "You better stay safe, brother."

I slowly nod my head. It's the first time she's ever referred to me as her brother and I like the sound of it more than I thought I would. Tatum has always been my friend, and she is an excellent member of our crew. But when it's official to be coven members, she will be my sister. It's been a long time since I've had any official family.

"Aww, Tatum's going soft. I just want to squish her." Monroe risks losing his fingers by squeezing Tatum's cheeks. "You don't have to worry about us, little sis. We're tough. We're going to be fine."

Tatum jerks her hands up and twists Monroe's wrist, flipping him onto his back before sinking her foot into his gut just hard enough to make him gasp. "Are you sure about that? Look how fast I put you down."

Monroe chuckles and knocks her off him, sending her to her ass. "Hell yeah. You know I let you do that."

"Sure, whatever. Just don't let it happen while you're out of the city. I mean it. You all need to be safe and bring Hayley back. The new deal can really change things for us." Tatum gets to her feet and hugs Monroe and Knox next. "And if things turn to shit, you better fucking call. We will figure out a way to get out of this city to save your bitch asses."

"You got it, Tate." I scoop up my duffel bag from the ground and swing it over my shoulder. The Aris Hotel car idles outside. The driver has already left, and it's up to us to get to The Whiskey on our own. Which is fine. We got this.

"Now don't destroy this place while we're gone. And stay the fuck out of my room. Got it?" Monroe says, following my gesture and grabbing his shit.

"Aye-aye, Monny. No going in your room." Tatum smiles. She's obviously going to fuck with his stuff now.

Before Monroe can respond, I grab him by the back of the jacket and drag him. I motion for Knox to pick up his things to follow.

Reaching the entrance, I bump my fist to a couple of the other crewmembers' outstretched hands. They don't say anything as I pull up my hood to shield myself from the sun.

Fuck. This is it. This is the moment that will truly test my power and prove my worth to Hayley.

"Let's do this. I want our fucking girl back," Knox says, striding out first.

I step out behind him and head toward the car. "Fuck yeah. We're going to get her back, and then we're going to take down all of fucking La Vega."

Monroe rubs his hands together, a wicked smile crossing his face. "And after that, maybe even the world."

"HOW IS THIS even fair? You have a fucking weapon, and I don't." I place my hands on my hips, scowling at Cooper as he stands across the ring, resting his back on the flexible wires. Bright lights shine above us, making it hard to see anything outside of this fighting ring.

"You'll thank me later. Most of the fighters only keep their weapon for a couple of minutes. You need to know how to protect yourself without anything. You need to learn how to punch, choke, break bones, bite, scratch to bleed someone out, and do anything you can to drop your opponent." Cooper smacks the flat side of his blade against his palm. "This is more than a performance. These strategies can save your life."

I'm already a dead woman walking. Even if I could manage to drop my opponent to their knees, it doesn't change anything. I'm still a prisoner. I'm still at risk of dying a second later. Just because Cooper wants to make sure I survive in the ring doesn't mean I can survive outside of it. Lawrence made himself clear. He's the only reason I'm alive right now. If I don't obey him or if I go against him, I'm dead.

"You mean save my life only to live a life of torture. Fucking awesome." I turn my back on him and stride toward the flexible wires wrapping around the fighting cage.

I realize a little too late that Cooper moved. My neck stings, and I feel blood trickling from the knife wound. He stands behind me and holds me by my stomach, stopping me from walking forward and directly into his blade, but I still nick myself.

What the actual fuck?

"Don't turn your back on anyone, including me, ever. Do you understand, Hayley? Look how easily you could've died." Cooper's deep voice vibrates against my ear. "I know you have no respect for your life, but if you die, I'm going to end up fucking dying, and I want to live. I have people who care about me and still need me."

I frown at his admission and lace my fingers around his wrist, forcing him to pull the blade from my throat. He eases back, allowing me to spin around to face him. His gaze darts from my eyes and to the blood on my neck, and he instinctively licks his lips.

Pulling up the front of my shirt, I staunch the bleeding and hide the cut from him. "Stop looking at me like you're going to bite me again. If you fucking bite me, I will show you what it's like to face someone who doesn't respect their life, as you said."

I brace myself to be slapped by him for talking back, but all Cooper does is put another foot of space between us. It's the strangest thing. It's unlike someone trying to control me not to physically hurt me to put me in my place. I don't know if I should be concerned or thankful. Maybe he's bottling it all up to unleash it on me later.

Groaning, Cooper throws his blade and sinks it into the concrete wall outside the fighting ring. The place we're practicing in isn't where we're going to perform, but Cooper said it was similar enough. I asked him about the others he mentioned before, and he told me the only time I will ever see them is in the ring. Lawrence doesn't allow the fighters to interact. He's afraid that if we do, we'll team up against him or something. Maybe refuse to fight. Because the Fright Fights are supposed to be us against them. Me against everyone else.

I don't know how I feel about it. I've never wanted to be against anyone in my life. I just want to dance and to be safe and loved. I want to go back to the Bella.

"This isn't fucking working. I don't know how to get through to you." Cooper scrubs his hands over his face and shakes his head. "There has to be something you're willing to fight for. If not yourself, what about someone else? Maybe Alex?"

Fury ignites inside me at his words. I would never in my life fight to survive for Alexander. It's his fault I'm in this situation.

Cooper raises his hands, his eyes widening as he drinks me in. He notices my reaction immediately, and if I didn't know any better, I'd think he was afraid of me. "Or not. I'm guessing he was a dick? Of course, he was. You were his property."

I tighten my mouth and don't respond. I'm not going to tell this asshole about my life or my past. I'm not going to let him try to get into my head to manipulate me into being the show's headliner. If I'm any good, it'll be the end.

I know what it's like to have the weight of acting as the perfect performer on my shoulders, and I know the consequences of letting people down. They're not good. I can't strive to be the best here. I'm taking Mya's approach and will only do what's necessary. With the thought of my best friend, a wave of worry crashes through me. I hope she's okay. Fuck.

Cooper clears his throat, tugging me from my sorrow. "How about we get you something to eat and sneak a peek at the Fright Fights happening tonight? We have to be careful not to get caught, though. Do you think you can manage that? Lawrence disagrees that it would be better for you to see one in advance, but I think it'll help you realize why you need to be my good little showgirl and listen to what I have to teach you." Cooper holds out his hand to me. "What do you say? We can even dress up. I bet you want a shower, don't you?"

This fucker. It's like he knows that I've never gone this long without bathing. The thought of cleaning up, eating, dressing in something other than these filthy clothes, and getting to see somewhere else besides the grimy basement of The Whiskey motivates me. I can't resist. I don't have it in me. At the Aris, I was taken care of far better than this, even though Alexander was a monster.

"I don't want to get in trouble." I try not to react and

keep my gaze trained on the floor.

Cooper smirks. "It wouldn't be you to get blamed. So don't worry your pretty little head, my showgirl. I'll take care of you. Promise."

I frown at his words. The way he says it makes me feel as if he's my caretaker. But he's not. He can't make these kinds of promises. He's a prisoner just as I am but has been given extra benefits for assisting Lawrence. In the end, he has no say or power.

But my damn human rationale wants me to trust him. All I have to say is that it better be the best fucking shower of my existence. Anything less and I'm sure I'll live the rest of my life regretting it.

I don't get a chance to respond because Cooper closes the space to me at vampire speed, hooks his arms under my legs and around my back, and lifts me off my feet. The world blurs as he carries me from the basement far too quickly to see our surroundings. It's like he doesn't want me to learn my way around this place. I can't plan my escape if I don't know.

One second, I'm in Cooper's arms, and in the next, I find myself standing in the middle of a tiled room with showerheads lined along the walls. It's completely open and without privacy curtains unlike anything I've seen before. This wasn't the kind of shower I had in mind.

Flicking on the water, Cooper turns on two of the faucets, sending steam through the air. I gape at him as he strips naked in front of me, showing off his ripped body. The guy has absolutely no shame and only smiles as he turns around and steps into the water, rinsing off the blood and dirt from however long it's been since he's last bathed.

"I'd hurry if I were you. The hot water only lasts for five minutes. After that, it turns ice cold." Cooper peeks at me from over his shoulder.

I'm torn between stripping in front of him and a hot shower. Of course, I'm going to choose the hot shower. Practically all the vampires in La Vega have seen me naked. At least my boobs.

With a sigh, I tug my shirt over my head and kick out of my pants, rushing toward the steaming shower. Keeping my eyes trained at the tile wall, I ignore Cooper the best I can. I wish he hadn't picked faucets next to each other, but it is what it is.

"That's a good girl. I knew you weren't shy." Cooper flashes his fangs and totally checks me out, flicking his gaze down to my boobs and then the rest of me.

Shivering under his scrutiny, I redirect my attention from the wall. I don't know where I summon the bravado, probably from my annoyance and adrenaline, but I drop my gaze down to his cock and lift an eyebrow. He's not the only one who can look without permission.

"What do you think? Do you like what you see?" This fucking asshole. I can't believe he calls me out.

His words cause me to avert my eyes as a blush burns up my cheeks. My first instinct is to tell him how attractive his body is, because that's how I've been trained to respond to someone seeking compliments, but all I do is ignore him. He gets a rise out of trying to get a reaction out of me.

"I'm probably average. Maybe a little above, at least here. I've seen a lot of fucking cock, so I know." Cooper stares at the side of my face, his gaze burning into my temple as if he can read my mind. "Not by choice, if I must add. Lawrence is a real son-of-a-twat. Mass showers. Guest entertainment. Erotic Fright Fights for special events."

"You don't have to explain." I shrug my shoulders and turn around, tipping my head back to wet my hair. "Doesn't matter to me either way."

Because it doesn't. It's none of my business.

"I just thought you'd be curious, is all, my showgirl. I'm sure the personal donors of Alexander are a bit like me. Doing what we have to do to survive." Cooper smacks his hand to a soap dispenser hooked to the wall and rubs his hands together to lather up. "Not all vampires have it easy. Around here, the donors are above vampires like me, who are put into the herd to keep the blood flowing."

I don't respond to his words. It's a lot to take in, listening to him describe to me something I had never in my life considered to be possible. I mean, a vampire being used as a donor for donors? It's insane. It would never go over well in La Vega. Maybe there are too many of them. I don't know. I have so many questions, but I know better than to ask.

"Do you think that's going to make me feel bad for you?" I follow his lead and soap up my body and hair, quickly rinsing off as the water turns from hot to warm.

"No. Because I don't feel bad for you either. The only thing you make me feel right now is hungry." He steps out of the stream and shuts off the water, leaving me staring at the ceiling.

I shriek as the shower suddenly turns ice cold and jump from the water and right into the open towel Cooper holds out for me.

"Is that why you're acting so nice? You want to feed on me? That's why I showered?" I shift on my feet and tighten the towel around my body.

Cooper runs his fingers through his wet hair, still standing naked before me, dripping wet and glistening.

My eyes betray me. I look at his body again, staring at the tattoos traveling along his chest and pecs and over his shoulders, working their way down his back like his body is a piece of artwork. It's mesmerizing yet disconcerting because I know that the ink is special for vampires and according to the Bella Crew, it stings.

"Are you offering?" Cooper smirks at me, his now clean face showing exactly how handsome he is. Scruff peppers his cheeks, but it doesn't look unkempt. He trims it just as he grooms the rest of his body.

I scrunch my face with a sneer. "No."

"Oh, that's a shame. Especially because you're going to leave me with a soaked towel. Wish you could give me something for hogging it." Cooper motions to the fact that he is dripping wet and naked. "You're not exactly helping my average size. It's cold."

I laugh in exasperation and throw the towel at him. He lets it hit him in the face, and I swear he sucks in a breath as if he's smelling my scent on the fabric.

"Where are some clothes? I'm not putting on those nasty dirty ones. You promised that we'd get dressed up." I move my weight from foot to foot, feeling incredibly exposed but trying not to show it. I could cover up with my hands the best I can. A part of me wants to, yet there's a bigger part of me that wants to act blasé and as if none of this bothers me. It wouldn't bother Ruby Vixen.

Unfortunately, she's no longer me.

Maybe Violent Violet will be the badass instead of the good little doll of Alexander Aris. She can help me kick ass and remain unfazed to all this bullshit. I just have to convince myself that I can be her and live up to those standards. Right now, all I feel is weak.

"I did, didn't I?" Cooper hands me back the wet towel, but I don't take it from his fingers.

I let it drop to the floor. "You have five seconds."

"Or what? You'll bite me? Beat me up? Try to spank my perky ass?" Cooper grins wider with his words. He loves teasing me. I kind of hate how cute he looks when he smiles. He's my enemy. He's my supposed trainer. I shouldn't feel anything but fear and anger towards him.

Ignoring him, I strut to the pile of dirty clothes and pick them up. "I'll force you to put these on."

He feigns being afraid, dropping his mouth open with fake shock. "Oh no. I'm shaking. Dirty clothes. Yuck. I just showered."

I can't stop the laugh from escaping my mouth at his dramatics. Chucking the T-shirt at him, I nearly get him in the face, but this time he moves out of the way. He vanishes from the spot in front of me at a speed far too quick for my eyes to follow only to return with a slinky navy-blue dress draped over his arm.

He swings it back-and-forth in front of me. "Will this work for you, my showgirl? I know it doesn't sparkle, but we're trying to blend in."

I snatch the dress from his fingers and shrug it over my head, the tight silhouette showing off all my curves and not leaving much to the imagination with a low-cut bodice and skimpy hemline. If I were to bend over, I'm sure my ass would show. It's probably the point, though.

"What about you? Is this so I blend in because you're going to walk around butt-ass naked as a distraction?" I twirl my finger and motion to his dick. "You know, that shrinkage isn't doing you any favors." It's a flat-out lie, but I won't admit to him that he's bigger than many in La Vega too. Not average.

He chuckles. "It does plenty. I don't want the attention anyway. It's already hard enough for me not to react to you checking me out. I'm getting tired of thinking about Bad Brad in a thong. It's a real boner killer, but I don't want to frighten you when you see just how much of a grower I can be."

Heat flushes my face, and I break his stare, closing my eyes. I wish I could disappear as I gather my shit together. I'm not used to someone's honesty like this. He talks to me as if he knows me. As if we're longtime friends.

"No amount of dick scares me. I grew up in La Vega. It was my job to entertain all the asshole guests of Alexander." I don't know why I say it, but it's as if I don't want him to think I'm some naïve, scared little donor. "Like you, I've seen a lot."

"Yet here you are, blushing and acting like a cute little virgin." Cooper's soft voice whispers against my earlobe. "But I'm glad you're not. I worry about what Lawrence has in store for you. The coven heads around here love the new and shiny. I just hope Lawrence doesn't treat you as such. How do you think so many of us vampires ended up as part of the herd? We stood up against them and their brutality."

I open my eyes and glance at him. Cooper stands a few feet away, now dressed in a pair of slacks and a button-down shirt that matches the blue of my dress.

"You stood against the other vampires?" I can't stop my mouth from voicing my question. It's the same as what the Bella Crew tries to do in La Vega, protecting donors.

Cooper shrugs his shoulders. "We're not all monsters. At least, I used to not be one."

"You do what you have to," I say, thinking about Sawyer, Monroe, and Knox and everything they do in the name of donors.

"That's right, my showgirl. Now let's get you something to eat and get our spots for the show. How does that sound?" Cooper opens his arms to me. It's as if he doesn't want to keep this particular conversation going, and I can't blame him.

"That's fine. Can we just walk? I want to see more of

The Whiskey." I rub my lips together and bounce on the balls of my bare feet, wishing he would've gotten me shoes.

"Sorry, Hayley. I can't allow that. It's far too dangerous around here. Hop up." Cooper wiggles his fingers.

I fold my arms over my chest in silent protest.

Flashing his fangs with a smile, Cooper launches for me, not giving me a choice. "Careful, my showgirl. I like it when you push back. It makes things more fun."

"You're an ass." I don't know what else to say.

"Could be worse." Cooper spins around, blurring the world.

He's right. He could be much, much worse.

HAYLEY

PUNISHMENT

MUSIC HUMS THROUGH the air, the intense beat sinking into my bones, entrancing me in a way that makes me sway my body. I forgot how addictive music could be, especially the quick beats of a song made seemingly for the soul.

Cooper sets me on my feet outside of a grand entrance to an auditorium with a brightly lit fighting ring in the center. The stadium seating climbs up to a second balcony, where it looks as if the cheap seats are located. If this were La Vega, that is where the Strip dwellers would sit. It's far away and hard to see the stage from there, but at least they still get to see the show.

"I'm sure you know the donor rules. They are the same here as they are in La Vega for the most part, except if a vampire catches you breaking them, they can punish you regardless of who you belong to. So, keep your eyes down, don't look at anyone apart from me and the performance, and stop looking so irresistible. You're going to make everyone extra bitey around here." Cooper takes my hand and pulls me in close until he drapes his arm over my shoulders. Leaning in, he adds, "Especially me. My hunger still hasn't subsided."

I peek at him in my peripheral vision, watching his eyes flash silver. At least they're not solid silver. If they start flickering too quickly where they look as if they're pure in color, then I know I'm in trouble. "Well, you haven't exactly had any blood. Does Lawrence starve you all the time?"

Cooper guides me toward a floor-lit aisle, leading closer to the ring. "Lawrence is not starving me. I have a blood source with me now, but I don't think she wants that kind of relationship. It's up to me to convince my blood source to feed me. Lawrence wants me just to take whatever I want, which I feel is inappropriate now that I'm of sound mind."

I shift my gaze from the ring and look at him. He's talking about me even though it sounds as if he speaks about someone else. A wave of confusion washes over me. I mean, what the fuck?

"I'm your blood source? Why didn't you tell me? You could've said something. I don't want you to get all volatile and psychotic again. You fucking hurt me last time. That's why I said you better not bite me." I tighten my jaw with my annoyance. "Giving you blood isn't a big deal."

He remains expressionless and takes me by the elbow, ushering me to a side aisle without a direct front view of the ring. We'll see everything from the corner instead of head-on. "It obviously is a big deal to you. I don't want to push you. I know this is all fucked up, and you don't want to be here just as badly as I don't. I just...I understand I must gain your trust to be able to ask for blood. Unfortunately, I suck at the whole teacher, trainer, caretaker aspect."

"That's because you're a prisoner. Usually, vampires in that sort of position aren't..." I let my voice trail off. The last thing I need is to give him any ideas about how to manipulate me into compliance.

"Nice? Sexy? Super easy-going and fun? A rule breaker?" Cooper taps his palm with his finger, saying everything that is definitely not on my mind. Well, until now.

"As threatening as a baby donor." I can't stop smirking

with my comment.

He brings his palm to his chest with a fake gasp. "Do you want me to be an asshole? A twisted sadist? If that's the only way you're going to comply, then...we're both dead. I don't have it in me. I barely survive the Fright Fights." Cooper motions to a pair of seats at the back of the section. He waits for me to sit down and then plops into the chair beside me. A few donors in glittering costumes stroll by with trays of crystal goblets filled with blood. Cooper's eyes flick away from mine as he stares at the donor for a long while, waiting for me to respond.

I don't exactly know what to say to him. It's obvious I don't want him to be a fucking dickhead. But I also don't believe him when he tells me he barely survives the Fright Fights. He's muscular, strong, and he obviously knows enough and is powerful enough for Lawrence to consider him a good trainer.

"Then I'm screwed, huh?" I ask instead of calling him out on what I'm sure is a lie. "Can I trade you in? How do you expect me to be confident if you aren't?"

Cooper tips his head back with a laugh, his voice echoing over that beating music. His laughter is contagious, and I smile at him. Leaning closer, he bumps his shoulder to mine.

"You're absolutely right, but unfortunately, any of the

other vampire performers would probably just devour you. Lawrence doesn't trust them. He barely trusts me, and he has something over my head that makes me comply."

I open my mouth to ask him what, but a bright spotlight beams over the crowd, and an emcee calls attention to the audience.

Okay, I wouldn't really even call us an audience. There are only a handful of people among the hundreds of seats. There's not even anyone in the nosebleed section.

"Welcome to the Fright Fights, ladies and gentlemen! We have a spectacular show for you tonight. Who is ready to see some blood wrestling? Some heart-stomping? Who's ready to feel the rain of death?" A woman steps out from a stage door, her two-piece costume glittering under the spotlight.

Fake cheers echo from huge speakers along the stage, and I lean forward and rest my elbows on my knees. I can already tell this is going to be one shitshow of a performance. The crowd doesn't even react. It's far from anything as good as Vampire Nights' was. I bet most of the other shows in La Vega beat this out as well. I almost feel bad for the vampire emcee. With her bored expression, I can tell she doesn't want to be here. I wonder if she is a prisoner too.

"No wonder there's no one here," I murmur, keeping my voice low.

"Shh, don't let anyone hear you. They don't know it's pure crap." Cooper bumps his shoulder to me again. "They're not exactly here for Bitchy Betty."

"Let me guess. You named her?" I ask, lifting an eyebrow.

"Just don't call her that to her face. Bodacious Betty will cut your tits off and give you a pussy punch that'll knock your insides around. Don't let her baby doll persona make you underestimate her. She is only the emcee on the nights Lawrence is out."

I puff out a breath between my lips. "Why am I not surprised that Lawrence runs the show? He's like a worse version of Alexander. An imposter."

Reaching over, Cooper covers my mouth with his hand. "You need to watch your mouth, my showgirl. You can't talk about our master like that, especially out here. There are consequences. I've seen him cut out people's tongues for less. You don't need to speak to fight."

My mouth trembles with his words. I'm so fucking stupid. I don't know what has gotten into me. I would never risk talking bad about Alex. What if Cooper has been messing with me this whole time? He could go to Lawrence and tell him what I said. Fuck, it wouldn't be the first time someone would use something against me to get ahead.

I shut down, my mood going from playful to fearful as

Bodacious Betty tries to rile up the crowd until another spotlight shines on the doorway. Two donor men, wearing only boxer briefs and painted with blue and pink body paint, hover in place. Confusion pinches their expressions, and they both shield their eyes. There's nothing intimidating about them, and I get the impression they have no idea what's going on. They're not fighters or performers. They look as if a single breath could knock them off their feet.

Thank goodness the music grows in volume, and I can ignore Cooper as he stares at the side of my face. I wouldn't be able to hear him talk anyways.

I think I'm done conversing for now. It's time for me to act as if I haven't been treated kindly. I need to act as if I'm not expecting my life to change.

"Oh, boys! Come to your master. I'll protect you from the big bad bubble butt bitch who thinks she can take both of you down in ten seconds flat." Bodacious Betty wiggles her fingers at the donors, and they shuffle forward, their eyes wide as they stare around the nearly empty venue. Like good donors, they obey the emcee and stick together as they meander toward the stage.

"Bodacious Betty June! Keep your filthy fingers off my blood sources." Another woman appears in the doorway to the backstage area. I've never seen anything like her. Her curly brown hair sparkles with glitter and gemstones are fastened to the strands. Her triangular bikini top barely covers her enormous boobs, begging to fall out. All she wears is a thong bottom with fishnet tights underneath, showing off her muscular legs. Opening her mouth, the vampire flashes her fangs, studded with sparkling diamonds that catch the light.

She steps forward, her glittering stilettos looking as if she stands on two knife points. And maybe she does.

The emcee widens her eyes and runs to hide behind the nearest audience member, a man in only a pair of jeans and a T-shirt. "Killer Kassandra, I'm not tryin' to steal your donors, babe. I was only tryin' to protect them from Fuck-You-Up Fine Girl."

Kassandra hollers with a feral scream. "What did you call me?" The vampire rushes forward too fast for my eyes to follow. She materializes in front of Betty and snatches her by the neck, lifting her off her feet.

"I'm sorry! I didn't mean anything by it, Killer. Please." Betty kicks her legs, trying to fight off the muscular woman.

"Put my sister down, you bitch!" a woman says from her seat between them. "Go back to your fucking cage."

"Yeah, Killer. Do what you're good for and take the criminals down." A man growls and points to the donors. "They tried to kill my lover, isn't that right, Katie May? We're here to see them pay."

Oh shit. This is how The Whiskey handles their disobedient and aggressive donors?

A smile crosses Killer's face, and she snaps the female audience member out of her seat, twisting her hair. "Boys? Is that true? Did you try to murder Katie?"

The donors gawk and thrash their heads back and forth.

It makes Killer smile wider. "That's what I thought. We have a liar on our hands. What should I do?" Killer unsheathes a knife, cutting her tiny bikini top open in the process, showing off her boobs. "She's caused us to sentence these two perfectly good donors to the Fright Fights."

"Let me go!" Katie screams, thrashing.

Bodacious Betty grabs hold of the man, jabbing him in the back with her knife, keeping him from interfering.

"Punch her pussy!" a man shouts from his seat.

"Shove your fist up her ass!" another yells.

My heart sinks into my stomach. What the actual fuck.

Killer wags her eyebrows. "You disgusting fools. I like that. But no. I'm going to take her mother-fucking, lying heart!"

Everything happened so fast that I can barely process anything as Killer spins the woman and jabs her blade into her chest hard enough to push her fist through too. Katie's scream cuts off with the exit of her heart through her back.

The emcee drops the man and cheers along with the fake soundtrack. "Get this bastard too, Killer! He bled on my shoe!"

I frown and glance at Cooper, meeting his gaze. "What the fuck?"

He smirks. "Stupid as fuck, right? It's staged. Sort of. Lawrence knew their coven was trying to steal donors and set them up."

I don't have a chance to ask him more as Killer goes after the man and tosses him toward the middle of the ring. She releases a whistle between her fingers, startling the two donors.

"Get in there and kill him. Show me you are worthy of being mine, boys." Killer Kassandra materializes behind the male donors and shoves them.

The expression the man from the audience gives when he realizes he is now a part of the show is priceless. There is something incredibly satisfying about watching his smug-ass be put to the test. He rips off his T-shirt and shows off the tattoos winding across his body, shifting and moving with his flexing muscles.

"Are you really going to let these pathetic donors fight for you, Killer Kassandra?" the vampire asks, running and hitting his back to the flexible wires to send him rushing toward the other end of the ring. He sticks his arm through, grabs one of the guys by the throat, and flips him into the arena. "You're all talk, you blood slave. Lawrence gave me a deal, you know. He fucked you over."

Killer Kassandra blinks a few times, and I realize she thought she had an advantage when the man has been acting this whole time. And shit. I didn't see it coming. This performance is chaotic and unbelievable. Twisted and fucked up.

I stare in utter shock as the vampire punches his hand into the donor's chest and pulls out his heart, taking a bite of it.

I gag and cover my eyes, the fear and disgust of the show getting to me. I can't believe they just killed a donor like this.

The other donor screams, but I refuse to look. I can't. I need to get out of here.

Without thinking, I stand up and run. I run faster than I ever have in my life as if Lawrence's venom bite triggers a side of me that I didn't know existed and it takes complete control.

"Hayley! Hayley, stop!" Cooper shouts from behind me.

I don't stop.

I reach the exit of the auditorium and rush into the casino. Lights sparkle and sounds bing through the air, drawing my attention to the slot machines. This place is far from nice. Even the Bella, though the casino has been closed for who knows how long, looks nicer than this. It's obvious that The Whiskey's main attraction is neither the Fright Fights nor the casino. There is no one here, really. I wonder if it's just all the front for the supposed herd that Lawrence keeps with the donors and vampires.

Cooper growls from somewhere behind me. "Hayley!"

I realize I unintentionally slow down, my speed diminishing from crazy, vampire-fast quickness to a normal jog. And now, I'm alone and unprotected. My stupid human fear instincts. They're going to get me killed. I'm not a fighter. I've always been good at fleeing, but running in a vampire establishment is never a smart idea.

Especially in a place like this.

Somebody snatches me by the back of the throat and throws me off my feet. The air knocks from my lungs as I roll across the scratchy carpet until I hit one of the slot machines. A shadow looms over me. I blink my eyes, trying to make out who the fuck just snatched me off my feet, but my eyes water too much. The pain only allows me to release a sob.

"Finder's keepers. This bitch is mine." An unfamiliar voice rings through the air. Fingernails bite into my wrists as a man yanks me from the floor and plops me on his shoulder.

Fuck my life. I can feel my ass and damn vagina exposed from underneath my short dress.

A snarl rips through the air and cuts through my very soul but not because I'm afraid. It's because I'm familiar with it. It's Sawyer.

One second, I'm on the man's shoulder, and then in the next, I land on the floor again. I scramble away, watching as Sawyer's massive form blurs in front of me as he attacks the strange vampire. My heart flutters at the sight of him. He found me. I knew he'd find me.

An alarm blares through the casino, and the lights turn off. I scream out Sawyer's name and try to run to him, but someone grabs me by my waist and drags me away.

"Are you fucking insane?" Cooper asks, his deep voice laced with his anger. "You could've been killed."

I thrash in his hold. "Let me go! Take me back!"

"You're fucking crazy!" Cooper hollers, spinning around and jetting through another door, taking me deeper into the hotel portion of The Whiskey.

Shrieking at the top of my lungs, I call out for Sawyer, hoping he can hear me and that he gets to me quick enough.

Cooper slaps his hand over my mouth and growls in my ear, silencing me the best he can. "Shut up, Hayley. If you know that guy and you want him to live, you need to shut your fucking mouth before someone hears you."

I still at his words. Why is he telling me this? Why does he care?

"Please, just be quiet. Security is flooding the place now. If they catch us out here, we'll lose any freedom we currently have. Do you want to find out what it's like to join the herd?" His chest presses against mine with his deep breaths.

I realize my legs wrap around him, but unless I fight him and throw myself back, he has a tight hold on me.

"Please, Cooper. Sawyer can help us. I'm sure the rest of the Bella Crew is here as well. If you can take me to them, they can help you too. They can get us both out of here." My voice shakes as I beg him, praying with everything in me that he listens to me.

"No one can help us, Hayley. I'm sorry. If Sawyer is in The Whiskey, there's no leaving. I'm sure Lawrence will either kill him or force him into the herd. He would have to have something useful to him otherwise to bargain with." Cooper strokes his hand up and down my spine as if the gesture will somehow settle my nerves.

"You don't know the Bella Crew. They're some of the most powerful vampires in all of La Vega." I lick my lips, trying to get my heart to calm down.

"If they're not a coven, then they aren't as powerful as you believe them to be. I know the leaders of La Vega, and they're not a part of the leadership. They can't help us." Again, Cooper shoots me down.

Anger rolls through me, and I dig my fingernails into his shoulders. I wiggle and squirm, hoping it's hard for him to keep a hold on me. If only my movements didn't backfire. Because Cooper growls and adjusts me, and I feel his body arousing from my closeness as I rub against him.

"Hayley," he mutters, shifting me to his hip. "Stop it."

I flick my attention to his and freeze. His eyes no longer show the emerald-green depths of his irises. They're now solid silver again. He's losing control. If he loses control...

"Cooper, don't hurt me. Please. If you're that hungry, I give you permission to bite me. I don't want you to lose control. I can see it in your eyes." I inhale and exhale a couple of short breaths.

He flashes his fangs. "No. Just be—"

The lights flicker on overhead, showing off the dirty storage room around us. Cooper tenses and sets me on my feet behind him, straightening his back and blocking me protectively.

The lock on the door clicks, and it slowly creaks open. I grab onto the back of Cooper's jacket, steadying myself. My legs weaken with fear, and I brace for an army of vampires to come in here to tear me apart.

"You have a lot of explaining to do, Cooper." Lawrence's guttural voice booms through the small room, turning my body cold. "Security caught Hayley running at vampire speed on camera. I had to kill one of my best men and put two others in the fucking herd. Give me one good reason why I shouldn't put you there too."

Cooper doesn't respond right away, his whole body rigid. He's afraid too. It's as if I can smell his fear.

"I'm sorry, Lawrence. I was working with Hayley, and fear set her off. It seems that her power derives from her instincts." Cooper steps a foot away from me.

"So, would you consider that progress?" Lawrence asks, standing tall in an attempt to peer at me.

"Yes, sir. Now that I know how to bring out her dhampir nature in particular, we can work with it." Cooper swivels and peeks at me from over his shoulder.

Lawrence flashes his fangs. "There still must be consequences."

Nodding, Cooper says, "I understand and will accept my punishment."

"Not for you, but for Hayley. I want you to show her what happens when she disobeys you or breaks one of the donor rules around here. It's of utmost importance that no one knows she is a dhampir." Lawrence materializes in front of Cooper, close enough to reach over and grab me by the throat. "Do you understand, Hayley? You'll now have to wear your collar. I can't have you running around here. You caused a lot of trouble and must pay for it." Lawrence retrieves the metal collar that he put around my neck to take me from the Bella. I don't even get a chance to fight him off or resist before he flicks and locks it around my throat. "Now for her punishment. I want you to give her three lashes."

Cooper growls under his breath. "Me?"

Lawrence snarls and shoves Cooper back, sending him crashing into me. I screech as my back slams into a metal shelf and digs into my skin. "Yes, fucking you. Do it now."

Tears burn my eyes, the thought of the oncoming pain already scaring the shit out of me. This can't be happening. I can't live through this again.

"No." Cooper's sharp word surprises me.

Lawrence glares and cocks his head. "What?"

Squaring his shoulders, Cooper faces Lawrence without fear. "You heard me. I said no. Hell-fucking-no." Cooper spins and faces me. "Run."

Before I can react, Cooper lunges at Lawrence and sends him colliding into the opposite wall.

I don't wait to see the fight.

I run.

BLOODLETTING

I RACE DOWN a hallway with a low ceiling in the direction where I think we came from. I can't hear the casino or any distinctive noises to guide me, and I try my best to navigate this old hotel. If there were ever pictures hung up along the guest hallway on this floor, they've been long gone. Actually, I doubt anyone stays here. It's quiet—too quiet—even for vampires.

I want to scream out for Sawyer. I want to scream out for help from anyone willing to listen to me. But I can't. If I yell, it's more likely that someone who would rather hurt me than help me would find me. I just need to make my way back to the casino. If I can, I have a better chance of finding Sawyer—or Monroe and Knox. I know he wouldn't be here without them.

Dozens of doors line the hallway, and I keep my pace until I reach the bend leading to a set of elevators. Cooper must've taken the stairs somewhere because I would've remembered the ride. He purposefully wouldn't let me see my way around, and I'm even more pissed off than I was.

I hit the button and bounce on my feet, wondering if taking the elevator will lead to my death sentence. Lawrence could've already called security, and they could be waiting for me. He could be in the casino and preparing to beat me in front of the patrons like Mr. Pala had.

But I can't stay here. My chance of finding one of the Bella Crew members isn't happening this deep in the hotel. I just need another minute. I need another dozen feet. I'll take the risk. Anything is better than the punishment Lawrence wants to dish out for an accident.

A lashing? Fuck. That's far worse than the paddle.

The elevator dings open, and I hesitate only long enough to make sure it's clear. I run in and slam my hand to the button with an L printed next to it, identifying the lobby.

The doors close with the rumble, and the floor shakes beneath my feet, more rickety than any of the elevators at the Aris Hotel. I never thought I would be afraid of an elevator. But here I am, clutching onto the sidebar for balance.

I stare at the shiny door, bracing for a fight I know I can never win. I don't even have a weapon. Now I really wish I had paid attention to Cooper in the fighting ring earlier. Instead, I might've screwed myself over. I can try my best, but in a situation like this, my best isn't enough.

The elevator jerks to a halt, and the door dings open. I stiffen and press my back to the wall, waiting a moment to see if anyone charges in. But no one's there.

I don't believe it.

And then I see him.

I gasp a breath and clutch my chest at the sight of Monroe standing three dozen feet away with blood spattering over his shirt.

"Fuck, there she is!" Monroe shouts, pointing the knife in my direction. "Hurry, Knox. The elevator."

I step out only to find myself in Knox's arms. He lifts me off my feet and kisses me immediately, his strong embrace enough to help me keep it together as the rest of me wants to fall apart.

"How did you find me? I've been so scared." I rest my forehead to his, trying not to cry, but my tears splash my cheeks and wet Knox's face as well.

"Did you really think we were just going to let some fucker kidnap our girl? Sorry it took so long, Hayley. Are you okay? Did anyone hurt you?" Knox kisses my earlobe with his questions.

"Who's fucking dick do I have to chop off to take back to Tatum as a souvenir?" Monroe materializes behind Knox and smiles at me from over his shoulder.

"The asshole you were with—" Sawyer's words cut off with the sound of an alarm, the screeching noise shocking my ears. But none of the Bella Crew falls. They manage to stand upright while the few guests lingering drop to their knees.

"Come on. We gotta go." Monroe points his bloody blade at the entrance. "Security at the town wall will only be down for two minutes."

Shit.

The three of them form a protective circle around me with Monroe leading the way and Sawyer by my side as Knox carries me. I cling onto him as if he's the only thing keeping me from losing my shit, and they race at vampire speed toward the entrance. Cool night air wafts around us, and I inhale a deep breath. The hotel and casino's air is stale. It smells like cigarettes and something grosser.

I peer over Knox's shoulder, keeping my eyes trained on the building. It's whimsical in a way with its fake towers that are supposed to look like some ancient storybook castle.

"I'll go ahead and make sure the gate is clear," Monroe says, peeking over his shoulder.

"No. Don't leave." I bite my lip with my plea, but I'm terrified if he runs ahead and leaves us that I might never see him again. This place is not La Vega. They have no allies here.

"You got it, little bird. I'm never leaving you again if I can help it. We are stronger together, right?" Monroe keeps his voice low, but he carries enough lightness to lift my mood.

"Right." I don't feel the truth of the word, despite knowing it's real. The Bella Crew is stronger together, and being here proves it. They left La Vega for me. They managed to get into The Whiskey. How? I don't even care.

The looming fence bordering the small desert town comes into view, and I dig my nails into Knox's shoulders, twisting to see a car parked right outside as if they just happened to stroll right in.

"Almost there, vixen. Hang tight. It's going to get messy." Knox unholsters a gun from his belt and aims it toward the fence.

He pulls the trigger, sending a loud pop ringing in my ears. I hadn't seen the shadowy figure until the second the vampire screamed out. It doesn't stop the man for long, and my guys close in tighter around me as more gunfire showers the night.

"Head east. We have to sneak up on the side. We're too open here." Knox whacks his hand into Monroe's side, getting him to follow his directions. "I don't want to risk Hayley getting shot because you aren't fazed by bullets, fuckhead."

"He's right." Sawyer takes the lead and runs east, heading to the chain-link fence surrounding the property.

Electricity hums and crackles, and I'm nearly certain that I wouldn't have been able to hear it before Lawrence bit me with his venom.

I clutch onto Knox tighter, inhaling the sweet scent of his skin. It's the only thing keeping my heart from escaping my chest. Fear radiates through my entire body, more so than I have ever experienced in my life. Even facing Alexander in a rage wasn't as scary as not knowing whether we'll make it out of here.

"Almost there, Hayley," Knox whispers, his voice tickling my skin. He presses his lips to my head and tries to reassure me with a kiss.

It's as if he knows what's swirling through my head and

can sense how frightened I am. I'm trying not to be, but I can't help it. I feel so much safer with the Bella Crew that I know I don't have to be as strong or brave or as capable as I would have to be alone.

I hate the thought of being alone and without them again.

Fuck, please. Please, universe, let us get out of here. I just want to go back to La Vega.

"I'll take care of the security. Knox, take her straight to the car. We'll catch up. I want you to fucking get driving immediately. We'll make sure no one follows us, and you can swing back around and pick us up at the rendezvous point." Monroe slows down only a little to be by my side. "Be good for Knox, little bird."

With a kiss to my cheek, Monroe abandons us, zooming ahead. Sawyer touches my chin with a smile and races to catch up to Monroe, leaving me and Knox behind.

Gunshots and growls sound through the air, setting off my fear instincts even more. I wish we could go in a different direction. I wish we didn't have to face anyone else at all. I'm just so tired of worrying about being hurt or caught or imprisoned. I just want to live without pain and torment. I never knew that it would be too much to ask.

"I'm going to put you on my back, so I can free my arms to fight. Is that okay?" Knox asks, rubbing his hand over my shoulder.

I slowly nod my head.

Flipping me over his shoulder, Knox repositions me to cling onto his back. I squeeze his torso between my thighs and lock my ankles around his stomach, ensuring that I won't fall.

He picks up his speed, blurring the world around me. I spot the bright lights of the exit leaving the community, and I puff a breath through my lips. This is too unreal. It's too easy. There's no way that Lawrence would rely on just security to keep threats in or out.

And then I feel it.

The metal collar around my throat vibrates just hard enough to startle me. I nearly lose my grip on Knox. It's been programmed to shock me if I try to leave. I know it. Lawrence is a smart man. He wouldn't risk losing me after going through the effort to bring me here. Cooper said it himself. If I'm here, Lawrence has already won.

"Knox, stop." The words barely come out of my mouth as the vibration intensifies in the collar.

"We're almost there." Knox rubs his hand over my forearm. "Don't be scared."

"Stop!" I scream, my voice ripping through the air as pain shoots through me. My muscles spasm, and I release Knox.

I don't hit the ground.

Spinning around, Knox catches me before my ass hits the gravel. I rip at the collar around my throat, but I can't get it off. It's stuck, and the shock only grows in intensity.

"Fuck. Sawyer! Monroe! She has a fucking shock collar on." Knox kneels beside me and shoves his fingers between the collar and my neck, but it only makes it zap me harder.

I throw myself back, my body convulsing. I can't do anything except lose myself to the pain.

"Don't move her. Don't touch it. You could cause serious damage." Knox grips my fingers in his, drawing my attention as the shock subsides.

I blink my hazy vision and spot Monroe and Sawyer standing a couple of feet away with blood splashed across their clothes. "I can't leave. You guys have to go. Don't get caught."

"We're not fucking leaving you. We'll figure it out." Monroe stomps forward and kneels beside me. "I don't care if someone catches me."

I inhale a couple of deep breaths, my chest heaving. "You have to go. If you're caught, Lawrence will put you in the herd. Or he'll kill you. Please, just go. You have to think of something else."

"We're strong," Sawyer argues. "He can't do shit to us."

"You don't understand. He's worse than Alexander. You haven't seen the blood collection room. If security gets you, Lawrence will force you to give blood to the donors he uses for gen. pop. blood. Even the strongest can't escape." I manage to get to my feet and hold my hands up, stopping anyone from getting closer. "Please, just go. Come back for me."

Monroe tries to close the space. "Shit. Hayley—"

I shake my head. "Go! Go now! I can't live with myself if something happens to you. You need a new plan. I'll be okay. He's not going to kill me. I can handle any punishment. But I can't handle something happening to you three."

A huge spotlight cuts across the ground, nearly illuminating us in its glow.

I screech and raise my hands, trying to draw attention away from Sawyer, Monroe, and Knox. The beam of light stops on me, and I clutch my arms around my body protectively. "I give up!"

"Hayley, be brave. We will be back. You're absolutely right. We are no use to you otherwise." Sawyer latches his hands to both Knox and Monroe's shirts. He forces them to go with him. "We will get you out of here. I swear."

I can feel the truth in his words.

If only I wouldn't feel the pain that comes with watching the three of them disappear. The same pain that grows with another shock in the collar.

I drop to my knees and lay on my stomach.

I blackout.

A sharp, stinging pain slashes across the backs of my legs, ripping me from unconsciousness. I cry out and arch my back. What the actual fuck? The agony doesn't subside, and I gasp, trying to get to my feet, but I can't.

"What did I tell you, Hayley?" Lawrence's voice snaps at me with a loud crack of a whip.

Pain cuts across my legs again, sending me planting my face to the muddy floor. I sob, my cries echoing around us. This is far worse than anything I have ever experienced. I never expected to be punished in such a savage way.

"Please, master. Don't hurt her anymore. It takes time for her to heal. If you're not going to let me give her blood, then show her mercy. She can't fight if she can't stand." Cooper's familiar voice drifts through the air.

"She also can't run either." Lawrence cracks the whip, but instead of hitting me, he lashes the ground a foot away.

I wince and bite my lip, trying to stifle my sob.

"Please. I'm begging you. I'll return to the herd. Just

don't do this." A shadow shifts in the corner of my vision, and Cooper comes into view. He's covered in mud and blood, probably in the same condition as when we first met.

"She needs to learn. And so do you." Lawrence flicks his wrist and lashes his whip at Cooper.

Cooper groans but doesn't fall back as a deep cut slices across the front of his shirt.

Again, Lawrence cracks his whip at Cooper, this time lashing him across the face. Cooper hollers in pain, but he doesn't back down. He moves closer until he kneels in front of me protectively.

"Lash me a thousand times if you want. Just don't hurt her. It's my fault. I'm to blame for all of this. I should've never taken her to watch the Fright Fights. I was just trying to—" His words cut off with another yell, and his body crashes to the ground.

I don't move. I don't try to run or fight. All I do is remain on my stomach and watch as Lawrence whips Cooper so many times I lose count.

My stomach twists with sick agony, but there's nothing left inside me to throw up. I can't believe this is happening. I can't believe this vampire has begged for mercy on my behalf. I don't understand him.

"Hayley," Lawrence snaps, his voice stabbing me as if

he plans to whip me again even though he doesn't. "If you ever run again, I will break your legs. I will heal you, and then I will break them again. Do you understand? What did I tell you about people discovering what you are? I'm only trying to protect you. If you would just obey and know your place, you would be fine. I don't like punishing you."

I grind my teeth at his words. It's not the first time I've been told that. It's a flat-out lie, and we both know it. But I'm not going to argue. I'm not sure I'll ever speak again unless demanded to otherwise. I can't face these kinds of consequences. I just can't.

The only thing that keeps me from wanting to die in this moment is that I know Sawyer, Knox, and Monroe are here. They will get me out. And when they do, I'll figure out how to kill Lawrence.

I don't have a choice. None of us do.

This monster must pay.

"Now, I want you to stay here and think about what you've done. Both of you." Lawrence flicks his hand again and whips Cooper once more.

I brace to get lashed as well, but Lawrence disappears, slamming the metal door closed and locking it.

I tremble in my spot, afraid to move. Afraid to breathe. I'm terrified to do anything except watch the door and wait for him to return for another round.

But he doesn't.

His footsteps fade.

"Hayley, I'm so sorry." Cooper's soft voice trickles to me. "I'm so, so sorry. I was only trying to help. I never wanted you getting hurt."

I don't respond to him. I can't.

The only thing I can do is cry.

6

HAYLEY

PUNISHMENT

COOPER GROANS FROM the corner of the room. He lays on his side, with his knees curled up to his stomach. I've never seen a vampire as tough as him look so weak and broken in my life. Pity courses through me the longer we share this cell. I don't know why Lawrence didn't separate us, but I'm glad I'm not alone, even though I feel bad for Cooper. If only my body didn't hurt so bad still.

"Cooper?" I keep my voice low, almost afraid to speak.

"Don't talk. Don't move either. I'm starving, and it's taking everything in me not to launch across the room and bite you, Hayley. These injuries aren't helping." Cooper jerks his head up and narrows his eyes at me. They're completely silver, showing off the fact that he's not joking. He's on the verge of turning feral, and if he does, he'll attack me. He lacks control and restraint. It makes me wonder how old he is and how long he's been a prisoner of Lawrence's.

I remain silent for only a moment, and then I summon my nerve and push to my hands and knees. My calves hurt too badly to get to my feet, and exhaustion wears me down, so I crawl my way closer.

"Let me feed you before you attack, Cooper. Please, I don't want you to get all vicious. You were already hungry before." I clench my jaw, my eyes watering with my movements. "And maybe after, you could help me."

Because his blood can heal me. I wouldn't even need to consume that much.

"I don't know. What if this is some sort of test, and Lawrence ends up retaliating? I'm already down with my guilt over what happened to you. I can't think of another reason he would leave us together." Cooper digs his fingers into the muddy ground with his fangs extended. His nostrils flare, and he growls as I continue my way to him.

"I don't think that's it. I think this is part of the pun-ishment. Maybe he thinks that I wouldn't let you, and he wants you to attack me like you did when he first put me in a cell with you." That would make better sense. It would serve me right. At least, that's what I think Lawrence would feel. I don't know him well enough. Not like Alexander. And in all honesty, I hope I never do. I just have to hold on a bit longer. It'll be better if I can get Cooper to cooperate and just drink my blood so I can drink his.

"Hayley…" His voice trails off, and he shifts, trying to get space between us, but he ends up cornered against the wall.

"Don't argue with me. Please, just let me feed you. It won't be for nothing. You can heal me after you eat. I'm hurting so bad." My voice cracks with my admission, and a tear splashes on my cheek.

Cooper groans again and rubs the heel of his hand into his eye. The cut across the other side of his face travels from his hairline, skipping his other eye, and then slices across his cheek all the way to his jaw. It no longer bleeds, but it's not healing as quickly as it should.

"I can try to just let you have my blood." Cooper growls again. I don't think he can control his deep-seated vampiric nature.

I shake my head, whipping my hair back and forth.

"No. Just drink."

I hold out my arm to him, putting it an inch from his mouth. He can't deny me because he's starving. I don't have a chance to brace myself before he snatches me and pulls me onto his lap, bringing my wrist to his lips. I have no choice but to straddle him in my torn and dirty dress. He locks his eyes with mine, his whole body rigid as he sucks my blood, letting it fill him up in a way that helps him regain control.

I pant the longer he drinks and pray silently that he doesn't drain me completely. The look in his eyes...it's so tormented. I can't help but wonder if that's how I look to him.

It's so strange being lost in his gaze. The green depths of his eyes shine even in the dim lighting. His messy blond hair flops to the side, lying limp on his head. The cleanliness from taking a shower hadn't lasted long, and I wonder if that's how it's going to be from now on. If our lives are just going to be a filthy, agonizing, terrifying existence for us. For me. I hope not.

A deep, guttural sound reverberates through my bones. Two big hands lock onto my sides and rip me away from Cooper. My mind whirls with fear, and I thrash and scream out. Cooper was right. This was a setup by Lawrence.

"You fucking monster. I'll cut your damn head off for touching my girl." Sawyer sets me on my feet behind him and lunges at Cooper. Grabbing the front of his shirt, Sawyer lifts Cooper off the ground and shoves his back to the wall. He snarls, sounding like a vicious animal as he threatens Cooper with his sheer size. "Your fangs are mine."

I don't even get a chance to respond as Cooper swings his fist out and punches Sawyer in the face. He drops him, and the two of them blur around the small room, hitting the walls and sending concrete dust through the air. I freeze in my place, watching in horror as the two vampires fight over me. Sawyer is trying to protect me, and I think Cooper might be as well, as neither of them really knows each other.

"Please," I say, getting my voice to work. "Sawyer, I gave him permission. I'm really hurt, and he was going to give me his blood to help me."

All it takes is my one line to get Sawyer to stop fighting Cooper and return by my side. He braves turning his back on Cooper, and he looks me up and down for the first time since entering the muddy cell.

Without even thinking, Sawyer sinks his fangs into his arm and holds it up to my lips. His familiar blood drips over my tongue, setting me off. It's as if my body and mind disconnect, and I can't control my actions. Sawyer's eyes widen as I bite my teeth deeper into his skin, opening up his puncture wounds enough for the blood to flow quickly into my mouth.

I expect him to shove me away. I expect him to demand that I stop. He doesn't do either. A husky moan escapes his lips, and he laces his arm around my back and pulls me to him until I find myself wrapped around his hulking, delectable body.

"Fuck, Hayley. Where did you learn to bite like that?" Sawyer adjusts his hand lower, holding me up against him by my ass. "Take whatever you need to feel better. I'm so sorry that I didn't get into the building fast enough."

"I see you still have it in your head that this donor belongs to you, Mr. Bella." Lawrence's sharp voice tears through me as he stands in the doorway of the cell.

Sawyer spins around, but he doesn't set me on my feet. He grips me tighter, ensuring Lawrence can't snatch me away. "She does. I have a contract for her. And it's Mr. Noble, to you. The Bella is merely my home. I never acquired the name. Perhaps if I'm ever granted approval to ally as a coven with my crew."

Lawrence cracks his mouth into a terrifying smile made for nightmares. I suck in a deep breath and try to get my heart to calm down. "Which will never happen under the authority of the La Vega Leadership."

"Maybe. I've been working my way up in power. Soon enough, they won't have a choice. They never expected so many Strip dwellers to unite and act together with purpose.

But you wouldn't know anything about that, considering Aris said you were cast out for...interesting reasons." Sawyer adjusts me to his hip, treating me as if I weigh only a pound.

A shadow moves in the corner of my vision, and I can't help glancing at Cooper as he silently moves to the corner of the cell. He's obviously uncomfortable and nervous about Lawrence and Sawyer talking with civility instead of breaking out into a fight.

Actually, it makes me a bit freaked out too.

"I'm sure he embellished the details of the situation." Lawrence crosses his arms over his chest, his annoyance over Alexander clearly scrunched on his face. "No matter, the donor is still mine. She is my heir because of my sister, who that fucker so unfairly sentenced to death. He's lucky this is all I take from him."

"That was unfortunate. I know Hayley was attached to Opal. But I don't care about your coven drama or whatever inheritance you think is owed to you. I'm willing to negotiate to take Hayley home. She is mine. If you disagree, you're going to have a war on your hands. I have a deal with Aris, and I have the resources to take this place down. I was hoping we could go about this in a more peaceful and civil manner." Sawyer keeps his voice even, and I can't read his expression. He has a deal with Alexander? Fuck. What kind of deal? I'm not even sure I want to know.

"You say that as if you think you're ever going to make it out of this room, Mr. Noble. I can take your heart before you can even call for backup." Lawrence smirks with his words, his confidence disheartening.

"I will. Because like I said, I'm willing to make a deal. Name your price." Sawyer's muscles ripple as he shifts on his feet, turning me slightly just in case Lawrence does try to attack.

"Nothing is worth more than my precious heir. She'll bring great wealth and power to my future." Lawrence takes a step closer, and he reaches into his jacket.

"One donor shouldn't mean that much to you. I can get you a lot more. I can help you take back what belonged to you in La Vega before the leadership cast you out. I have far more resources than you realize, and I have trust." Sawyer keeps his eyes locked on Lawrence.

His words ignite something unsettling and dark inside me. He can't be offering to work with Lawrence to give him part of La Vega. I'm going to have to agree with whatever reasons the leadership had that separated Lawrence from them, because Lawrence is a fucking psycho.

"I need to think about it." Lawrence holds his hands out. "Now give me Hayley."

"No. She's mine," he repeats. "There shouldn't be anything for you to think about. I'm not letting you have her."

Lawrence rushes us, but Sawyer spins out of the way. I screech with the quick movements, my fear instincts driving me crazy as Lawrence tries to capture me. Swinging his fist, Sawyer punches Lawrence in the gut, knocking him back.

Snarling, Lawrence materializes in the doorway. He unsheathes a knife and points it at Cooper. "Get over here. You're going back to the herd until I think things through." He turns his attention to Sawyer next. "If you want Hayley, then you can fucking stay here."

"Fine by me. The offer stands until the next nightfall. If my crew doesn't hear from me, they'll be coming. I wouldn't wait too long. Monroe is impatient when he wants to fuck shit up, right, Hayley?" Sawyer squeezes my ass.

I open and close my mouth, my words stuck on my tongue.

Everything happens so fast that I can't keep up. Cooper yells out, and the door slams. Lawrence slides the lock into place, abandoning me alone with Sawyer in the cell. I gawk at the door in shock, expecting him to return at any second with a team of security personnel. Silence lingers. The only noise thrumming through the air are both our hearts beating. Sawyer's is the most musical sound I've ever heard in my life, the rhythm a perfect melody to make my soul sing. I could sway to the thudding of his heart, the music his body creates from my closeness practically intoxicating. Because he's not scared. He remains guarded and aware, but Lawrence doesn't freak him out like he does me. To him, he's another asshole vampire on a power trip. Something he's used to.

"Hayley," Sawyer murmurs, gliding his finger along my jawbone, tracing the curve of my chin until he guides my face away from staring at the door and to him. His blue eyes light with blips of silver. "You have no idea how much I've missed you. Did the fucker hurt you more than I can see?"

I rub my lips together, knowing he's referring to more than getting whipped. For the first time tonight, fear lines his eyes. My silence scares him. So does my hesitation. I wish the words would spill from my mouth, because I am okay. I just—I lean in and kiss him, desperately needing his closeness.

He moans against my mouth, kissing me once more before easing back. "Hayley—"

I rapidly blink, trying to control my tears. "I'm fine. He didn't hurt me like that. Now please, I've missed you. Just kiss me for a minute. It might be all the time we have."

My command sets Sawyer off, and he crashes his mouth mine, kissing me deeply as he slides his tongue into my mouth and tastes my lips. I run my fingers through his soft hair and keep him close, not letting him pull away even if he wanted to. I can't get enough of him. Of his touch. Of his taste. Of the way I feel so safe wrapped in his arms. It's as if we're not in a filthy cell and in a beautiful paradise together as long as we are alone.

I break my mouth from his lips and work my way down his jaw until I lick my tongue across his throat. Something savage inside me awakens, and the faint memory of the taste of his blood explodes in my mind, setting off a hunger deep inside me.

"Fuck. Fuck. Fuck." I jerk away and cover my hand with my mouth. "You have to put me down. Hurry."

Without hesitating or questioning me, Sawyer sets me on my feet. He remains in my personal space, clutching my hands between his as if even the thought of letting go of me pains him.

"What's wrong? No one's here. I can hear Lawrence coming from a mile away. I recognize him now." Sawyer lowers his brows on his forehead with his frown, his mouth pouting yet managing to stay sharp instead of softening.

I lick my lips and puff a breath out. "It's not that." It's now that I realize that he doesn't know what I am. He doesn't know I'm some sort of mutated being. I'm afraid to tell him I'm not the donor he thought I was. What if he...no, Sawyer wouldn't ever think of me like Lawrence does. I know him better than that.

"You know you can tell me anything," Sawyer murmurs, rubbing his thumb over the side of mine. "In your own time when you feel comfortable. I know it's not easy for you to speak freely, but I won't stop reminding you that you can with me."

I smile with his words. It's such a strange concept to be able to say anything without having to worry about getting punished for saying something wrong, and it's still hard for me, especially now, but I want to try. Just not right this second.

Right now, I want to feel Sawyer on a level that I haven't gotten to yet. I want to show him how much I've missed him. How much I want him. I want to use him to help me forget all the shitty things that happened to me, even if it's only temporary.

"I know I can, and I will. I promise. I just...kiss me again. I'm okay now." I clutch his face and lean in, brushing my lips to his, feeling the softness of his tongue caressing mine as his hands glide through my short hair and down my back as he picks me up once more.

He doesn't push me to talk to him and instead gives in to my desire to just be with him in this moment despite the fucked up shitshow around us. Reaching between us, I rub my hand over his cock, feeling the hardness of his shaft through his pants. It turns me on knowing how excited he is to be with me, and I can't help thinking about what it would be like if he would just unzip his pants and fuck me right here and right now. He could easily do it. I'm not even wearing underwear under this filthy dress. I never expected my first time with Sawyer to be in a cell, covered in mud and blood. I thought it would be in his room in the Bella. I thought it would be more romantic, but I realize I don't need romance. I don't need anything except for Sawyer and his desire for me.

"Do you want me?" I ask, my breath whispering against his lips.

"Always." Sawyer's big hand shifts my dress up from behind, and he slides his fingers between my legs, feeling my slick lust for him.

I moan and rock my hips, bouncing slightly in his arms, getting him to finger me in a way that leaves me breathless.

"How does that feel?" Sawyer murmurs, his voice vibrating across my lips. It's not often someone asks me if I like something, and I respond with a moan in agreement, my words refusing to come out. "You're so wet for me. I want to taste you."

My breathing quickens at the thought, and the state of my body makes me hesitate for a second, but Sawyer picks me up higher and rests my back to the wall. He doesn't care if there's dirt on me. He kisses my thigh anyway and gets me to wrap my legs around his shoulders. My head brushes the top of the cell because of his height, and I bow forward a bit and hold on for dear life, though I know he would never drop me.

His tongue glides across the seam of my legs, and he buries his face between my thighs and flicks his tongue, teasing and tasting me, sucking my clit just right and in a way that I have to clench my jaw to keep quiet. All I want to do is scream out my pleasure. I want him to know exactly how he makes me feel and how much I like this. Bouncing on his shoulders exhilarates me.

"I'm going to cum," I say, gasping as my body zings with pleasure. "I'm scared I'll be loud. Someone will hear us."

He slows down his mouth and eases back, denying my body what it craves in this moment. "I can help."

Sawyer surprises me by digging his fingers into my hips and bringing me back down until I land on my feet. He doesn't finish me with his mouth and instead bows in and kisses me while sliding his finger between my legs to rub my clit with just the right pressure to bring me back to my peak. This time it's more intense, and I feel my knees weakening. Sawyer doesn't let much noise escape my mouth, kissing me deeper and silencing me as my muscles spasm and I orgasm, the sensation so intense that my body stiffens, and I lose myself to the pleasure he ignites in me.

Sawyer smiles through a kiss. I can feel his lips stretching as if he enjoys that he makes me orgasm as if it's his sole purpose in life. And now I want to do the same for him. I want him to have me any way he pleases.

I grab his pants and slide the zipper down, reaching in to pull out his cock, lacing my fingers around the thick girth. I wonder if it's going to hurt as it slides inside me. I wonder if Sawyer will enjoy my body as much as I enjoy his. Because this is what I want. I don't care where we are. The only thing that matters is we're together.

I stretch my leg up, resting it on his chest, and use my strength to lift myself high enough to align my body to his, standing on my tiptoe. I'm not exactly perfectly aligned to him, but I can rub his tip between my legs to let him feel just how wet he makes me as I silently give him permission.

"Are you sure, Hayley?" Sawyer asks, his voice deepening with his desire. His muscles ripple as I slide my fingers up and down the length of the shaft.

"More than ever. Give me what I want. Take what you want." I adjust him just enough to feel the pressure of his thick girth, ready to stretch me in a way that might make me sore for days. But I don't care. I want to feel it for days. I want the reminder every time I take a step just how incredible Sawyer makes me feel.

Sawyer releases the sexiest growling noise from his throat, taking my words as a command. He shifts his fingers and digs them into my ass cheek, raising me up another foot while propping me against the wall. He glides into me, bowing his head down to watch our bodies connect. I moan at the sight and the sensation of my body adjusting to let him in.

Sawyer's the biggest man I've ever been with on any sort of level, and I savor every second of it. I love his intimidating height and how he can tower over someone with enough threat to make them back down. I also love how small I feel in his arms and how safe and protective he is with me. He treats me as if I'm fragile and priceless. I don't need to be tough with him. I like being able to have my guard down. I shouldn't have to be tough in moments I feel safe.

Sawyer thrusts harder and faster, moaning every time he sinks deep inside me. I clutch onto him and lean my head back, devouring his affection every time he kisses me. Our eyes meet, and he locks me in his gaze. I smile at him through my panting, murmuring how amazing he feels. He graces me with a sexy look that smolders me deep to my soul. I feel as if I'm his perfect woman. His appreciation of me is so hot and heavy that it's almost tangible.

With his free hand, he strums his thumb over my clit and plays with my body as if the melody of my breathy moans gets him off even more. He doesn't stop massaging my clit until I orgasm again. I watch my body do something it has never done, and I squirt him. I gasp in surprise only to have Sawyer steal my breath away as he kisses me more intensely, gliding his tongue over mine and keeping me quiet as he rocks his body into me, the motion bouncing my back against the wall and scraping my skin. But I don't care. I don't care about anything except for him and the passion we share in this moment. With a soft moan against my mouth, Sawyer pulls out and cums on the wall beside us. Watching him gets me off even more, and I smile and cling to him. I know why he did it. He doesn't know when we will get out of here to clean up, and his thoughtfulness gets me good. It keeps me going and craving more.

"Bite me. Drink from me. Get everything you need from me, Sawyer. Let me take care of you as amazingly as you protect me." I kiss his earlobe and suck it into my mouth, nipping him gently.

"I'm fucking falling in love with you, Hayley. I want you to know that. No, that's not right. I'm not really falling in love with you. I already love you. I want to destroy the world on your behalf. I will decimate everyone who tries to hurt you. That I promise you. I will do everything it takes to keep you safe." Sawyer kisses down my throat, using his teeth to pull the strap off my shoulder. Sinking his fangs into my skin, he bites me so quickly that I don't even feel the prick before his mouth molds over the puncture wounds, and he begins to suck.

My heart soars with his declaration. I never knew that I'd want someone to destroy anything on my behalf. I never expected I would crave to see him fuck someone up, to hurt someone all in my name. and I love it more than I should. I think I might love him more than I should. There's always that constant hesitation lingering over me. Because I've seen love get destroyed in unimaginable ways. I know that my parents' love was ruined. Love is something that has to be protected with everything in us to survive in our world. Can this last? Are we strong enough?

It doesn't matter.

Nothing matters except that we are willing to fight. Sawyer, Monroe, and Knox proved they would do anything for me. No other vampire would face this kind of threat unless they were in it with their entire beings.

The edges of my vision shadow, and I comb my fingers into Sawyer's hair as he continues to drink. My body tingles, and the wild hunger that nearly caused me to bite him earlier returns at full force. I don't even realize I'm jerking my head toward his shoulder until it's too late. I sink my teeth into his skin, biting him hard enough to break it open, sending blood flowing into my throat.

Sawyer grunts and releases me, his body awakening all over again as my bite turns him on. It's not what I had expected. I never thought he would like it. But he does.

"You are so fucking sexy. It's taking everything in me not to ravish you all over again. Your mouth excites me. Do you enjoy how I taste?" he asks, his voice all raspy and sexy.

I ease away from his skin. I can't resist dragging my tongue across the blood once more. "You taste amazing. I'm so hungry for you. Starved."

He chuckles and combs my hair from my face. "Is that so?"

I release a weird-ass growl from my throat and bare my teeth at him, jerking my mouth toward his throat next until I bite him. He inhales a sharp breath, and I moan as his blood fills my mouth and travels down to bloom tingles in my stomach.

"Damn. Hayley, your eyes..." The hitch in his voice startles me.

I jerk away, fear clutching my chest. His features shift from desire to confusion, and his eyes flick across mine as he stares at me as if he sees something different in me.

I cover my mouth with my hand. "I'm so sorry. I couldn't help myself.

"I don't understand. You're not a vampire." Sawyer reaches up and drags his thumb across my lip, smearing the blood staining my mouth. "Right? You don't have fangs. You taste better than any donor. But your eyes…"

I inhale a deep breath and slowly exhale. Sawyer doesn't put me down like I expect him to, but he does readjust my body so that I can lock my legs around his waist. Fixing his pants, he lowers us to the floor, allowing me to sit on his lap.

"Talk to me, Hayley. Please. When did this start?" Sawyer rubs his big hands up and down my spine, smoothing out my nerves the best he can.

I lick my lips and clear my throat. "I have something I need to tell you, but I don't know how. I had no idea about any of this until Lawrence bit me with his venom on the way here. Alexander wasn't just a cruel monster because I was his best performer. I'm not like other donors. He created me."

Sawyer's frown deepens as he tries to process my words. I can't even process them myself. What I'm about to say is completely outlandish. Impossible. Insane. Yet, here I am, living proof that anything is possible.

"Have you ever heard of a dhampir?" I ask, keeping my voice low.

Sawyer's eyes widen with shock. "What?"

"You do know." I can tell. It's written all over his face. And Lawrence might've been right. Because Sawyer almost looks afraid. Lawrence said that vampires fear us because we drink their blood.

My lip trembles, but I can't get my voice to work. I can't explain any of this because I just don't know anything yet.

"I knew there was something amazing about you," Sawyer finally says after a moment of silence. "A dhampir. You're a fucking unicorn. You're incredible, Hayley. You're mine. Just because you're a dhampir doesn't change anything. It just makes sense. It explains why it's so easy to be with you and why Aris is horrible."

I smirk at his words, watching his confusion and fear morph into something indescribable. Maybe fascination. Maybe wonder. All I know is that in this moment, I feel like the most precious being in the world. I feel so very loved.

"Do you know anything about dhampirs? Lawrence didn't tell me anything. I'm afraid." I lean forward and rest my head on his shoulder, just listening to the sound of our hearts beating.

"I only know the stories, but I'll tell you anything I can. And I'll get you out of here. I swear. My promise to you stands. You're my woman. I want you to be my entire existence, too. I will do anything." Sawyer hugs me tighter.

And I believe him.

For the first time in days, I feel as if I'm going to be okay. I'll be better off than okay.

I think I finally found my strength.

Lawrence was wrong about me being just a donor even though I'm a dhampir.

I want to prove the stories right.

Lawrence will learn. He will see that I'm not a donor. I'm part of the Bella Crew.

We will take him down.

I SMIRK AT Monroe, listening as silence falls between Hayley and Sawyer in a fucked up prison room. He won the game of Rock-Paper-Scissors to get her in the first place, and I'm glad he did. Had it been Monroe or even myself to win, there would've been a huge problem. It was bad enough Sawyer started a fight with the shadow dweller. But thankfully, when Lawrence showed up, he got his shit together and remembered not to do anything stupid. Monroe would've lost his head or some shit. Me? Who knows. Sawyer has always been incredible at thinking on his feet. I make a lot of judgment calls with my heart. And my cock. Right now? My damn cock aches as I think about Hayley. Sawyer got to fuck her in a way that I crave. Our short time trying to leave wasn't enough. I don't know how long Sawyer will be with Hayley in that cell, but I wish it were me.

"I feel like a fucking psycho right now." Monroe keeps his voice low and stabs his blade into the concrete floor, chipping away at the foundation.

"Only right now?" I ask him teasingly.

He jerks his hand and stabs the blade an inch away from my leg, missing me on purpose. "Fuck off. You know what I mean. A part of me wants to rub one out because I'm so damn horny, and I can't stop staring at this weird-ass setup. I thought the leadership was bad. Can you imagine what it's like for these guys here? Like what the hell."

He's right about that. These bunk beds filled with bodies are unlike anything I've ever seen in my life, and I've lived a long time. I didn't notice them at first until Lawrence dragged out the young vampire from the cell with Hayley and hooked him up to the top bunk in the far corner, knocking him the fuck out only to jab him to send blood into a tube feeding an unconscious donor. It's twisted.

And I can't help the curiosity coursing through me. That guy might know things. It seemed as if Lawrence trusted him enough to keep him with Hayley. And now that Sawyer can focus on the world outside of Hayley since he's not screwing her, I can focus on other things too.

I push to my feet. "Keep an eye on the security feeds and watch the door. I'm going to free the asshole Lawrence had in the room with Hayley."

"Fine, but you better fuck him up a bit. He drank from our girl." Monroe cracks his knuckles and gets to his feet, dusting off his pants. He pulls his com device from his pocket and taps the screen, peering the security feeds around The Whiskey. We managed to hack into the system, and while we can't do certain things like unlock the gates, we can at least have a visual of what's monitored.

"Sure thing, dickhead." I don't plan to do what he says, because the guy is obviously a prisoner. I doubt that he would stand up beside Lawrence, and if I can get him to trust us, he might be able to help us. He knows more about this place than we do. We might be able to make a deal to get him out of here.

Monroe flicks my shoulder. "Fucking liar."

I shake my head and stride away from him, not giving him a chance to stab me in the back or something. It bothers him more than it does me. I heard Hayley offer her blood to the guy. She wanted his in exchange. I might dislike the idea, but I know she was doing what she had to do.

Making my way through the aisles of stacked beds, I glance at the bodies, wondering if they ever get out of this state or if they're basically flesh bags of blood on tap for the duration of their lives. Lawrence keeps them like animals—fuck, maybe worse. It's one of the few things that La Vega doesn't allow. Because when humans are treated like animals, they are more likely to fight back. I know this because I would too. I didn't suddenly lose my morals when I transformed. I remember certain parts of my life, and I don't think of donors as any less. That's why I stand with the Bella Crew. That's why I want to change La Vega. I think donors need better. They would thrive if the circumstances weren't so fucked up. If they thrive, so do we.

I reach the corner of the room where Lawrence forced the vampire onto the top bunk, and I tilt my head and stare at him in silence. He's gagged, but he's no longer unconscious. And what the fuck. He's strapped down in such a way that he could never escape, forced to lie here and have his blood pumped into what looks like an old man beneath him. From the gray hair of the donor, the old man doesn't look like he's going to last much longer in these conditions. His body might heal to regenerate more blood, but donors need more than that.

I step closer and peer down at the young vampire. He can't be much older than the age he turned as a mortal. How do I know? Because he was too compliant. Whatever got him into this mess probably involved his transformation. He still has the demeanor of a donor. He wouldn't have it if he were as old as the Vampire Uprising or The Divide. Sure, I could be wrong, but I'm usually not. I used to see this type of shit all the time.

The vampire's eyes widen at the sight of me, and he mumbles something I can't hear with the gag. It could be a plea for help or a warning. I guess I'll find out. Darting out my hand, I rip off his gag and pull it out of his mouth. A long tube drags from his throat, and the guy coughs and groans, but he can't sit up because of the restraints.

I aim my knife and cut at the heavy straps, keeping only the ones on his legs in place just in case he decides he's going to try to fight me or some shit. I need a chance to move out of the way.

"Are you fucking crazy? You're going to get us both killed. Who are you?" The vampire has a lot of fucking questions when all he should do is thank me.

"It depends on who you ask. I'm Knox, and Hayley is my girl. We came for her." I motion toward the prison cell. "I saw you with her."

He stiffens on the bed, shifting his gaze in the direction of my fingers. "She gave me permission to bite her. Please, don't hurt me. I'm just trying to fucking survive."

"You're lucky it was me and not Monroe to get you right now. Because I don't plan on hurting you. I want to help you, but I need you to help us first. What do you say? Are you going to be Lawrence's little bitch, or are you going to show me that you don't deserve this fate?" I wave my arm around.

The guy frowns and twists his lips to the side. "What the fuck kind of question is that?"

I bob my head. "Good answer. Now tell me about this bullshit. Why are you here? Why were you with Hayley?"

The guy swallows and licks his dry lips. "How about you start by asking me my name? I'm not just going to give you answers to your questions. I want to talk to Hayley first. You said she was yours, but another vampire is with her. He could—"

Monroe materializes on the guy's other side. "Careful what you say, asshole. Sawyer would never hurt her. You, on the other hand..." Jabbing his hand, Monroe pops the vampire in the jaw, sending his head cracking to the side. "That's for putting your fangs in my woman. You're lucky I don't restrain you and remove them."

I shove Monroe, forcing him back. "Damn it. Watch

the feeds. I'm handling this."

"Fucking fine. Handle it, goddamn it." Monroe disappears and reappears outside of the cell door. He quietly knocks his knuckles against the metal, and I regret sending him away. I don't want Hayley getting disturbed right after she fucked Sawyer for the first time. She deserves his sole attention despite everything.

I make a mental note for his ass about this later. I have to focus on the vampire in front of me now.

Turning my attention away from Monroe as he whispers something to Sawyer, I look to the vampire again. "Sorry about Monroe. He's protective of our girl. He's an act first, think about it later type of guy, which is necessary in La Vega. We're part of the Bella Crew and part owner of the Bella hotel. Where are you from?"

The vampire shifts his gaze from staring behind me at Monroe and back to me. I'm not the only one distracted. "My name's Cooper. I'm from here. I grew up here, I was transformed here, and I'm sure I'll fucking die here. I've been caring for Hayley and preparing her for the Fright Fights, until tonight, that is."

He scrubs his fingers into his scruffy face, groaning with the gesture. His jaw looks a bit swollen and bruised, and he's on the verge of turning feral from his lack of blood but seems to be able to keep his shit together. I've seen outcasts far worse. Some Strip dwellers as well.

"What the fuck are those?" I ask, imagining some sort of wrestling match. But worse. If Lawrence keeps donors like this, I can only think of different fucked up ways he'd make a show with them. Before I was bitten and transformed during the uprising, I sometimes caught a wrestling match after a long day at the hospital at a bar. If it's even remotely like those matches...shit. Hayley isn't a fighter.

"The hotel's lame entertainment. Vampires parading in glittery costumes and...killing donors for fake sport. No donor lasts more than a fight or two." Cooper clenches his jaw tight enough for me to hear his teeth grind together.

My stomach twists at the thought of Hayley being thrown into a ring to participate in a deathmatch. "Why the hell would Lawrence go through all this trouble to sentence Hayley to death for a show? What the actual fuck?" I almost don't believe it.

"She's...not expected to lose. I'm training her." Cooper remains expressionless with his words. His silver eyes glow with his hunger, and I wish he'd give more away. He's refraining from saying whatever the fuck is on his mind. I wanted to approach him as an ally and someone who can help him, but if he doesn't spill the details soon, I won't have a choice but to spill his guts until he talks—or have Monroe do it.

Cooper doesn't get a chance to respond to my silent threat because Monroe releases a little whistle. I flick my attention towards the entrance to the room, listening as a key turns in the lock. I haven't seen places that have an actual key lock in who knows how long. Most of the stuff in La Vega is automatic.

"Fuck. It's Lawrence. Why the fuck is he back so quickly? I thought he would leave Hayley to suffer until she starved." Cooper lies back and adjusts the machine, pretending to hook himself up again. "Better hide if you don't want to end up in one of these bunks."

I unsheathe my weapon and tighten my fingers around the hilt of my blade. "Don't say anything. If you can prove that you are not on Lawrence's side, we will get you out."

Cooper doesn't say anything, and I join Monroe near that storage closet with huge racks of equipment, making it easy to remain out of sight.

Lawrence creeps into the building at human speed, slowly drinking in the sight of his collection of donors. The twisted fucker draws his fingers along the row of beds closest to the central aisle, and he smiles as if he's staring at the most precious thing in his world. He's psychotic enough that it probably is to him. I still can't believe he created this monstrous place.

"I know you can hear me coming, Mr. Noble. I hope

you know that I have thought long and hard about your offering, and I think you can do better." Lawrence calls the words out with a smile cracking across his face. The old man looks twisted as fuck. He reminds me of one of the brutal human serial killers in the old classic movies. This guy should've never been transformed into a vampire. He might be strong, but he will be the ruin of everyone. That is if he ever got out of this small town. The leadership probably realized it, which is why he is here in the first place.

It makes me question Sawyer's deal just a bit. I know he can't be serious about helping Lawrence take La Vega, but I know he is confident enough to risk it anyway. Our crew would be furious if they knew. Our ideals are completely opposite of this. We want donors and vampires to coincide more evenly. Well, at least, not this way. Because the vampires here have the shitty end of Mr. Pala's cane. I can imagine what that fuckhead would do if he knew and created a new alliance with Lawrence.

"Are you not going to respond to me, Mr. Noble?" Lawrence asks, raising his voice louder over the humming machines.

A deep growl hums from the metal door. "I am listening. I don't need the dramatics. Just tell me what the fuck you want to sweeten the deal. I already expected as much from you. You're a lot like Aris, you know."

I cringe as I watch Lawrence's features sharpen with his anger. He obviously hates being compared to Aris.

"Far from it. He doesn't have the backbone or the nerve to do what is necessary. His power is wasted. Look how he had such a precious, priceless commodity in his hands for so long, and he didn't raise her to her proper potential." Lawrence saunters closer to the door, taking his sweet time. I hate bastards like this, who think that it is some kind of torture to leave someone waiting and impatient. If anything, it just makes me more stabby.

"I agree with you on that matter. Hayley deserves far better than what she's been given for who she is and what she is." Sawyer's voice deepens with his comment.

I side-eye Monroe. What the fuck is Sawyer talking about? He just said *what* Hayley is. The way he says it makes it sound as if she's not a donor. I don't get it.

Lawrence clicks his tongue and shakes his head. "My heir, you gave away our little secret. I should kill Mr. Noble because of it."

Hayley gasps. "Don't you fucking dare. If you even touch him—"

Lawrence flies at the cell door, unlocks it, and swings it open. He snarls and snaps his fangs, looking as if he's about to charge Hayley. I jerk my hand out and grab Monroe by the shirt, hoisting him back. He's about to start a fight, and even though we could win, there are other more powerful vampires in this town. I've seen them on the feeds. They won't let us leave either. We need the entire Bella Crew to take this place down. And if we tried, I don't know what the leadership would do. They do have some sort of alliance with The Whiskey and Lawrence, and they'd be obligated to do something. The only thing we were supposed to do coming here was to get Hayley and take her back to La Vega. Nothing else. It was in the contract we have with Aris.

Sawyer straightens his shoulders and shoves his palms into Lawrence's chest, knocking him out of the doorway. Lawrence twists and grabs onto Sawyer, flipping him off his feet. He aims a knife at Sawyer's heart, his quick movement and strength proof enough that it would take all three of us to destroy the bastard.

"You're going to have to be tougher than that to best me, Mr. Noble." Lawrence extends his long fangs, growling deep in his chest, the rumble making Hayley back up out of view.

"Don't threaten me. I was going easy on you. I will not let you threaten Hayley or try to scare her. Like I've said before, she's mine. You have no claim on her. Now get the fuck back and tell me what you want to sweeten the deal. My patience runs thin." Sawyer glowers at Lawrence until the vampire backs up and raises his hands in surrender.

Monroe relaxes next to me, but he bounces on his feet in anticipation to charge Lawrence just in case he tries anything.

"I have decided that I will accept your offer if you can prove to me your worth. I think you would make a great headliner of the Fright Fights here. You'll also be the perfect partner to my beautiful dhampir and help keep her secret during the show. If you agree, I will arrange a shared contract with Aris. She can stay here half a year and in La Vega for half a year. You and your crew will be responsible for not only her travel but also her protection. Without benefits. Hayley will be responsible for satisfying any needs or wants you have. Those are my terms. You must get the leadership to agree." Lawrence widens his smile with his words, and he straightens his back and peers around the blood room.

Sawyer hops up and dusts off his pants. "Make it three months and spread out through the year so I don't have to leave my hotel for that long, and you have a deal. I'll see to it that it gets arranged."

"Then you must also donate blood to my collection," Lawrence counters, motioning toward the room. "Agree or no deal. No more discussions. No more bartering. You must have a permanent spot on my show, cater to Hayley, provide blood, and help me take down the La Vega Leadership. If you can do that, Hayley is yours. And you know what that means. It's not just for a human lifespan. It's forever."

I frown at his words. What the actual fuck?

I expect Sawyer to tell him that he needs to discuss it with us, but Sawyer proffers his hand. The two of them shake in silence, and I can't help the sickening feeling rolling through me. It's the first time since turning that I actually feel as if I might get sick. What the fuck?

"You have yourself a deal," Sawyer says, affirming his decision.

"Please call your crew here. I know they linger nearby. I need to make a couple of things clear." Lawrence swivels on his feet and looks around. "Come out, come out, wherever you are."

I scowl at the same time Monroe does. Neither of us moves, waiting for Sawyer to give us the sign. Pursing his lips, Sawyer whistles and calls us to him.

With a heavy sigh, I follow Monroe to the center aisle to show ourselves without getting within reach of Lawrence. I hate this. I want nothing to do with this fucking deal Sawyer made without even discussing with me.

But then I see Hayley standing in the cell behind the two of them. Our eyes meet, and I understand exactly why Sawyer agreed to do what Lawrence asked. Because if I were him, I would've agreed too. Hayley deserves a better life, and it is our job to provide it to her because she can't do it for herself.

"Lawrence, these are my crewmembers Knox and Monroe. They are what I consider my seconds in command." Sawyer slowly nods his head.

Monroe and I both remain silent.

"Then they understand the importance of keeping their mouths shut regarding Hayley and what she is." Lawrence steps closer, clenching his fingers into fists at his sides. "It's imperative that nobody knows she's a dhampir. If I find out either of you shares her secret, I will take your heads. Do you understand?"

A dhampir? The fuck? I've never heard that term before.

"They agree. I'll do it myself if they betray me and our agreement." Sawyer tips his head, giving us both a look to trust him.

"I understand," Monroe says first, though his confusion is as clear as mine.

Lawrence looks at me. "I need you to say it as well."

I flick my gaze to Hayley and Sawyer and finally back to Lawrence. "I understand. I will not share the secret."

Lawrence smiles. "I'll have Cooper catch you up on what you need to do to prepare for the show, Mr. Noble.

Until then, you may stay in room number five-oh-five with your crew. I apologize for the lack of three beds, but it is important that we have space for our guests. I hope you don't mind sharing."

I suppress my smirk.

"That won't be a problem." Sawyer steps back and holds his hand out to Hayley, coaxing her to leave the cell to join his side.

"Good. Now get some rest, and we will meet tomorrow at dusk. I expect you to have everything in order by then." Without another word, Lawrence disappears.

Before Sawyer has a chance to open his mouth, I charge him and knock him back into the cell, crashing his back to the wall. I snarl and snap my fangs, my whole body rigid with my anger. What the actual fuck is happening? This was supposed to be an in-and-out operation. We weren't supposed to make this kind of deal with an asshole. We already have one that is just shitting all over us back in La Vega.

"You better have a fucking good reason as to why you made this deal without even talking to us first. And second in command? We are fucking equals, Sawyer." I fist his shirt in my hand, tightening the collar around his neck.

"Knox, please. Calm down." Hayley's soft voice whispers from behind me, and it's the only reason I don't punch Sawyer in the face.

I know he did what he did because he was protecting Hayley, but he needs to know that even if I might've done the same thing if I were in his place, he can't start making decisions on everyone's behalf. We always agree on what to do together as a crew. It's how things work between us and how it will always work. Hayley isn't just his. She's our girl, and the future he chooses affects everyone.

Slowly swiveling around, I face Hayley and her big blue eyes and quivering lip. I can't stand the sorrow on her face, so I close the space to her and kiss her, trying to stop her mouth from trembling. I hug my arms around her and pull her in close, savoring her touch and how perfect she feels in my arms.

"I'm sorry. This whole situation is just fucked up. All I want is to take you back to the Bella. I want to kiss you and show you how much you mean to me and to get Sawyer's smell off you. It's making me incredibly horny. I've missed you." I try to keep my voice light despite the darkness burning through me. "Can I at least take you back to the room here since I know taking you home is impossible? I'd like to make sure you are physically okay."

"As long as you promise to shower with me first," Hayley says, tilting her head back to look into my eyes.

"Absolutely. I'd like nothing more than that." I lick my lips and kiss her again. "And then we need to talk." Shifting, I look at Sawyer and Monroe. "All of us."

The two of them nod in agreement.

Sawyer motions for us to follow behind him. "Tell me about it. Our lives are about to change. Not only that, so will our eternities."

A part of me hopes for the better, but the more realistic part of me knows that it's going to be hard. Things could get worse.

I have a feeling that the only way we are going to get the life we want is if we succeed at taking La Vega from the leadership and stopping Lawrence from trying to move in.

Humanity depends on it.

So does the Bella Crew.

"THIS COULD ULTIMATELY be a good thing. We'll have access in and out of the city. Do you know what we could accomplish with that kind of clearance?" Sawyer sits on the edge of a queen bed, his long legs bent as he rests his elbows on them.

"I don't fucking care about any of that. Tell me about dhampirs. How the hell did you even know about them?"

Turning in the rolling chair, Knox meets my gaze. "How are you taking it? It had to be one helluva information bomb. I can't even imagine, vixen. I can barely wrap my mind around it myself. I need to know what you're going through. I need to figure out if there's anything I can do to help you."

Monroe bounces the balls of his feet, moving me up and down on his lap. He rests his chin to the crook of my neck and kisses my skin softly. "Can I just fuck someone up already? Maybe I can take your damn place at whatever the fuck these Fright Fights are. I'm not going to lie. If I can fuck up some crazy vampire, I'm good."

I can't stop the laughter bubbling from my throat. Shifting on his lap, I turn sideways to get a better look at his face. Monroe grins at me, showing off his fangs, and I stretch closer and kiss him. I can't help myself. He's so hot when he's all riled up and needing to embrace his murdery, crazy-ass side.

"You would be amazing." I nuzzle my nose to his, feeling his beard tickle my chin.

"He might be skilled enough, but look at Sawyer. He's a fucking freakshow. He might have tons of people lining up, and Lawrence knows that." Knox links his fingers together.

I crinkle my nose. "Freakshow? Far from it. He's sexy

and tall. Handsome. I can't get enough of him."

My words light Sawyer's face with a cute smile.

"Yeah, yeah. We get it, little bird. You want to bone him all the time now. I think I could still put on a better show." Pulling his knife out, Monroe twists his hand and spins it by the hilt in front of me. "We could have a lot of fun. Just imagine all of the training I'll put you through."

I giggle as he growls and kisses my throat again. "I'll even let you pin me on occasion. Maybe. I rather enjoy seeing you beneath me."

Heat flushes my face at how easy it is for Monroe to talk about these kinds of things in front of Sawyer and Knox. Actually, they all are comfortable with it. I can tell that since he mentions it, they're all now thinking about having sex with me. And I know for sure that Monroe is, because I feel his dick harden under my ass.

So I wiggle. I roll my hips teasingly, just wanting to do anything to distract him.

Two strong hands grab my waist and lift me away from Monroe. "Don't even start, vixen. Monroe wouldn't hesitate to take you to the bathroom, and I really fucking want to talk. I hate to say it, but this conversation takes precedence. I want to know more about dhampirs too badly. It's driving me crazy not having all the information here." He taps his head. "I need to know every little thing about you."

Knox adjusts me in his arms until he cradles me like a blushing bride. He spins far too quickly for Monroe to try to grab away and uses his sturdy, muscular frame as a shield, pinning me to the wall.

"Sawyer can tell you all of that business, since apparently he knows. You guys can have that little gossip session you want. I just want to hear Hayley scream my name and feel her wet pussy tighten around my cock with her orgasm. I'll let her bite the hell out of me too. I need her mark." Monroe snaps his teeth, his presence looming ultra-close to Knox's back. At least he's honest about his desires.

I stretch up and look at him, watching him glide his tongue across his lip before he sucks it into his mouth. And damn. I want that too. I didn't know how much I did until this very second. I love how much he wants me and my body and doesn't care about anything else except for what makes me happy.

"You like that," Monroe says, stretching out his fingers to caress my cheek. "Be my badass girl and sucker punch Knox, so I can steal you from him. We will have so much fun. Just think about it." Monroe teases me by sinking his fangs into his arm. He waves it a foot away, trying to entice me.

My breathing quickens, and I can't take my eyes from the blood trailing over his skin.

Sawyer tips his head back and laughs. "Shit, Knox watch out. She's considering his offer. Look at her eyes. That's her dhampir nature peeking through. She has similar qualities to vampires, but instead of feeding on humans, she needs vampire blood along with food. She'll get sick otherwise."

His words steal the warmth from my body, and now all I want to do is talk as well. Because Sawyer has answers. He'll tell me things that Lawrence won't.

"Goddamn it, Sawyer. You fucking cock-block. You just killed her lady boner." Monroe chucks his knife at Sawyer, but Sawyer moves too fast and the sharp point thunks into the wall behind him.

"Chill out, you bastard. It's important that we know everything we can about Hayley." Knox rubs the back of his neck and sets me on my feet. "One of the few advantages our enemies have over us is information. If we can sort this out, we can use it against them. Both Aris and Lawrence know something about dhampirs that makes them risk shit to fight over her. I'm assuming power. Aris abused her to keep her weak and controllable. Lawrence wants to test her."

"Lawrence called me his eternal blood source." I shiver at the words.

I turn to Monroe and hold my hands out until he steps

closer. Grabbing him by his belt, I pull him to me and caress my fingers over the bulge in his pants. "If you let us all talk and process everything, I will suck your cock and swallow after."

Monroe raises an eyebrow. "Fuck. You're such a bad girl. You have no idea about all the things I want to do to you because of it."

A wink at him. "Maybe I'll let you do those too."

Monroe play-growls and tries to scoop me up, but Knox intervenes and tosses me towards Sawyer. I screech a laugh as I fly through the air and land in his arms. Sawyer sets me on the bed and rolls on top of me, kissing me as he wraps the blankets over us, blocking Monroe.

"Dammit. Fine. Just keep laughing like that, little bird. I love the hell out of hearing it. Like a little psychotic hyena." Monroe flops onto the bed beside me and Sawyer and drapes his arm over the two of us, not even caring. He sandwiches me between them.

I tilt my head. What the hell is that? Sounds cute.

"Now to get you to act like one." Monroe gives me a shake. "I'm here for it. We can fuck shit up together."

"La Vega better watch out, if that's what you plan for Hayley." Knox joins us and sits cross-legged at the edge of the bed. It's far too small for the four of us, but no one complains. It's just so nice to be together.

If only a knock didn't sound on the door.

If there's one thing that can set off my guys, it's a damn unwanted interruption.

"This better be fucking room service because I can tell it's not Lawrence. It's not a donor either." Monroe abandons the bed first and thrusts the door open, aiming his knife at Cooper's groin.

Cooper flies back and hits the hallway wall behind him, clutching himself protectively. "Don't hurt me. I have orders."

I rush off the bed and attempt to go to Monroe, but Knox intercepts me, scooping me up protectively.

"What kind of fucking orders? We were told to get some rest here for a few hours." Monroe aims his knife again.

"Monroe, it's okay. Cooper isn't our enemy. Let him in." I hope my voice is as steady as I feel. Because I'm not afraid to speak up to Monroe. I don't want him hurting someone who could be a possible ally. I know that Cooper can help us in the long run. He knows the Fright Fights. He knows the competitors. And lastly, he knows about me.

Monroe peeks at me over his shoulder. Narrowing his eyes, he attempts to see if I'll back down, but I wiggle in Knox's arms until he sets me on my feet.

Begrudgingly, Monroe steps aside, points his blade at

Cooper and then into the room. "You heard Hayley. Get your ass inside now. Don't touch anything. Maybe stand across the room. I don't know you, and I still want to cut you up for earlier."

Cooper flares his nostrils and steps into the room. He straightens his back more, giving himself another inch of height. It doesn't do much considering that all three of them are taller than him, but whatever makes him not as intimidated.

"Monroe, you don't have to be such a dick. If Hayley thinks this guy is chill, then we need to trust her judgment." Knox laces his fingers through mine, offering me a smile. I can't tell if he fully believes his words, but at least he's try-ing.

"He's the dude that is supposed to be telling us more about whatever the fuck is going on anyway." Sawyer scoots to the edge of the bed and points at a small desk with a roll-ing chair. "Sit. Tell us a little bit about yourself. Don't ex-pect us to be commanded by you. We're here for no other reason except for Hayley. Don't try anything stupid, and we can all get along."

Cooper follows Sawyer's instructions and plops into the rolling chair, swiveling it from side to side with his nerves. Monroe remains by the door, refusing to settle down and relax again. I can't blame him. This whole situation is fucked up, and he doesn't trust Cooper. If he knew what had gone down between me and the vampire when I first arrived, things would probably get violent. But just over the last day or so, I know Cooper is only trying to survive. He's not a bad guy. He just has limited options.

"I don't know exactly what to say." Cooper fidgets and brushes his fingers through his blond hair. "If you have questions, just fucking ask them. Treat this like the interrogation it is and not like we're about to become friends. I know we're not. I know my place around here."

Something about Cooper's words bothers me. He automatically shrugs us off, considering my guys as threats to him.

"Don't make this awkward, you guys. It's already hard enough. Cooper was part of the herd that you saw. He's one of the vampire performers at the Fright Fights, and he's been...feeding me." I regret my words immediately, because Cooper's eyes flash silver. It's obvious that I wasn't the only one being fed. "And I've been providing blood for him. If he doesn't get blood from me, he doesn't get blood at all."

Sawyer growls deep in his throat, his body turning rigid at the thought. "Not anymore. Now that we are here, Lawrence better figure something else out."

Silence follows his comment, and the five of us stare at each other. I should speak up and try to redirect the conversation, but I don't know how. I'm not used to this. I need somebody else to do it.

"You don't have to worry about me. Hayley only felt bad. I didn't even ask her. And I won't ever ask her. I can go a while without blood, and I can always just..." His words trail off.

"Finish what you were going to say," Monroe snaps, leaning his back against the door. "What can you always do?"

Cooper sighs and shakes his head. "I can drink from one of the donors at the Fright Fights. That's how most of the performers get blood anyway."

"Why does it sound like the donors aren't cool with that?" Monroe asks. He finally decides to move from the door and comes to my side. I sit back on the bed, and both Knox and Monroe take places at my sides while Sawyer decides to perch on the corner edge of the bed.

"Because they're not. They're prisoners and sentenced to death. The Fright Fights make their punishments a spectacle. People pay to see this bullshit. But what can we do? We can't leave. If we don't fight, we'll never get any time away from the herd. Some donors choose to compete just to end things. Death is better to some." Cooper droops his shoulders and drops his gaze to the floor.

I scrunch my face, remembering the part of the show I

saw. It was absolutely horrifying. I couldn't imagine having to perform in it over and over again. Except I'm going to have to. I heard the deal Sawyer made with Lawrence. He agreed to participate as my partner. I never in my wildest dreams imagined such a thing, yet here we are. How will we ever get through? Sawyer is a badass. He can take down a ton of vampires. Fuck, he even cut off someone's dick on my behalf. But killing donors? He doesn't have that monstrous gene inside him. He appreciates donors, unlike other vampires. He sees a future where donors and vampires can coincide. I'm afraid that if he goes through with this, it could change him. It could change me.

"You can't be fucking serious. What's the fun in watching someone far less powerful than their opponent get slaughtered? That's not an interesting fight. That's just sick." Monroe scratches his beard, combing his fingers through it. "It's weak and shows nothing. If Lawrence wants a fucking good show, he needs to pit vampire against vampire."

Knox reaches over and smacks Monroe on the chest. "Don't give anyone any ideas. We can't leave a mess in our wake. Remember our rule. We leave things better than what we started with."

I blink a few times, tipping my head to meet Knox's eyes. I've never heard that rule before, but it resonates with me. It makes me appreciate him and the Bella Crew more than ever.

It gives me hope.

"I'd prefer it. I don't like fighting donors, but I also don't want to spend all my time fucking generating blood. That's torture. At least I can do my best to give swift, merciful deaths." Cooper leans back in the chair and tips his head toward the ceiling. "Don't judge me for it either. You'll get it when you actually do something besides sneaking around here like tough guys, acting as if you matter in the grand scheme of things."

I raise my eyebrows in surprise.

"Nothing matters. Not here." Cooper turns his gaze to me for a second, but he once again looks away.

"Damn, you're fucking depressing. If that's what you think, then why even bother showing up here. Why don't you just go do whatever the fuck you do? We don't need you." Sawyer reaches out and touches my knee. "We'll figure it out. Hayley gives us a reason. Our crew gives us a reason. And we matter to them. That's what's important. I don't need to change history. I need to make things good for the people I care about."

"Whatever. Like I said, I'm following orders. I'm not here to do anything except make sure you know the rules. I was also told that I need to make sure Hayley gets enough blood. She's going to need it. Dhampirs require a lot after triggering their innate nature, especially if they are expected to remain in control. They're worse than vampires when they're starving."

"Not happening. Hayley will get everything she needs from us. Do you understand?" Sawyer proves his point by biting his arm and holding it out to me.

I freeze, staring at the dark ruby rivulets of his blood dripping over his skin. It's so shocking that he so easily offers blood like he's my donor. I don't move. I'm not even sure if I'm breathing. My chest tightens as I continue to stare.

Monroe barks a laugh and drapes his arm over my shoulders, giving me a little shake. "Come on, little bird. Don't leave Sawyer hanging. We can tell you want to lick it. There's no shame. Unless you're in the mood for me."

I giggle in nervousness, shaking my head. "You're too damn much, Monroe. You guys keep acting like this is so normal."

"It will be if you just would act like a good little dhampir and take what you want." Monroe's playful voice turns husky, and my smile fades.

I can't believe I'm about to do this. All four of them watch me as if I'm the most fascinating creature in the world. Blood exchanges are known to be intimate, but here

I am about to treat Sawyer as a food source.

I tighten my jaw. "You know what? No. I'm not going to treat you like you're my personal donor. If we're doing this, I want you to bite me too."

I expect Sawyer to protest, because the others watch us. But he accepts my challenge and pulls me to him until I face him and straddle his lap. Brushing my hair from my shoulder, he leans in and tears at my collar with his teeth, exposing my skin. And I feel like the sexiest woman in the world. Heavy silence fills the air, and no one says anything as Sawyer sinks his fangs into my shoulder. I gasp and cling onto him, the sensation of his mouth just as incredible now as it was in our moment of passion in the prison cell.

Sawyer moans and eases away, licking his lips. "Your turn, Hayley."

"Yeah, Hayley, be a vicious little dhampir and bite the hell out of Sawyer for making me jealous as fuck. He's not the only hungry one." Monroe bounces on the bed, shifting closer, peeking at me.

This cute bastard wants to watch. Actually, so does Knox. It should be weirder than it is, but it's not. It feels exhilarating and perfect, even with Cooper frozen in his seat as if he's afraid to speak or move or even breathe. My guys act as if he no longer exists, so I go with it. I know I invited him into the room.

"You can bite me too, Monroe. I don't mind." I lick my lips and bat my eyelashes at him, loving the heavy lust darkening his gaze.

"Careful, Hayley. You need to drink first. If you don't—" Cooper snaps his mouth shut as all three of my guys growl at him, finally acknowledging that he's still in the room. "I mean it. You guys can act like assholes all you want toward me, but I'm trying to help Hayley. If you drink too much, and she doesn't get any, she will fucking attack you. I've seen it happen."

His words are enough to snap all of us out of our playful mood to turn to him. He just said that he's seen a dhampir attack someone. If he has seen it, that means he knows of another person like me.

"That's why Lawrence chose you to care for Hayley before we got here," Sawyer says, musing my thoughts for me. "I was wondering why you. You're obviously young and not very powerful. You carry yourself as if you were newly transformed."

Cooper purses his lips. "Yeah, my grandmother. She was taking care of me when I was a child, and I saw it happen. That's when I realized the woman I thought was my mother was actually my grandmother. She ripped a vampire's heart out that broke into our house."

His story captures my attention completely, and I lean

forward. His grandmother was a dhampir? Whoa. If that was the case, that means she had a child. But what about Cooper? He's a vampire. Dhampirs can't change. At least, that's what Lawrence said. His venom bite proved as much. I didn't transform, and I didn't die.

"How? You should be one too, right? And your mom? What about her?" I peer at Sawyer, wondering if he knows the answers. He remains silent, and I don't think he does. He only knows the stories. Cooper? He lived the dhampir life with his family. "I have so many questions. Why didn't you tell me this?"

Cooper's fangs peek from his full top lip, and he brings his emerald gaze to mine. His eyes drink in my face as he stares at me for a long, silent moment. I'm not sure if he's going to answer me. He looks as if he might try to flee the room to avoid this conversation. Whatever happened in his childhood must've been traumatic enough that it's hard for him to talk about. I should know. I understand what it's like to live through torment and torture and abuse. Cooper might be a vampire. He might be strong. But we aren't that different, and I realize it more and more now.

None of my guys move as I stand up and close the couple feet of space between me and Cooper. I rest my hand on his shoulder, unable to stop myself from trying to comfort him.

"I'm sorry. I don't mean to pry," I add, trying to force my mouth to smile. "You don't have to tell me anything. I get it."

"Like hell—" Monroe groans as Knox punches him in his gut, stopping him from speaking his mind. I can tell he's as invested in answers as I am. It does take a lot for me not to keep pushing Cooper, but I don't want him to shut down.

Cooper reaches up and rests his hand on mine. "You don't have to apologize. I do want to tell you. I just...it's hard for me. I've been carrying the secret all my life. The only ones who've ever known were Lawrence and Opal."

Hearing Opal's name awakens a deep cut inside of me, releasing the grief I've been trying to suppress since Alexander murdered her. I still can't believe she's gone. This all feels like a nightmare.

"What about the rest of your family?" I ask, hoping if I redirect the conversation to just work through my questions one at a time, it might be easier for him to talk.

"My grandmother was sentenced to death. My mother died when my little sister was born. She carried the dhampir gene but isn't like you. Males can't be like you either, at least, of what I know. It was possible for me to pass it down if I chose to have offspring, but there was no fucking way we were ever going to let that happen. No one in my family was going to live a life as what Lawrence wanted." Cooper clenches his jaws with his words. He doesn't want his family to have the life that I find myself in now.

"Your sister is a vampire too?" Knox asks, speaking up. Sawyer and Monroe remain silent, taking in the whole conversation and letting me direct it.

Cooper nods his head. "We managed to get one of the guests to transform both of us in exchange for our older sister. It was her idea. She saved us." Shaking his head, Cooper blinks his eyes, and the sheen in his gaze disappears.

How fucking awful his situation was. I can't believe that his older sister made a deal with a vampire to transform the rest of her siblings. I understand desperation, but I still just can't imagine it.

"You can see how it turned out for me. My little sister, Lilac, works across the way at Falo Ills. I agreed to become part of the herd, so she wouldn't have to be. Lawrence threatens to put her in all the time, which is why I do what he says. It is what it is, but she's family. She deserves better. I don't want Daisy's sacrifice to have been for nothing. Her master murdered her because she tried to take him out in his sleep. We were hoping that we could transform her later, but it's just..." He lets his voice trail off. "Life is shitty. But you already know that."

It's so much to take in. I still have so many questions,

and I want to know more about his family and life, about his grandmother and what she was like as a dhampir. I want to know everything about him.

I don't get the chance to ask.

An alarm blares through the air, and the lights shut off.

My guys materialize around me protectively.

"What the fuck is going on?" Sawyer asks, linking his fingers through mine, ensuring that no one can take me.

"It's a drill. Lawrence has them to keep everyone on their toes in case of a threat. We have to go." Cooper stands up from his chair, unfazed by the strange alarm.

"We're not going anywhere," Monroe says.

The door to our room swings open, and a team of security personnel aims guns at us. "Everyone out. Boss's order."

"What is this about?" Sawyer asks.

No one responds.

The security personnel open fire.

BLOOD SPRAYS ACROSS my face. Monroe swears as a bullet sinks into his shoulder. Rushing forward, he stabs the first security personnel in the neck. Knox spins me away, shielding me with his body while taking several shots to the back. Sawyer grabs another one of the personnel and manages to cut his head clean off, leaving blood pouring everywhere.

My eyes widen at the strangely intoxicating scent permeating the air. It sets me off in a hungry panic. My stomach roars, the pain so intense that I bow forward. It feels as if I haven't eaten in weeks. The starvation gripping at my very essence consumes my every thought. Shadows crowd my vision, and I spin in Knox's protective arms. I shove against him, trying to get him to move. I can't control myself. It's as if I'm watching my body from beside myself.

"Hayley, stop." Knox meets my sudden strength with his, forcing me against the wall.

I growl and snap my teeth at him like a damn animal. His eyes bulge in shock, but he refuses to let me go. Instead, he tilts his head to the side and exposes his neck to me. And holy shit. My teeth sink into his flesh hard enough to send blood gushing into my mouth. I groan as his delicious taste cascades down my throat as I suck harder and harder. He adjusts me in his arms, rubbing his hand down the length of my back. He tastes so fucking good. I can't get enough.

"Hayley, slow down. You're going to drain me completely." Knox puffs a breath in my ear, but he doesn't try to force me away. I'm nearly certain he won't. All he does is continue to hold me and let me have my way with him.

"Fuck, someone grab her." Cooper's voice cuts through the air. "Be careful though. She's lost control. She could hurt you. You don't understand a dhampir's strength. Once it's triggered, she can do serious damage."

"She's fine. I can handle her." Knox groans again, his body wobbling. It's as if I somehow entrance him, because he no longer asks me to slow down.

Sawyer comes up behind Knox and rests his hands on his shoulders. A deep, scary-ass growl escapes Knox's mouth. He doesn't want Sawyer separating us. It's the craziest thing, and I can't get my mouth to stop sucking and biting for more. Neither of us can resist each other.

"He won't be able to make her stop. There's something about dhampirs that hypnotizes vampires, especially if they're emotionally connected. He's going to let her kill him." Cooper remains a couple feet away as if he's afraid of me.

I try to convince myself to release Knox, but my mouth still refuses to. I only stop to bite him again, opening another wound, leaving another mark. I'm a fucking savage. My brain won't connect to my body and obey me, and Knox's lustful moans do nothing to help.

"Damn it. I want her mouth on me next. Hold Knox. I'm going to see if I can get the starving minx to latch onto me next." Monroe bites his arm, and the scent of his blood wafts to me as he waves it near my face.

Whatever he does works, because I manage to pull myself away and launch into his arms, grabbing his wrist to drink from him next. He laughs as we fall to the floor, and I pounce on top of him, sucking him hard enough to make him moan.

"Hey, little bird. Look at you all badass and bitey. You sexy, naughty girl. Careful. I'm gonna want more." Monroe releases what sounds like a purr from his throat, and I gasp in anticipation as he clutches my thigh.

My hunger morphs into lust, and I slide myself lower.

Sawyer hooks his arms around my waist and yanks me off Monroe before things get carried away. He holds me out like a savage beast, dangling me in front of him.

It's enough to smack some sense into me, and I stop thrashing and hang forward like a doll in his arms. Cooper, Knox, and Monroe all stand in front of me and stare at me with strange expressions crossing their faces. Cooper's face is hard with indecipherable emotions. Maybe fear. Maybe annoyance. As for Knox and Monroe, they look as if they want me to bite them again. They look as if they were about to take off their clothes to let me have more of them.

"This is what I warned you about. All the blood you just spilled set her off." Cooper takes a few steps away as if he's afraid the others will go after him. "You guys need to realize the woman you knew before she came here has changed. Being bitten with a vampire's venom makes her stronger. It makes her crave blood more. I'm sure before that, Alex had given her just enough to keep her satiated and healthy. All bets are off now. At least, as long as she has the venom in her system. It won't last forever. She will have to be bitten again and again over her life to keep the power."

What the actual fuck? I can go back to how I was? Do I want to? If it means that I won't be so out-of-control...then yes.

"Does Lawrence know that?" Sawyer asks.

Cooper shakes his head. "No. I couldn't give him all of the answers."

"Good. Don't tell him. I think we need to come up with some sort of plan and agreement. We could really use your help, Cooper. What do you say?" Sawyer offers his hand to the vampire.

Cooper hesitates. "I won't tell him, but I don't know if I can risk helping you. My sister—"

"What if we can get her out of this town? Will you help us then?" Monroe cracks his knuckles and rotates his head, cracking his neck next. "I think we can arrange that."

"He will know it was me." Cooper shifts on his feet. "I don't think Lilac would agree if it meant something happening to me. I mean, something worse than what I experience now."

"We'll come up with something. If that's what it takes

to help Hayley, we'll get it done. Your life is about to change, Cooper." Sawyer glances from Cooper to me and then to the others. "All you have to do is agree to be on the Bella Crew. And who knows. Maybe we can get you out of here too. But you can't be afraid. You have to know that even if someone is more powerful than you, it doesn't mean you're weak."

Cooper inhales and exhales, thinking over Sawyer's words. Just when I think he's about to reject his offer, Cooper holds out his hand and shakes Sawyer's. "If it means getting out of the herd and making sure my sister is safe, then yes. I don't really have anything else to lose."

"Just don't fuck up or betray us. Don't think we won't cut off your cock." Monroe tightens his mouth, squaring his shoulders. "If you join Bella, it's for life."

"You mean forever." Knox proffers his hand to Cooper next.

"If we can even make it out of here," Cooper says, scrubbing his hands to his cheeks.

"We will, little buddy," Sawyer says, teasingly. "You'll see. Watch how we handle things now. My com device detected movement from Lawrence's office. He's probably heading our way since security failed to take us to him." Turning to me, Sawyer grabs my hand. "Hayley, bite me. Do that sexy thing, and don't stop. Monroe, shoot Cooper a couple of times. Knox, play the good guy."

I can barely process what's happening as I bite into his throat, obeying his command. I don't have to ask him to know there is a reason for it, especially if he knows Lawrence is coming.

I close my eyes and suck on Sawyer's throat, his blood filling me up with something that warms me from the inside out. Growls rumble through the air from Monroe and Knox, and Cooper shouts with the sound of a gunshot. A few more ricochet through the air, ringing in my ears. I'm too afraid to pull away from Sawyer, so I bite him again and pretend none of this is happening. I pretend this is foreplay leading up to a passionate moment between us.

Lawrence shatters my fantasy, his raging holler booming through the air. "Hayley! Release him now!"

"Whoa, calm down. It's not what it looks like. She's starving. Let Sawyer care for her. She needs to heal from her injuries as well. We were attacked." Knox intercepts Lawrence, not allowing him to get within reach of me and Sawyer.

Lawrence growls, and something crashes. "She will hurt him. Stand back!"

"Hey, stop. I'm fine. Don't come near us. I don't know what the fuck you've done to my girl, but she's turned a bit wild. The second she was threatened, she started acting like a starved Strip dweller." Sawyer swivels, using his body to block me against the wall.

"I'll handle her. While you're in my hotel—" Lawrence heaves a breath and snarls in exasperation. I think Monroe must've gotten between us and hit him.

I want so badly to see, but another part of me is still too afraid.

"Handle her? Fuck that. I've seen how you've handled her so far. If I ever see you fucking hurt our girl again, you will regret it, deal or not. I don't give a fuck if she attacked someone. I don't even give a fuck that she lost control. She has to learn, and I'd rather her learn to control herself with me than devour any more of these assholes. They interrupted our training meeting with Cooper. Which you forgot to mention, might I add. He's lucky Hayley trusts him, or else he would probably be on the floor too." Sawyer rubs his big palm between my shoulder blades and whispers for me to release him.

I get my shit together and pull back, but I keep my face hidden against the crook of his neck. Unease clenches my chest. Despite my guys surrounding me, I can't control my fear instincts. It doesn't help that I can still smell the blood filling the air. And there's a lot of it.

"These were my best guards. You're telling me that Hayley did this?" Lawrence shuffles across the floor, his footsteps thudding as he hops over the bodies.

"No, but she helped. These assholes started firing without even giving us a chance to figure out if they were legit or not. Look at what they've done to Cooper. They shot him. They shot all of us. Can you blame us for fighting back? They came in here and just demanded we go with them. The same would happen to them if this were La Vega." Monroe deepens his voice, his annoyance grating into me. "Hayley could've been killed."

He's absolutely right about everything, and if Lawrence thinks otherwise, he's an idiot.

"I apologize for my guards' rash behavior, but they were informed not to allow you to push them around. I'll not have you coming into my hotel and acting as if you're in charge. You're alive as a courtesy. Don't forget it. You have a place, and despite where you think it is, it is beneath me. I could end all of you, but I find you useful at the moment. I have wanted someone who had some influence within La Vega outside of the leadership. Just remember, if it falls through, or you don't hold up your end of our agreement, you'll end up dead. Or better yet, you'll be part of my blood donors."

My guys are smart, and they do choose their battles wisely. That is one of the things I have learned from them. There are times where they wish with everything in them that they could just destroy the world, but strategizing how to get everybody through this alive is far more important than trying to flex their power and prove Lawrence wrong. It's what makes them who they are. Even the hotels and Alexander in La Vega know better than to truly underestimate them.

"You can cut that shit out. We don't need the reminder. What we need is to know what the fuck all of this was about. Cooper had mentioned something about a drill, but you can't expect us to follow along without being properly informed. If you want an alliance to work between us, then you need to give a little as well and not expect so much in return." Sawyer sounds so sexy confronting Lawrence and his bullshit.

It's almost weird how Lawrence doesn't react like Alexander. If he were Alexander, I'd be able to tell exactly what he was thinking and plotting. It scares me even more that I can't. Because it's obvious Lawrence doesn't appreciate being told what to do.

"I suppose that's fair. It seems we need to work out the details now that I'm certain you'll be a good fit here." He waves around the room. "Not a single survivor. Perhaps I can barter with you to also train new security personnel. I would offer you a position, but I don't trust you. Not yet." Lawrence shifts in my peripheral vision, and I finally get the courage to lift my face from Sawyer's throat.

Sticky blood covers my body, and I try not to look at myself in the wall mirror. I look as if I just finished a performance in the blood rain back at Vampire Nights. It's like I can never get through a day without having blood all over me. At least the majority that's on me belongs to Sawyer. It makes licking my lips not so gross. Actually, it tastes incredible. Just like him.

I shake my head, pushing the thoughts away. Lawrence's gaze burns into me. I can feel it scraping at the side of my face as if he is cutting me with his sharp nails.

I refuse to look.

"I think that is an excellent idea." Sawyer loosens his hold on me, and I realize he wants to set me on my feet.

I tighten my legs around him. "Please don't," I whisper. I'm just so afraid that if he's not holding me that Lawrence will snatch me away, and there won't be anything anyone can do about it.

Sawyer shifts me until I feel Monroe's strong fingers lace around my sides and ease me away from him. That's the only reason I let go.

"Why don't you allow Cooper to take Hayley to the gym to continue with her practice for the show while we work out the contracts. I would also like to listen in as you call Alexander. We need that portion of the deal in place before anything else. If you can't accomplish that, then there's no point in pursuing this alliance." Lawrence steps closer. He's circling us like a damn predator, and it makes me squirm in Monroe's arms.

"I will escort Hayley," Monroe says, speaking up. "I'm an excellent fighter, and I want to ensure she truly knows how to handle herself in the supposed Fright Fights." Monroe twists and looks at Cooper. "Is that okay?"

Copper shrugs his shoulders. Having Monroe ask him if it's okay is probably the last thing he expected. Lawrence doesn't say anything as Cooper finally agrees. He probably prefers that the Bella Crew separates.

I don't like it, but I know I don't have a choice. Sawyer, Knox, and Monroe have a plan. They always have a plan.

Turning to Sawyer and Knox next, Monroe adds, "You know how to alert me if you need me. I'll also inform Tate of what's going on. I'm sure she's waiting for my call."

Sawyer whacks Monroe on the back with a nod. "Don't get into too much trouble."

Monroe chuckles without another word.

Grabbing Cooper from his spot sitting on the floor, Monroe hoists him to his feet.

The three of us disappear at vampire speed. I say a silent prayer to the universe. This is my new life now. I hope it's better than before. But I won't hold my breath. Because I don't even know if that's possible. How could it be with me?

"First of all, you have to show her how to hold her weapon, so she doesn't lose it." Monroe curls his fingers around his dagger, showing me how to jab and swipe while also protecting myself. "It might help your ass too."

Instead of arguing with Monroe, Cooper listens and readjusts his grip on his own daggers. I realize the only fighting experience Cooper might have is in the ring. That won't help either of us when it comes to outside threats.

"It's also better for you to wear out your opponent first. You're a sexy little minx, Hayley. Use your talents to your advantage. I've seen you in the air. If you can get up in the corner of the ring, you can jump and reach that beam up there. Maybe we can rig the stage for a better show that will also benefit you. Make it a lot more fun and entertaining while also keeping you safe. You could help the donors as well. I'm sure we can figure out how to get to them." Monroe runs toward the side of the ring and climbs on the ropes, repositioning himself. Without warning, he jumps at Cooper and tackles him.

I screech and hop out of the way, watching as Monroe pins Cooper in a matter of seconds, aiming his blade at his neck.

"It could benefit your ass too. We're going to need you to work on your damn skills if you're going to survive. Everyone must toughen the hell up. The Bella Crew has a lot of threats, even among our allies." Monroe catapults off Cooper and holds his hand out to him, helping him to his feet.

Cooper rolls his shoulders, shaking off the fact that Monroe beat him so quickly.

"Things are really going to fucking change around here. I don't even know what the point is for me to even think I could help you guys." Cooper steps back and leans against the flexible wires. "I might be in over my head, and I hate it."

Monroe surprises me again by crossing the space and leaning next to Cooper. "Fuck yeah, you are, but that doesn't mean anything. It just means that you know your strengths and weaknesses. You don't just assume you're a fucking badass because you're a vampire now. You have intelligence that can benefit everyone. You know the other fighters. You can teach us about them."

Cooper smiles, his whole face lighting up. It makes me appreciate Monroe even more. Sure, he can be psychotic and aggressive. He can be a handful when it comes to others outside of the Bella Crew. But at his heart, he's a softy. He understands boundaries and respect, and he gives them where they are due. He's always been careful and kind with me, and I love to see him act the same with others.

Cooper meets my gaze. "Uh-oh. You just set the dhampir off. She seems to have two switches. She's triggered by violence and by kindness. Look at her eyes. You might want to brace yourself."

I laugh and shake my head. "Yeah, you better. I'm about to attack you with my fucking lips. You're so cute. I can't even stand it."

Monroe chuckles and opens his arms for me, and I race to him and hop into his embrace, letting him spin me around. I kiss him, sliding my tongue into his mouth, savoring his closeness.

"You're utterly irresistible," I moan against his mouth.

"Hell yeah. Do you whatever you want, little bird. You know I don't have shame." Monroe falls back and grins, flicking his hands at Cooper. "You better turn around. This sexy girl is about to have at me."

My giggle echoes through the air, and I wiggle in his arms until he puts me down. "No. Remember, I need to work on my control. I'm okay. You were just extra adorable. I wanted to show you my appreciation."

"Don't let me be a fucking cock-block. I know dhampirs' natures. The connections to the vampires who claim them are important. That's how you'll be able to survive. My grandmother always told me that she would've been better off had she found a coven to take her in, but she was too scared because she had my mom already. She grew up among rebels against the uprising and just adapted to live as a donor out of sight. She wasn't bitten with venom until much later in her life." Cooper bounces on the tethers and pushes himself toward the middle of the ring. He scoops up the weapons and performs a couple of jabs like Monroe had shown me. He's already ten times better than before, adapting quickly. But I guess he would have to.

"That makes sense. I'm sure it was hard for her if she needed vampire blood to survive." Monroe moves behind me and positions my stance, getting me to spread my legs wider as he adjusts my arms, having me bring one up to block my face.

"She did what she had to, if you know what I mean. Vampires are easily persuaded when males severely outnumber females in this town." Cooper purses his lips, grimacing at the thought. And I can't blame him.

I know what it's like to be a woman in La Vega. I know what a lot of the men want, which is why I performed a lot of sexual favors for Alexander. It was just part of life as a performer. I'd probably still do the same now if I didn't have the Bella Crew.

"Fucking hell. Just the thought pisses me off. These asshole leaders and their twisted ways have to fucking stop. They need to earn that kind of right to be with a woman. This is why we always go for the cocks." Monroe flares his nostrils. "You tell me if there's any twisted fuckers around here. I'm cool with risking my ass to clean the house."

Cooper nods his head, his face twisting with his appreciation. He smirks, and I can tell that he agrees with Monroe's morals. "Damn. I wish you guys could've come a lot sooner. This shitty hellhole could really use someone like you around here."

"La Vega is my home. It's Hayley's home too. But if you know a couple of assholes we can trust, I don't mind training them too." Monroe nudges me with his big palm to my lower back. "Now, let's get some practice in. I want to see my girl sweat. I want to see you bleed a bit too. You got to earn your place, man. Hayley, don't go easy on him. I know you have a thing for those who need to be coddled a bit."

I laugh as he smacks my ass, shocked by the fact that he mentions he knows I could possibly like Cooper a little bit, and he doesn't have a problem with it anymore. Well, at least just in this fighting ring.

"Monroe, stop it. It's not like that. I barely know him." I spin on my feet and swipe the blade at Monroe, getting him to hop back.

He just laughs again. "I know, little bird. But he doesn't. I've seen you get riled up. And if you accidentally attack him and bite his throat, I want you to know I'm not going to be jealous. I know you're mine."

Cooper clears his throat and shifts awkwardly on his feet. "I know that too. You don't have to worry. I know my place. It's always been clear in my life where I belong. Hayley needs you guys."

I don't know how to respond, the conversation turning in a direction that I had no idea it could take.

Charging forward, I rush Cooper throwing him off guard. He didn't expect me to start trying out the moves Monroe taught me, but I need to do something, anything, to get my mind off things and to stop thinking about biting him. It's fucking weird now that Monroe mentioned it. I can't stop thinking about it. His blood tastes just as good as the others.

"Oh fuck. I didn't know you could fly so fast, little bird. Do that leg thing. You know what I'm talking about. Don't think I can ever forget you stealing that damn banana from my fingers. That's the one you're going to use to get these guys on the ground." Monroe claps his hands, encouraging me to fight.

I smile as I swing my leg up, catching it just right on Cooper's neck while jumping into the air. I climb up him, squeezing his head between my thighs. He gasps and grabs my ass instinctively, but instead of throwing me off him, he freezes. I thrust my body forward, throwing him off balance. Landing on top of him, I practically suffocate him as my knees hit the mat. I use his distraction against him and swivel, stabbing my knife into his stomach, making him groan.

I regret it immediately. I knew I was supposed to fight. We all agreed that it would be okay if I stabbed instead of faked it because I need to get used to it, but what I didn't expect was to have such a strong reaction to Cooper's blood. It pours from the wound, startling me. I try to throw myself off him to put space between us, but Cooper digs his fingers into my thighs and rolls me off and onto my back. He pins me down with his hand to my throat. It's as if my body decides now that I can't fight him, because all I do is cry out. My fear instincts get the best of me, and I fail to push him off. I fail to do anything. If we were in the ring, and he was out to kill me, I'd be dead.

Cooper rushes to get off me and clutches his hand over the knife wound. "Fuck. I'm sorry, Hayley."

Monroe growls, but he doesn't try to attack Cooper or

anything. He rushes to my side and kneels. Grabbing me under my arms, he pulls me up and sits me upright. Touching my chin, he gets me to look at him.

"Little bird, don't give up so quickly. I know you don't want to hurt anyone, but you have to remember Cooper is tough. You need to redirect your fears. What I want you to do is not think about how you could get hurt. I want you to be pissed off that he managed to overpower you. I want you to think about something else instead of fighting. Maybe think about a little blood exchange. If you can focus and teach yourself that this isn't life and death, you might be able to push past those fears. I will make sure to talk to Sawyer. He might be able to do something about it." Monroe leans in and kisses me. "Don't be hard on yourself either. You did fucking amazing. Exactly what I wanted you to do."

I blow out a breath and nod my head. How am I ever going to do this?

"I don't know, Monroe." I rest my head on his shoulder. "This isn't me."

"Damn right, it's not you. You need to figure out who it is, though. I know you used Ruby Vixen to get you through the performances and all the sexual bullshit Alexander always made you do. If you use another persona, maybe you could do the same here." Monroe looks to

Cooper. "Do you have costumes and shit around here?"

Cooper bobs his head and motions toward the door. "The dressing room is down the hall. And I agree with you about the persona." Strolling closer to me, Cooper looks down and offers me a smile. "Would you like me to pick you out something?"

"Yeah, thanks. I think Monroe's right, and it'll help me." I lick my lips and inhale and exhale a couple of breaths. "I think it's time I just shut down. I don't know how else to deal."

Cooper reaches out and pokes my nose playfully. "It's okay if you do. I think it'll be good for you. I think it's best for you to embrace your new persona."

I look at Monroe and force myself to smile. "Are you ready to meet Violent Violet?" I ask, watching his face morph into curiosity.

"Fuck yeah. The name is awesome. I bet she's one ba-dass bitch." Monroe combs my hair behind my ear.

"I hope so." And I really do. Because I need it. I won't survive otherwise.

10

HAYLEY

BONDING

A SOFT GROAN hums from behind me. "I'd offer to help you get dressed, but it would be too painful to do so. Ripping your clothes off is more of my expertise." Knox stands in the doorway of the tiny dressing room, which is more like a closet compared to what I'm used to.

Monroe chuckles and grabs a tiny two-piece costume from the rack. Gemstones glitter across the dark fabric, sparkling in the harsh lighting that will ensure my makeup doesn't look as perfect as I'm used to. "Then get your ass out of here. I don't mind dolling her up. Look at this thing. Doesn't it scream Violent Violet? I have the perfect wig for you as well." Monroe snatches a colorful wig of the blues, purples, and pinks from its place on a small shelf. He flips it onto his own head and grins at me, tossing the strands over his shoulder. "What do you think?"

I laugh in amusement, swiveling in my makeup chair to face him. "It looks amazing on you. I think you should keep it. You can be Murderous Marilyn."

Tipping his head back, Monroe cackles like a maniac. He rips the wig from his head and puts it on Knox instead. Knox growls and darts from the doorway and into the room, dodging out of his way until he reaches me and sets it on the vanity table.

"This fucker loves this shit far too much." Knox slides his arm around my waist and pulls me into him. "Maybe he can just take your place. I'm sure if he shaved that fucking beard, no one would question it."

Monroe hugs his arms around the two of us. "Aw, Knox-baby. I always knew you thought I was beautiful."

It's my turn to laugh hysterically like the hyena he teased me of being. "You guys are too much."

I devour their playfulness, loving every second of it. It's

far too easy for them to be broody and serious that I've only ever seen them loosen up at the Bella. So, seeing them act like this here warms my heart and gets me good.

"And you like it." Sawyer appears in the doorway, sporting the tiniest speedo I've ever seen in my life.

My mouth drops open, and I shift from my vanity table and stand. I give Sawyer a slow, long once-over, drinking in the sight of his muscular body on full display. He flexes his muscles, showing off as if he's about to perform, and I can't stop the laughter bubbling from my mouth.

"Damn. I don't know whether I should be jealous that the world is going to see you like this or if I should rush you, jump into your arms, and devour you. I was not expecting you to be wearing that." I fan myself and stroll closer, circling him as if he's about to become my prey.

Silence falls through the dressing room, and Monroe and Knox stare at us in anticipation like we might put on some freaky-ass, hot performance for them. And who knows? We might. Boundaries currently don't exist between the four of us. Not with having to share a room. I think they're all waiting for me to make a move before they try anything in front of each other. I don't know whether or not I should. What if it turns into something weird? What if they start becoming jealous? I'm not sure I'm ready to invite all of them to participate in anything sexual with me.

But it has crossed my mind. Is that wrong? I honestly don't know. I don't know how they feel apart from them wanting to be with me despite having to share.

"Hayley, what are you doing? I'm not sure what's going through your mind, but whatever it is...I need you to say something." Sawyer touches my cheek, and I realize that I had stopped in front of him while lost in my thoughts. I don't move or speak, probably looking freaky as I stare at his abs without truly looking at him. He's going to think I'm so spacey.

I force my lips to smile. "Sorry. Your body kind of hypnotized me for a second."

"Damn. Now I need to up my game. I want your brain to turn to mush in front of me." Monroe comes up behind me and hugs me, resting his chin on my shoulder.

His words knock some sense back into me, and I spin and cup his cheeks. Standing on my tiptoes, I kiss him, purposely smearing my lipstick across his mouth. If I was performing at Vampire Nights, my makeup wouldn't budge. I think this cheap stuff is purposeful. Lawrence wants the performers to start off nice and then to finish looking like a wreck.

"There's no need. I love seeing my lipstick all over you." Turning on the balls of my feet, I look in Knox's direction. "What about you? Do you want to know what it's like to be kissed and devoured by Violent Violet?"

I don't know what gets into me. Maybe the nerves of the upcoming fight. Maybe the fact that I feel so good in this moment. All I know is that I shed my hesitation, needing to give all three of them the attention they crave. It's something I imagine Violent Violet doing. She's a tough badass and unafraid of any vampires with a desire to devour every man in her path.

Knox raises his eyebrow, realizing I've gone from being Hayley to turning into my stage persona. "It all depends. Are you sure you can handle me, vixen?"

"You should be asking if she can handle all of us," Monroe says, grabbing my hand, spinning me back toward him. "Because I can't get enough of her right now. I fucking love your playfulness, little bird. It's rare to see you like this, and I need more."

"Careful." Sawyer joins the three of us and traces his finger along my jaw. "She's a bit mysterious right now. You don't know what to expect. If you push her..."

I shiver under his words. "I need you to push me. I need you to stop being so careful with me. I can handle it. I can handle all of you."

My body hums with my words as I slide out from in between them. I don't know how they take my comment, but I hope they realize I'm okay with anything. I don't want things to be weird. I just want things to be normal between us all. I want things to be open. I don't want to feel nervous all the time.

"We know you can handle us, but the question is if you want to. I need you to speak up and tell me what it is you want and what you feel you need, Hayley. I'll never make assumptions with you as much as I want to right now. Because the way you just said what you said...fuck. You want us all, and I'm okay with that." Knox licks his lips and shifts his gaze to Monroe and Sawyer. "I don't know about these fuckers, though."

I can't stop the smile from crossing my lips. Sawyer and Monroe don't say anything for a moment, thinking about what I said, and Knox confirmed.

Nerves bunch in my stomach, but I try not to let it faze me. I know they don't intentionally not respond. They're just careful. I think they want to hear more of what I have to say instead of assuming that Knox is right.

Talking has never been my strong suit, so I suck in a breath, gather my confidence, and close the space to Knox. Linking my fingers to the front of his shirt, I surprise him by pulling it up and over his head. Showing him is easier.

"You assumed right. I feel because the situation has changed, my boundaries changed as well. I don't need you guys separately. I think I'm comfortable with showing you affection in front of each other. Like this." I kiss Knox on his peck and work my way down, gliding my tongue along the middle of his abs until I get to my knees. I don't know where this comes from, but I realize how much I like this part of me. I love how I feel in this moment. All three of them watch me, their gazes smoldering over me with all their hot intensity. They want to see how far I take things. I want to find out for myself as well.

Unfastening Knox's belt, I pull it off and drop it to the floor. Tipping my head back, I stare at his heavy-lidded gaze. "I mean, if you're all okay with it. I want you all to be comfortable and happy. It just isn't about me. You're all mine."

Monroe shifts on his feet, his muscles rippling with his movements. "I'm down to see where this goes. What about you, Sawyer? Are you cool? I think our girl needs to hear it."

"I'm good. I just want to see exactly what Hayley means." Sawyer moves closer. "I won't lie, though. I wish I were Knox right now. This is just like that first night."

"Except this time, Hayley might let you watch." Knox combs his fingers through my hair, pulling it out of my face.

His words excite me on a level I had no idea I'd enjoy. Because I know how sexy they think I am, and they don't care who I kneel in front of as long as I like what I'm doing.

I don't respond to him and unfasten Knox's button and slide the zipper down. My heart races with excitement, knowing that none of them will protest. And for once, this is on my terms. I can keep going, or I can change my mind. I don't have to worry about the consequences of what can happen if I don't. Because there are no consequences between us. There are only rewards. And I want to reward them all.

Knox moans as I reach my hand into his pants and pull out his hard-on, stroking it. Our eyes lock in a stare, and I lick my lips and glide my tongue from his balls all the way up his shaft until I swirl it around his tip. But I don't suck him into my mouth. Instead, I reach out and grab onto Monroe. He inhales a small breath, his body tensing as he straightens his back. I leave Knox's cock just pointing out and get Monroe to come closer. I unbuckle his belt next, letting it hang on his pants. The three of them watch me as I do the same with him as I did Knox, and I pull his cock out and stroke it while working his tip.

"Damn, little tease." Monroe rubs his hand over his cock, stroking himself as I move to Sawyer and pull down the speedo, barely containing his massive dick, hard and ready for my attention.

I smile at Monroe and then turn my attention to Sawyer, taking my time to explore his body by cupping his balls and rubbing him with my thumb, teasing him more than the others just because I can. I don't know why, but I want to see what I can get away with before they react. I could be walking a dangerous line with three horny, hungry vampires, but it doesn't feel like that. It just feels exciting. I can feel the anticipation in my very bones.

"You're so beautiful, Hayley. Don't think that you have to treat us all equally. I'm good with whatever you want. If you don't want me right now, you don't have to do anything. I'm happy to just be with you." Sawyer plays with the strands of my hair, peering down at me as I continue to tease him.

"I know." And I do know. I know he's not lying. I know he's not only saying it to make me feel better. "I'm going to do what I want, and what I want is to just figure out how all of this is going to work. I mean, are you guys really that patient? Can you handle me taking my time to taste and explore you?"

Knox groans and jerks himself off, totally turned on by my words.

I reach out and stop him. "Not so fast. I want to do that."

I take over for him and glide my fingers across the length of his shaft. He moves closer to touch me on my shoulder. Sawyer continues to play with my hair, drawing my attention back to him, and I finally give him what he wants. I glide my tongue over his cock, tasting his pre-cum and exactly what I do to him. Monroe doesn't stand beside Knox for long, surprising me by joining me on the floor. He kisses my shoulder and positions himself behind me, sliding his hands around my body and down the length of my torso. His hard-on presses against me, and he trails his fingers into the front of my pants, dipping them between my legs until he can feel my wetness.

"Little bird, I know you want to tease us, but it's not in me to let you do all the work. I want you too badly. I don't care if you ever touch me as long as I can have you how I want." Monroe's voice deepens, and I moan at the sensation of his fingers putting pressure on my clit as he rubs me.

I open my legs a bit wider and then turn my focus back to Sawyer, sucking his cock into my mouth. He releases the sexiest noise, his attention burning across me as I lick and suck him, tasting him how I want. I continue to stroke Knox, who helps guide my fingers the way he likes. Everything in this moment is so exhilarating that I let my guard down completely and just enjoy being with the three of them.

And I want more.

"Monroe, fuck me. I want you to fuck me so badly." I lean back as I rub my slobbery hand over Sawyer's cock and suck Knox's into my mouth. "If that's okay. My body craves more."

Monroe hums deep in his throat. "You fuckers better get on the floor if we're going to make this work. I'm taking Hayley bent over on her hands and knees."

One second, I'm in front of Knox, and then the next, my palms lie flat on the floor as Monroe rips my pants down and kisses my ass cheek, nipping me with his fangs.

I gasp with a laugh and moan so incredibly loud as he licks my clit, tasting me how he wants. Sawyer and Knox follow his command and drop to the floor, the four of us still trying to figure things out but managing to still give each other attention. Sawyer kisses me and tilts my head so I can kiss Knox too. I get Knox to lie down in front of me, and I give him a blowjob again, bobbing my head up and down, slobbering all over him to get him slick.

"Let me hold you up a bit, so you can show Sawyer some attention too," Knox says, flattening his palm against my clavicle.

I nod in silence and balance on one hand, using his strength to support me. I love how he instructs me without making me feel as if I'm clueless. Because I'm a bit unsure. I've never been with three vampires at once like this.

I know for sure that they haven't shared anyone like this either, but they still know how to make me feel comfortable. Completely sexy. And loved. I never in my life expected to feel loved like this. It's hard for me to even wrap my mind around the emotions.

"Are you ready, little bird? I'm dying for you. I want to give you whatever you want." Monroe positions himself behind me, massaging his fingers into my ass cheeks, slowly spreading and closing my body playfully. He draws his fingers between my legs again, teasing and testing my reaction as Sawyer tips my head back to kiss me once more.

I bite my lip with a smile. "I am. I want this so badly."

Monroe slides into me, our bodies connecting and feeling as if he ignites a bomb of ecstasy through my body.

Sawyer and Knox both watch my expression, their eyes flashing silver with their desire. My short hair hangs around my cheeks, and I bow forward with Knox's guidance until I can suck his cock the way he wants. Sawyer moves in closer, his body now within my reach. I show off my talents, being able to stretch in ways that allow me to take care of him as well with my hand. He guides my movements as Knox arches his hips up and down, making it easier for me. Monroe bows in, his strong arm around my waist. He kisses each of my shoulder blades, his body moving in sync with mine, and he reaches between us until he can strum his thumb over my clit, making it really hard to focus on anything but pleasure. I give in to my bliss, just existing and savoring the sensations rolling through my body. I let the three of them guide and move me the way they want like I solely exist for them in this moment. But they also exist for me, too, whispering how beautiful I am and how lucky they are to be with me. It's unlike anything in the world. I never knew how easy it was to be with the three of them. It's as if their friendship and closeness make it possible. They're not competing. They work together as a team to ensure that I'm perfect.

"Fuck, her pussy is so tight. She's so wet. She loves this." Monroe thrusts over and over again, his deep voice and new position hotter than I realized it could be. Even though he's talking about me to them, I still feel the heat of his words and how much he loves this moment. It's not just about the sex. It's about the four of us bonding. How we almost merge as one entity in this wave of passion.

"Her mouth is fucking intoxicating. Her tongue and how she rolls it just right, sucking me just hard enough...you're so incredible, Hayley." Knox caresses my cheek, his gaze penetrating the side of my face.

Sawyer leans over and kisses my shoulder, unfazed by my closeness to Knox. "Can I bite you? I want to taste you."

I hum my agreement, making Knox tense his body with the sensation. He groans and tightens his hand to my hip, savoring how good it feels.

So, I do it again. I hum louder, moaning with his cock in my mouth, loving how his breathing picks up.

"Do you like that, Knox? Just wait. Wait until she screams in pleasure. I'm going to make her cum." Monroe bumps his hips harder to mine, increasing the pressure as he uses his vampire speed, vibrating his fingers to my clit at the same time he thrusts over and over. I can't even think through the motions, and I feel my body tingling all over until my muscles spasm, and I scream out, allowing my orgasm to control my body and voice. I stiffen, savoring the bliss. Monroe leans in and kisses my spine while Sawyer bites my shoulder, the prick enough to set me off again, his fangs making me cum.

"Fuck, I'm about to cum, Hayley." Knox slows my head down as his cock flexes. "Will you swallow for me?"

I moan my agreement, bobbing my head until his sweet flavor floods my mouth. I pull back and swallow, licking my lips. That's one of the things about certain vampires. Their cum can sometimes taste like dessert, and Knox is no exception.

"So damn sexy," Monroe says, thrusting faster as he works my body over again, acting as if there's no way he's going to let me get away with only having one orgasm.

Sawyer leans down, smiling at me and touching my cheek. Knox holds me up completely, allowing me to just hang in his arms. I reach out finally and grab onto Sawyer, pulling him to me, so he kneels beside me. I'm tall enough that he could fuck my face if he wanted to, and I lick the tip of his cock to silently tell him as much.

"Are you sure?" Sawyer asks. "You don't have to."

"I want you to finish too." I lick my tongue over his tip again, getting him to position himself just right to where he can rock his hips into my mouth, doing the work while I concentrate on just giving him the right amount of pressure.

"She is the most incredible, caring woman in the world, isn't she?" Monroe says, moving his finger quicker over my clit, my whole body clenching again with another orgasm.

Sawyer grips my hair as he grunts, my voice and tongue enough to get him off. He cums in my mouth next, and I slow down and swallow, tilting my head to smile at him at the same time Monroe finishes with a groan and a few more thrusts.

Hugging me from behind, Monroe flips me over as he flops on the floor, holding me on top of him. We smile at each other, and he kisses me, not even caring that I was just sucking Knox and Sawyer off. None of them care.

I feel so incredibly adored and appreciated. Being able to choose to be with all of them like this without strings or consequences or being manipulated into it...I need this. I want this always.

"I could get used to banging our girl with you," Monroe says, caressing his fingers to my shoulders. "Look at her face. She's so incredibly happy right now. I never want to see her stop smiling."

I grin wider. "And I'm going to have to get used to you talking about me to them."

The three of them chuckle, and Knox laces his fingers through mine and swings our arms back-and-forth.

"We can't help ourselves. It's surreal. We knew we were close, but this is closer than we could've ever imagined. And funny enough, I enjoy it. I love having them to talk to about you. I love being able to ensure you're perfect because if I'm incapable of doing something, I know they can pick up my slack." Knox play-punches Sawyer in the shoulder. "But don't forget who saw her first."

"You never let us," Monroe quips, sitting up with me on his lap. "If you want to be sp—"

Knox covers Monroe's mouth, shutting him up. But not to stop him from arguing.

A holler rips through the air, and someone laughs, the feminine voice echoing from the hallway outside of the dressing room. Knox rushes to the door and blocks it, ensuring no one can enter as I quickly clean up with Monroe in the small bathroom. I put on my costume and let Sawyer help me with my wig.

"Hey there, handsome," a sultry voice says, jerking my attention to a woman in the hallway.

"Careful, Killer. He's not a performer." Cooper's voice sounds over the laughter. "He's also not available, so unless you want to piss off our new headliner, then you'd better back off."

A hiss startles me, setting off my fear instincts. "Fuck off, Coop. I'm not afraid of some little donor. I don't give a fuck what Lawrence said. Obviously, she's not that tough if she has a bodyguard."

Knox growls under his breath, stepping away from the door. "I would be careful what you say. Hayley is mine. You should be scared. I don't know who the fuck you are, but you need to mind your own business."

Something crashes from the hallway, and I hear Cooper groan. I don't have a chance to prepare myself as someone flies into the room in a blur, knocking Knox onto his back.

I stare in shock.

A familiar, beautiful vampire aims a dagger and stabs him in the chest.

My vision turns red.

SHOCK AND ANGER snap through me, drawing me from the warmth and love of the passion I shared with my guys. Watching as this vampire stabs Knox ignites the savage part of me thirsty for blood. I scream and scramble to my feet, wanting nothing more than to punch this bitch right in her perfect nose. Sawyer beats me to the woman, grabbing the back of her glittery costume, and yanks her away. Spinning, he throws her toward the wall, and one of the mirrors shatters, sending pieces of sparkling glass across the stained floor.

"You better fucking knock it off before you lose that goddamn hand of yours. Don't think I won't cut it off." Sawyer snarls and flashes his fangs, grabbing the woman from the floor to hold her by her wrist. He proves he's not joking by slicing his blade across her skin.

"Let me go, asshole! Lawrence will take your balls if you hurt me. I'm the most popular act in that damn Fright Fight ring." The vampire snaps her teeth, trying to bite Sawyer, but he's at least two feet taller than her and a good hundred pounds more. She looks like a little doll hanging from his grip. A psychotic, possessed doll but tiny nonetheless.

"Chill out, Killer. He has a deal with Lawrence. You can't talk to him like you do me. He's only humoring our master by participating in the show." Cooper rushes up and presses his hand to Sawyer's muscular chest. He looks up at him. "Give me a minute with her, and I'll get her to relax. She's always on edge right before a performance."

I scrunch my nose. I highly doubt that it's only right before a performance. She just came rushing in here, blades stabbing, without even considering the situation. What the actual fuck? If she's this savage outside of the ring, I'd hate to face her in it.

"You don't need to intervene, Savage." Killer uses Cooper's stage name. He did mention that some of the performers stay in their personas all the time. It's kind of like some of the gems back at Vampire Nights. Almost all of them kept their stage names.

"Fine. You don't want your hand, then I don't give a fuck." Cooper heaves a breath and turns away from Sawyer and Killer. She really does stay true to her name.

Killer huffs and thrashes, getting Sawyer to release her. He remains guarded and aims his weapon at her. Monroe unholsters his gun, drawing her attention to him. I think she finally realizes she's outnumbered and overpowered. This is not the stage.

She adjusts her sparkly top and searches the room, narrowing her eyes on me. "Get your little servants under control, or we're going to have a big fucking problem, donor. I was told I couldn't kill you but don't think I won't make you wish you were dead."

What the hell am I getting into? The only thing keeping me calm is the fact that I know Sawyer will be with me. I also know that I'm capable of summoning strength if I'm freaked out enough, and I'm pretty sure I'm going to be fucking strong during the fight.

"Oh, fuck no. You're not threatening my girl." Monroe

aims and fires his gun without warning, shooting Killer in her stomach. The scent of her blood smacks me like a shockwave, and Knox snatches me before I tackle the woman and really test my ability to fight against someone who isn't afraid to hurt me. It's one thing to practice with Monroe and Cooper. It's a completely different story to face a raging bitch of a vampire who has taken on fighting as her entire existence.

I shouldn't feel sad for her, but I do. Just a bit. I don't know what kind of situation she was in before. If she has a background like Cooper, I know things aren't good for her.

"Damn it, you asshole! You ruined my costume!" Killer tugs at her crop top and stares at the bloody holes. Her attention goes from annoyance to worry. She gives me whiplash with her change in demeanor. "I can't go on stage like this. Tonight's match is supposed to be packed. I need to look amazing."

Monroe raises an eyebrow, shifting his attention to Sawyer and Knox. He doesn't know how to handle the situation either. I'm sure he expected the woman to try to fight him instead of complaining about her wardrobe. I guess the vampire entertainers aren't that different from donors, because Mya has complained about costume malfunctions as well. So have I.

Someone taps on the door, and I take an automatic

step back as Lawrence fills the doorframe and bangs a cane to the tile floor. He searches the room, assessing the situation. From the sounds of other voices in the hallway, I wonder if someone called him to interrupt us.

Killer pouts her bottom lip, looking sad as hell as she faces Lawrence. She's a far better actress than I realize. I can already tell that she's going to blame everything on us.

"Master, look at my costume. You didn't tell me I had to prepare myself for these assholes. That one shot me. I didn't even do anything." Killer shifts her gaze and motions at Monroe. "He shouldn't even be in here. This room is for performers only, and he said he's not participating."

Lawrence remains expressionless to her comment, continuing to tap his cane on the ground. I can't take my eyes away from it, imagining that he probably hits donors with it like Mr. Pala had.

"If you don't get her in control, we're going to have a far bigger problem than her acting as if she's innocent. We weren't aware this dressing room wasn't private. It was in our agreement." Sawyer steps forward, his bulging muscles even more defined because he only wears a speedo. Even with so few clothes on, he's intimidating as fuck. And sexy. The thought of him wrestling anyone like that prods at my deep-seated jealousy. I already want to attack Killer, and the fight hasn't even begun.

Lawrence sighs. "Always with the dramatics, Kassandra." Turning to Killer, he adds, "Leave it for the stage. If you can't handle the consequences of your actions, perhaps being one of my fighters isn't for you. I told you things were going to evolve around here. We finally have the opportunity to bring in more patrons than before. More patrons means more blood. It means better facilities. More time away from the herd for you. You should thank me because of how thoughtful I am, thinking about you."

I expect the woman to open her mouth and argue, but she bows her head.

Staring at the floor, she says, "Thank you, master. I'm sorry. You know how I get before going into the ring. I must be in the right mindset to make sure the show is unforgettable. Please punish me for my actions as a reminder."

I gawk at her as she bends over and touches her toes, shaking her ass at Lawrence. I don't think I've ever seen someone ask for a punishment like this, and I'm nearly certain she's only doing it because it gets her off and not because she feels she deserves it. And from the look on Lawrence's face...gross.

Swinging his cane, he whacks Killer hard on her ass, knocking her to her hands and knees. I cover my mouth in surprise, trying to hide my shock.

Lawrence smiles with enjoyment, just as sadistic as Alexander, and he steps closer to Killer and holds out his hand to her. "That's my good fighter, Kassandra. Now, why don't you gather the donors and head to the stage? You're up first tonight."

"First? But—" Killer snaps her mouth shut and drops her gaze to the floor again.

Lawrence ignores her and turns to Sawyer. "I've decided I want Hayley to fight against Kassandra without you. You may stand by, but I have something far more entertaining for your portion."

Sawyer clenches his fingers into fists. "She's not ready. We had a deal that it would just be me tonight with her riling up the crowd."

Flaring his nostrils, Lawrence crosses the space to Sawyer. "It's my show. Get used to it. I find things are better when they're unexpected. Which is only a test for tonight. I need to ensure you will follow through. We have a meeting with Alexander coming up, so if you expect me to participate instead of ending this deal and keeping Hayley for myself, you must obey. If you have a problem, then you can—"

"What if we do a tag team, and I partner with Hayley?" Cooper asks, keeping his distance. "Killer can have a donor as well. It could be interesting."

Lawrence shifts his gaze to Cooper, silently staring at him for a minute in consideration. I expect him to deny him. I expect him to do something crazy like smack him upside the head with his cane. What I don't expect is for him to nod his agreement. "I think that is a marvelous idea. But I want Hayley to kill the donor."

My heart sinks in my stomach. "What?"

"You got it, master. It'll be an excellent show." Cooper frowns with his words, flicking his gaze to me.

Lawrence smiles, his eyes flashing silver. "I'm sure it will be. Good luck, everyone. I'll see you all on stage."

I'm going to be sick. I'm going to be so fucking sick. How am I ever going to survive getting into the ring and murdering someone? It won't even be out of self-preservation. I have to kill someone for fun.

Fuck my life.

Whenever things look up or I feel okay, the universe likes to push me back down to remind me of my place. I'm a donor. I will always be a donor even though I know I'm a dhampir.

"Hayley, you don't have to do this. We'll fight and cancel any negotiations we had. I'm not allowing you to be in this situation." Sawyer ruffles his fingers through his brown hair, staring at the brightly lit ring. The place is half-packed with a lot more people in the audience tonight than before.

"You make it sound so easy. I know what will happen if I don't do this. I can't risk it. I don't want you guys getting hurt because of me. Even if you weren't here, I'd have to do it. This is my new fucked up life now. I just want to get through it. I want it to be over already." I bounce on the balls of my feet, my whole body trembling with my nerves. This wouldn't be the first time I've done something that I've had to do. I've grown up knowing things won't ever be my way, and I must do stuff I disagree with. Like killing someone.

Fuck, I'm so sick. My stomach twists and turns.

Sawyer bends down and gets in my face. He pinches my chin and guides me to lock my eyes with him. "Hayley, look at me, and don't look away. I'm going to manipulate you to help you get through this."

My whole body relaxes, and only his big hand holds me up, preventing me from spilling to the floor. Lawrence didn't allow me to drink any blood, hoping it makes me more aggressive. Or compliant. I'm not sure.

"Is that okay? I can help you suppress your emotions. I don't want you to feel this terrible. If you're not going to let me break the contract, please let me do this." Sawyer begs me with his beautiful blue eyes. They light with silver in anticipation.

"Please, help me. Please, stop me from feeling anything." My voice comes out automatically as the words escape my mouth without me even thinking about them.

How twisted is it to want what he offers? I just want to be numb. I need not to care anymore. Without feeling anything, I might actually survive.

Sawyer offers me a whisper of a smile, though his eyes don't shine with the happiness I wish they would carry. He leans in closer until he fills my gaze completely, his eyes turning solid silver as he prods into my mind. "Hayley, first, I want you to know that you're safe. You don't have to be afraid for your life or your well-being. I will take care of you. Do you understand?"

"Yes." My voice barely sounds above a whisper.

"Good," Sawyer says, leaning in close enough to touch the tip of his nose to mine. We share our breathing space, and it helps me relax even more. "Whatever happens tonight is not going to affect you mentally. You're not responsible for the death of the donor. It is Lawrence. You're not going to dwell on it because the donor has been given a death sentence. You're brave and strong. You will not care about your opponents. The donor will try to kill you otherwise. You know you have to do what is best for you. Do you understand?"

"Yes." A strange sensation crawls across my face and travels down my neck and into the rest of my body. The sickness gripping me fades, and I manage to straighten my back as Sawyer releases me from his mind manipulation.

A smile crosses my face. I listen to the crowd growing wild. They cheer louder than I remember the crowd at Vampire Nights, which pumps me up even more.

"How do you feel?" Sawyer asks me, drawing my attention back to him.

I snap my teeth at him, the strange sensation consuming me. All I want to do is bite him. I realize I'm starving, and the sickness clutching my stomach might be my blood hunger.

"Shit. One of you needs to give her some of your blood. Right now." Cooper clenches his fingers into fists, staring at Lawrence entering the ring, wearing a fitted tuxedo with a red bowtie. It's far from the same extravagant costumes that Alexander encompassed, but he still looks showworthy. "I mean it. Do it. I don't care what Lawrence wanted. She needs to be at least a bit in control."

Knox bites his arm and extends it out to me. Like a wild beast, I close the space to him and lace my fingers around his wrist, pulling his arm to my mouth. I don't know if it's because of my nerves or because I'm starving, but I can't control myself. His blood smells too good. It tastes even better.

I groan and suck harder, ensuring I'll leave a mark behind.

Knox slides his hand around my back and pulls me to him, the only thing separating us now being his arm. It doesn't last for long, because he manages to detach me and kisses me to redirect my focus. His lips mold against mine, kissing me softly. It's enough to help ease the fear and anxiety crashing through me.

"I love you. I love you more than I knew I could love someone in so little time." Knox caresses his fingers to my cheeks, smoothing out the tightness of my jaw. "You're strong. You're brave and capable. Just know that I doubt Lawrence would destroy a blood source if the man didn't deserve it. Maybe he did something really fucked up."

I hold onto his words, hoping he's right. But I wouldn't put it past Lawrence to be so sadistic. Regardless of my thoughts, I don't feel as bad as I thought I would. The only thing I feel right now is lust and hunger and the need to just get this over with. I have an intense desire to turn into Violent Violet.

"You're right," I say, bouncing on the balls of my bare feet. I look up. "I'm sure it was terrible, and he needs to pay. So does Killer Kassandra. She's going to get her ass beat down for even touching you, Knox."

Monroe chuckles and extends a dagger out to me. It belongs to him with the Bella Crew emblem etched onto the hilt.

"Don't lose my lucky knife, little bird. I'm letting you use it because I know that if you have something that belongs to me, you'll take better care not to accidentally let somebody disarm you." Monroe silently reminds me of a couple of moves, jabbing the knife and then flipping it around to hand it to me.

I inhale a deep breath. "I guess this is it, huh?" I turn to Cooper. "Keep up with me, okay? I don't want to have to save your ass."

Cooper tips his head back and laughs in amazement. "All right, my showgirl. Let's do this."

I take Cooper's hand and let him lead me to the door with the aisle where we'll run to the stage. The music blares with an upbeat rock song, and Lawrence announces the arrival of Killer Kassandra and her pet donor Naked Steve.

Killer shoves past Cooper, dragging a naked man, true to his name, behind her by his hair. He screams and shouts, kicking his legs and trying to fight, but he can't escape the vampire's death grip. I should feel bad for him, but all I can do is laugh because his flaccid cock bounces around, looking pathetic as hell like the rest of him.

"Remind me not to jog naked by you," Cooper murmurs under his breath, watching me watch Naked Steve with a smile on my face. I can't help it. It's funnier than I thought it would be, and I know it's because Sawyer helped change my emotions to prepare for this moment. I would usually be horrified, but I'm not. I'm amused.

"I wouldn't mind that. You're not exactly Naked Steve material. I've seen you in the shower." Heat blooms across my cheeks with my words. I know I shouldn't tease him, but it helps ease the anxiety.

"Careful, my showgirl. Your dudes can hear you. I don't need that kind of problem. I know my place." Cooper tightens his jaw and rolls his shoulders, readying himself to carry me into the ring.

"And in the opposing corner, I bring to you a new deathly duo that'll surely leave blood splatting across your eager faces. Let's give it up for Savage Saint and Violent Violet!" Lawrence's voice booms into the microphone, echoing over the music.

Without hesitating, Cooper bends down in front of me, encouraging me to get onto his shoulders. I swallow my nerves and do as he instructs, unsure of what to expect. We haven't even had much time to train, and the arrival of the Bella Crew changed the plans, not giving us extra time to practice, but I've grown used to thinking on my feet. If Naked Steve is my opponent, I think I'm pretty safe. I could probably flash the guy my boobs and stab him. At least, that's the plan. I haven't told anybody, but I'll do whatever it takes, and they know it. The Bella Crew is okay with it.

Cooper runs at vampire speed, and I clench my jaw, stopping my voice from screeching out in surprise. I tighten my thighs around his neck, now distracted because I can't stop thinking about how he's probably hyper-aware of how close I am. He might even be able to feel the heat between my legs, especially because his quick movements practically make him vibrate against me.

Damn body.

I'd rather be turned on than terrified though. I tuck the information into the back of my mind to remember to tell Monroe about it later. I bet he'd love knowing that something as simple as being carried on his shoulders could lead to a lot of fun.

A sharp hiss snags my attention away from my thoughts, and the world spins as Cooper tosses me from his shoulders. I land on my feet and throw my arms in the air. The landing comes so automatically to me that my body just does it. Killer rattles the flexible ropes around the ring, trying to intimidate us as she waits for the bell to ring.

As for Naked Steve? He cries in the corner, cupping his junk in his hands, completely mortified.

I blow out a breath in relief because I don't care. I

don't feel anything toward that guy. No sympathy. No pity. All I feel is the need to end him and put him out of the misery.

I guess I'm a bit psycho, after all. That's what this vicious world does.

"So, you're going to be up first, Hayley," Cooper mutters under his breath. "That guy is not going to want to fight. You'll be able to get in a few punches before he realizes he doesn't have a choice. Because of it, one of two things is going to happen. He's either going to refuse to fight as not to hurt you, or he's going to turn into a monster. Be prepared. Don't kill him immediately. If you do, Lawrence will bring out another donor. Remember, first and foremost, this is a performance. Give them a good show."

I stretch my leg behind me and then pull it up over my head, balancing on the ball of my foot and showing off my flexibility to the crowd. The few guys in the front row scream out my name, catcalling and shouting the disgusting things they want to do to me.

I brush them off, so incredibly used to being treated like this, that I put on my show smile and blow them kisses. "I don't think you can handle me, gentlemen," I say, raising my voice.

I can hear Monroe swear under his breath from here. It only takes a minute before something blurs within the hazy light blocking my view of the crowd, and I spot Monroe threatening one of the guys with a fisted hand.

"Remember, anything goes. This is a fight to the death. Only one donor will make it out alive. We'll see who the better vampire is tonight. Will it be Killer Kassandra of my Blood Princesses, or will it be Savage Saint of my Executioners?" Lawrence waves his hands to each of us and backs toward the side of the ring. "Let the Fright Fights begin!"

A loud gong rings in the air, nearly deafening me. Killer acts first, grabbing Naked Steve by the wrist and spinning him, throwing him in my direction.

The man tumbles across the ring.

He groans and pushes onto his hands and knees, tipping his head up to look at me. Our eyes meet, and I give him a once-over, preparing to fight.

Killer tosses a blade at the man, and it smacks into the mat beside him. He looks from me and to the blade. This is it. This will determine what I'll have to do.

The guy sucks in his top lip and his face morphs from fear to anger. Jerking his hand out, he grabs for the knife. He's not going to beg for mercy. Cooper's speculation about him was right. This man isn't innocent. I've seen the look he gives me in the eyes of many vampires. He might be a donor, but he's still a monster.

"Hey, pretty girl. You're going to be mine tonight. Do

you know why they put you against me?" The donor sneers with his words pushing to his feet and positioning his stance.

I remain expressionless and stare at him, trailing my gaze from his dirty face down to his limp dick. "Yeah, actually. They know I'm not afraid to cut off the cock of a man who deserves it."

The man scowls. "Fuck you. They want me to put you in your damn place to be the broken little bitch you are."

Except I'm not broken. I'm stronger than ever.

I'm no longer a donor.

I'm Violent Violet, and I have no fucks to give assholes. All I have is a taste for blood.

NAKED STEVE IS a dead man. Not because he has been sentenced to death by Lawrence, but because he just put his hand on Hayley. The tension radiating through the audience is enough to heat up my cold skin. I try to block out the growls of the Bella Crew. They're pissed off that I haven't stepped forward to intervene. But I can't.

Hayley isn't fragile. She could possibly be the most

powerful being in the world if she's given the proper care and training. The fact that she has spent her entire life sheltered and unknowing about her own nature really fucking sucks. I feel bad for her. I wish she wasn't here in the first place. Except for another part of me, my instinct as a vampire, loves that she is. I never expected to meet another dhampir in my life. My grandmother was special to me, and she told me a lot about her life. It was shocking the day she murdered that vampire, because I had no idea that she was my grandmother. She looked young. I thought she was my mother, but even then, it was as if she didn't age at all over the years. Technically, she didn't. Because her genes derive from a vampire, she didn't age. Neither will Hayley. She will forever remain in her current adult state, a beautiful, stunning woman who now faces a murderous rapist who desires to pin her down and overpower her in front of everyone.

I won't let that happen. There's no fucking way he will get close to her. He's lucky to even have his hand, because there's nothing I hate more than disgusting men who think they can treat a woman like this.

It's men like this that make the Fright Fights easier. It's not always terrible men, but when it is, I feel as if I'm serving justice, even if it's all for entertainment in this boring town.

Hayley yells out, her voice setting off the crowd even more. Those sick son-of-a-bastards love hearing her. I don't usually get queasy, but my stomach twists in knots just knowing that some of them get off on the idea of her getting hurt or worse.

"You got this, Violet," I call, clapping my hands and trying to pump her up. "Get him right in the dick. Then I'll drop him."

Hayley screeches out, trying to pull away from Steve to get some space between them. Kicking her leg, she whacks the fucker in the balls. He hollers and lets her go, but he doesn't stay away for long.

"Come on, baby. Get her. If you can get her, I'll suck your dick. Wouldn't you like that?" Kassandra waves her hands over her head, her sparkly costume glittering in the light. She climbs on the ropes and stands taller, looking over the crowd.

She used to not always be like this. Kassandra grew into a monster because of Lawrence. She was once human with me. She's not one from the uprising either. But her persona quickly changed when she realized Lawrence would do more for her the crazier she acted. And then she became one of the headlining vampires of the Fright Fights.

"Fuck off!" Naked Steve shouts, spinning to block Hayley from striking his balls again. "I don't want your fucking fangs anywhere near me."

"Then what about your Freaky Fine Girl, Daddy-Boy? Will you do it for me?" Brandy Ray's voice echoes through the speaker as Lawrence wags his eyebrows. The Cloos Coven must've fucked Lawrence over if their only female donor presents herself on stage. Strolling forward, she acts almost robotic in her movements.

Fucking hell. Hayley's going to lose her concentration if she realizes the donor has been mind manipulated. No one in their right mind would suck Naked Steve's cock.

"Fuck off, Brandy! You're the bitch who—" Hayley uses the theatrics to her advantage, launching at Naked Steve again. She lands on top of him and scratches his face, trying to claw his eyes out.

"Yeah! Get him!" I shout, excitement coursing through me.

Naked Steve's screams for mercy set Kassandra off, and she propels from the ropes and onto him. Because she enters the ring and touches him, the rules state they switch places. Hayley widens her eyes, the fear obvious on her face. Kassandra snarls, jerking her hand forward to snatch Hayley. Neither of them sees the manipulated donor until Brandy turns into Freaky Fine Girl and sinks a knife into Kassandra's back. Spinning, Kassandra punches her fist into the donor, ripping her heart out before she realizes what happens.

I charge toward Hayley, thanking the universe for the bloody interruption, and grab her hand, spinning her toward the corner. I take her place and roar, embodying my Savage Saint persona. Kassandra realizes her mistake, jerking her attention to me. It's too late. Jabbing my knife, I stab her in the shoulder, sending her blood squirting all over Naked Steve.

"Whoa, folks! Looks like we got some bloodshed! You know what that means!" Lawrence's voice bursts through the speakers, the guttural noise vibrating the mat of the ring.

I clench my jaw and brace myself for the wave of disgusting gen. pop. blood about to flood the stage, turning this fight into blood wrestling. Lawrence is going all out tonight.

I swivel on my feet. "Cover your face, Violet!" I shout, trying my best to prepare her for the waterfall. A lot of times the blood screws with the donors more than the vampires, blinding them for a split second.

The words barely escape my lips before the buckets tip over above us, spraying blood everywhere. Abandoning their seats, the people in the crowd tip their heads back around the rings, getting a taste. The security team ushers everyone away, and I try not to let it distract me as Kassandra hops up and flings her hair back, sending blood spraying again. Instead of automatically coming after me, she shakes her hips and flashes the crowd her tits. Hayley groans in disgust from behind me, but I don't turn to look. I stride forward and start circling Kassandra as if I'm the predator and she's the prey. This is a game that we've played many times before in the ring. The crowd loves seeing women get overpowered. They are so twisted, but what else can I do? This is a performance, after all, and as Lawrence has said time and time again, what the crowd wants, the crowd gets. The only line he draws is fucking on stage. That's for the Erotic Fright Fights, but the cost is far too expensive for most to attend. Thank the fucking universe.

"Do you like what you see, handsome?" Kassandra's voice bellows through the air. She grabs her top and rips it off completely, choosing to stand in the middle of the ring, covered in blood, with her massive tits on full display. And damn it. I know what she plans. It wouldn't be the first time she's tried to smother me and incapacitate me.

I flash my fangs, flexing my muscles. "You love the idea that I do, don't you, Killer?" I retort, pretending to draw the silhouette of her body with my hands.

Kassandra hisses, keeping a couple of feet of space between us. "The only thing I like the sound of is suffocating you with my tits. You're going down, Savage."

Lunging at me, Kassandra flies in my direction. I don't move and let her shove me off my feet, getting the crowd riled up. They shout about my manhood and how I'm a weak piece of shit because Kassandra got me down so easily. But it's all part of the show.

Kassandra does exactly what she threatens and leans in, smashing her boobs into my face. I pretend I can't breathe and thrash beneath her until she arches back up and grins, pulling a knife from the sheath on her hip to point at me.

I tense, preparing myself to be stabbed either in my side or chest. Kassandra loves stabbing the hell out of me.

She doesn't get the chance.

Hayley surprises her and enters the ring, shoving Kassandra back. I realize something triggers her dhampir nature, and she lands on top of Kassandra, looking ready to sink her teeth into her.

If Naked Steve didn't run from the side of the ring toward Hayley, I would intervene. I hate the idea of Hayley sucking on Kassandra's neck.

"You little bitch, you're mine." Naked Steve latches his fingers onto Hayley's arm and yanks her back. "You owe me, Killer!" he shouts at Kassandra, dragging Hayley away.

Swinging her body, Hayley manages to hook her leg around Naked Steve's neck. She flips up onto his shoulders and throws herself forward, forcing him to the ground. He hollers as her knees hit the mat on each side of his face, and she jabs her fingers into his eyes, blinding him.

"You disgusting asshole! You don't deserve to see anyone's boobs." Hayley's voice screeches, sounding over the cheering crowd. They're as invested in what she plans to do as I am.

"Cut his dick off, vixen!" Knox shouts, his encouragement poking at Hayley's dhampir nature. He doesn't know it, but he and the other Bella Crew members are triggers for her. Because she has claimed them as her own, she can play off their emotions.

Hayley clenches her jaw and manages to slide down Naked Steve's body, dragging Monroe's lucky knife along his chest. He screams and flails, but he can't do anything because Hayley's quick. She uses the blood to slide down him as if she's on an old Slip and Slide until she glides her ass right over his cock. The guy's body reacts to her movements, and the fucker gets a hard-on. He's definitely not a grower, and Hayley cringes as she laces her fingers around his shaft and slices the knife through so quickly with a maniacal scream. She gawks at his severed dick in her hand for a second before she chucks it and hits Kassandra in the face.

Naked Steve wails, the high pitch of his voice deafening. He falls into utter shock and passes out. Kassandra shrieks and rushes Hayley, lifting her off her feet. She bites her fangs into Hayley's shoulder, chomping so hard I'm sure she penetrates Hayley's bone. My vision turns red with anger, and I rush toward the two of them only to have someone crash into me. I snarl and punch my fist at the stranger from the crowd.

"Don't fucking ruin the fight!" the vampire shouts, getting in my face.

I jam my knife into his stomach and stab it in a couple of times until he falls away from me. I hop to my feet and kick him in the side, rolling him out of the ring.

His distraction was long enough for Kassandra to pin Hayley down. I yell as Kassandra grabs Hayley's wrists and forces them over her head. She proceeds to smash her boobs in Hayley's face, suffocating her in the process.

Growls sound from the audience, and I hear Lawrence cheer Kassandra on with the microphone. A part of me explodes fury, because I failed to get to her quickly.

But I won't fail her now. I promised her I'd keep her safe in the ring.

I launch at Kassandra and grab her hair, yanking her off and dragging her a few feet. Hayley gathers her bearings and scrambles up. I expect her to go after Naked Steve, but she follows me and Kassandra, her eyes blinking silver. I smash my hand across Kassandra's eyes, blocking her vision so she can't see, and Hayley collides into us and bites Kassandra's neck, ripping a chunk of her skin away in the process.

"Naked Steve," I say, flashing my fangs at Hayley, hoping I can get her to stop sucking on Kassandra's neck. "Kill him. Kill him now and get this fight over with."

Hayley jerks her head back, her face covered in blood, and she growls at me, the noise far sexier than I expected coming from her mouth. Part of me wishes she would come for me next and sink her teeth into me, sucking me with her pouty mouth and luscious lips.

"Kill him!" I repeat, using my hand to nudge her back.

Naked Steve sobs and clutches the bloody wound where his cock was, probably wishing he remained unconscious. He realizes Hayley zones in on him, his survival instincts kicking on and helping him get to his feet.

"Fuck," Hayley mutters under her breath, straightening her shoulders as she prepares to face the man.

Racing toward him, she drops to the mat and sweeps her leg out, knocking his feet out from under him. He hits the ground with a thud and a grunt, and she hops on top of him and aims her knife.

I expect her to hesitate. I expect her to change her mind and get off him. But something dark twists around Hayley, stealing away her morals and putting her into survival mode as well. She will kill as not to be killed.

Except she's utterly and completely ruthless.

Jerking the knife down, Hayley stabs Naked Steve in his stomach, and she doesn't stop. One. Two. Three. Four. Five, six, seven, eight, nine, ten. Her movements turn impossibly fast, and I lose count until his guts fall from him, the mess, unlike anything I've seen. I don't know what Sawyer did to her while he was manipulating her mind, but it's like he unleashed a beast and put her in the ring.

The crowd roars and cheers, crowding around to watch as Hayley proceeds to slice the knife across Naked Steve's throat, finally silencing his screams. I stand in shock, watching as she manages to sever his head and then throws it at Kassandra hard enough to knock her back.

I do the only thing I can think of. I attack Kassandra and slice my own dagger across her throat, bleeding her out enough to knock her unconscious. She'll heal, but it will stop her from trying to do anything.

Hayley heaves a breath, her chest rising and falling, and she grabs a handful of guts and throws them at the crowd. Tipping her head back, she screams, the noise far from evil. She sounds desperate and broken. She sounds as if she might've just snapped out of Sawyer's mind manipulation to have everything crash back onto her.

Dropping to her knees, she lands in the blood and curls in on herself. I don't leave her there for long, rushing to her side and scooping her into my arms.

Lawrence rings the gong, announcing the fight is over, and he hops into the ring and grabs my hand raising it over my head. Hayley recoils from him as he does the same with her, and the audience goes ballistic and unlike any time I've ever heard in all my time performing for the Fright Fights.

"What a fight!" Lawrence calls, kicking the body of Naked Steve out of the ring.

Some of the vampires fight over his remains, licking the fresh blood from his skin without care.

"Don't forget to spread the word about our newest fighters. The night's still young, and we have a lot of blood left to shed around here. What do you guys say? Do you want to see another round?" Lawrence laughs with excitement, his voice rising to a pitch I've never heard. It weirds me out and makes me shuffle away from him. I'm afraid he's going to demand we stay in the ring, and I don't think Hayley can handle any more.

Sawyer must realize what could happen, because he hops the tethers and lands in the ring in front of Lawrence.

"Get out of the fucking ring!" Sawyer says, his voice booming over the crowd. "It's my fucking time to show these assholes what a real fight looks like."

I release a breath and nod my head, abandoning the ring without waiting to see if Lawrence complies. Sawyer snatches one of the vampires from the crowd and tosses him into the ring, towering over the man and making the crowd cheer. They love the fact that he is crazy enough to bring in somebody not even part of the show.

"Please take me back to the room," Hayley whispers, her voice tickling my ear as she hides against my neck. "Something's wrong with me."

I rub my hand across her back. "You need some more blood. You were injured. Go ahead and bite me."

I should wait for Monroe or Knox, but I'm afraid. I don't want Hayley to experience any more pain than she has to. I don't know what it is about her, but I'm drawn to her unlike anyone I've ever been around before. It's no longer me trying to save myself and asking her to help me. I want to help her. I don't know if it's because of the Bella Crew or because she's a dhampir, or what, but all I know is that something inside me is changing.

"Are you sure?" she asks, instead of sinking her teeth into me like she would if it were one of the guys she's claimed.

"Absolutely. Take whatever you need." Hayley rips into my flesh, the strength of her bite enough to make me gasp. The pain only lasts until she moves her mouth over her mark and begins to suck, sending a wave of energy through me.

I hug her tighter and run from the auditorium. I rush with vampire speed all the way back to her room. I close the door, resting my back to it for a moment until I slide to the floor.

Hayley eases away from my throat, her eyes watery with tears. The look of sadness and shock on her face strikes my heart, and I feel her pain as if it's my own. "Make it stop. Something happened, and Sawyer's manipulation didn't stick. I can't believe I did that. I'm a fucking monster. I'm no better than Lawrence or Alexander. Maybe I do deserve to be caged."

Fucking damn it. Rage explodes through me that she even feels an ounce of pain over the situation she was forced into.

I cup her face and lean in. "I can't. You drank too much blood, and there's no way I'll be able to break into your mind. I'm so sorry. You're not a monster, Hayley. You're far from it. Monsters don't feel remorse. They don't have pity for hurting someone who deserved it either. That man out there was a rapist. He probably killed someone. He wanted to kill you. He didn't even beg for mercy. Please, just take a breath."

Her lips quiver and I can't stop staring at her pouty mouth and how I suddenly want to kiss her. But I can't. I won't. I'm not going to take advantage of her in a situation where she's vulnerable. It's not my place. She's not mine. I can only be here for her as a friend.

She hugs me, her soft cries stirring something inside me I haven't felt since I transformed into a vampire. In a moment where I should feel hopeless, I feel as if I'm stronger than ever. Because of her fragility, it gives me the strength to want to fight back. And fight harder. To do whatever it takes to stop this bullshit. I'm not a damn vampire donor for Lawrence any longer. I'm a new member of the Bella Crew. I won't let them down.

The door to the room hits my back as someone tries to open it, and I shift out of the way and let Knox into the room. He swears under his breath and drops to his knees beside us, combing Hayley's hair from her bloody face.

"Oh, vixen. Come here. Let me see you." Knox holds his arms out and silently demands that I hand her over to him.

I don't argue and do as he asks.

I watch in silence as Hayley throws her arms around Knox, crying louder as he holds her. He turns away from me and strolls toward the bathroom. I want so badly to follow to make sure she's really okay, but Knox closes the door without a word.

I stare at the wood for only a moment. If I stay, I'm afraid I'll lose control and demand to be near her. I'll demand to help.

But again, it's not my place. My place is to obey orders. My place is to just survive.

If only these emotions awakening inside me didn't consume me.

It takes everything in me to stroll to the door. I can't catch my breath until I open it and stare into the empty hallway.

Clearing my throat, I say, "Call me if you need me. I'll go grab a couple of things for Hayley and come back later."

Knox shouts his thanks, and I force myself to exit. I force myself to let Hayley go. She is safe. She will be okay.

As for me? I'm not sure. I don't think I'll ever be.

AFTERPARTY

I SIT ON the counter and stare at my bloody hands. The events of tonight replay in my mind over and over again. I killed a man. I mutilated his body. I stabbed him so many times that his intestines fell out. If I was a vampire, I'd probably have sucked on them. Instead, I let the audience do the job of licking them clean.

I shudder at the thought. What the actual fuck? Who

knew I could be so vicious and violent when my emotions were suppressed? It was as if everything bad that happened to me in my life came crashing down, turning me into a fucking monster. And then, all of a sudden, it was as if the wall Sawyer built in my mind crumbled. I felt everything ten times more intensely. Disgust about what I had done still lingers with me now. I'm not sure I'll ever get the blood and guts and tissue out from beneath my nails. I can still taste the splash of his blood on my lips, the metallic rancid flavor nasty in comparison to the blood of my guys.

And what was worse? The look Cooper gave me. I'm pretty sure he regrets ever agreeing to be on our side. He looked at me like...

"Hayley, hey? Will you look at me? I need to know that you're listening. I want to check your wounds, but I can't see them properly with the blood. Can I help you shower?" Knox links our fingers together, keeping my hands close to his heart. His gesture gets to me. He trusts me with one of the most vital parts of him even still. He doesn't look at me as if I've done the worst thing in the world. He looks at me as if he's worried that I'm somehow broken beyond his ability to repair me.

I tilt my head up and finally meet his blue eyes, the depths endless in a shining pool I want to drown in. His bottom lip puckers out the longer he stares at me, and I reach up and tap it with my thumb. Grabbing my wrist faster than I can pull away, Knox sucks my index finger into his mouth and hums as he pulls it out slowly. The gesture shouldn't be as hot as it is, especially because of where the blood came from.

"You taste like a champion," he teases, finally getting his mouth to smile, though I know it takes everything in him to do so.

He wants to frown as much as I already am, but he also wants to be okay on my behalf. Because if he's worried and sullen, it doesn't help my mood. I know he wants to do everything he can to see me smile again. I just...I don't know if I can. I'm not sure if I should try to fake it. I never want to be fake around him, but I also don't want him to feel as if he's a failure for not being able to just kiss me better. My wounds aren't just of flesh. They cut deep into my soul. Into my very being. Tonight changed me. Tonight proved exactly what kind of monster I can be. No, not the monster I *can* be. The monster I *am*.

"It's better than being a loser, I suppose. There was no way I was going to let that asshole kill me. Plus, I think if I hadn't put on a good show, Lawrence would've done something far worse. I don't know what, but I'm sure it would've been fucking twisted. I just wish...I don't know how to explain it."

"Well, you don't have to explain anything to me. I'm here for you regardless." Sliding me off the sink, Knox carries me in his arms to the shower. He reaches in and turns on the hot water, but he doesn't set me on my feet. I don't think he's going to. Not that I want him to put me down. "I'm proud of you, Hayley. I know what you did tonight sucked. I understand that acting like that goes against everything you are. I also know the weight murder carries on someone, which is why I'm not a huge fighter. But you need to know that none of this was your choice. His death was not your fault. It was Lawrence's and his own. He was a criminal."

I sigh and nod my head, chanting his words in my mind as if they're my new mantra. It's not my fault. I didn't do it for fun. I did it because it was that guy or me. If only it would make me feel better.

I blink my eyes, suppressing another round of unwanted tears. "I just want to go home. I wish I was never put in this position. I wish I never dragged you guys into it, either. It's not fair. I know you had plans, and you were going to change La Vega—"

Knox silences me with a kiss, cutting off my words in the most delectable rude interruption. I'm okay with him doing it again and again as long as our souls are together, and I can feel his adoration and desire for me in a single brush of our lips.

He doesn't lean away until he's sure I won't say anything else. Opening the shower door, he kicks his pants off, and I help him with his shirt. He carries me into the hot stream of blissful shower water that stains red the moment it touches me.

"I never want you to think you've ruined anything." Knox sets me on the deep ledge intended for bath products but empty except for a small bottle of soap. This place is severely lacking, but I don't need much as long as whatever is in that clear bottle cleanses my skin of tonight. "You're lucky it was me you said that to, vixen. Monroe would spank you if he knew you assumed we weren't still going to change La Vega. Because we are. This doesn't change our plans. It doesn't even change the timeframe we're hoping for. We're not alone. Tatum, Govan, and Walcott are all there running things on our behalf."

I bite my lip. "It's a shame that Monroe is the only one brave enough to spank me, Knox. I feel as if I'm punished just a little that I'll feel better about tonight."

The look he gives me speaks volumes. He loves the hell out of me making such a suggestion, the both of us knowing the true intent of my words. He's not one to assume. He loves for me to say things as they are and wants me to be vocal when it comes to everything, but I also know he enjoys filling in the fantasy I begin to create. I think he's more comfortable now than he was in the beginning. He knows I'm not with him because I have to be. I'm with him because I choose to be.

"You naughty, naughty vixen. You want to get me in trouble, don't you? I'm not supposed to do anything except care for you and tend to you as a former medical practitioner. We both know I'm incapable of being professional when you tease me like that...especially with how fucking sexy you look right now. It doesn't help that you're enticing me with traces of blood. It's not as good as yours, but you make me incredibly hungry."

I smirk, loving everything about this moment. I love how just being with Knox eases the ache inside me.

I break his stare, tracing my gaze along his rippling muscles, following the line of his abs to the V of his hips, pointing out that he's far more than hungry. He's desperate for my attention.

I'm not going to pass up the opportunity to point it out. It's far better to think about how much he desires me than anything else going on right now.

I gently lace my fingers around his hard-on, slowly stroking him. "I think you're more than hungry for me."

He chuckles and reaches out, helping me unpin the disgusting, sopping wet wig from my hair. He hangs it over the glass, and blood drips from the fake strands in rivers along the door.

"Always, vixen. I want to ravish you and satiate my ravenous desire. You have no idea what you truly do to me and how much I wanted to be alone with you. I was thanking my luck that I'm the one in charge of ensuring you're uninjured and healthy, because it means I get you all to myself until the Fright Fights are over." Knox traces his hand from my jaw and down my neck, slowly following the curve of my clavicle until he rubs his fingers over my tight nipples, pebbling from the coolness of his skin against the hotness of the water.

I continue stroking him with my fingers, tipping my head back into the hot shower stream and enjoying his exploration of my body. "I think I do. Because you do the same to me. I can't even go another minute without thinking how much I want you. I want to use you. I want nothing more than to enjoy everything about you. Because when I think about you, and you alone right now, I don't think about other things."

Knox leans in and kisses me, pulling me close by my hips until our bodies press flush together. His cock has nowhere else to go except between my legs, so I slide off and stand on my tiptoes, squeezing him between my thighs without letting him enter me. He kisses my neck and works his lips lower, exploring the length of my body inch by inch with his tongue and lips and teeth. He nips me on the top of my boob, tasting my blood for a second before sucking on my nipple until I moan. I grab onto the shower wall and let him continue until he kneels on one knee and grabs my leg, positioning it onto his shoulder. I balance on the edge of the small ledge, my whole body buzzing in anticipation as he nips my thigh, his fangs drawing blood and making my whole body clench.

"You taste like the vanilla ice cream my mother used to make when I was human." Knox moves from his bite mark and kisses my thigh, using his right hand to spread me open with his fingers until he licks his tongue over my clit, the sensation capturing my breath and every thought trying to steal my attention.

"I can't get enough of you," he mumbles, licking me faster and harder at the same time he fingers me, rubbing me in a way that strikes me with electric pleasure.

I can't even form words, my moan being the only thing sounding through the air. Knox watches me as an orgasm builds until I bow forward and scratch my nails into his back. Blood seeps from his skin, the potent scent hypnotizing me. I drag him up and lick across his shoulder, unable to stop myself. Blood fills me with warmth, setting off what I can only describe as blood lust. I just want to devour him in every way. I need more.

"Can I bite you?" I ask, my voice breathy with my desire.

"As much as you like, vixen." Knox bends his neck, exposing his throat to me. Grabbing my leg, he stretches my body up until I balance on one foot, doing the standing splits. He sandwiches me to the wall, steadying me in place.

I moan and sink my teeth into a sweet skin as he aligns our bodies. With a groan of his own, he thrusts into me, the pressure of his cock igniting tingles through my body. I feel so good, and he tastes incredible. I lose myself to him, enjoying how hard he rocks into me, how he tangles his fingers through my hair and reciprocates a bite to my shoulder. I cling on to him and gasp, my moans coming in bursts of screams. Knox rubs one of my nipples and takes a moment to silence my mouth with his, exploring my tongue.

Knox moans with our passion, rocking his hips and teasing me with his fangs. His hand slides between us, and he increases my ecstasy by rubbing my clit, bringing me to my peak again. My whole body tenses with my orgasm, and I bite him harder, throwing myself at him until we crash through the glass door. He manages to catch us by smashing his hand into the wall behind him. He doesn't let anything stop him from ensuring we get what we want from each other.

The world spins and my back lands on the bed, now wet with shower water from our bodies and blood from each other. I force him over and get on top, riding him hard until he grunts with his orgasm. I lay on top of him, only for him to grab the covers and shift back onto me, hiding us from the world in the blankets.

He smiles and kisses my throat as if he can't get enough. If a tap didn't sound on the door, interrupting our moment, he might even want to go at it again.

"We're busy!" Knox calls, grinning at the sound of a groan muffling in the hallway. It's Monroe. "You and Sawyer already got to fuck our girl since we arrived. It's my turn and I'm going to savor every second of it."

I laugh, rubbing my nose to his, kissing him once more. "You don't have to wait outside, Monroe. I think we're beyond those boundaries. But...be pre—"

"Fucking hell. This place is a mess, and my damn balls feel as if they're going to explode just from the scent." Monroe kicks the door closed behind him, folding his arms over his chest.

I hide my face in the crook of Knox's throat. "Keep that kind of talk up, and you're going to end up in a cold shower. It's weird."

"Weird? Fuck that. I want you to know all the time how much you get to me. How much I desire you. It's taking all my strength not to fly toward that bed, unwrap you like the gift you are, and have my way. I don't care if Knox watches. He's a voyeur and doesn't know it yet." I listen as Monroe's boots thud across the floor, and the bed shifts as he sits on the end.

I laugh and squirm as he grabs my ankle, trying to yank me toward him, but Knox doesn't let me go. "Careful, you two. I'm still in the mood to wrestle."

Monroe flops next to me, sandwiching me to Knox through the blankets. He messes with them, looking for an opening and manages to sneak his hand inside our blanket burrito until he squeezes my bare ass. "I like the sound of that. Give it to me wild, Hayley. Scratch me, bite me, growl at me. Let's just let our primal desires take over. But be careful. It'll be me claiming you."

I giggle with his words, squirming as he tries to make his way between my legs with his fingers. He's not even fazed that I just fucked Knox.

Knox chuckles and throws the blanket off, linking his fingers around my wrist and pulling my hands over my head. Monroe purrs deep in his throat, his gaze devouring the sight of my body as I lie on the bed, still damp with the bloodstains that only belong to me and Knox.

His tongue glides across his lips until he sucks in his bottom lip with a smile. "Damn. Sawyer is going to be pissed if we celebrate without him, but I might just accept his wrath. I'm sure he'll be back in a couple of hours. I can't imagine an afterparty going on for that long with donors."

My eyes widen with his words, and I use all my strength to break free of Knox, stopping Monroe from trying to tease me with his hands.

"You damn mood killer. You could've waited just a bit longer." Knox swings his fist and clocks Monroe in the shoulder, knocking him onto his back.

Positioning his hands behind his head, Monroe crosses his legs and gets comfortable. All he does is smile, his sharp fangs extended and ready to bite at my command. Either that, or he's really fucking excited. I know vampires extend their fangs when they're in certain moods. Hungry and horny. Both, maybe.

"An afterparty? We never had those with Vampire Nights except to entertain Alexander's guests. Is it like that? I need to know what to prepare for. I don't like surprises." My stomach bunches with nerves, and I try to shimmy my way out from between Knox and Monroe, but they both fling an arm around me, sandwiching me between their bodies again.

"It doesn't sound like it. Lawrence doesn't seem to have many friends. He controls this whole town and doesn't trust anyone. I couldn't imagine him trusting his sole form of entertainment in the hands of another. It's not like dhampirs are easy to come by. Plus, I would never fucking allow it. The only one you're ever going to entertain after hours and off the stage is us, and only if you want to. Like now. Sawyer can handle his ass. He probably needs a moment to chill after his fight anyway. You should've seen him. He—"

Knox growls and slaps his hand over Monroe's mouth, covering it. "Let Sawyer tell her what he wants to tell her."

My eyebrows knit together with my concern. I know that Sawyer isn't a killer. At least, he doesn't do so to donors. And now that I think about it, I need to go to him. He might be worried about me as well.

Groaning, Monroe rolls off the bed and scrubs his hands into his beard. I realize that blood splatters across his face, lingering from the show. His shirt fares no better. "Fine. I'll grab her something to wear. You have to fend for yourself, though. Maybe she can shower again. I don't want anyone else to smell her as she is right now. You really worked her over good."

Blush burns my cheeks, and I cover my face with my hands, inhaling a few breaths, trying to calm my nerves. My emotions run rampant, and I try to process how many I've gone through tonight. Fear, anger, pride, lust, happiness, grief, numbness. It's far more than I've felt in a long time.

I'm used to always leveling between fear and anxiousness, and now I'm getting whiplash with this rollercoaster my life turned into.

Without arguing, Knox lifts me from the bed and into his arms, carefully carrying me over the glass still glittering on the floor in the bathroom. He helps me the entire time we shower until he relocates me back into the room, where I spot Monroe holding out a mini dress covered in sequins. Beside it, he lays down a pretty navy-blue wig along with a bunch of glittering jewelry. I've never worn much in my life because of my performance. I smile and pick up one of the necklaces, running my finger over the sapphire stone.

"This is beautiful," I say, smiling at Monroe. I lift my hair up and allow him to fasten it around my neck.

"It has a tracker in it. All of the jewelry does." Monroe stands super close and fastens the chain. "Sorry if I'm a bit paranoid. You should've heard the disgusting assholes at the show and how much they wanted you. I wouldn't put it past anyone trying to kidnap you, and we don't really know our way around here that well. We don't have the same access and power that we had in La Vega. It was already bad enough there with Alexander arranging other hotels to get you."

Relief floods through me, his thoughtfulness getting to me on a level that makes me feel as if I'm as precious as the gemstone hanging around my neck.

"I love them all. And I love that you want to make sure I'm okay all the time. How did you even get these?" I ask, turning my arm back-and-forth, watching the light reflect off of the diamonds of the bracelet.

"We brought them. We brought a lot of things that we haven't declared in front of Lawrence. He can't know." Monroe purses his lips, hiding them within his beard. "We need to have an advantage all the time. We also have a communication line open with Aris."

"You talk to Alexander?" My heart races just thinking his name. I knew Sawyer had something in the works with him, but I hate to even think about it. I hate that he's working with Alexander and Lawrence at all.

Knox thins his lips together, bobbing his head, answering for Monroe. "I guess we haven't had too much time to go over everything, have we? I'm sorry for that, but yes, we have arrangements with Alexander. But now that Lawrence is in the picture and Sawyer changed things a bit, we aren't exactly sure where we stand. We're still waiting for him to contact us with what exactly he wants us to do, considering that Lawrence wants you part of the year."

"Oh." I don't know what else to say. My mind shuts down, and all I can do is stare at the glittering sequins on the tight dress.

Knox and Monroe realize I'm not going to say anything else, and Monroe helps me get into the dress and zips it up from behind. It accentuates my curves, the low-cut bodice showing off my cleavage. It covers more than a lot of the costumes I wore for Vampire Nights, but I still feel incredibly sexy and exposed.

"I almost forgot the most important thing," Monroe says, holding up a holster with a knife sheath. He straps it to my thigh like a garter belt. He doesn't try to hide it or anything, making it clear to anyone who looks at me that I'm armed. Not that they would think much of it. I'm better off just staying between Knox and Monroe anyway.

Someone bangs on the door, startling me, and none of us has the chance to move as it flies open and clatters against the wall. Lawrence stands in the doorframe, his face twisted with annoyance, and I take an automatic step back as he dangles a collar and leash from his fingers.

I shake my head, holding my hands up in defense. "Please, no."

Monroe gets between us and growls. "What the fuck do you think you're doing? You can't just come in here uninvited, dangling a damn collar that should be intended only for fucking animals at my girl."

Lawrence rushes Monroe, grabbing the front of a shirt and overpowering him by jamming a knife into his side.

Unlike Sawyer, Lawrence doesn't even humor Monroe. I know that Knox and Sawyer have more influence with the Bella Crew, but they treat Monroe as an equal. Seeing Lawrence treat him as less than pisses me off.

Knox grabs my hand, stopping me from trying to start something I can't win. There's no point in yelling at Lawrence. I don't know what I'm even thinking. I really need to smarten up when it comes to him and learn to separate my attitude between how I am with the Bella Crew and how I am with everyone else.

"She will wear it as all of the donors do. Do not make me grab another one to put around you. This is for her safety. It has a tracker in it and will ensure she stays in complete control. I cannot risk her lashing out at any of my guests." Lawrence flashes his fangs and punches Monroe so hard that he falls to his knees, heaving a breath.

Fuck.

"Stop! Please! I'll put on the collar. Don't hurt him. He's just protective of me." I strut forward and pull my wig from my neck, straightening my shoulders to face Lawrence head-on. I refuse to let him see me afraid of him. I'll do what it takes to protect Monroe and Knox. If wearing a collar is what I have to do, then I'll fucking do it.

"That's my good heir." Lawrence kicks Monroe one more time, keeping him down, and then he spins toward me and hooks the shock collar around my neck. "Let this be a lesson. She'll obey me regardless of what you want. You've given me a better hand at things, because now all it takes is threatening you to get her to comply."

No. No, no, no. This is not what I wanted. I just need things to stop. I want to go back to the Bella and not be the downfall of my guys because they'll do anything to protect me. They've had long lives, and I'm just a...I guess I'm not a donor. It's still hard for me to think otherwise, even though my vision turns red with my anger, and I have to dig my fingernails into my palms to keep myself from trying to lash out at Lawrence. If I do, he will shock me. He'll probably shock me so much that I blackout. I'm not immune to pain. I think I'm more susceptible.

"I'll do whatever. You were right. I just want to be with them. I don't care about anything else." I inhale slow breaths with my words, trying to keep my voice from shaking.

I expect Monroe and Knox to argue, but they remain silent. They want to do something by the sharp features of their expressions, but they won't. I have silently demanded they stand down and let me handle the situation without even having to tell them. It's like they can read my mind. We must pick our battles, like Sawyer has said before, and this isn't one of them. I've been through worse.

"Very good. I have had a couple of guests, quite power-ful ones if I might add, and they have requested a taste of your blood. I hope you don't have a problem with that, Violent Violet." Lawrence smirks with his words, turning his attention to grin at Monroe and Knox.

I bob my head. "I don't mind. I'm used to it."

One look at my guys proves that they're not. They're far from okay with what happens, and I don't know what to expect. What if they decide to try to take down The Whis-key?

No, Sawyer will handle it. He'll smooth things over. Until then, I just need to be a complacent donor.

Lawrence tugs me by the leash, guiding me out of the room and into the hallway. Monroe and Knox remain near-by, but Lawrence doesn't let them surround me like they want, parading me onto the empty elevator and to the casi-no.

It's far more packed than the last time I saw it, and I bow my head, staring at the floor.

"Hey, Vi! Violet!" a vampire calls out. "Hey, Lawrence! I'll give you a donor to force her to the floor and crawl. Let me see up her dress. Come on. Give us a show."

Lawrence doesn't react, ignoring the guy.

I release a breath. I thought he might comply, but he's far more concerned with whoever waits for us at the afterparty to humor the casino dwellers.

We reach the back of the casino, where a crowd of people hang out in what used to be a human bar before the Vampire Uprising. Several vampires grin and catcall me, and Lawrence tugs me to a halt.

"Give the audience a smile, Violet. Show them you're happy for their attention." Lawrence jerks my collar, forcing me to react.

A vampire materializes in front of me. "Mmmm. Pretty girl. Why don't you give us something better? Perhaps a taste?"

Lawrence shakes his head. "You'll have to negotiate with the king of the hour. He has won his choice of the first bite of this delectable Blood Princess."

"Damn-fucking-straight. Bring her to me." Sawyer's voice echoes through the air.

I stare in shock as he stands near a throne, placing his hands on his hips. Shoving me in the back, Lawrence pushes me forward hard enough to stumble in his direction. I cringe and cower, one look in Sawyer's eyes igniting my human fear instincts. But he doesn't yank me up or put on a show.

Swinging his arms over my head, he grabs another vampire by the neck and cracks the asshole's head on the floor. Blood sprays across my feet, and I stare in shock as the guy passes out. It's not a death blow, but it's enough to incapacitate him.

Throwing the man over his head, Sawyer tosses the guy toward the main aisle of the casino, where patrons watch in anticipation. I realize it was the guy from earlier who wanted me on my hands and knees. He was going to try to grab me, and Sawyer saved me.

I don't even get a chance to move before a female donor in a two-piece bikini and a fluorescent green wig jumps at Sawyer, forcing him to catch her because he's not the type to just let someone fall.

I frown as she plants a kiss on his cheek, ignoring the fact that he stretches away and treats her as if she might have a viral disease or something similar to the flu that went around a couple of years ago, killing many donors outside of the Aris Hotel where Alexander quarantined us.

"What a king! You saved our headliner! Let me repay you. Come on, you sexy beast of a man. Bite me. You know you want to. I can see the hunger in your eyes." The performer bends her neck, exposing her throat to Sawyer.

Something unsettling crashes over me, flicking on the switch I'm pretty sure contains the detonator for my psychotic side. I never knew I could be jealous like this. And right now, I want to snatch the woman by her hair and yank her away.

And then I find myself doing as much, twisting my hand through her wig and dragging her off Sawyer.

Shocking pain sizzles across my neck, stopping me in my tracks.

My legs buckle and a screech, falling to the floor, unable to control my body.

The donor laughs and tips her head toward Sawyer. "She's not so tough after all, is she? She doesn't deserve to be yours tonight."

Striding forward, she pulls a blade from a sheath on her glittery belt. She stands over me and grins. "You're not worthy of being the headliner. I've been fighting and winning for a year. Just wait. You're not taking my spot."

She jabs her knife at me.

My dhampir nature takes over.

Not even the shock collar can stop me.

THE PAIN SHOCKING my neck only pushes me forward, and I straddle the performer and wrap my hands around her neck, choking her hard enough to make her eyes bulge. It's as if I'm looking at myself from the outside, watching this monster version of me take control of my body as if I'm possessed.

No one runs to intervene. All the crowd does is gather

around, treating this as another spectacle of a show with me in the middle.

"You're far from worthy. He's mine. He chose me. Do you understand?" I ask, my voice growling.

The performer's eyes widen, a strange reflection flashing at me. I realize that along with my vicious nature, she can see the part of me that has been hidden all my life until Lawrence triggered it with his venom. She knows something's different about me. It's written all over her face.

She locks her fingers around my wrists, trying to stop me from choking her, but I can't let go. I'm afraid if I do, she'll yell out that I'm different. She might tell the whole casino the reason I'm as strong as I am is that I'm not a donor. Yet, I'm not a vampire either.

A cold hand grabs the skirt of my dress, dragging me away from the performer. My back slams against the hard floor, and I gasp as the air escapes my lungs. My eyes burn with tears born from my fear and anger. I need to do something. I can't just act complacent.

"You bad, bad donor, Laura Rose. I have my eyes set on Violet, and it'll be me who ends her life the moment I get the chance," Killer snaps, her voice ringing through the air as she abandons me and towers over the woman. The performer cowers under the vampire's scrutiny, her tough attitude vanishing as she faces someone who she considers a predator.

"It's Velvet Rose, Killer Kassandra. Don't call me otherwise." For being so scared, the donor still manages to force her performance, though I'm not sure anyone apart from the two of us heard her. Killer seems like the type to cut out tongues for backtalk. "I was only trying to prove my place. You know I deserve to be the headliner. You've seen me." The performer rubs her reddening neck, already starting to shift colors with the bruises my strength left behind in the shape of my fingers.

Clapping his hands, Lawrence grabs everyone's attention. He hollers a laugh and pulls a cane from his pocket, thumbing a button to send it unfolding with a deafening click. I imagine he plans to hit someone with it. Whether it will be me or the donor performer, possibly Killer, I don't want to find out.

Sawyer steps between me and Lawrence protectively, and he reaches out his hands and pulls me to my feet, surprising the hell out of me by swinging me onto his shoulder as if I'm just a piece of property to be tossed around.

And fuck. I love that he does it. I love that he growls at everyone nearby as he ignores the whole room. He strides back to his throne and plops down, positioning me on his lap.

He shifts my hair out of the way and brushes his lips to

the back of my ear. "I need to bite you. Is that okay?"

Without responding verbally, I just nod my head, keeping my gaze focused on Lawrence, trying to figure out what he plans to do.

"It looks like the Carnage King has claimed the one he wants, which means one of you will fall before him. Who will it be? Who will face the consequences of failing to prove their worth?" He raises his hand and points to both the performer and Killer. I can't believe he continues to act as if this casino is a stage. It's as if his whole life is one big show for the masses, and I'm caught up like a little puppet within it because my strings tangle and try to strangle me to death in the process.

"I didn't fail!" Velvet Rose screeches, getting to her feet and grabbing her knife from the floor.

Sawyer shifts my hair again, teasing me with his fangs, knowing that half the crowd still watches us in anticipation. He won't allow the commotion to break his current performance, his acting skills better than I knew they were.

"The anticipation is killing me," I whisper, encouraging him to proceed.

I dig my fingers into his legs as he sinks his fangs into me, and I try not to react with a moan, though the fact that he does it so sensually, easing away to lick and kiss the spot turns me on. I don't want people to know I enjoy being bitten by him. I don't want to give them any ideas. It wouldn't be the first time someone has tried to just take a bite. I already know they expect as much. I'll be on one of those tables soon enough because of Lawrence, but I'll put it off as long as possible. I know Sawyer will too. The fight unfolding between Killer and the performing donor is my saving grace. It's another distraction I can use to prepare myself better for what's to come.

Killer screams out a war call, using her vampire speed to circle the donor, causing her to spin on her feet as she tries to determine which direction Killer will attack her from. The crowd taunts Velvet Rose, misleading her. A part of me wants to feel bad, but she brought this upon herself.

"Put her in her place!" a man shouts.

Another man whistles. "Eat her heart out!"

Lawrence rubs his hands together, getting between Killer and Velvet Rose, grabbing the two of them by their hair. "Now, now. That kind of afterparty performance costs extra."

Whistling, a vampire raises her hand. She might be the only female patron at the party. "Five percent of my rations!"

I blink a few times, listening in shock as the crowd offers part of their blood stipends to Lawrence as if he needs anymore.

Lawrence rubs his chin, grinning.

"I'll give you this bitch. But watch out. She's not easy." A muscular vampire drags an older gagged woman by her feet and tosses her toward Lawrence. "Sickly."

Lawrence claps his hands again. "Sold! You may thank this gentleman for the show." Turning to Killer, Lawrence adds, "Get to it. Give the crowd what they want, Killer Kassandra! Eat her heart out."

"No!" Velvet screams, spinning to look for an escape. But there's no point. She's a dead woman already.

Sawyer touches my chin, pulling my attention to him. "Face me, Violet," he commands, using my stage name. "I want your sole attention." He obviously doesn't want me to watch the fight.

I ignore him, twisting more. I search the crowd, spotting Monroe and Knox standing nearby. Not far behind them, I see Cooper sitting up on the table with a bite on his thigh, and I can't help my frown. Why is he on a donor table? And then I realize that some of the vampires take the other donors to drink from him, healing them so they can consume as much as they like.

Fuck. This is so twisted.

Everything is fucked.

Velvet screams again, her voice stinging my ears. "Please—"

Sawyer spins me around, covering my ears at the same time he kisses me. I try to pull away until his big hand slides down my back, pulling my body even closer. Slipping his tongue into my mouth, he kisses me with such passion that I can't ignore his need to protect me.

I comb my fingers into his dark hair, sitting up higher on my knees, enjoying the taste of his mouth. I savor the softness of his lips and how safe I feel in his arms despite the chaotic horrors unfolding around me. I love how in this moment the world is fighting and at war, but it doesn't get to me in the safety of Sawyer's arms.

"Kill her!" a man yells, his voice trying to snatch my attention.

But nothing can steal me from Sawyer.

At least, not until my shock collar buzzes and electrocutes me, stealing my breath and making me scream in pain. Sawyer growls and stands up. The world blurs around me, making my teary eyes water more. He flies at Lawrence and snatches the com device from his hand, not allowing him to shock me again.

"She's behaving. You know our agreement." Sawyer flashes his fangs and squeezes the com device so hard that it crumbles within his fingers, the pieces of metal and plastic and glass raining toward the floor.

Lawrence surprises me by remaining expressionless yet

silver flashes in his eyes. I think if the crowd wasn't focused elsewhere, he would react. He would probably punch Sawyer's heart out if he could.

"You were showing your possessiveness too much. I have guests here who want to feed on her tonight. It's imperative that we allow it, especially if we need more alliances to overthrow the leadership of La Vega." Lawrence flares his nostrils, his muscles rippling under his suit. He's not built like anyone in the Bella Crew, but I know he is just as strong. "You need to understand one thing. I'm allowing you to be with Hayley, but she also has duties. She must maintain an appearance as one of my donors. If anyone were to find out—"

Sawyer leans in, growling deep in his throat. "No more collars." The demand jabs into me, and if I were Lawrence, I'd be afraid. Sawyer isn't kidding.

Lawrence remains silent, and it takes everything in me not to look at him. "Then you must come up with another idea to ensure her safety. You have no idea what anyone here is capable of. We're not welcome in La Vega for a reason."

Sawyer adjusts me in his arms. "I will ensure it. She doesn't need a collar when she has me and my crew. Understand?"

"Heed my warning, Mr. Noble. If anything happens to

her, the consequences will be far worse than anything you could ever imagine." Lawrence's jaw twitches with his words.

Sawyer doesn't respond and instead turns and strides away, heading in the direction where Knox and Monroe watch the fight while also glancing at us. I can't help but look past them at Cooper, wondering what's going through his mind. He can't seem to take his eyes away from me, his expression a mixture of indecipherable emotions. The way he handled me after the fight, how he treated me with such care, doesn't disappear from my mind. Actually, it lingers.

"This is turning into a real shitshow." Sawyer still doesn't put me on my feet, and I'm pretty sure he won't the whole time we are out here among the patrons.

"It shouldn't last long. I can already tell the crowd grows bored by how long Killer Kassandra takes with her prey." Monroe crosses his arms, shifting on his feet. "Plus, Lawrence is going to want to leave any second. I just got word from La Vega. The meeting is on."

My eyes widened, and I want to ask more questions, but a scream, followed by utter silence, cuts through the casino. Sawyer can't stop me from looking before it's too late. I stare from his arms as Killer slides her hand from Velvet Rose's chest, pulling out her heart. She glides her tongue over it and then tosses it at the man who offered the old woman donor in exchange for the show.

I cover my mouth with my hand. I don't want anyone to see my grimace. But I can't help it. I can't get over how unimportant a donor's life is here. Unlike La Vega, it takes a lot for one of the covens to end a life. But this place? I guess I would consider it a mercy.

Knox grumbles under his breath, flicking his attention to me. "You're being summoned, Sawyer. Lawrence wants Hayley."

Sawyer tenses, looking around. "Fuck. I don't want to take her. They'll have to get through me first."

I sigh and touch his cheek. "Sawyer, it's okay. I'm fine with this. It won't be forever. The consequences are worse if I don't comply."

He opens and closes his mouth to argue with me, but I kiss him again and wiggle enough that he has no choice but to either let me fall or set me down.

I need to be brave. I need to have confidence despite the nerves bunching my stomach. I need to act like a good little donor. Vampires love when donors put up a fight, and I refuse to get to their innate need as predators.

"I'll be okay. I promise." I lick my lips and hold his stare until he finally gives in to my need to protect him.

"It's fucking hard to tell her no, huh?" Monroe asks, rubbing his fingers along my arm.

"Why don't we take you to a table by Cooper. It might make things a little easier. He can intervene if our jealousy controls us." Knox motions to Cooper as he still watches me. "He's proved himself capable of taking care of Hayley."

Sawyer squeezes his eyes shut for a second, gathering his thoughts and possibly his nerve to follow through with Knox's suggestion. "Fine, I'll take her there, but I need you to tell Lawrence about the meeting. Maybe he'll decide to just let us go to prepare."

I'm not going to hold my breath. I'll die first before Lawrence shows me any mercy. I know this is him trying to prove a point that regardless of the deal he made with the Bella Crew, he still holds power and is in control. He'll flex his authority if he has to. I hate it.

Monroe smacks Sawyer's back. "You got it. Maybe I can make an interruption or something."

I sigh. "Please, don't do anything crazy. It's just a couple of bites. I've been through worse."

Knox scowls at the thought. "Keep our girl safe, Sawyer. Don't let any fucker get handsy."

He doesn't wait for Sawyer to respond, because he already knows Sawyer will do whatever it takes to keep me safe. He and Monroe abandon our sides, leaving us near the feeding tables. I watch them cross the casino to where Lawrence stands with several men in suits around him. They all look at me while talking to each other, weirding me out. I'm used to being stared at, but it doesn't mean I like it. I'm not sure how to react here. I would smile and wink back at Aris, but here? Ugh.

Sawyer tugs me toward Cooper, who slides from the table to offer me his place. There are a couple of empty spots, but I appreciate his gesture.

"Hayley, it's best to keep your gaze down. Don't look or speak to anyone. They'll try to get you to but ignore them the best you can." Cooper murmurs the words, stiff in posture.

I can't help flicking my gaze over his body, his speedo not leaving much to the imagination. My damn curiosity gets the best of me, and I use my new fascination with him to keep my eyes from betraying me as voices draw closer.

The hairs on my arms rise, the familiarity of Lawrence's low rumbly voice setting off my fear. I wish I didn't have such an intense reaction to him. I wish I could be strong. Fuck, I wish I could just get myself to be numb.

Sawyer helps me position myself on the table, but he doesn't back away. He remains at my head, staring down at me while I continue to drink Cooper in.

"The guys coming are fucking disgusting. I suggest you keep your limbs close to your body. Cross your legs at your ankles." Cooper tightens his jaw, his disdain for whoever approaches clear on his face.

I don't react. He doesn't understand I've been trained to deal with being groped. I've had my boundaries pushed over and over again and beaten if I even reacted negatively toward unwanted affection. The only thing that was ever off-limits was full-on sex. Most men weren't interested in anything except getting off themselves. They didn't care where they stuck their cocks, so I was okay with parting my mouth open for them.

I close my eyes, trying to push away my memories. I want to think differently. I want to not be okay with this kind of treatment. I deserve better. The Bella Crew showed me that. It's as if the ingrained part of me knows that if I do think I deserve better, it'll just be that much harder because I'll never get that. As long as I'm in someone else's control, my life will be shit.

"Your new addition is stunning, Lawrence. Wherever did you find this donor? Surely, she's not from the herd, is she? Have you been keeping her all to yourself until you realized what an asset you were wasting?" A man stands by the table, shoving Cooper out of the way.

What a fucking asshole. It's so strange to see a vampire treated like a donor. It makes me so angry. I know it happens to him all the time, but I feel as if Cooper was cheated out of a better life. All donors think that transforming into a vampire would change everything. Sometimes, they don't even care if they end up on the Strip. Because being on the Strip was better than being under the fangs of some bastard. At least, that is if they were vampires. Donors on the Strip don't survive.

"A parting gift from my beloved sister," Lawrence mutters, keeping a couple of feet of space between the man and himself. He doesn't join the others as they create a circle around me like I'm the most exquisite meal they've ever had lie in front of them.

Another man clears his throat, placing his hands on my thigh and digging his nails in as if he wants to see my reaction. I tense my body but don't react to the pain. That's what he wants. I won't give him the satisfaction of knowing he hurts me. Letting him drink my blood is already bad enough.

"At least she was good for something. The traitor. I'm surprised you even managed to survive the trip to La Vega." The vampire bends over, flashing his fangs. Sinking his teeth into me, he takes the first bite and sucks my blood.

I flick my gaze up and stare at Sawyer, his whole body rigid as if it takes all of his control not to launch at the vampire and tear him apart. He realizes I watch him and gazes into my eyes, locking me in a silent stare.

He manages to open my mind with a whisper under his

breath, and he commands me to only think about him in this moment.

"It was easy enough. It seems there is a bit of weakness in the leadership. Some of the lower covens plan to rebel. Those who are even less have also banded together, and it won't be long before they overthrow the leadership." Lawrence comes closer and shadows over me, getting next to Sawyer. "That is if things go according to plan. Isn't that right, Mr. Noble? You see, gentlemen, my newest headliner, Carnage King, is the leader of the Bella Crew. He has the numbers to really shake things up."

Another vampire bites into me, drinking my blood, acting as if I'm nothing but a blood bag for him. Small mercies. I'd prefer this over him considering me his plaything. "Interesting. We should talk sometime, Lawrence. Do you know I have a few allies within the city limits? Not enough to make a dent, but enough to assist."

Lawrence hums under his breath. "Perhaps. I would need more details and Mr. Noble's opinion. He's the greatest threat to the leadership, which is why he's here. Alexander has a deal with him, but because of how smart a man Mr. Noble is, he came here to make a deal with me to cross the bastard."

Sawyer rests his hands on my shoulders. "I'm not interested in bowing to Alexander. I see a great opportunity with

Lawrence."

My heart sinks into my stomach at even a thought, but I know Sawyer has a different plan. I just can't really think beyond this moment and how it makes me feel with him agreeing with Lawrence after everything.

"And Lawrence? What of us? You brought us here for a reason." The last man says, finally speaking up for the first time. He doesn't wait for Lawrence to respond and grabs my arm, yanking my wrist to his lips to bite me. He sucks slowly, groaning deep in his throat, his body awakening right next to me, so I can feel his boner touch my side.

I try not to react, but I shift enough as to not feel it.

"That all depends. If you want an alliance and the chance to help me take power, I'm going to need something from you." Lawrence smiles with his words. "I'm going to need you to prove your worth."

"And how would you prefer that? Would you accept a percentage of my donors?" the first man asks.

"No. I have something more useful in mind. There is supposed to be a meeting happening between me and Alexander. He believes we can somehow negotiate through the differences we have involving this particular donor. I want you to go with the Bella Crew and bring something more valuable to me. I want more of his performers."

My heart races at the thought of Lawrence getting his

hands on any of the Gemstones from Vampire Nights.

"And how do you expect us to do that?" the man who bit me on my thigh asks. "I'm sure he keeps them under lock and key in his hotel."

"You'll figure out a way. Perhaps Mr. Noble can help you." He reaches down and grabs my chin, forcing me to look at him. "Maybe even this beautiful dhampir."

My mouth opens and closes at his words.

He told me how imperative it was for my existence to remain a secret, yet here he is sharing it with three vampires that could very well try to do something crazy.

The three men fall silent. Sawyer grabs Lawrence's wrist and forces his hand off me. He growls deep in his throat and flashes his fangs.

"You will keep Hayley out of it. It will be me and me alone." Sawyer smacks his hands on the table, the strength of his hand shaking me to my core.

"We shall see, Mr. Noble. But first, help yourselves, gentlemen. Let her blood be an incentive. There can be more where that came from. All you have to do is bow to me." Lawrence straightens his shoulders and steps back, giving them room. "Bow to me and prove your alliance to The Whiskey."

I stare in shock as the three vampires kneel before him. I can't believe he wants more than just La Vega. He wants the dancers.

He wants to be Alexander.

There are already enough monsters in the world.

I can't let this happen.

Lawrence must die.

15

HAYLEY

BAD BLOOD

"WE WON'T BE long, vixen. We'll just be across the casino in Lawrence's private office. Try not to get into any trouble, okay?" Knox kisses the top of my head and winks at me. "But if you do, make sure you kick some ass. Have your weapons?"

I tap the five different spots Monroe had fun securing weapons on me in plain sight. He said it was pointless being subtle. Most donors seem to have at least a knife, though it's futile when you can't even move as fast as a vampire. I think it's like a security blanket, making them feel better. For me? It's a hit or miss. When it comes down to it, I know I can do it. I just wish I didn't have to. Fighting doesn't come naturally to me.

"Fuck yeah, she does. I gave her my lucky knife as well. I know that's the one thing she'll never lose, because it belongs to me." Monroe kisses me next, grinning at me. "And I'll keep reminding her until she knows how important she is to me. I don't let anyone touch the hilt except for her now. She's my lucky charm as much as it is. I can imagine her cutting up a lot of enemies with it." Meeting my eyes, he winks. "I expect it, little bird. Their ghosts give it extra power."

I laugh and shake my head. "As long as it works, right?"

"Just be aware of everything. We know that you will be, but we just have to say it." Sawyer opens the door to the hotel suite. "Cooper will pick you up within the hour for some more practice. We don't expect you to have to go through another fight until we get back from our trip to La Vega, but we've all agreed you're training every day regardless. If it's not for the show, it's just for you."

"I do wish that I could dance instead. But I get it. You guys want to keep me safe." I sigh, thinking about all the days I've spent training on the aerial ring and doing floor routines with the other dancers. That was far more fun.

"It won't be like this forever. You'll get a handle of things. Once you can kick Monroe's ass, we'll add in some fun stuff. Maybe we'll even consider what you had mentioned about a show at the Bella. It would be nice if it's something you want to do."

His words surprise me. I remember how upset they were at the thought of me having to perform. But I guess it's different when they know I actually want to do it. And my own show? I could create something spectacular. I never thought about it. I've always just followed the rules and did whatever my caretaker made me do.

A smile crosses my face. "Seriously? You'd let me?"

Sawyer tilts his head. "Let you? Come on, Hayley. You don't ever need permission to do things you want with us. You're our girl and not our property."

I jump at him, wrapping my legs around his waist and kiss him deeply. He chuckles against my mouth. I don't let him pull away until I'm done and had enough of the taste of his soft lips.

"You guys go without me. I don't think I'm capable of detaching her." Sawyer tightens his hands around my waist, hugging me even closer.

"Fuck. If you stay, I stay." Knox sandwiches me to

Sawyer from behind.

"I'd cover for you guys, but would you really want me to? It'll end with a stabbing," Monroe teases and sticks his hand between mine and Sawyer's faces, blocking us from kissing again.

I snatch his finger with my teeth and bite him, not letting go even as he struggles to pull away. Monroe swears and laughs, trying to shake his hand free, and Sawyer finally puts me on my feet.

"You should know there are consequences for interfering with a dhampir's affection." Sawyer wags his brows. "Show him, Hayley. Teach him a lesson."

Play-growling, Monroe tugs his hand again. "You little vicious minx. I'm warning you. Keep it up and—"

I smile wider and add pressure to his finger between my teeth.

"That's it. You're in trouble now." Monroe surprises me by slipping his hand between my legs. "I know how to get you to let go of me."

I shriek and laugh, releasing him. "Damn it. That wasn't fair."

Snatching my shirt, he drags me closer, a bit rougher and more demanding. And fuck, he looks so hot. "All is fair in fighting and fucking when it comes to me. If you can't handle the pushback, then maybe you should beh—"

I retaliate by grabbing his cock through his pants and stroking it. "I should what?"

Knox hooks his arms around Monroe and yanks him away, shoving him into the hallway. "All right, vixen. You've teased us enough that we're late. Keep it up, and I'll allow Monroe to tie you up for punishment later."

I stick my tongue out at them. "Try not to kill Lawrence. I want the chance to do that myself. And come to the gym when you're done, okay? I want to wrestle with you all."

"Naked." Monroe grins with his word, adjusting his pants out in the hallway.

I giggle, my cheeks flushing with heat. "Definitely."

The three of them punch and play-fight each other until Monroe kicks the door closed, and I listen to the three of them vanish. I don't know what I got myself into, but I'm pretty sure Monroe was serious about naked wrestling. I don't mind, though. I have an advantage. It's nice having the distraction of my boobs smothering them in the way they like.

A knock sounds on the door, and I rush to open it, expecting to see Cooper on the other side. I startle at the sight of Killer standing in the hallway with her hands planted on her hips.

She flashes her fangs at me, the sharp points white

against the red of her ruby lipstick. The holographic strands of her wig hair glitter in the soft lighting, and she wears a one-piece costume made of fishnet over a sexy rhinestone bikini.

I don't know if I should slam the door in her face, so I just keep it cracked. "Can I help you?" I ask, my nerves getting the best of me.

"I'm your escort to the gym. Something came up with Cooper. I figured we'd get an early start since I'm pretty fucking sure we're going to be together in the ring again." Killer remains firm in her spot, staring at me with a wicked, confident smile on her face. "So, hurry up. I don't like being in this trash section of the hotel."

Something's wrong. My human instincts go crazy, and I know damn well that if my guys said Cooper was coming, then he would be coming. I don't think Lawrence would even allow Killer to come and get me.

I try to slam the door in her face, but she's too quick. She shoves her hands to the wood hard enough to send the door flying into my face. It smacks me off my feet, and I fall to the ground on my ass.

I don't get a chance to move before she jumps on me and grabs my throat. Instead of biting into me, she squeezes, cutting off my airway. I thrash and try to break free of her grip, but nothing seems to work. I scratch her and kick my legs, doing everything I can think of to get her to let me go. She wants to knock me out. Why? Probably to drain me later. I don't think she'll do it here. There are too many chances of being caught. If I pass out, I'm probably dead.

"Stop fighting and make this easy on both of us. You're not getting away from me. You made me kill my most compliant donor, and there is no way in hell I'm dealing with you at the show. I don't want to fucking fight you night after night. It's going to get fucking old." Killer hisses with her words, leaning down and getting into my face. She tries to make eye contact with me, but I don't let her. I look up and away.

With one hand, she holds my throat, and with her other, she pinches my chin, trying to get me to look at her again.

It's the only thing that gets her to let me go. I swing my arm and punch her in the side of the face, knocking her off me. I roll over and get on my hands and knees, reaching for my side to pull out one of the knives Monroe armed me with. Her fingers lock around my wrist, squeezing so tightly that I scream and yank away, afraid she's going to break my arm.

"Make this easy on yourself. You have five seconds to comply, or I'm going to make it fucking hurt." Killer growls deep in her throat, the noise more animalistic than human.

She grabs a fist full of my hair and drags me back. Using my legs, I swing my body up and tumble toward her, kicking her in the stomach. It's only enough to get her to drop me for a moment. But that's all I need.

I grab for another knife and manage to jerk my hand out and stab her in the side. She wails and snarls, her anger more powerful than her pain. She launches at me with vampire speed and snaps her teeth, sinking them deep into my shoulder.

Pain swells through me, and I stab her again, trying everything I can to get her off.

The scent of her potent blood wafts through the air, stealing my attention. My stomach roars with a sudden angry hunger, giving me the strength to shove her off again. She yells and catches herself on one hand, using her other to block me.

"What the fuck! You shouldn't be this strong!" Killer screeches, hitting her back on the floor.

I ignore her as I climb on top of her and pin her by her throat. "I'm going to fucking kill you. I'm going to kill you and eat your damn heart."

Killer startles at my words...no, she startles at my expression. I'm nearly certain my eyes look similar to a vampire's as my dhampir nature controls me.

"Oh, shit," she mutters, grabbing at my hair. She tries

to yank me close to her to take another bite, but I resist her strength, tensing and steeling myself toward her power.

"Fuck! Hayley!" Cooper's voice rings through the air. The door slams, and he materializes next to me, his shadow looming over Killer.

"Get her off me!" Killer screams, struggling against my death grip.

"She knows I'm different. We have to do something. My secret can't get out. It's already bad enough that so many know." I heave a couple of breaths, trying to control the raging savage inside me. It takes everything in me not to sink my teeth into Killer's throat. I want so badly to bite her. I want so badly to taste her blood and have her know what it's like to be someone's prey for once.

She would deserve it. She deserves a terrible, painful death for everything she's done. I don't give a fuck if she was forced into this position. She's taken this role so seriously but I'm certain it has consumed her. Cooper was right about the performers. They do take on their persona, shutting out their previous lives.

"Cooper!" The high pitch of Killer's scream stings my ears, and I slam my hand over her mouth, muffling the noise. She sinks her fangs into my palm, sending shooting pain up my wrist and into my shoulder, but I don't release her. I can't.

Growling and baring my teeth, I prepare to bite her. She hollers against my palm. I don't know if it's the sudden fear scrunching her face or my savage blood hunger, but I jerk my head down and bite her hard on her neck, yanking her head to the side in the process. I rip and spit a chunk of her skin, my brain screaming at me in disgust, but my body refuses to listen. This is what I need to do to survive.

"Hayley, slow down. Let me help you." Cooper shifts beside me, not rushing to yank me off. "I can hold her. I'm afraid she's going to overpower you."

I don't say anything to him as he reaches down and locks his fingers under Killer's arms, hoisting her to her feet. I cling on to her, and he drags me up at the same time. Killer flails her arms, trying to fight, but she can't. I tear into her throat too much, so she can't even make a noise any longer.

"Hayley, please. I know you want her blood, but no one deserves this slow and painful of a death. Please." Cooper's voice whispers to my ear. He speaks as if I might attack him next if he talks any louder.

It's the only thing that gets me to stop sucking. Easing away, I inhale a deep breath and stare into Killer's wide eyes. Her mouth opens and closes as she gasps, but I'm nearly certain she's suffocating. Maybe drowning on her blood. I might've crushed her chest in the process as well. I don't know. She looks weird.

"I can do this for you. Just give me a bit of space." Cooper locks his gaze onto mine, but he doesn't react. He remains expressionless.

"No." The sharp tone of my voice makes him hesitate. My mind whirls. I need to do this. I don't know what it is about this moment, but I feel as if the only way I'll ever be okay is if I end this monster's life myself. I want to do it so that Cooper doesn't have to.

Unsheathing another knife, I grind my teeth and jab it into Killer's chest. It slides in, her sternum broken already. Blood pools over my hand, and I retract the knife and drop it to the floor. I can't help myself as I bring my fingers to my mouth and lick her blood. It satiates a feral, sadistic part of me I never knew existed. Cooper's eyes flash silver as he watches me, but he doesn't say anything. All he does is hold Killer tighter, but it's pointless. She's not going anywhere. She no longer has any fight left in her as her body sags. But it's not over yet. She's not dead.

Shoving my hand into the gaping wound from my knife, I cringe as I touch something soft and slimy yet pieces of something hard mix with it. And then I yank, pulling out her insides, not even sure if I grabbed her whole heart. I've never done this before. I hope to never do this again.

Cooper drops Killer's body to the ground and kicks her

away, sending her toward the wall. Without hesitating, he rushes me and lifts me into his arms. The world blurs as he relocates me, leaving behind the mess of my fight with one of the headlining vampires. My mind can't even orient itself as Cooper shuts the door to another hotel room and strides across to the bathroom. He sets me down on the sink and turns on the hot water to the shower as if he can't stand the thought of Killer's blood all over me.

I remain frozen, wringing my hands together. I can't think of anything to say. I'm not even sure if my mouth will work if I wanted it to.

And then I see myself in the mirror.

Holy fuck. I don't even recognize whoever stares back at me in the reflection. The bloody savage looks like a starved Strip dweller. My eyes remain silver, and blood drips down my chin and stains the front of my shirt. If I didn't bare my teeth, I'd think fangs were hiding beneath my lips. But they're not. I'm still a dhampir. I'm not a vampire regardless of what I look like.

I'm worse.

"I'll go get one of the Bella Crew members," Cooper says, shifting his weight as if he doesn't even know what to do with me.

I shake my head in silence. I don't want them to see me like this. I don't want Lawrence to know.

I still can't get my mouth to speak, and Cooper obeys my silent disagreement with his plan.

"Okay. I get it. Are you injured?" he asks, strolling closer, his eyes roving over my body as if he can assess my injuries under the thick layer of blood coating my skin.

Again, I shake my head.

He exhales a long breath, his whole body shuddering with the gesture.

I wish he would tell me what goes through his mind, because his face still remains expressionless. My body refuses to cooperate, and I know he's worried. I just don't know how to deal with myself. There's a darkness inside me ready to unleash itself on the world. I just don't know how I will survive if I can't get myself under control.

"Focus on me, my showgirl. I know you're in shock. I can't imagine what it's like being a dhampir, but I clearly remember what it was like after I first transitioned." Cooper stands between my legs, resting his hands on my aching shoulders.

I try not to wince, but I forgot Killer bit me. Darting his eyes from my face, he realizes that beneath the blood is a bite mark. He frowns, his eyes flashing silver, and for the first time, he reacts. Grabbing a washcloth from the rack, he holds it under the sink and wets it. I try not to squirm as he squeezes cool water from the cloth and over my wound, cleaning it so he can see it better.

"She got you good. If she wasn't dead already, I'd kill her myself." He flares his nostrils, studying the puncture wounds and the teeth marks. She didn't just get me with her fangs. She wanted me to hurt.

"But she *is* dead. *I* killed her." My words come hoarsely from my mouth. I don't know how I managed to even speak, but it's like I have to say what's on my mind. It's the only thought coursing through my head apart from the pain. I killed her. I killed her, and I don't feel bad about it. All I feel is numb. A part of me might even be a bit exhilarated. It freaks me out. I just imagine killing terrible vampires until there's no more left.

"She was trying to kill you first. You did absolutely nothing wrong. I want you to remember that, okay? You killed her because she came in here and attacked you. She was not a good person, and who knows how many lives you saved by ending her life and getting rid of Lawrence's little plaything." Cooper manages to get his frown in control, and he smooths his features out with a soft smile. "I'm impressed, my showgirl. I knew you had it in you, but seeing you in action...I'm proud of you."

It's obvious that he wasn't going to say he was proud of me and something else instead, but he changed his mind. And now I really want to know.

"You're proud of me for killing someone? You kind of have things a bit twisted." I lick my lips, still tasting the blood of Killer. I want it off of me. I want to taste something else.

As if Cooper reads my mind, he wets the washcloth again and rubs it across my mouth, cleaning my face up. He grabs one of the water cups from the counter and fills it up, offering it to me to drink. "I am. You did everything right. I think the only reason Lawrence will be mad is because this didn't happen on stage in front of an audience. But don't worry. He's not going to do anything to you."

I intake a sharp breath, my shock melting into fear as I process his words. "Fuck. You don't know that." This is bad. Oh-fucking-no. What have I done?

All I can think about is him whipping me and how painful it was. What if he does it again? I would take Alexander's paddle any day over that damn whip.

"Fuck," I repeat, pushing Cooper back.

I slide off the counter and get to my feet. I don't know what I'm doing, but I need to do something. Anything. I need to hide Killer's body.

Cooper snatches my wrist, stopping me. "Hayley, wait. Let me help you get cleaned up and give you some blood."

I shake my head and yank away from him. "No. I

need to go. I need to take care of her body. Lawrence can't know."

Realization crosses his face as he realizes why I'm afraid. Instead of arguing with me, he slowly nods his head. "If that's what you want to do, then let me help you."

I squeeze my eyes shut. "If he catches you—"

"I can handle myself. Now, come on. I have an idea." Cooper doesn't give me a chance to prepare myself as he picks me up again.

I suppress my scream at the quick relocation.

Cooper stops short, his whole body tensing.

Oh fuck.

Another vampire rushes us and rips me away.

16

HAYLEY

COVETED

"BEAUTIFUL VIOLET. DON'T fight me. I won't hurt you." The strangely familiar voice hums in my ear. "I'm a friend."

My body cools as my mind registers that he's one of the vampires who drank from me at the afterparty. "Let me go."

Shockingly, the vampire releases me, but he spins me away from Cooper, not allowing him to get close. Holding out a knife, he keeps Cooper back. I nearly shout for him to run for help, but another vampire...no, a human man, exits the room beside mine and trains his gun at Cooper.

"No need for aggressive tactics, my pet," the vampire says, motioning to the human. "Mr. Saint won't try anything because he's going to want to hear me out."

Cooper hesitates, his gaze darting from mine and to the man. "If you so much as hurt her, Mr. Falo, it'll be the end for you."

Mr. Falo? That's the hotel across the way. I saw it when we entered the gates to the town. He must be the owner or ruling coven there. I know Lawrence is the true authority, though.

"Do you really think I want to hurt someone as coveted as she is? She is worth quite a bit, according to my sources. It also seems her true master wants her back badly enough to negotiate a deal. I need your help, Mr. Saint. It seems she trusts you." Mr. Falo doesn't look at me as he says the words. "I would like to release your blood sister from a contract in return for you assisting me in returning this lovely specimen to La Vega."

The look that crosses Cooper's face speaks volumes. I knew he wanted to get his sister back. I knew he joined the Bella Crew because Sawyer said they would help him. But that's no guarantee. What this guy offers? It is a guarantee if

Cooper hears him out.

Oh-fucking-no.

Cooper owes me nothing. I could just be a means to an end to him, considering that he agreed to train me to get out of the herd.

I push the thought away. I can't think like that. It's just so hard for me to trust anyone, and he doesn't have the same life as Sawyer, Knox, and Monroe do. He could be attracted to me, but that could be it. He must think of himself first, and in all honesty, I wouldn't blame him. I know what it's like to be enslaved to a vampire. I know what it's like to have to do things you don't want to do.

If only neither of us was put into this position.

"Why should I trust you?" Cooper steps closer, peering at me from around the vampire. He assesses whether he could reach me if he tries. "Right now, I have a pretty good deal going on."

"You need higher standards, Mr. Saint. Your current living situation is far from acceptable. If you agree to help me, I'll give you a position among my coven. I'm going to need someone to overlook the hotel here when I claim one in La Vega. Perhaps you can visit this lovely woman on occasion. Mr. Aris has agreed that if we go through with this that we may have time with her."

My heart sinks in my stomach. What the actual fuck?

Not only do I have to worry about Lawrence and Alexander now, but I also have to worry about this guy. I knew Lawrence was a fool for sharing my secret. I can't imagine someone not wanting the opportunity to claim me, considering I'm basically a damn forever donor.

"You'll bring me onto your coven?" Cooper's expression softens with his husky voice. "Why? I'm not powerful. The vampire who transformed me was a mere outcasted shadow dweller."

"That means nothing to me. A coven comes together to create power, not be pieced apart. I'm sure you can prove your worth. I've seen you fight. I think your abilities are rather appealing when it comes to getting shit done." The man looks at me. "You'll also prove useful with your knowledge. Lawrence was quite impressed with you. If he is impressed, then I'm sold."

I don't like the way they both look at me. Even the human guy standing in silence blocking the hallway stares at me. I need to run. I need to get out of here. If I stay, I don't know what Cooper will do or if he will agree. We had a plan.

"I need you to prove something to me first. You're asking quite a bit for me, so I need you to do something. I need you to get rid of a body." Cooper motions to the door of my hotel room. "If you can do that, then we'll talk."

"Cooper." I cover my mouth with my hand, wishing I didn't speak.

Cooper's mouth twitches as his fangs peek from beneath his lip. "Is it a deal? We'll have to discuss things in detail later when the sun rises. This donor is protected by the Bella Crew. They also have a deal with Lawrence."

"I think that'll be acceptable. Just know if you speak even a syllable of this conversation to anyone, your sister is dead." The vampire smiles, stretches his hand out, and pats my cheek. "Be a good girl and mind your mouth. If you speak, I will remove your tongue."

I don't even get a chance to say anything before the vampire enters my room, grabs the body of Killer, and vanishes with his human associate.

I heave a couple of breaths and dig my nails into the palms of my hands.

I'm so confused. I can't believe this just happened. How can Cooper think he can get away with this? It puts me on guard, and I hold my hands up when he tries to close the space to me.

"You asshole! How could you do this?" My voice rises in pitch, and I take another step back. He can rush me if he wants to. He can steal me away and hide me until Mr. Falo is ready to speak to him.

"Hayley, please. You have to calm down before you attack me. I'm not your enemy. I understand you're pissed and in shock, but I had to make a deal. You realize he could've overpowered me and just taken you, right? There would've been a chance that somebody would've stopped him, but there would've also been a chance that he was successful. I wasn't going to risk you getting hurt." Cooper tries to close the space to me again. His features twist, and he stops short.

I catch sight of my reflection in the mirror. I'm a monster again. I'm on the verge of losing control, and he's the one I crave to go after. It's hard for me to even process his words. That asshole vampire threatened to kill his sister and cut out my tongue. Fuck.

"But your sister. You could break her contract for her." It's the only thing I can think to say. I mean, I wouldn't blame him for wanting to help his family. It's not as if he would be sacrificing himself. It's the same situation as with the gemstones and my best friend Mya. Alexander threatened them because of me, so of course I wasn't going to put up a big fight. I wasn't going to leave when others were at stake, but that's me. I care about them as if they're my family just as Cooper cares about his sister.

"My sister would understand. She was raised by my grandma too. Plus, she's tougher than me." He offers me a pathetic smile that convinces me of absolutely nothing except that he's not sure of himself.

"Cooper..." I don't know what else to say. This is too much. He's put me in a terrible position. He should've just gone and got help and risked the asshole vampire kidnapping me. I'm sure my guys would've gotten me back. No one wants me to die if I don't have to because they can use me for my blood. I have faith in the Bella Crew.

"Please, forgive me. I hate that I agreed to anything, but I know we can get out of it. We could use this to our advantage. Mr. Falo said that he was working with Aris, which means Aris is going to try to betray the Bella Crew. Since we know that, we can outsmart him and strategize."

I shake my head, my features scrunching. "But he said—"

Cooper risks me devouring him by closing the space and grabbing my hands, cupping them between his. "Hayley, I know I'm not some powerful vampire. I know I don't have anything to offer you apart from knowledge and experience. But I made myself a promise long ago that I would fight for humanity. If I got the chance to get out of here, I would fucking rebel against my own kind. I would fight like the rebels the Bella Crew are. I would do it because of my sister and my grandmother. I would do it for any other dhampirs like you in the world. I don't have anything to lose. All I see right now is a new life I can gain. I want it."

I study his face, his green eyes flashing silver. He smolders me with his intensity, trying to get me to believe what he says. And it's not that I don't believe him, it's just that...so much can happen. When I thought my life couldn't get worse, it turned fucking awful. And I'm at the point where I know it could just be unbearable.

I've lost a lot of my faith in life. I've been born to serve vampires. I've been cursed as an eternal donor, and I sometimes wonder if this fight would even be worth it in the end if anything were to happen to the Bella Crew and what they want for the future of La Vega. This bullshit shouldn't land on my shoulders like this.

"But I also don't want it at your expense," he adds when I'm not quick to respond.

"If it came down to it, would you do something at my expense? I wouldn't blame you. I know what it's like to be less than and treated as property and a performer." I lick my lips with my words, the lingering taste of blood still tainting my lips.

"I wouldn't. I swear. You have to trust me." Cooper furrows his brows, keeping his gaze locked on mine. "Please."

Can I trust him?

Should I?

"Why? Why should I? I already know that you only

started this whole thing to get away from the herd." I pull my hands away and cross my arms over my chest. "I need a good reason."

He swallows, his Adam's apple bobbing in his throat. He doesn't rush to say anything. All he does is continue to stare at me as if he can read what I want him to say on my mind. But I don't know what I expect. I lost the ability to create expectations as a way to protect myself.

He lifts and drops his shoulders. "I have given you my reasons, Hayley. I made a promise."

"That's not enough. I've had too many damn promises in my life. I don't have a good reason to trust you, and you don't have a good reason as to why. But I know you're going to do whatever you're going to do regardless. Just be upfront about it, okay? I don't want to be let down." I step back and turn away from him, my whole body aching in a way that I haven't felt before.

"You're right. I don't have a good reason, and I don't think I ever will. I also can't promise that I won't let you down. I'm not your hero...but I was hoping that maybe you could be mine." He touches my shoulder, trying to get me to turn around, but I don't.

I won't.

"I can't. I can't even save myself." Words have never felt truer.

I'm not a hero.

I'm a donor. And apparently, I'll be one forever.

I stare at the ceiling, listening as the door creaks open. Cooper silently did the best he could to remove all the evidence of the fight between me and Killer. Cleaning up blood is kind of a thing for vampires, and he did a decent job, considering how much blood had spilled. I'm sure they have a billion different techniques, but it still doesn't change the fact that it happened, and we're hiding it. That Cooper asked Mr. Falo to get rid of the body.

"Little bird, you have something to tell me, don't you?" Monroe closes the door behind him. He doesn't come any closer and waits for me to turn around to look at him. "You do know that the trackers you wear give us both sound and visuals, right?"

I suck in a breath and sit up, jerking my attention to him. "You know?"

"Fuck yeah. I watched the whole thing at least twenty times in the last hour. It was so fucking hard not to rush here, but you're being watched by the fucking traitor." Monroe crosses the room and plops down on the bed beside me, engulfing me in a hug and rolling on top of me.

Leaning down, he kisses me without hesitation as if he wants nothing more than to get rid of the pout crossing my face. And it works. The relief I feel in this moment, knowing that I don't have to explain anything is like a weight eases off my chest. I was going to risk my tongue to do so.

I pull away from him and meet his eyes. "Should we be worried? What if he does something because you know? Did you hear what he said about Alex? Where are Knox and Sawyer?" The questions tumble out of my mouth one after another, and I search Monroe's gaze for answers.

He raises an eyebrow. "I need to work on my distracting skills, little bird. You shouldn't even be able to think with me on top of you."

Blush creeps over my face, warming my cheeks. I feel his body arouse against mine. His hard-on presses into my leg as I squirm under his hot scrutiny.

"That's why you're here," I say, biting my bottom lip between my teeth. He doesn't give me any answers except for kissing me again. He came to check on me and to ensure I was okay—distracted instead of freaked the fuck out.

The desperation of his mouth speaks volumes. I don't think he has the answers, or he doesn't want to share them with me just yet. He wants to be with me and help settle my racing heart first before anything else.

And I allow him to.

Monroe breaks from my mouth, knowing I'm not going to talk anymore. He kisses my jaw and glides his tongue down my throat, kissing me inch-by-inch as he works his way lower. He shimmies between my legs, pulling up my shirt to kiss my boobs, and he makes me laugh by blowing against my cleavage.

"You can stop me if you'd prefer to talk, Hayley." His mumbling voice vibrates against my skin. "But you need to know that nothing, and I mean fucking nothing, takes precedence over taking care of you right now. Not when you look as if you're going to break at any second. We have everything under control. Sawyer and Knox are strategizing and getting shit together. We're good. You're going to be better as long as you let me have my way. I'll tie you up and silence you otherwise until you can't think about anything outside of me." Monroe watches me for a reaction. "Is that okay?"

I shift my body, spreading my legs wider. It's as if he knows exactly what I want and need. I hate stressing and worrying. I hate feeling as if the world will explode. I hate even more thinking that I had to deal with this alone. I'm so used to it that it's like his playful, sexy demands banish the whirlwind emotions from me, leaving behind only desire and the need to do as he says.

"Yes. It's more than okay. Do what you think is best

for me. I just...I don't want to think anymore. Fuck me until I can't." I know he always wants me to speak up because he'll never assume with me. It's gotten easier and easier to do so. And his constant affirmation and reminding me helps. He likes when I tell him everything on my mind. He's insistent that he doesn't have to guess. I know it's because he worries. One day, I hope he doesn't have to. I hope none of us have to worry about anything except each other. "I know you wanted to earn that right, and you have. I'm yours. I need you to take care of me."

He graces me with a sexy smile, his eyes trailing down my arms to my hands, linking our fingers together. "You really want to be my good girl, little bird? I know your dhampir side has a naughty streak I know I'll want to tame. Seeing you embrace your savage side drives me wild."

"Maybe I need that." I comb my fingers through his hair. "I don't know how to control myself on my own."

Stretching my arms up, he kneels between my legs and leans in, pressing his mouth to my ear. "Fuck, you're so sexy. So hot. I feel like the luckiest man because you trust me enough to allow me this power over you. If there's something I do that you don't like, just say so. I don't need a special word or anything. I don't want things to get complicated. If you like something, tell me you want more of that. If you don't like something, all you have to say is stop or not that. Use your voice. It's important to me. I want you to speak up. Always. You have to speak freely with me." Monroe loosens his grip on my wrists, guiding my hands to rest on his shoulders as he reaches around to my back until he can unclasp my bra.

"I want you to hold still," he says, exposing my boobs and nudging me to lie back. "If you move, I'll stop. No squirming. No scratching or biting until I say so. You're going to be my good little dhampir as I kiss your whole body before I taste your blood and leave my mark."

My heart races, my body reacting to his words. Heat burns over me, thinking about his mouth all over me. The thought alone makes it impossible not to shift. "I want to bite you so badly. Maybe it'll help me." My voice remains soft as I say the words, my wants hard to voice out loud. I'm not used to telling someone what I want from them.

His eyes flash silver, and he tightens his jaw. "No. If I give you your way now, I'll keep doing so. Trust me to satiate you how you need. You can't bite me until I make you cum first. It will be your reward. You'll get everything you want but on my terms. Do you understand?" His need to dominate my pleasure sets me off in a good way. I fill with excitement, knowing that he will stay true to his word. I wasn't lying about him earning this from me. Look at everything he's done already for me. If he wants me to be his good little bird and let him have his way, I will. I want it more than I realize. It's freeing and comforting knowing that he'll handle his power over me with care.

"Yes. I understand." I smile with my words, leaning back just watching him watch me. "You need to tell me what to do then. How do you want me?"

Monroe purrs deep in his throat, the raspy, sexy noise reverberating through my very being. He glides his fingers over my torso at a torturous pace until he touches my boobs and plays with my nipples, rolling them between his fingers, making them hard from the coolness of his touch and the sensation.

"I want you just like this. You're going to stay utterly still as I lick you from your throat all the way down to your pussy. If you squirm too much, I will restrain you." Monroe leans forward and glides his tongue over my neck, the sensation soft and cool, sending a wave of tingles through me.

"This is going to be torturous, but I'll try my best," I say, my voice moaning as he continues his way down.

"You better, my naughty dhampir." He looks up at me with a smile, his eyes heavy-lidded with his lust. "You're going to have to be especially obedient these next few days with everything going on. This will help you. I know how you like getting your way with me, and I'll allow it, but not now. You're mine. Your pleasure. Your excitement. Everything in this moment is mine to give you."

I release a ragged breath, my whole body singing in response to his words. I've never had someone treat me like Monroe does, and I love everything about it. I love that he controls me with pleasure instead of pain. He wants me to voice what's on my mind instead of being silent. It makes me want to obey him and not rebel. I want to be his good girl. I want to be his perfect little bird. It's exhilarating.

"After I make you cum, I want you to just let go. Give in to your instincts. Keep your control and obey until I say so. I just need to ensure that you're taken care of first." Monroe eases lower, repositioning my legs until he bends my knees. He lifts my hips with one hand and tugs down my pants with his other, watching me with enough intensity I can feel his look burning across my skin in a good way. He tilts his head and drinks in the sight of me in just my thong. The anticipation prods at me in a way that awakens the beast inside me. And she wants out. My stomach burns, the hunger turning into blood lust, but I tense and try to control myself the best I can.

"Hayley, focus on me. On what I'm doing. You're on the verge of losing control already, and we can't have that, can we?" Monroe asks, slowly touching between my legs with his fingers, rubbing circles to get me warmed up though I'm about to overheat with my lust. I'm about to explode already. My body wants him so badly in ways I never really considered.

A whimper of agreement escapes my lips, the sound pathetic, but it only makes Monroe smile wider. He loves that he does this to me.

"If you lose control, it'll be okay, little bird. It's nothing a little punishment can't fix." And by punishment, he doesn't mean anything like I've experienced before. His punishment will leave me craving for more.

"I want that. I need that," I whisper through another moan.

He eases his hand away, stopping. "You don't. You want to be my good dhampir. I'm not continuing until you lie back. I want to do this without the restraints. You will be your own restraint...unless you don't want more."

I hadn't realized I sat up. I catch my eyes flashing silver with my nature in the broken pieces of the mirror in the frame on the wall. "Please, I do." I fall to my back again and cling onto the blankets around me.

Monroe tests me, tracing his finger along my thigh, ensuring I'll remain in my spot. It takes everything in me to do so. I never imagined not jumping on him would be so hard. His self-control amazes me. He doesn't rush or anything, slowly starting again.

"That's better. Just savor my touch." He increases the

pressure of his fingers and lowers himself, spreading my body open until he rests my legs on his shoulders and glides his tongue across the seam of my lips and licks my clit. He sucks it into his mouth, rolling his tongue in a way that has me gripping the blankets harder. Fuck. It's unbelievably hard not to move as he instructed, so I turn my head and bite a pillow.

"No, Hayley. I want to hear your voice." Monroe steals the pillow away and tosses it across the room. "I want to see you fight to stay in control."

My whole body hums and aches from the pleasure he creates. I scratch at the blankets and lose myself to the ecstasy of the moment until an orgasm builds, and my body pulses and shudders through the divine experience. He sinks his fangs into my thigh, biting me at the same time as I lose control. I can't stop myself. It's as if my orgasm triggers me, my deep-seated nature taking his commands seriously to let go when I came.

I scream out and grab him, using my newfound strength to pull him up to me. He chuckles and growls, the sound melodious and so seductive.

He doesn't resist me and leans his head to the side, exposing his throat to me. "Go on. Take your reward, Hayley. Devour me."

I give him what he wants and bite him, sinking my

teeth into his flesh hard enough to draw his blood. He doesn't let me roll on top of him and grabs my hands in one of his. Using his other, he keeps going, using his fingers to touch me again at the same time he slides his hard cock between my legs. The pressure makes me gasp and release him only for my mouth to bite him again. He thrusts hard and deep, and I scratch my nails into his back, letting him adjust my legs to stretch them over my head. We stare at each other with a foot of space between us, my body contorted and restrained with my feet planted on the wall above the bed. His eyes flicker with silver, and he leans down and bites me on the boob this time, letting the blood pool and drip down my nipple before he slows his thrust to lick it off, not allowing himself to fuck me as hard and fast as he wants. He's going to stop and start and torture me in the best way, ensuring that my pleasure is everything that I need it to be while taking his share and controlling my body.

"You feel so good. You taste so fucking delectable. I'm never going to let you go. Never." He doesn't mean letting me go from the passion in this moment but from our eternity together. An eternity I never even considered possible. It's so strange to think about, but it also makes me feel even more powerful. I don't feel like a weak eternal donor like Lawrence has claimed me to be. Right now, I feel as if I am the source of Monroe's power, and we can survive on each other forever.

"I love you," I say, the words coming out softly, shaky with my voice. I've been afraid to admit as much, but it's true. I know we've claimed each other. I just never really considered love being something for me. I've never considered it obtainable because with Alexander it was impossible.

Monroe hums his satisfaction and opens my legs to nestle between them, being able to cup my face. "I love you too. I had no idea how much I could, but it's as if you're all I ever think about. All I ever want and need. You've made my purpose with the Bella Crew even more crucial than ever. I don't want to only fight for donors. I want to fight for you, Hayley."

I smile at his words, and he kisses me, rocking harder and faster until the only thing that fills the air is our passion and moans.

He remains gentle, but I know he has a wild side to him, and I can't wait to unleash it. Flipping him over, I get on top of him and pin him down the best I can, getting in one bite before he growls and rolls me off.

"I don't think so, little bird. You're mine." He growls and drags me to the end of the bed by my ankles, not letting me attempt to get on him again.

He stands up and lifts my legs, curling me in on myself and pinning me in place with his strength. He flashes his fangs and bites my ankle, letting his innate beastly side take control of him.

It's so incredibly sexy. His carnal nature matches how I feel inside, and it strokes my monster in a way that leaves me compliant.

Monroe rubs my clit as he finishes, ensuring that I experience another wave of pleasure, and I tear the fabric of the blanket with my strength, holding on as my body takes me to the edge of an imaginary cliff and thrusts me off.

Climbing back onto the bed beside me, Monroe pulls me into his arms, kissing and hugging me, thanking me for trusting him. He shows me such affection that my heart fills with warmth, and I feel as if I can survive forever in this moment.

If only we didn't hear the sound of the voices in the hallway. But it's not a threat. It's just a slight interruption.

"Hayley? I know you're busy, but you're needed in the training room," Cooper says, his voice remaining even.

I squeeze my eyes shut, and panic tightens my chest. I know what this is about. I know he wants to take me to see Mr. Falo again.

"You heard him, little bird. You're needed for a performance." Monroe winks at me with his words, leaning in to whisper, "Don't worry. It'll be safe. I won't let anything happen to you."

I nod my head and gather my nerve.

Monroe gives me the strength to push forward.

His confidence gives me the strength to face another threat.

I should be used to it.

The whole world will always be against me.

I CREEP DOWN the hallway, keeping my distance as Hayley meanders next to Cooper. He touches her lower back, and I can't stop staring at his hand. I know the fucker is attracted to Hayley. I'd be offended if he wasn't. She's the most beautiful, sexy, talented woman in existence. But I don't know if I can trust him. He hasn't tried to reach out to any of us after the shitshow bitch attack, and I don't know what exactly he plans with this meeting.

The fucker from Falo Ills is nothing more than a wan-nabe Mr. Pala. I can take him myself. Actually, I'm fucking positive I'm going to. Sawyer and Knox remain with Lawrence, discussing the details of the trip to La Vega we plan to make tomorrow night. I had no idea how much I missed home, and I look forward to returning. There's no way in hell I'm coming back to this shithole. If we can get Hayley into La Vega, we can keep her there.

As for Aris, I wish I fucking knew. We have a deal with him, but he knows we might not hold up our end. He's not an idiot. He's infuriatingly strategic and suspects our back-up plan involving Lawrence. What he doesn't know is the only reason it's in place is to ensure we can get back to La Vega. It would be easy enough for him to intervene and steal Hayley before we step foot back in the city. If Lawrence confronts him, it'll be easier. I'd rather those two fuckers fight each other. Maybe they can take each other out, and the world would be a better place.

Fuck wishful thinking.

It doesn't work. You can't just hope and pray that things work out. You have to stab and punch and fight like one evil bastard to ensure things stay in your favor.

"Keep your head down. Don't look at anyone." Cooper slides his hand from Hayley's back and to her side, but she doesn't pull away from him in fear like I expect. I don't know if it's because she doesn't consider him a threat or what, but now I have to know more about her feelings. Why doesn't he set her off? Even Walcott, the damn puppy dog dickhole, wannabe asshole, sets her off. And that guy's tame in comparison. I've seen what Cooper can do. I saw how he pinned Killer Bitch Woman instead of trying to break them up. He wanted her to die as much as she did.

"Don't worry, Cooper. I know what is expected of me," Hayley mutters, and I tighten my jaw to stop from smiling. "I don't need you to keep reminding me to act like a fucking donor."

Good girl. My little bird needs to put him in his place. She doesn't take orders from him, because she knows how to handle herself under vampire scrutiny.

"I'm sorry. I can't help myself. I worry you might accidentally break one of the rules. We can't draw any attention to us. We have enough already. We're being watched." Cooper straightens his back, clenching his fingers into a fist. He senses me behind him but chooses to search around the lobby of the hotel, leading to the casino floor, instead of peeking.

He thinks that it's the Falo fucker watching, but I took care of his watch guard already. There's one headless, dickless, handless vampire shoved in the stall of one of the old closed-off bathrooms. The guy's security camera is now tapped into mine, and I have it aimed at the ground. He's not going to see shit except for the boots I stole. It was my lucky day that they actually fit me, and I didn't have to squeeze my big-ass feet in. I plan to keep them too.

"You better have a good fucking plan, Cooper." Hayley softens her voice, but she needs to lower it quite a fucking bit more if I can hear her from this distance. I'm going to have to work on her pitch and tone and get her to learn how to whisper properly. It might have to be my next thing. Get her to be quiet while I fuck her hard enough to make her walk funny for days. And that's saying a lot, considering how flexible she is. I can contort her in any position I please, and I look forward to it.

Damn it. Stupid fucking boner.

I push the thought of bending Hayley over out of my mind the best I can.

It's hard as hell seeing her sway her hips right in front of me, her body moving in ways I want to feel against my hands. She's intoxicating in scent and taste, in sound and touch. I just want her every second of every day.

I shake my head, shoving my list away. *Think of that severed dick you touched. Think of the severed dick you touched. Think of the severed dick you touched. Remind yourself it's in your pocket for Tatum. Remind yourself that you better fucking find some ice soon, or else you're going to have a rotting fucking dick in your pocket.*

The thoughts are enough to kill my boner, and I concentrate on the lump pressing against my leg. I was rather unimpressed at the size of the security guard. It's nowhere close to the giant cock Tate requested, which means I'm going to have to find a couple more before we get back. Maybe I'll even give her a special present. Maybe she'll enjoy a bouquet of the cocks belonging to the leadership and the owners of this twisted town.

"Just up ahead. It shouldn't take too long. He's only supposed to show proof that he got rid of the body." Cooper twists to look over his shoulder, and I duck behind one of the old slot machines.

I remain hidden and out of sight from the security cameras. They all hit certain spots but not everywhere. I don't think Lawrence cares enough about this place to really have strong security measures. It's not like anyone's going to want it. They're more likely to go after his donor zoo.

"I hate this. I don't want to be here. I don't know why you couldn't just do this without me." Hayley plays along with everything, voicing her fears out loud, but she doesn't sound as scared as she would've been even a week ago. She knows I'm here. She trusts me to keep her safe, and I won't let her down. Never again. I would rather get my heart kicked out than put her in a position like she was before. This one is bad enough.

"Because he wants to make sure that you obey me. If he thinks you don't, things will get messy. I don't want him to take extreme measures. The vampires around here are vicious, and he could send anyone after us." Cooper stops and turns toward Hayley, reaching out to touch her shoulder. He pushes her hair to her back, and I can tell he sees one of the bite marks I left on her. Her strapless dress doesn't leave much to the imagination, just how I like it.

"Whatever. Do what you have to do, so I can go back. Monroe is going to be waiting. You interrupted our time together." She shifts on her feet and glances around, and I pop into view so she can see that I'm here.

I duck before Cooper can see where she looks.

"I'm sorry about that." Cooper touches her arm, getting her to walk with him again.

This fucker isn't sorry. I'm sure he's a bit happy that he stopped me from going at it again with my girl. I'd do so all night and all day. All week and maybe all year. Fuck, not maybe. I would.

Hayley doesn't respond to him and just shakes her head, releasing a sigh of annoyance. She remains stiff in posture, keeping her gaze on the ground, but I know she's dying to look around.

I wait a couple of minutes, watching as Cooper guides Hayley toward the back of the casino, where there's an elevator leading to a parking structure. They could pretend to be going to the basement, but my visuals of the Falo bastard show him lurking like a pervert in the shadows in one of the stairwell alcoves. Because no one parks in that structure. I don't think there are even more than a handful of cars in this whole town. People live there. I'm sure that's where the vampires without wealth and power stay during the day.

"Take my hand. I need to keep you close and ensure nothing happens to you." Cooper clasps Hayley's fingers. Unsheathing a knife, he arms himself. And then he gets Hayley one as well. Good man. I hate fuckers who think they're tough enough that they can protect anyone. People have to be able to protect themselves. Especially Hayley.

I creep behind the two of them, following them at a distance until they reach the level where the Falo fuckhead waits.

And he's not alone. A shadowy figure stands beside him, and I realize it's a woman. A vampire. She hangs back with her arms over her chest, but I can't see her face. She keeps just out of sight of the visual on my com device.

Hayley stops short, squeezing Cooper's hand, getting him to halt in his place. I watch her posture change. She turns rigid, and I swear I can hear her heart beating louder.

Faster. Something is setting her off.

"It's okay, dhampir. No one is going to hurt you." Mr. Falo's voice rumbles through the air, echoing through the stairwell. "I'm only holding up my end of the bargain and proving that my word is good to Mr. Saint."

"Cooper? Oh, God. Cooper. I had no idea that Lawrence let you out of the blood swap contract." The soft feminine voice snags everyone's attention, and I realize that the female vampire is Cooper's blood sister. I knew he had one, and it was part of the deal that we would help her get out of here too, but I missed this part of the negotiation from the videos. I think I was too concentrated on Hayley that I didn't catch this stipulation.

Fuck. Cooper is going to be a problem. I know it.

"Lilac, shit." Cooper drags Hayley with him as he closes the space to the woman and throws his arms around her. "I'm so fucking happy to see you. I've missed you."

"Same, brother. When Kingman came to me, I almost couldn't believe it. You've been caring for a dhampir. And now you get to help ensure she gets back to where she belongs. Grandma would be so proud." Lilac eases away and turns to Hayley. The way she refers to the fucker Falo digs under my skin. No one enslaved to another would speak almost lovingly and so informally about the one who controls them.

I tense as she cups Hayley's face. I hate it. She's about to lose her damn hands for touching my girl. I don't care if she knows about dhampirs or if she is Cooper's blood sister. I don't trust her. Fuck I don't even trust Cooper right now.

"Where I belong? He's trying to send me back to my master in La Vega who sold me around the Strip." Hayley's voice snaps through the air as she speaks up.

Cooper pulls her away from his sister and plants his palm over her mouth, silencing her. "Don't speak again. This isn't the place you speak freely. Do you understand? Your concerns aren't warranted either. Anything is better than this bullshit."

I ball my hands into fists, my rage consuming me. It takes everything in me not to charge forward and stab Cooper in the gut. I don't like the way he handles Hayley. I understand that he treats her as it's expected in front of the other vampires, but I'm not cool with it. I'm not cool with any of this. It has to end here.

"You are a slave in La Vega?" Lilac turns to fuckhead Falo. "You didn't mention this. I thought you said she wanted to go back."

Oh hell. I was right. Cooper's sister isn't enslaved or being forced to stay with Falo. I thought it was weird when Cooper said she was being held against her will and treated like trash. But that's not the case. I wonder how long it's been since he has seen his sister. She talks to Falo as if he's of equal level.

"I don't consider it enslavement, honey. Don't you think being a performer in a safer environment is better? We'll be getting a hotel of our own and able to finally leave this shithole." Fucker Falo puts his arm around Lilac's shoulders. "You have to trust me."

Cooper straightens his back, the same realization that hit me now hitting him. "Lilac? Are you with him?" His voice comes out softly, hesitantly, as if he's afraid to hear the confirmation.

Lilac purses her lips. "We have a blood union, Cooper. I thought you knew."

Cooper flashes his fangs, growling deep in his throat. "You lied to me. How is this freeing my sister if she's willingly with you? You said—"

Fucker Falo rushes Cooper, pushing him into the concrete wall. Hayley screeches and scrambles out of his reach, and I can't stand hiding from them any longer.

I fly forward and grab the back of fucker Falo's suit jacket, yanking him away. He snarls, surprised by my attack, and I slice my blade across his throat, sending blood spilling down his white shirt.

"You traitor bastard! Did your dumbass think you could get away with making a deal with Aris without us finding out?" I hold Falo in place, aiming my knife at Lilac, keeping her back. "This kind of bullshit isn't tolerated. I'm going to need one damn good reason why I shouldn't decapitate you right here."

Falo opens and closes his mouth, the gurgling noise sending more blood spilling. I should've gone for the gut, but he was pissing me off.

"Wait, please. Don't hurt him. He's only doing what is best for our coven. You have to understand." Lilac holds her hands up in surrender, risking her safety by stepping forward.

"Cooper, you need to help us. You're part of this. Come on, don't you want to have a better life? Falo told me about your deal, but ours is better, don't you think? I know it seems bad to return Hayley to her master, but we have to make decisions that are best for us. Grandma would understand. Help me with this asshole."

Because of her words, I stab Falo in the side next, making him holler. His throat already heals some, letting him get enough air to make noise.

"Lilac...no. I was doing this for you. I was...fuck. I can't believe this bullshit. You've been safe and unharmed this whole time when I imagined the worst fate possible. Why didn't you come for me? Why didn't you try to negotiate a deal to bring me to Falo Ill instead of leaving me to the herd?" Cooper's voice shakes with his words. He's been played, and he realizes it now. But he's not angry. He's hurt.

"I was working on it." Lilac keeps her hands up in surrender, darting her eyes to me and back to her brother.

"It's been two years. I've lost two years and have experienced unimaginable fucking things." Cooper's chest rises and falls, and he growls in frustration.

"I'm so sorry for that. Do you remember what grandma used to say? We do things we have to do to survive." Lilac puckers out her bottom lip. "Please, Cooper. You must understand. We are vampires now. We don't have that same bond anymore. Blood bonds are weak for a reason. They just keep you down."

"You bitch! You're a fucking bitch! He has only thought of you, and you didn't deserve it." Hayley surprises the hell out of me and launches at Lilac. She shoves her back into the concrete wall, putting her in place with her strength.

Cooper just stands there and watches in awe, and so do I, because damn. I'm a bit jealous she attacks a vampire on his behalf. I don't even think she realizes it. She's so caught up in her new hunger that it consumes her.

"Little bird, don't kill her. We're going to need them both alive. Their treachery has given us an opportunity. We can use this to our advantage if they agree. Because Aris offered them a hotel. We can take it. We can use his betrayal. It'll be fun. If you need to bite someone, go ahead and bite Cooper. He deserves a little teeth." He'll also enjoy it and won't fight back. I can see how much he thinks about it now, his expression morphing from anger to lust like the horny bastard he is. I know that look because I'm sure it's written all over my face now.

Hayley doesn't let go of Lilac. "How can we trust her? How can we trust them?"

A wicked grin crosses my face, my deep psychotic nature threatening to rise. "Because they won't have a choice. I'm going to start by cutting off one of Falo's fingers. And if he tries anything, I'll cut off his dick next. I'm sure that will be saddening for the two of them. And as for Cooper's sister, she can take his spot in the herd. I will put her there myself."

Cooper flashes his fangs, but he doesn't yell at me or argue. "No, I'll fucking put her there myself. She needs to know what she's done. It's not like she's my sister anymore."

I slowly nod my head in approval. "Don't worry, Cooper. You're part of the Bella Crew now. You'll always have allies and family who are worthy of you." I know it's hard for me to trust him, but this proves a lot. Some vampires side with whoever they feel is strongest, and I know it's not the case for Cooper. He believes in our cause because it's his cause too.

"You have my loyalty. I hope you know that I was never going to put Hayley into danger. I was saving her by going along with this." Cooper grabs his sister from Hayley and proves his point and allegiance by stabbing her in the back and making her scream. It helps that he hasn't seen her in a couple of years. She's probably not even close to the same person he knew as a donor. This life changes you.

I turn to Hayley. "You want to do the honors and take one of his fingers?"

Hayley hesitates as the thought crosses her mind. She slowly shuffles closer and stands in front of Falo. He growls and gnashes his teeth, trying to bite at her, but there's no way he could get within her reach. Darting out her hand, she snatches his wrist and yanks his arm away from his body. I expect her to reach for a knife, but she surprises the hell out of me once more and brings the fucker's finger to her mouth.

I stare in amazement as she chomps down as hard as she can, using her teeth until she snaps his index finger clean off. She spits it out, and drops of blood trickle down her chin. Holy shit. That's my fucking woman. Fucking glorious.

Falo hollers in pain, his voice echoing through the concrete stairwell. Hayley's eyes flash silver, and she punches him in the bloody throat, silencing him for a second.

"You're a dead man if you betray us. I'm part of the Bella Crew, and everyone will know soon enough. If you try anything, your fate will be worse than losing your fucking cock. I'll devour you inch by inch and spit you out to the masses. You're not in control anymore. I am." Hayley pinches his chin and lifts up his lip. I can see what's on her mind clearly written on her face. She wants to do more than remove his finger.

And after everything she's been through, I'm going to give her what she wants.

"Do you want to take his fangs, little bird? I'm down with that." I smile at her, gripping Falo tighter.

"You psycho!" Lilac shouts.

I jerk my attention to Cooper. "Go take her now and meet us back in the room. Make sure she's secure."

Cooper disappears without hesitation, obeying me as if I'm the one in charge. And maybe I am in this moment. I've gone a little bit rogue, considering Sawyer and Knox aren't here. But I know they would be on my side. They would want me to do this, because this is an opportunity we can't lose. We have surprise on our hands. Both Lawrence and Aris think we're on their sides but also trying to cross them, and now we're on our own and can take care of them all.

I'll see to it.

"I have some pliers in my pocket, little bird. Do as you wish. I'll hold him tight. Don't worry." I grin at Hayley as her hand slides into my pocket, and she rubs her fingers along the hard curve of my cock, fully ready to go at it again with her.

She smiles and positions the pliers to Falo's right fang. "You're never going to fucking bite anyone again."

I had no idea I could love her even more.

I savor the sound of Falo's screams.

"You should've seen the little minx. It was so fucking hot, watching her get her revenge and justice for being treated like a fucking piece of property. The whole world is going to know that she's not. She's part of the Bella Crew." I shake Hayley by her shoulders, leaning in and kissing her neck. "I just want to fuck the hell out of her and reward her for being such a little badass."

She laughs as I give her a little hump, showing her exactly what she does to me. I know she still might be trying to grasp everything that's happening and process the whirlwind of emotions coursing through her, but I want her to always know that it's okay to be as bad as our enemies. She'll never be a villain or a monster. She'll just be my badass woman.

Knox cocks his head, his face expressionless, but I can tell he's not pleased. He worries far more than I do. So does Sawyer. They need to learn that our girl can handle a lot more, even if they don't think she should. I don't think she should, but on the other hand, I'd prefer to know that she can. I'll support her in all her savagery. She'll never feel as if she's done something wrong or crazy. It's hard to beat me anyways. The world better watch out.

I glower and bare my fangs at Knox as he closes the space, ignoring me as he searches Hayley's eyes.

"Are you okay? You've been through so much in just a few hours. Do you need help? You know we're here for you." He's referring to mind manipulation. That's Sawyer's specialty, but I don't like it. I think it's more important for her to be able to learn how to handle everything on her own instead of having us just wipe it away.

I would never say as much, though. If it's what Hayley wants, then she'll get it. What she wants is the most important thing, regardless of how I feel.

I just hate the idea of being able to prod around inside of someone's head and mess with their mental state. It gets a lot of donors in trouble and is one of their biggest weak-nesses. It's how Lawrence keeps everyone compliant. The same goes for other covens running the hotels. It's a lot of work constantly manipulating donors' minds, as things can break them out of the manipulation, but they do it any-ways. I bet some hotels line them up daily and have their ways. Fuckers. It pisses me off thinking about it.

Hayley audibly swallows, and I wish I could see her face. I know she worries about how we perceive her. "I'm surprisingly fine. I don't know. It felt..." Her skin warms under my touch, her blush clearly showing her embarrass-ment over her thoughts. She doesn't have to say it out loud for us to know that she liked the feeling of being in control. She liked putting a fucking bastard in his place.

I groan and kiss her throat again. "It was fucking amaz-ing, wasn't it? He cried like a weak little bastard."

Hayley laughs in exasperation, her muscles finally loos-ening. "I never thought I would enjoy something so...gross. A bit psycho. But damn. He deserved it. I bet he's done worse."

"Fuck yeah, he has. I can already tell just by the way he has shit set up. He would be doing no favors to La Vega, and we have enough twisted assholes against humanity." Sawyer finally speaks up, trying to show his support in a way that makes Hayley not feel as if he judges her. Because he doesn't. It's just hard knowing exactly how to handle certain things with her. A simple sentence could throw her off completely and shut her down. It's going to take a long time to help her work past the years of abuse. It's why we're so cautious. But on the other hand, that's why I feel as I do about mind manipulation.

"Well, you know if you need us for anything, we are here for you. If you just want to talk it through or if you want us to help you, you know, forget, we can do that too." Knox glides his knuckles over her cheek and leans in to kiss her. I finally let her go, because she wraps her arms around his neck and kisses him deeper, sensually, so fucking seductively that if I remain within reach of her, I'll want to join in. I don't even care if I have to take turns with Knox. She can give both of us attention. All three of us. She's already proved as much, and she enjoys it. But we need to stay focused. We need to ensure at least one of us has attention on what's happening outside of this damn room. Cooper still hasn't come yet, and if he doesn't in the next couple minutes, I know I'm going to be the one who has to go find his ass. Sawyer and Knox are still up in the air about him. They're a bit angry that he was in that position in the first place. But they don't know what it's like to constantly have to face other vampires that are stronger than them. They can hold their own around mostly anyone. But Cooper?

He's untrained. He has a weak bloodline, and because he's kept practically starved all the time, he doesn't have the same power.

A knock sounds on the door, sending relief through me. I didn't want to have to hunt him down. I'm sure I'd have to mutilate a dozen guys in the process. I've already showered and have a clean shirt on. I'm running low on what to wear, and I doubt Knox and Sawyer would appreciate me just roaming around naked all the time. But I might anyway, because now that I think about it, I'd love to see Hayley's reaction. I saw the way she devoured Sawyer in that dumbass, tiny speedo costume. He's lucky that the thing wasn't a thong. If it was? His ass would've been whipped by me for fun. He can't have his ass hanging out and expect me not to fuck with him. It takes a lot out of me not to squeeze Hayley's cute ass all the time when she's wearing those tiny pieces of fabric that I just want to tear off.

"It's Coop," Cooper says, his voice low as he whispers against the wood. It's obvious that the dude is scared out of his fucking mind, thinking about everything he's getting into. He's going to have to really knock that shit off, because while fear keeps you on your toes, you have to be brave. Confidence can really help him in a fight. He can't be going into this thinking we're going to lose. That kind of negativity is bullshit. He just has to be smart.

I beat the others to the door and crack it open, not letting him in right away. "Were you followed? I can verify on the security feeds. So, you better fucking know."

Cooper shakes his head. "I wasn't. Lawrence is making arrangements in his office. I mind manipulated all of his donor security, and the one vampire isn't a concern at the moment. He's currently out of the building and burning his ass off as he tries to find one of the missing headliners."

He's referring to Killer Bitch. No one will ever find the body. I saw Falo incinerate her myself on one of the feeds. He left her in the sun to burn all day, and with her dead, she wouldn't heal. Her ashes would scatter on the wind. Comes in handy.

I pull out my com device anyway, showing him that I'm not going to take his word for it especially after the bullshit. I thumb through the feeds and study them, verifying that he knows his shit. "Good. Because things need to remain a secret for the next day. We're going to be leaving for La Vega tonight. If anyone suspects anything, you better be prepared to fight like hell if you're going to escape with us."

"It's going to be fine. Everything is in place, and we've confirmed with Aris that he knew we were playing Lawrence. He just doesn't know we're playing him too. You were a fucking smart asshole with your plan, Monroe." Sawyer nods his head at me, his approval not necessary but appreciated.

"How are you going to reward me? Suck my dick?" I laugh at his frown. I love fucking with the bastard.

Hayley gasps and laughs, her musical voice chiming through the air. "Hey, now. That cock is mine."

Damn it. My balls throb at her words.

I rush her, stealing her away from Knox. Flipping her onto my shoulder, I relocate her into the bathroom, kick the door closed, lock it, and then sit her ass on the sink. "You gotta watch that naughty mouth of yours, little bird. I can't control my urge to fuck you over and over again."

The door crashes open, and Sawyer hauls me back by my shirt, dragging me into the room. I swing and punch him in the balls, dropping him a peg, but he recovers and punches me right back.

I tense and grind my teeth, but a little ball punching doesn't drop me. It's one of the things I'm proud of. I can handle a lot of fucking shit. Walcott and I have always been a bit crazy in our fighting techniques. We've learned how to ignore the intense pain with these weak-ass nuts. They've been cracked open a dozen times over the years. It's a good thing vampires can't have children, because I'm pretty sure baby batter bags are useless now.

"Oh, come on, Sawyer. You're really going to cock-block?" Hayley laughs from the doorway of the bathroom. And damn. I fucking love what she says. She really knows how to tease us in unimaginable ways.

Sawyer tightens his jaw, and if Knox didn't get between me and Hayley, I'm nearly certain she would've motioned for me to return to her. We're all wrapped around her little finger.

None of us can even deny it.

"I—" Sawyer's com device chimes, and he snaps his mouth shut. Yanking it from his pocket, he stares at the screen.

I materialize behind him and stare at the bullshit message. "Fucking again? This guy is screwing with us." I'm nearly certain he's going to try to stop us from even reaching La Vega while taking those other bastards with him instead.

"What is it?" Hayley asks, the smile vanishing from her face.

I don't want to tell her. None of us really do. But we have to keep her in on things. She deserves it.

"Lawrence has demanded one last meeting with everyone, except you and Cooper. He wants to starve you, and he knows that we'll give in and give you blood." Sawyer speaks up, telling her first so none of us has to. "He claims it's because dhampirs are stronger when they're hungry, but I'm afraid he's going to try to manipulate your mind to ensure that you can't do anything."

A bang sounds on the door. "Mr. Noble. I'm here to escort you."

I twist my lips and stare at Sawyer. "This fucker. I don't like this."

"Just be ready to fight. We can take him together." Sawyer straightens his back and stands tall. He turns to Hayley. "We'll be back as soon as we can. I'm going to give you one of the com devices, so you can watch our every move. If anything happens—"

"I'll fucking destroy this whole casino." Hayley flares her nostrils, her eyes flashing silver.

It wasn't what Sawyer was going to tell her, but it works for me. I like her plan better.

"We can still do that, little bird. Just pack your things and be ready, okay?" I kiss her once more.

"They're going to regret ever messing with us." Hayley nods her head, reassuring herself. That's the confidence I'm talking about.

Because with her words, I believe her.

We will burn this place to the ground.

PREPARATIONS

I'M GROWING ANTSY. I've been stuck in my room for what feels like days. Without a window, I can't even tell how much time passes. At least I'm not in a cell. But I wish Sawyer, Monroe, and Knox would hurry up. They're with Lawrence now. I know the meeting with Alexander draws near, and they're strategizing exactly how to handle things. Alexander wants me back, and Lawrence plans on working something out with him, giving him temporary access to La Vega in exchange for peace. But as for everything else? I have no fucking idea. It's going to be a shitshow.

A knock sounds on the door, but I don't even move to answer it. I don't call out either. I can't even get out, so there's no point in doing anything other than waiting for whoever is on the other side to barge in.

"Hayley?" Cooper's muffled voice sounds through the door. "Are you awake? May I come in?"

I close my eyes and think whether or not I should. What happened with his sister still lingers in my mind.

"I was told to bring you something to eat. We have to be prepared for the trip to La Vega." Cooper knocks again, this time cracking the door open. I force myself to open my eyes and catch him peeking at me through the small opening. I roll to my side and rest on my elbow, but I don't bother moving.

"I don't really need to be prepared. I doubt I'll even get to leave the car. They'll probably just show me on a com device or some shit to prove I'm alive." I flop back on the pillow and stare at the ceiling. "Plus, I'm too nervous to eat anything. I have a terrible feeling."

"Those are your dhampir instincts. Never ignore them. My grandma used to say that. She wanted us to always remember it in case we decided to have children. Of course, she probably never expected this." Cooper waves at himself, referring to the fact that he is no longer a donor.

I sit up on the bed and rest my elbows on my knees. "Tell me more about her. What was she like?"

Cooper offers me a soft smile. "That's a hard subject for me, my showgirl. It still feels as if I just lost her, even though it's been years. I guess that's what happens when you stop aging."

I pat the bed beside me. "Then tell me more about yourself. I need a distraction. How are you feeling? You have to be upset over your sister."

He rubs his hands over his cheeks. "Not as upset as I am over putting you in that position, Hayley. You're not the only one in need of a distraction. I feel as if I'm always talking about myself, and I'd love to know more about you. I know you were enslaved to Alexander but tell me more about your life in La Vega. What's it like being a donor in the city? Did you have to donate blood like the donor's here? Do they have herds?"

His questions ignite memories inside me, and I can't stop the frown crossing my face. It's hard for me to imagine him ever being a donor.

I crinkle my nose and shake my head. "The human population wouldn't stand for that, but I don't know much outside of the Aris. I had never left until I met the Bella

Crew."

"It must be strange for you." He doesn't pry with more questions. He understands from experience that these conversations aren't exactly easy. "All of this."

I shrug without a word, unsure if my voice will come out shaky. I pat the spot on the bed next to me again. "You brought food?" I manage to say, changing the subject.

"Shit, yeah. Sorry. I bet you're famished." Cooper plops down beside me and reaches into the bag hanging on his arm and pulls out an orange. It's been a while since I've had one, and I zone in on it as if he'll peel and feed it to me if I look at it long enough.

And sure enough, he digs his nails into it and pulls at the rind until he can get a piece for me. He holds it out in his palm, and I bow forward and snatch it with my teeth, surprising the hell out of him. I could've taken it with my fingers, but some vampires love handfeeding donors, and I figured it wouldn't hurt to show him my appreciation. This kind of distraction is far better, and I'm not one to be ungrateful for food.

"Shit. I thought you were going to bite me." He grins with his words, peeling another piece and holding it out. "I'm not supposed to give you blood. So, control yourself, my showgirl." The tease of his words makes me want to test him even more.

I grab his wrist and bring it to my mouth, playfully nipping him. It helps ease the weirdness between us over Falo. "I can't. I'm just so hungry. I'm going to devour—"

Cooper rips away from me, abandoning my side to rush toward the door. He rests his back to it, a strange look on his face. The playfulness between us disappears, and I gawk at him in silence. Fuck. I took things too far. I'm just so used to being able to tease Monroe, Knox, and Sawyer.

"I'm sorry," I say, scrunching my face. "I was only teasing you. I didn't mean to scare you. I don't think I have the stomach to drain you dry anyway."

Cooper's chest rises and falls as he pulls himself together. His eyes flick from the floor and to me. He gapes at me with such an intensity that I'm nearly certain he might set my body ablaze. I shift on the bed, wishing he would look away. I can't seem to get myself to do so, though I know I'm not trapped in his mind manipulation.

I cross and uncross my legs, fidgeting with the comforter by balling it in my fists. "I'm sorry," I repeat. I don't know what else to say, and I hate the sound of the silence in the air.

Cooper palms his forehead and scrubs his fingers into his blond hair, finally breaking eye contact. I fall back, bouncing on the bed, my body buzzing and out of whack. But at least I can breathe again. I don't know what it was about his gaze, but I felt completely enthralled.

Snatching the pillow, I cover my face with it. "Cooper, please say something. I can't tell what you're thinking." I mumble the words into the pillow, refusing to look at him again.

The bed shakes as he returns to it, and I feel the coolness of his hand touch my knee. He clears his throat, but he doesn't speak right away. He gathers his thoughts, and I let him. I'm afraid if I say anything right now, he might just leave. I really want to know what the fuck is going on and why he acted the way he did.

"Fuck, Hayley. I'm sorry. You probably think I'm out of my goddamn mind." Cooper shifts on the bed again, bouncing me. "It's just...you can't tease me like that. Okay? It's dangerous."

I frown at his words. "Why?"

I'm not dense. I know he's attracted to me but dangerous? Hardly. We've exchanged blood before. He's seen me naked. I thought we were okay with playing around.

Cooper groans and covers his hands with his face, rubbing them as if he's trying to scrub the thoughts from his mind. "Because you are claimed, and I don't want to jeopardize what you have. I don't want to jeopardize what the Bella Crew has offered me. I know they have a weird-ass ability to not tear each other apart when it comes to you, but I don't know. I find you...beautiful. Strong. There's something about you I feel a connection to beyond the fact that we were both put into this shitty situation. My feelings aren't good for either of us. I shouldn't even be admitting them."

I don't say anything for a minute, letting his words sink in. I guess I was used to the way Sawyer, Knox, and Monroe were with each other that I didn't think it was a big deal.

"Oh." What else can I say? I find him hot, and he's been so nice to me. I'm afraid of making him uncomfortable. "I'm sorry. I wasn't thinking...and now this is fucking awkward. I'm sorry."

He twists his lips. "Hey, no. Don't apologize. I just know my place. I'm not like them."

"You keep saying that. You keep saying you know your place as if you are beneath them. They don't think like that. Everyone in the Bella Crew has their strengths and weaknesses. They recognize them, and they know how to use them to work stronger together." I smile as I think about it. Monroe is the first one to admit that he doesn't have the same kind of power that Knox and Sawyer do. It never really affected us. I doubt it would affect Cooper.

What am I thinking? He's not talking about the power within the crew. I'm pretty sure he's talking solely about me. And now? I don't know what to do. I don't know what to think.

He groans with a chuckle, clearly realizing we talk about two different things. But I don't want to push him. I don't really know him, but that didn't stop me from being drawn to Knox, Monroe, and Sawyer. This is a bad idea. I can't think about it. I could be putting too much thought into something that is nothing.

"I'm sorry. I'm not good at this. Talking. I usually just do what I'm told." I sit up and scoot to the edge of the bed.

"Hayley, you've done nothing wrong. It's all me. I should be more careful anyways. It's just...you have this presence about you. I feel a connection. Relatability. It might be part of our natures too. I carried the dhampir gene before I transitioned." Cooper gets to his feet, scooping up the rest of the orange from the bed. He holds it out to me until I take it. "I don't know. Whatever it is...I just can't think about it right now. It's dangerous."

"Cooper..." I feel him shutting down, and I want so desperately to latch onto him and keep him open. His honesty digs into me.

He shakes his head at me. I've lost him. "Why don't you finish eating this, and I can wait in the hallway until the others return? It shouldn't be long. Maybe even minutes."

I open and close my mouth, wondering if I should beg him to stay, but he clearly wants to go. I'm so confused by everything. Am I overthinking things? Fuck. I don't know.

I bow my head in silent agreement, popping the orange pieces into my mouth, stopping myself from speaking. Cooper leaves the room and clicks the door closed, but I can still hear him in the hallway. His body thumps against the wood. Taking a few deep breaths, I close the space to the door and press my hand on it.

"Cooper," I murmur, hoping that he'll still talk to me. "I hope you know that I appreciate everything you've done for me."

He thuds his head to the door, sounding as if he drops to sit on the floor, resting his back to the wood. I imagine mimicking him and get down on the ground as well. "I wish I could do more for you. It's just hard. I don't have the power or the strength. I can't stop thinking about things that I shouldn't be thinking about involving you, either. It takes all my control not to act."

"You say that as if it's a bad thing. It's okay, you know. I sometimes think about it too." I hate that I keep apologizing. "You fascinate me. I can't help wanting to know more. You're right about the connection. You understand things others can't." Maybe this is a dangerous line. I know better than speaking freely, but I can't help myself.

"Your fascination might be a bit different, my showgirl. You want to know things while I want to experience them."

He thuds his head to the door again. "It'll get my dick cut off."

I frown and shake my head, though he can't see me. "None of them will touch your dick. I'll ensure it." Fuck me. Did I offer to protect his cock? "I'm sorry. I'm...I'm going to shut up now."

He chuckles. "It's funny. I never thought I could talk to someone like this. I've kept secrets for so long." Cooper redirects the subject, helping me not feel as awkward. "You make it so easy. My grandmother would've whacked me over the head for being such a moron. It's like a part of me doesn't ever want to function when I'm around you."

"Do you think that it's because of what I am? I've always had a lot of attention on me. Maybe it's my dhampir nature. Because I survive on vampire blood, I would need something to help me get it, considering how powerful vampires can be, right?" The longer I think about it, the more sense it makes.

"Hmm. Perhaps. I didn't really get to see that side of my grandmother. She never told us where she got blood from. She didn't need that much." He releases a heavy breath. "I can see how and why you would be able to attract us. You use that sexy body and sweet personality to lure some asshole in and then you can devour him like a maneater. A perfect seductress predator to those who wrong you." He chuckled with his words.

My mouth drops open, and I crinkle my nose. "And to think I thought I was simply irresistible."

"Oh, my showgirl. You are. It makes you especially dangerous for me. Because I don't even think I'll fight you if you decide you want to drain me dry. I might die a happy man." Cooper groans like he's thinking about it.

Blush heats my cheeks with his words. "I'll take that into consideration next time you attack me out of starvation." I giggle with my words, because if I think seriously about it, I'll frown. I can't help thinking about if that happened. What if I somehow continue to act like a monster like the persona I channel in the Fright Fights? It came so easily, but then it broke me so deeply. I couldn't imagine killing Cooper or even Sawyer, Monroe, and Knox for that matter by accident.

"Good. You should. That sounds like a far better way to go than any other way." Cooper's voice remains soft as if he thinks about me ending his life. It's twisted and dark, but I get it. I thought about it before. Especially in moments where all seems lost.

"You're ridiculous," I say, stretching my legs out in front of me. "That doesn't seem fun at all. I would think you would prefer me to fuck you as I murder your ass instead of draining you."

"Damn it, my showgirl. You can't put those images in my head." I can't see his face, but Cooper might be thinking about it in detail. I'm sure he's creative. He's known how to survive all this time, even managing to turn from donor to vampire.

"That's too bad. If you can't handle my teasing, then maybe you shouldn't suggest that you'd prefer to die by my hands. It's kind of a dick move. Not cool. I don't want to kill anybody that I like." I stare at my glittering fingernails, wondering if blood lingers beneath the dark polish.

"You're right. I should fantasize about you murdering everyone on my behalf. I know you're capable of it. You just need the right training. The right protection. Fuck, if you get worked up enough, you could probably take on an army of assholes. Rip their hearts out." Cooper chuckles at the thought, the seriousness of his voice finally lightening.

"All while wearing stilettos in a bikini." I can't stop the smile from crossing my face, hearing him laugh a bit harder.

"That visual is fucking sexy, isn't it, Coop? I can see why you're out here in the hallway. Is the little minx teasing you too much? She just loves going straight for the balls. I swear her number one weapon is the ability to summon eternal boners." Monroe's deep voice laughs huskily, the sound so musical. I could listen to him forever.

"Nah, it's not like that. She looked kind of bitey, and

you heard what Lawrence demanded." Cooper remains even-toned.

I frown because I might've thought it was like that. Am I disappointed? Maybe.

Monroe growls and something crashes against the door. "Let's get one thing straight. I'm not stupid. I know what Hayley does to people, and I'm offended if you lie and deny your attraction toward her. I don't like that shit. Be honest. I'm not going to cut your dick off. We've made an alliance. But don't think I won't stab you for not being upfront."

Shit. What he says is confusing. I feel as if I need to talk to him. Sawyer and Knox too. Because I never expected this sort of reaction. I mean, they cut people up and steal and stab and all sorts of crazy-ass shit on my behalf. I know they include Cooper in the Bella Crew because he knows things that we don't, but...

The door clicks open and nudges my back as if Monroe knows I'm leaning against it. I scramble to my feet and hug my arms across my body, meeting his silver flashing gaze.

"Hey, little bird. Are you trying to get Cooper to let his guard down so you can bite the hell out of him?" Monroe runs at me, his fangs peeking out. "Or do you enjoy his company?"

I blink a few times, not exactly sure how to respond or react.

My first instinct is to say what I think he wants to hear. That's how I always respond to things that could end badly. I wish it were easier to remember Monroe wants me to be truthful and to never pretend.

"Hayley, you don't have to be afraid to tell me anything. It's fucking fine if you like hanging out with this baby vampire. He's all right looking. Gives you blood sometimes. He even brought you a lame-ass orange, which was smart of him. He couldn't have survived watching you eat a damn banana. Not with how your hunger makes you deep throat the phallic fruit." He cracks up at his own comment, his laughter making me giggle and shake my head. Even Cooper can't help himself, because he chuckles from behind Monroe.

I lift and drop my shoulders, knowing he's still waiting for me to respond. "That's only when you tease me. That guy was handfeeding me how I like. And to answer your question..." I stroll closer and step into Monroe's open arms. Cooper stares at me, our eyes meeting from over Monroe's shoulder, but I try to pretend that he's not hanging onto my every word. Standing on my tiptoes, I brush my lips to Monroe's ear and say, "He's nice. Cute. I'm not sure what else you want me to say."

"Do you want me to tell you what I want you to say? Because you know that shit's not going to happen. I'm not putting words in your mouth. I'm just trying to let you know that you don't have to be worried. I know you're my girl. I also know that flirting is how you survived. I just don't know if there's anything behind it." His voice remains low, the whisper at a pitch that I don't think Cooper could hear.

"I don't know either. You're mine. I belong to you, Knox, and Sawyer. Right now, that's what matters to me, okay? Everything else is just in the air. I don't even want to think about it. I don't really want to talk about this either, if that's okay." Because it's true. If I think about it, I might start getting anxiety. Like I just said, Cooper is nice to me. He's attractive.

Monroe leans back and touches my cheek. "That is perfectly fine, little bird. I can't help my need to remind you that you can talk to me about anything. I'm not going anywhere. I'm not going to get pissed off if you like someone that isn't me...if it wasn't obvious."

I nod my head. "I'm sorry. I'm just...thanks for reassuring me. This is hard to wrap my mind around. I love you. I never want you to be pissed off at me."

He raises an eyebrow. "That will never happen...unless you go trying to save my ass and get hurt or some shit when you know I can take care of myself."

I smirk at Monroe. "What? So, I can't be your hero?"

"Aw shit. Sounds like someone is going to test Monroe's fragile masculinity if he keeps that attitude up. I mean, come on. I'd let Hayley save my ass any day. Would be so hot. I know she has it in her, especially after seeing her during the Fright Fights." Knox materializes in the hallway with Sawyer by his side. The two of them give me a long look as if they want to rush into the room and have another moment, just the four of us, but neither of them tries.

"As much as I want to talk about how badass our girl can be, we have to prep. The vehicles are ready and Lawrence is waiting outside. I don't want him to act like a fucking worse asshole than he already is, so let's not keep them waiting. We have to pick our battles carefully the next day or so. We're going to be on our home turf, but we have to consider everyone as our enemies at this point." Sawyer stands tall, his biceps pressing against the tight fabric of his T-shirt.

"Cooper, get your shit too. You're coming with us. Lawrence sees value in having someone he knows he can use to fight." Knox pats him on the back. "But don't get too excited. I don't think you're going to get to see much of La Vega. You might have to stay with him for the meeting. I'm not exactly sure. He's not telling us anything."

Without a word, Cooper disappears to head back to the room he now calls his own to grab a couple of things.

Sawyer and Knox enter our hotel room, and they shut the door. I realize they might've sent him away for a reason. They obviously want to talk to me.

"Hayley, we're going to be heading into La Vega, and you're coming with us. We need you to be prepared for anything. We're not on either of their sides, and the plan is to make sure they stay against each other. If they are enemies, then it's easier for us to sneak by. We're going to get in contact with the Strip crews, and we're going to keep you there. You're not coming back here. Do you understand?" Sawyer keeps his voice a whisper against my earlobe. "Lawrence isn't making it back here either. He's not going to survive. I promise you that."

I slowly nod my head in agreement. I want so badly to believe his promise, but if I do, I might be let down if it doesn't work out.

All I can hope for is to survive all of this myself.

I have a feeling if I get stuck between Alexander and Lawrence, I won't be going anywhere with the Bella Crew. The two of them will rip me apart.

HOMEBOUND

I SQUEEZE SAWYER'S leg, pinching him out of nervousness. He doesn't react to the pressure and only slides his hand under mine, so I can grip it instead. We look at each other in silence. This whole car ride has been ridiculously quiet. No one wants to talk. No one wants to strategize. I think everyone just wants to get home, despite not going into La Vega yet. We have to ensure Lawrence makes it to his meeting location outside the wall. I'm sure the entire leadership anticipates this moment. Unless Alexander is doing it in secret. I have no clue. All I know is that I don't want to go. I want to be done with these assholes and find myself back at the Bella. I never even got a chance to truly call it my home yet, but Sawyer's presence gives me hope.

If only Lawrence didn't make the others ride separately in another car. He said it's better to have two vehicles in case something happens. I think he just wants to make sure that we can't all team up and overpower him. It doesn't help that his so-called allies are with us. Well, two of them. Mr. Falo is with Monroe, Knox, and Cooper. I hope they make the whole car ride truly unbearable for him. Show off their fangs to remind him what he's missing and what happens to people like him. I hope they tell him everything they'll do if he even so much as looks at me wrong.

Damn. I wish I could hear it.

"When we get there, Hayley, you're going to stay in the vehicle. This is only a scare tactic to prove to Alex that he can't fool us with his betrayal. Understand?" Lawrence looks at me in the rearview mirror. "This is a warning to him about going behind my back. He only needs to see you long enough to know that you're alive and under my control."

I don't respond to him. I don't feel the need because

there's nothing I can really say. It is what it is, and I will be the obedient little dhampir he expects me to be until he turns his back. He thinks he's in charge, but he's not. Neither is Alexander. Lawrence thinks he has the advantage because Alexander doesn't know his alliance with Falo failed, and we can use it against him. No one trusts anyone at this point, and hopefully Monroe was right about them taking each other down.

I was nervous telling Lawrence about the situation, but if he knows about the betrayal, he can surprise Alexander and catch him off guard. The attention won't be on us. It's all so complicated, but this is all part of the Bella Crew's plan to get back into the city and remain there. Sawyer has done an amazing job playing the role as someone who needs help. He knows how to work the power-hungry over, and convinced Lawrence that we'll even bring him the performers from the Aris, but what we're actually going to do is plan an attack. We're not giving anyone anything.

Sawyer drops his arm over my shoulders and kisses my temple. "Look, we're almost there." He flicks his hand, motioning to the city lights in the distance. I don't think I've ever seen La Vega from this perspective as an outsider looking in at night. Last time, I only saw the city vanish in the daytime. And now, I realize just how beautiful it is. If only under the glittering lights wasn't such a terrible, monstrous city. I can't help but wonder what it once was like when donors ruled. If only we can turn back to those days, or at least be able to bring donors back up as equals instead of as blood sources.

"I wish I could see more of it. It's so strange to see it from a distance. I've only ever been able to look out my room window at the Bella's fountain." I stretch up a bit in my seat as if I could see more of it beyond the wall. But I can only see the tops of the towering skyscrapers of the run-down hotels.

"You will, my heir. You'll see more than La Vega. I plan on taking you to many places over your eternity." Lawrence offers me a creepy smile, turning slightly in his seat to look over his shoulder instead of at my reflection in the mirror.

I shiver at his words. There's no way in hell I want to spend even another day with him, let alone an eternity. And traveling? Where to? I didn't even know that the vampires around here got out much. It's safer to remain in their hotels, especially when they have power. I would be okay spending the rest of my existence in the Bella as long as I had my guys by my side.

"Where's that exactly? The nearest territory is still quite far away. They are also completely locked down and walled off. At least, that's what I remember." This comes from the silent man sitting in the front seat beside Lawrence. I wish the front had three seats, so I didn't have to be so close to the other strange vampire, who has been staring at my wrist for what feels like the entire car ride so far. I know he's thinking about how he got to drink from me, and I'm probably making him hungry by just existing. Thankfully, Sawyer was allowed to ride with us. All it takes is him glowering to get the guy to look out the window.

"I have my ways, Mr. Primm. You know there is far more to this world than incorporated territories. There is a whole land of wilderness and pockets of humans untouched by vampires. I'd like to explore with my heir and her...protectors. Taking La Vega will give me the means to conquer more of the world."

This man is truly evil. There seems to be no end to his desire and craving for power. It makes me hate him even more.

"That's pure folklore. There are no pockets of untouched human civilizations, Lawrence." The man beside me finally speaks up, leaning forward to get a view of the side of Lawrence's face.

I don't even have a chance to react before Lawrence swings his hand out and smacks the guy across the cheek hard enough to send his head jerking into me. Stars pepper my vision with the force of his head smashing into mine, and Sawyer snarls, lifts me up, and puts me on his lap and away from the man.

"Hayley, you're bleeding." Sawyer touches his hand to my head where it hurts the worst.

Oh fuck.

Slamming on the brakes, Lawrence skids the car to a stop. He flies out from behind the wheel and flings the back door open. Sawyer tightens his hold on me, not allowing Lawrence to drag me out without him. He catches himself on the door, keeping me locked under his arm as if I'm a little doll. Bright headlights flash behind us, and I squint my eyes as Monroe screeches to a stop, kicking up dirt with the tires on this old back-world road that hasn't seen much travel. "Are you fucking crazy?" Sawyer says, growling, aiming his blade at Lawrence.

The others join his side, and Knox and Monroe create a wall of muscle between me and the asshole.

"She's bleeding. I had to get her out of the car. Those bastards are already addicted to her blood, and the last thing I need is for a damn fight to break out. I didn't want to have to give her blood, but she needs to heal." Lawrence flashes his fangs and bites his arm. "Give my heir to me. It will be my blood and only my blood she consumes."

I grimace at his words. The last thing I want is to put my mouth anywhere near him. Just the thought twists my stomach. This is his fault to begin with. If he hadn't slapped the vampire, he would've never smashed his head into me.

"Lawrence, don't be so foolish to think that we lack restraint," Mr. Primm says, exiting the vehicle.

The other man follows suit, remaining silent but never taking his eyes away from me. I squirm under his scrutiny, wondering if Lawrence might be right about him. I cling onto Sawyer tighter, wanting nothing more than for him to back up and add more space between us.

"Yeah, Lawrence. Get back in the car. You know there are outcasts and rebels out here. You want to make it to our destination, don't you?" This comes from Falo as he exits the other vehicle with Cooper.

"The destination you've picked? Hardly. You probably have a plan in mind to try to take what doesn't belong to you." Lawrence growls deep in his throat. His eyes flash with hunger and then he looks at me.

My heart sinks into my stomach. What the fuck? He looks absolutely crazy right now. I don't know what set him off, but I'm not sure we're ever going to make it to our destination.

"You have five seconds to give me my heir," Lawrence says, taking a step closer.

"I think Hayley will be okay. She's not bleeding that much. She's already healing. Giving her your blood is unnecessary. I think we need to stick to the plan." Sawyer straightens his back, looming over everyone. "We're almost there. Why don't we just rearrange who sits in what car?"

Lawrence doesn't have a chance to respond because someone materializes from behind the car. Who the fuck is that? And then I notice the filth covering the vampire. He must be one of the outcast vampires they mentioned.

He heads for me, but then Lawrence intervenes and cuts the guy's head clean off him, putting him out of his starving misery.

"Everyone get back into the vehicles. We must go. If one is here, more will follow. It's a mere inconvenience, but they have nothing to lose and will try to disable the vehicles." Lawrence swivels on his feet. "Come now."

Sawyer reluctantly heads back to the vehicle, and we climb into the backseat. Lawrence gets behind the wheel and Monroe and Knox fill the other seats, forcing the other two guys to go with Cooper. I can't help looking at Cooper out the back window. He sits in the front seat, letting Falo drive.

We only get rolling for a minute before something smashes into the side of the vehicle, and I stare in shock at a vampire, flashing his fangs. Shadows dance and move around us, managing to keep up with the pace of the vehicle. I don't know how vampires move so fast, or maybe this car just goes too slow, considering that it is an ancient gas guzzler, as Sawyer called it.

"Fuck, I've never seen so many." Monroe shifts in the front seat and peers out the window. "It's like they knew we were coming."

His words strike something deep inside me. What if they did know we were coming? What if Alexander decided he was going to try something else to get me back. I wouldn't put it past him. He could offer any of these guys a chance at a better life if they get to me.

"This is purposeful. It's obviously a planned attack. Fucking Aris." Knox grabs my hand, holding it even though Sawyer has a firm grip on me. "These guys aren't outcasts. They're Strip dwellers. I've seen some of them before. I can—"

Lawrence jerks the wheel, swerving as a vampire darts in the road. The Strip dweller wants to face us head-on. He launches at the windshield, smashing it with his fist. I screech out in fear. The window shouldn't shatter so easily, but this vintage car can't withstand the same amount of force as the newer ones. It makes me wonder why Lawrence even bothers with it.

Dust engulfs the vehicle, and we bounce and hit the dirt. We're so close to La Vega, yet I'm not sure we're going to make it.

"Fuck. We have a flat tire. We're going to have to go by foot." Lawrence throws his door open, stabbing a vampire in the chest with his blade, sending him back. "Sawyer, keep Hayley safe. Keep her up on your shoulders and out of reach."

The world blurs as Sawyer flips me up and onto his shoulders. I squeeze his neck with my thighs, gripping onto his hair to not fall over. The last thing I need is to crash to the ground when it looks like at least two dozen vampires circle us as if we're their prey. My fear instincts go crazy, and I intake a couple deep breaths.

Alexander isn't in power because he's dumb. His intelligence helps him hold control. Of course, he would think we would go against him. His inability to trust anyone makes it easier for him.

"Head for the city!" Knox calls, rushing ahead and swinging his fist, knocking another Strip dweller out of the way.

The world blurs around me as the vampires speed forward too quickly for me to focus on anything, my mind disoriented from the sudden movement. I hold on for dear life, praying that we make it. I close my eyes, choosing to shut the world out as blood splashes over me and hollers and screams fill the air. The scent of rancid blood permeates my skin, the strip dwellers' blood nothing like my guys. I don't want to devour them. I want to run away. I want them to stop. "We need to fucking split up from Lawrence." Sawyer keeps his voice low, managing to whisper the words to Knox. "This might be our chance. If we can get away, we can strategize better."

"I think we need to wait. We need to get her to the destination first." Knox remains by Sawyer's side, ensuring no vampires get within reach of me.

The terrain changes the closer we get to the wall, and old houses and other buildings grow up around us as if the city once expanded far beyond the main Strip. Except whatever is out there isn't on our side. It's as if it's an urban wilderness. I'm sure it's monitored by the leadership as not to allow anyone to live here, though I don't think it's livable with how none of the houses seem to have any tinted windows or windows at all. Many roofs are gone. It's a complete war zone from the past. And it doesn't expand out for very long. Just up until we reach the towering wall.

"Alex! Show yourself! You think you can send your army to stop us, but you've severely underestimated our ability. We have a deal to make." Lawrence stops at the wall and spins on the balls of his feet. "You have one minute before we return to The Whiskey and prepare an attack on your city. Don't think we aren't capable. My reach and alliances expand far and wide. Opal was always rather open and discussed many things in great detail. How do you think I managed to get into your city in the first place? I've only been nice because of her. Now that she's gone, you better fucking show yourself is all I have to say."

A figure blurs from one of the houses, and an unfamiliar vampire in an Aris uniform jumps on Lawrence's back, stabbing him in the process.

He growls and spins, throwing the guy off him. It doesn't take long for Lawrence to decapitate him, sending his head flying across the broken street.

"You still have it in you, you dirtbag. This was all a test to see if you were worthy of such a deal." Alexander materializes a dozen feet away, and a spotlight shines down on all of us. I shield my eyes from the blinding light, trying my best to keep my shit together.

"Fuck you. You were just attempting to destroy any possible alliances I had brought with me. If you weren't afraid, you'd have met me face-to-face and alone. I see that you still have the leadership under your boot." Lawrence tips his head up toward the wall and wiggles his fingers. "Maybe they'll reconsider your position and their decision from years ago."

Baring his fangs, Alexander says, "Never. You're not worthy of the city."

Alexander is one to talk. My anger rushes through me

when he locks his gaze on mine. Something indecipherable crosses his face, and he raises an eyebrow. It brings me back to being his baby doll and his property. Just being near him reminds me of all the pain and heartache, all the abuse and the disgusting situation he put me in. It opens up a wound that I thought healed over, but now I realize it wasn't healed. It was just bandaged.

I clutch onto Sawyer, trying to remain in control. He holds me by my knees. I realize I might be choking him with my thighs, but he doesn't complain as he tries to get me to loosen my hold.

And then I do.

But it's not to relax on his shoulders.

I manage to use him to stand up, balancing on his shoulders for the second it takes for me to position my body for a leap. No one has a chance to stop me as I fly toward Alexander, my body and mind disconnecting as I let my dhampir nature take control.

Alexander's eyes widen, and he opens his arms and braces for my impact.

Except this time, I'm more powerful. I'm not his weak little donor. I'm not afraid of him.

I'm going to rip his fucking throat out.

20

HAYLEY

ALLIANCES

I SINK MY teeth into Alexander's throat, ripping and spitting his skin and filling my mouth with his blood. It tastes different than I remember, more bitter and less exhilarating. Tasting blood far superior to his has turned me into a bit of a blood snob, I guess.

Alexander snarls and punches both of his fists into my back, forcing the air to escape my lungs. I instinctively release him out of self-preservation. He can't touch me again as Monroe rips me off Alexander and pulls me to him. I can't control my nature, and I accidentally sink my teeth into Monroe next. He grunts and tightens his fingers in my hair, fisting it, but he doesn't pull me away and lets me drink. The burning in my stomach is too much. I'm starving, and the stress and anxiety of this night clobbers my self-control. I need to be wild and savage. It's the only way to survive. Alexander won't accept my obedience. Not now. He'll destroy me, knowing I can and will fight back.

"Get her out of here. I'll take care of Alexander." Lawrence darts past us and charges Alexander. "If you dare try to kidnap her or betray me, I will destroy you. Do you understand?"

No one responds to him. Not that we have to. His focus turns solely to Alexander. And with the start of their fight, more security personnel materialize around us, creating a circle. Of course, he came with backup. This is far more than his usual array of vampire security. I think he still has ties to some of the crews that weren't allied with the Bella. The three vampires that came along with Lawrence back him up, tearing down vampire after vampire as Lawrence and Alexander blur in a fight.

"Stay together. Keep Hayley within our circle. We're going back to the Bella." Knox takes me from Monroe and positions me in his arms to where I hug him with my whole body, allowing his hands to be free in case we're attacked.

Cooper stands by his side, allowing Monroe to lead the way and Sawyer to block us from behind. My heart pounds, the heavy beats rapping against my ribcage, threatening to break through it at any second. The edges of my vision shadow, and I can't help wondering what's truly happening. We expected a fight, but it was nothing like this. All I can hope for now is that maybe those two bastards do actually kill each other. But then again, they're not the only threat. The leadership stands behind Alexander. They would inherit his hotel and disperse it accordingly if something were to happen to him. Or the rest of his mysterious coven brothers would take over. They could be worse. I still have a contract under the Aris Coven name. I'm his lifelong property, and they can do whatever they want with me. If it's not one enemy, it's another.

"Head to the south wall. Lawrence said there was an access tunnel there. Very few know about it, and it's how he got in the first time. It's guarded by a couple of Strip dwellers that ensure no one can enter or leave the city, but we can handle them. I think the leadership feeds them to ensure their loyalty." Sawyer pulls out a gun from its holster and prepares to shoot to keep people at a distance. It's not often he uses a gun because they don't do much to vampires, but he's willing to do anything right now.

"Those fuckers better be ready to negotiate with us or lose their fucking heads. I'm not in the mood for any more bullshit tonight. I just want to take our girl home. If we can get her there, we can protect her." Monroe also pulls out a gun, aiming it forward as we round a pile of rubble next to the looming wall.

"Are you guys crazy? You can't take her back to the Bella. They all know that's exactly where you'll go with her. If you want even a chance to keep Hayley safe and hidden, you're going to need somewhere else. This city is fucking huge." Cooper speaks up for the first time, turning to look at me.

No one responds to him right away. Everyone knows he's right, because if they want to keep me forever, they're going to have to give up the familiarity of their hotel until they can reach out to the Strip crews for back up. If they take me there now, Lawrence knows where to find us. He could just come in and start shit. Same with the leadership. It's obvious that Alexander doesn't plan to negotiate with anyone, and he'll do whatever it takes to get me. I don't know what his plans are, but the look on his face...he finally realizes what he's dealing with. I'm not the same person he sold off at auction. I'm no longer a little weak, scared donor. I'm a dhampir and will devour every damn vampire I can. I bit off a guy's finger for fuck's sake. I realize now more than ever that I'll do anything. I'll be anyone I have to be.

If I'm going to survive, I need to fight harder. I need to be ruthless. I need to prove myself as a Bella Crew member. I can't expect my guys to take care of me. I can't expect the world to show me mercy. I need to get the world to bow down and beg me for mercy instead.

Starting now.

I spot the silhouette of a vampire darting from the wall, and I point him out to Monroe. He charges the bastard and stabs him in the gut, pushing him all the way back to the wall, slamming his head against it.

"Who runs the city access?" Monroe asks, his fangs peeking out from beneath his lip. "We need entrance without fighting. We would prefer not to destroy all of you."

The vampire gnashes his teeth, trying to fight Monroe, except he's not of the same power. But that doesn't matter. A dozen more figures materialize around us, showing their numbers. There are only so many vampires even the most powerful can handle, which is why there is the leadership and the alliances keeping the covens in control safe.

"If we let you through, they'll starve us. We can't allow it." This comes from a female vampire and the first one I've seen tonight. There are very few of them outside of the big hotels, and I can't help wondering how she found herself a part of this group.

"We can provide blood for you. We're from the Bella Crew, and if you help us, we'll help you. That's how shit works on the Strip." Sawyer steps forward, taking his leadership position.

"You have nothing with you. How do we know you don't want to just fuck us over?" The woman steps forward, leaving her group behind.

I clear my throat. I don't know where I get the courage, but I know I must do something. We don't have time to fight. We just need to go through. We need more people on our side.

Straightening my shoulders, I say, "I'll let you all bite me and drink my blood if you let us through. It'll hold you over until we can make arrangements."

My guys tense around me, clearly shocked by my offer.

"We really don't want to fight. Aren't you tired of how the leadership treats you? We're trying to change things. But you have to let us back in," I add.

"You're in no position to make such an offering, donor. By the looks on your master's face, he clearly doesn't want to share." The woman continues to saunter closer, risking getting within a few feet of me.

Monroe has the nerve to chuckle. It sounds oddly musical in this moment. Of course, he would chuckle at her words. "She doesn't belong to only one of us. I give you permission. If Hayley wants to let you bite her, that's all her. But I swear if you hurt her or try to take more than you should, I'll cut your tits off." He jerks his attention to the guys of the group. "And don't think I won't cut your dicks. I owe someone a cock bouquet."

"Fucking asshole," Sawyer mutters under his breath. "You're going to get your ass fucking beat for this."

I wiggle from Knox's arms, forcing him to let me go. "This is my decision, Sawyer. We need to get through. We need more alliances. If we have an alliance with these guys, they can help us. This is one of the few accesses that isn't heavily guarded by the leadership."

Knox stays by my side and locks his fingers through mine. "Listen to vixen. She has a point."

I suck in a deep breath and allow Knox to guide me toward the group of vampires. I feel as if I'm a delicacy waiting on a table to be devoured even though I stand in front of them. I hold out my arms, and the woman rushes me first as if she can hardly contain herself. She bites me so quickly that I don't even feel the prick of her fangs, and I exhale a breath and close my eyes, just thinking about how this might all soon be over.

"You may pass. But I'm going with you to ensure you

uphold your end of the bargain." The woman cracks her knuckles and then wipes the drop of blood from her lips. She turns to the rest of the group. "Don't allow anyone else in until I return."

I blink in surprise. I wasn't expecting that kind of offer. "Thank you. You won't regret this."

We follow the woman through a tunnel the size of a large vehicle. It might have once been used to bring in supplies, but it has now been converted into a shelter for this den of vampires.

I don't get long to look around. It's too dark anyway, the place not having electricity.

My guys pick up speed, following behind the woman as she leads the way.

I can't believe we made it. I can't believe we are back in La Vega. The lights of the city glow around me, and I stare up at the first hotel that resembles what was once a donor landmark long ago. I can't recall the name, but it's as tall, if not taller, than the monument at the Aris.

The world hums with life, and I can sense Strip dwellers lurking around but keeping their distance. I'm sure they can't enter this area as it's a part of whatever crew or group this woman is the leader of. She looks like she does the same amount of damage the Bella Crew does to those who try to threaten their territory. She also has the backing of the leadership, so it does give her an advantage.

"You can't take the main street. It's heavily monitored by the leadership. There is a back alley that goes along the Sphere and will take you to the old tracks. That's your best route." The woman motions for Sawyer to lead the way. "I'll take the shortcut and meet you there."

Something doesn't feel right, and I grip on to Knox. Leaning down, I whisper in his ear, "Don't follow her directions. Something's wrong."

Sawyer and Monroe hear my words, and they flick their attention to me. Cooper darts ahead, turning to peek at me for a second.

I don't even get the chance to call out before the woman jumps on Cooper, sending him crashing to the ground.

"I'll hold her off!" he yells, grabbing the woman by her hair and flipping her off him.

I expect my guys to hesitate, but they don't. The world blurs as they rush past, leaving Cooper behind. I watch in horror as the woman jabs her fist into his chest.

She's going to kill him.

A part of me wants to run away, but another part of me knows that I can't run from this. I can't let him die on my behalf. We promised him a better life, and he has done his best to be here for me even if it's only been for a short while.

I throw myself from Knox's arms, and he can't keep his grip on me, my dhampir speed and strength kicking on. I launch at the woman and grab her wrist, stopping her from pulling out Cooper's heart.

She screams at the pressure of my grip, and her fingers loosen. One second, she screams, and then the next, her head pops from her body and smacks Cooper in the chest. I stare in shock as she collapses on top of him, and it takes my mind a minute to catch up with everything.

"Warn us next time, little bird." Monroe kicks the body of the woman off and hauls me up. "You're keeping me on my fucking toes, and it's driving me crazy."

"You're not the only one," Knox says, inspecting every inch of me, ensuring I'm uninjured. I laugh, but mostly out of nerves. There's nothing funny about the situation. If my adrenaline wasn't running so hot, I'd be a mess. It helps that my thoughts of revenge consume me. All I can think about is what I'm going to do to Alexander if he survives the fight with Lawrence. I can't help it. I feel stronger than ever. My surprise attack on him has left me more confident than I knew possible. Because I can hurt him. I can be a worthy enemy to him.

"Come on. We have to move." Sawyer helps Cooper to his feet and pats him on his back. "Hayley, can you give him some blood so he can heal faster?"

I slowly nod my head. Instead of waiting for him to bite me, Sawyer holds me up for Cooper to take me in his arms.

"You better hold on tight to her. Don't drink too much. She's already had enough taken tonight. We'll lead the rest of the way." Sawyer pulls out his com device and taps the screen a couple of times.

"We can head toward the Ri. Mesquite might have somewhere we can stay." Monroe motions with his knife in the direction we're supposed to go. I can't remember anyone named Mesquite, but I hope the guy isn't as treacherous as the rest of this damn town seems to be.

"He fucking better. If we don't find shelter soon, we're going to have to face the sun," Knox says, picking up his pace.

"Don't worry. My cousin has our back. He'll be able to contact the Bella for us as well. It's Walcott's time to shine. The bastard has been dying for another moment to murder at a whim, and it'll be a good distraction to draw attention away from us. Tatum can get the Strip dwellers riled up as well. We have to make it hard for Aris and Lawrence to look." Monroe's voice rises with his anticipation. I'm sure he'd prefer to be out taking down the monstrous masses instead of hiding, but he won't leave me to do so.

"That should work—" Sawyer snarls and jabs his knife,

gutting a Strip dweller.

Vampires crowd the area, loitering outside the front of the Sphere. I don't know how far the Ri is, but I'm afraid we'll never make it by foot. There are too many threats and people getting in our way. It doesn't help that blood coats my skin and clothes, turning me into a spectacle—actually, we all are.

I peer around from Cooper's arms, trying to get a visual, but we move too fast. It doesn't help that Cooper carries me like a child. It's as if he doesn't want to give me the chance to push away from him if need be. I cling onto his neck, resting my cheek to his shoulder blade. He smells different with the blood of the female vampire on him. It's not bad, but I don't like it either. I hate the thought he even had to experience such pain. That he felt the need to sacrifice himself for me. Why does he feel my life is worth more than his? That's a rare occurrence, and something I haven't really experienced until I met the Bella Crew.

"If you need to bite me, go ahead," Cooper whispers the words under his breath.

"I'm good." Now is definitely not the time for me to be sucking on Cooper's neck. I need him to stay focused, and I'm nearly certain that if I bite him, Monroe, Knox, and Sawyer will also lose their focus. They can't help it.

"Are you sure? You're sniffing me." He adjusts me in

his arms, changing my position until I wrap my legs around his waist.

"Because you smell. I mean…fuck. Why do you have to point it out?" I can't stop laughing with my words, embarrassment rushing through me. Now is not the time for me to lose focus either. Bastard.

"My state of filth didn't bother you when we first met," he teases, relaxing his muscles.

I groan and bury my face into the crook of his throat. He's right about that. But this is different. I don't want to explain it either.

"We're almost there. Good job at keeping Hayley calm. She didn't even notice the heads flying." Monroe materializes behind Cooper, grinning at me with blood spattering across his face and soaking his beard. It looks like he bit a couple of people, and I don't like the fact that others' blood is on him either. What the actual fuck? Something like this wouldn't have bothered me before the same way it does now.

At least it's not human. That makes it a teensy bit better.

"Both of you shut up and pay attention. There's—" Sawyer can't get the words out as a car screeches from the parking structure in front of us, nearly taking us out.

Sawyer jumps on the hood, holding on as the driver

stomps the brakes, trying to send him flying off.

"Fuck. Run!" Knox throws his arm out and steals me from Cooper, not giving him a chance to run with me. He's going possessive, and only trusts my safety in his arms.

"They must've fucking settled their disagreement. They took the back road into this damn place. I thought it was blocked off." Monroe aims his gun, shooting it at the window of Lawrence's vehicle.

Fear tightens my chest, and I squeeze my eyes shut. They shouldn't be here. They should've killed each other already. And now, it looks as if Alexander and Lawrence have teamed up because they share the car. The three other vampires ride in the back as well.

Oh fucking no.

No. No. No.

Lawrence flies at me and Knox, knocking Sawyer out of the way with a swing of his fist. I scream at the force of Lawrence's body ramming into me, and pain swells across my back and spine.

We tumble over the ground, and Knox skids, probably getting road rash in the process. He grunts but doesn't complain, and he doesn't loosen his hold either.

"Listen very carefully, Hayley. I don't have an alliance with Alexander, but you need to act as if I do. This is all part of the plan. I'll be taking you to the Aris. Do you understand?" Lawrence growls, shoving his hand against Knox's chest hard enough to pierce his fingers into his skin.

Panic rises inside me, and I grab Lawrence's wrist. "Don't hurt him. If you hurt him, I'll kill you."

"It must look authentic. I need the Bella Crew to act as if they're not on my side." Lawrence bares his teeth, threatening us with another growl. "If you don't let her go, I'll end you. I don't need the weakest link."

Fuck. I'm insulted, but there's nothing I can do.

"Take me as a prisoner. It's the only way." Knox refuses to let me go, and I try not to lose control.

"Then you'll be treated like one." Lawrence hooks his arms around both me and Knox, using his super-strength to pull us from the ground.

The world blurs as he relocates us and throws us into the back of his vehicle. He punches Knox hard enough to knock him out, and he slips into the front seat.

Sawyer and Monroe yell out, but Alexander blocks their way. They all blur in a fight until Lawrence hits the accelerator and sends us barreling forward.

I watch Alexander grab Cooper by the throat and drag him away, leaving Sawyer and Monroe chasing after us.

I hold my arm out of the window, waving and clanking the jewelry I haven't taken off. I press my finger to the button, opening the line, but I keep it muted.

Lawrence flicks his gaze to the rearview mirror. "This is going to be a hostile takeover, Hayley. Alexander believes we have a truce. We're going to put on a performance, initiating this new alliance. And when we do, you're going to show him your true nature. You're going to eat his heart."

THIS IS GOING to be an utter shitshow. I know it, Monroe knows it, and I'm pretty fucking sure all of La Vega might know it. Word in the city travels fast. Walcott isn't the only one with a big-ass mouth, and Aris has called in every one of his damn alliances and every blood debt owed to him to ensure that nothing shakes his power.

Lawrence probably knows it, but he's so confident in

himself that he's willing to risk the safety of Hayley and Knox to test exactly how powerful Aris is. It doesn't help that he's sent the three assholes he claims as allies to us for a so-called strategy plan. It has the entire Bella Crew up in arms—literally—and the five of us have at least twenty-something guns trained in our direction with Walcott's trigger-happy finger ensuring the fuckers don't forget whose domain they're in.

I stab my knife into the roulette wheel and give it a spin. "All right. You three go fucking stand in that corner while I discuss this bullshit." I curl my fingers, calling over Tatum, Govan, and Walcott.

Walcott snaps his fangs and pretends to try to stab Fa-lo. Falo jumps and scrambles back, acting like a scared little ball sack now that he's no longer in his territory. He doesn't even have fucking fangs and should've been put into Lawrence's sadistic herd. He's a worthless piece of shit. I don't know why Lawrence ever considered him to have enough power to control anything. He can't even control his damn nerves.

Whistling, Walcott motions to the group of onlookers. "Hey, shitheads! Why don't you show these three our hospitality and give them some blood, will you? You know the kind."

Damn. I wish I had thought of that. I'd love to see

these assholes drink the rotten blood Walcott keeps on hand for the bastards who try to start shit.

One of the guys materializes behind Primm and jabs his gun into the vampire's back, forcing him to walk. If only they were all we had to worry about.

"Why don't we just murder them and get it over with? You know that is the best strategy." Monroe waves his knife and pretends to draw it over his throat. "It's going to happen sooner or later."

I tighten my jaw. "As soon as we have Hayley and Knox in sight, you can have your fun, dickhole."

"I really fucking hate that they're with Aris. What were you thinking?" Tatum taps her fingers to the table, leaning forward to snatch my knife from the wheel.

"Knox made the decision for us. He wasn't given much choice, but at least he's with her and another new crew member. Cooper is from The Whiskey, but he's decent," I say, strumming my fingers on the sleek wood rimming the table.

"Is he hot?" Tatum wags her eyebrows. "I could use a new dick around here, and I'm tired of looking at Walcott's ugly mug." Tatum snatches Walcott by the chin and smacks his cheek.

"He's taken, Tate. My little bird already sunk her teeth into him. You'd have to fight her, and...she's changed."

Monroe remains expressionless with his words. We haven't told anyone about Hayley yet, and I'm not sure that I want to.

"What the fuck? She really is the queen of cocks." Tatum fists her hand, swinging her arm in an attempt to punch Monroe in the balls. "You know what? Let me handle this. I'll have our cock-babe back in thirty minutes. I need her around to teach me her ways. It can't all be about her blood. Maybe we can be the—"

I slam my hands on the table. "Hayley is a dhampir."

There. I fucking said it. I'm not even sure any of them know what a dhampir is. Walcott looks confused as hell, Govan cocks his head, and Tatum raises her eyebrows, her mouth dropping open.

"I heard about those when I was on the Strip. Some of the rebels mentioned them, wishing they were real. Apparently, they're supposed to be super vampire killers." Tatum keeps her voice low. "That doesn't really look like something Hayley is. You can take total offense to this, but she's not exactly a badass."

"You haven't seen her fight recently," Monroe says, clearly taking offense to Tatum's comment.

I don't, though. I know her heart is in the right place, and I'd prefer her not to think of Hayley as a threat or some kind of vampire hunter or killer. She is one of us, regardless of what she's capable of or her nature.

"She couldn't have changed that much." Walcott crosses his arms over his chest. "Whatever the fuck a dhampir is."

I scrub my hand over my cheeks, trying to keep my cool. I want to flick him in the balls and tell him to let me finish. I don't need this kind of argument. It's not important whether they think Hayley is capable of holding her own in a fight or not. What's important is they know she's different and why it's so important we fight to get her back. She's not just a donor. She's not just the woman that I'm madly in love with. She is an amazing being on a whole new level. She's like a magical fucking unicorn that bites like a zombie, attacks at random, and really knows how to get me on my knees in a good way. Because I would bow to her if she asked. I don't know what it is, but she entrances me. She makes me see just how lucky I am that she has deemed me as hers.

"Aren't dhampirs basically mutants? I'm not as old as some of you guys, but I do remember the rumors about it among some of the Strip dwellers before I joined your crew. Some people were considering trying to make them before The Divide. It never worked. There were a lot of casualties." Govan purses his lips, his eyes darting around the empty casino floor as if he recalls a time from long ago. And he is. It's been decades since the divisions. The Vampire Uprising was probably over a century ago now, though I can't really remember much. It was a savage time. While La Vega is a bit volatile and crude, it's nothing in comparison to what it was like when I was transformed. I remember it being such a fucking scary time before I realized what was truly happening, and I was bitten by a random bastard on my way to get to my parents.

I shake my head, pushing the thoughts away. I don't want to think about my blood family. They've been dead for a long time, and it's almost as if it was another life altogether. I can't dwell on things that I can't change, and it's best to focus on the present. On the future. The one thing I do miss is how life felt more important being a donor, because we didn't have what we do now. All I have is time. I'll keep going until one day someone ends my life. And if they don't, then I better fucking keep Hayley safe. Because eternity doesn't seem like something I want unless I have her by my side. Unless the Bella Crew makes it through this.

I don't know how much longer I can handle being treated as if I'm some weak, powerless vampire when I have control over a hotel and over donors and others. But the leadership doesn't like how I run things. I don't treat people as if they are here to serve me. This is a community to thrive in.

I might not be a rebel, but I'm the leader of the Bella

Crew, and change is a must. I realize it starts with Hayley. She's the one we've been waiting for. She's important to both the donor and vampire worlds.

"That sounds fucked up. Thank God I was fucking single." Tatum rests her elbows on the roulette table, staring at the faded colors. I missed everything else that Govan said, but I think he was talking about the fact that a lot of donor women who were pregnant during the uprising died. A lot of women in general died. Men too. But it seems as if females were the target. Vampires like those in the leadership didn't want to transform a bunch of women into vampires, because female donors bring new life and a new blood. A man can impregnate far more women in a short time compared to how often a woman can have a child. It's really fucked up to think about it, which is another reason why we fight. I grew up with four sisters, and females were important to our family. My dad taught me how to treat and respect them, and I still carry that to this day.

"It was, but Hayley isn't from an old line. It was Alex who created her. He bit her mother while she was pregnant and managed to create Hayley's dhampir mutation. We don't know the extent of what she's capable of, but it's life-changing. Aris had no clue what the fuck he was doing. But Lawrence? He knows about dhampirs, and he managed to awaken her deep-seated nature. I guess venom triggers it." I lick my lips and scrub my fingers through my hair again. I don't want to talk about this anymore, but I know they have questions. The problem is I'm not sure I can answer them. Cooper was someone I was relying on because he knew a dhampir in real life. I only know of the stories. The folklore. There's just so many factors that we can't predict because of how rare Hayley is.

I'm relying on Knox and his medical background to look into it more once this bullshit gets settled. It's hard for us to figure shit out if we're constantly having to be on guard and to fight.

"Damn, this is all so crazy. Does she have fangs now?" Walcott bounces on his feet, rubbing his palms together as if he imagines Hayley as the monstrous killer Tatum described.

"No, she's still technically a donor. But she's stronger. She's fast when something triggers her. And I did see her bite off the finger of a bastard. It was fucking glorious. You would've been so impressed, but fucking stay away from her, asshole." Monroe grins at Walcott and swings his arm out, punching him back. "She'll never be the queen of your cock. You got it?"

"Oh, come on. You're just afraid she's going to want me and only me. I'm such a fucking catch." Walcott wags his eyebrows.

Tatum tips her head back and laughs. "With your ugly ass mug? Maybe after that face tattoo bullshit fades. I still can't believe you let me tattoo that on you."

It's hard to tell, but Walcott's tattoo is actually a pussy that Tatum gave him when he was trying to teach her. He knew it and still let her, because I'm pretty certain even though they aren't together, and they only fuck around when they're horny, he does have a thing for her.

She doesn't exactly feel the same, but he takes what he can get. He also finds shit to do with some of the dudes around here.

I don't think he could give Hayley the loyalty she wants and needs. It's obvious that even though we're okay to share her, she's not okay to share us. I realized really fast that I think her dhampir nature doesn't allow it. Her possessiveness is twice as much as a vampire's. Usually, we wouldn't be able to share a donor like we do, but there's just something about Hayley.

"That's fucking enough. We need to strategize a plan. I know that Lawrence is setting some kind of bullshit up with Aris, and we need to get everything in line. We need to start a battle that the leadership can't ignore. There's no way we can sit back and let Aris get away with whatever the fuck he's planning. We also need to make sure Lawrence doesn't swoop in and try anything either. He's worse. You should see how he has his donors at The Whiskey. It's literally like cattle. And it's not only humans." I look at each of my crewmembers, letting them know with my eyes just how fucked up it is.

I usually have a tolerance for the messed up, but I've never seen anything like it. That was one of the few things that I agreed with when the leadership came into power. They weren't to treat donors so unfairly and disgustingly. That's why they all have places and hotels. They are fed and given jobs and allowed to have family and lives. It's why they have blood withdrawal centers that collect blood and add it to pools to feed vampires from.

Sure, there are personal donors out there at every hotel, but they're given better benefits. We don't do any of that here. Everyone is treated equally, and we protect everyone to the best of our ability. No one in power truly knows exactly how many donors we have and how much blood we can put together. Because our donors are happy, and they are free from vampire control, they willingly donate and they thrive.

Tatum has done an excellent job. We only require twenty-five percent of the donors to give blood. That's only because it does take effort and wealth to provide for them. It's not that they really take it as a requirement though. Sometimes, they will offer more when they know we might need something. Tatum keeps them in the loop.

She's also going to have to tell them about Hayley. We have our donor warriors who can fight. We don't have them just sitting around in hotel rooms all day long just living and existing. They know what's coming. They've been preparing for this their entire lives. They know that if they stay with us, and they trust us, that we'll change La Vega. We'll change their lives and the lives of their children. They're the true rebels in this grand scheme of things.

"Tell us what you think we should do. I stand behind you fully. You know that I would die for our cause, and if you think Hayley can help us, then I'm here for it." Tatum looks at Walcott and punches his shoulder. "And this asshole will be here for it as long as he wants me to ride him anytime soon."

Walcott bursts out in laughter, grabs Tatum by the hips, and pulls her to him. He fake humps her until she stabs him in the stomach. "I just want to fucking see Hayley in action."

Govan doesn't laugh or react. All he does is continue to stare at the roulette table, his mind wandering as he loses himself in his thoughts.

Monroe swings his arm over Govan's shoulders. "What about you, dude? Your opinion matters to us as well."

Govan lifts and drops his shoulders. "You guys are going to think I'm selfish, but I want to get Mya. She'll be the first one Aris goes after because Hayley cares about her. I know you guys don't think much—"

I raise my hand, cutting him off. "We'll get Mya. I promise. I agree with you. If we get her first, then Hayley is less likely to do something crazy. She loves those performers like family, and she'll sacrifice herself to ensure they're okay. That's just one of the things about her."

It's infuriating, but I do understand it. She feels responsible for the other performers at the Aris. She feels as if this is all her fault, and that Alexander wouldn't treat them so poorly had it not been for her.

But she's wrong. He would've done so regardless. He's just using her to make her feel as if she's to blame. And I hate it. That fucker needs to be held accountable. He needs to fucking get his head chopped off for gaslighting her and making her feel as if all of the pain he put her through was her fault.

"Yeah?" Govan's face changes as a soft smile spreads across his lips.

Monroe gives him one hell of a shake. "Of fucking course, man. You're a Bella Crew member. If it's important to you, it's important to us."

I open my mouth to agree with Monroe, but my com device chirps. I quickly yank it from my pocket because the chime is the one that I have set for Hayley. She's activated one of her trackers, even though I know exactly where she is. She is in the gym at the Aris. I can see her on the map.

I turn away from the others and stroll a couple of feet away to put distance between us. Monroe materializes by my side and pulls out his own com device to look at the screen.

It's not Hayley.

It's Cooper.

"You fuckers need to get here quickly. Lawrence was too fucking confident in himself. Things have changed. We need you." Cooper grinds his teeth, a deep growl reverberating from his throat.

The world blurs on the video feed, and Cooper hollers in pain. Static crackles across my com device, and I lose the visual.

I hear Hayley scream next. And then the weirdest thing. Another yell rips through the air. It's not Knox though. It's fucking Lawrence.

The connection drops.

Fucking shit.

The attack alarm blares through the hotel, alerting the

fighters that we're meeting in the lobby. This is it. We're going to hit hard and fast and unexpectedly. Walcott and Govan are already in contact with our allies. But we're not going to attack the Aris. We're going to attack the walls. We're going to the streets and riling up the Strip dwellers. We won't be doing any damage that could possibly cause donors to get hurt. We'll hit the vampire areas hard. And right now is the perfect time. The sun is out, and it's not easy for them to move.

This should give enough of a distraction to keep Aris from calling upon his so-called allies. It'll also hopefully put a crack in the leadership. It's time they realize we're only complying because we don't want donors to be hurt. They need to know we're just as powerful as they are. If we want the city, we can take it. I think there are enough people fed up with the way things are being handled that we can overthrow them.

We're going to have to. If we don't, I'm nearly fucking certain they will destroy us all.

"I have connection. It looks as if Aris is going to fucking reveal what Hayley is. He's going to show her as a dhampir." Monroe growls with his words.

My chest tightens at the thought. This isn't good news. It's important no one knows that she's a dhampir. There's too much speculation and folklore. I don't want word getting out, and if it does...what will happen to the donors? I think this could open up a shitshow in the city.

"Tate!" I yell, calling attention to her as she prepares to leave. "I have a new task for you. I need you to put a team together and get every damn woman you come across and bring them here. I don't care who they belong to, but I especially need you to round up the pregnant ones. I'm afraid shits about to go down, and we have to protect them. Have your donors put out word to the hotels. They need to be in sight for you. We don't have time to search."

Because if people realize how dhampirs are made, they're going to try to make their own. Depends on the rumors.

Fuck. "I'm all set. I got in touch with one of the security personnel and paid them off to let us into the hotel through the side entrance. We'll have to be quick. You know how Ally's doesn't like people going through." Monroe rolls his shoulders, stretching his body as if he plans charging in and murdering everyone he comes across. And who knows, he might.

Ally's is connected to the Aris, and it's the fastest way to get to the elevators. That'll be our best bet to sneaking around until we get to the gym.

"They're going to fucking let us, even if I have to overthrow whoever Aris has under his boot." I double check my weapons and tap my com device, scrolling through all the feeds again. We're going to rush straight across the Strip to the other side, moving in direct sunlight. It'll hurt like a bitch if we get caught out there too long, because the sun protective gear can only protect us so much before we start overheating, but I'm willing to risk it. I would walk butt-ass naked across the empty road in the sun to get to Hayley if I had to, burning my cock and all. She's worth it.

"You got the extra sun gear?" I ask, adjusting a duffel bag on my arm with far more weapons than I could ever use. But they're not just for me. I'm arming up every single fucking donor I come across, and they're going to fight like hell.

This is it.

Monroe grabs his backpack from the floor, unzips it, and shows me the extra blankets and facemasks. We have enough for Knox and Cooper. Any other asshole is just going to have to figure shit out for themselves.

"Good. I think I'm ready. We're going straight to where we see Cooper's location. I'm fucking certain he's the one with Hayley's jewelry now. He was a smart bastard to pick it up if Aris took it off her. We'll have to make sure to reward him or some shit. Throw a party after all this is done." I straighten my shoulders and peer around the chaotic casino, wondering if this is what it would look like if we opened the hotel to the public. I don't know if I want to find out though. There's a lot of bullshit that goes into people looking for shelter. The Strip travelers can be ruthless. I just want to keep my crew and my donors safe. But things are going to have to change. Hopefully for the better.

Monroe leads the way to the hotel exit, and I stare at the bright sun, shielding my eyes even though the shade blocks us from the beams of white.

"Our girl is going to be okay. She's going to fuck some shit up. I hope you know that." Monroe whacks me on the back. "Who knows. Maybe she'll have already devoured the assholes by the time we get there."

If only I had that kind of wishful thinking.

I put on my hood and brace myself.

Dashing forward, I race into the sun.

TEARS BURN MY cheeks, and I rest on my hands and knees, trying to breathe through the pain. I can't believe this is happening. My fear and anger battle it out, and my mind fights with my body to get the fuck up. If I stay down, Alexander will beat me again. He'll hurt me, force me to drink his blood to heal me, and then beat me again. I don't know how much more I can handle. It's like he wants me to beg to die. And I'm about to.

"Get the fuck up and fight, Hayley. Show me you're as powerful as Lawrence says you are. If you get up and prove to me you can in fact be of some use, then maybe I'll let your little blood donor live." Alexander snarls and smacks me with his paddle, sending me forward onto my stomach. I can barely move. I think my ankle might be broken. I know that my wrist is because I've broken it before. He twisted it so hard that I blacked out. That's what I get for slapping him.

"Come on, Hayley. You can do it. Get up and show him exactly who he's created." Cooper's soft voice whispers to me from his spot chained to the wall. Lawrence and Alexander forced him to call the Bella Crew, setting them up. I knew that whatever Lawrence had planned was going to be a shitshow. I don't know if he is actually against Alexander or not. He has been ruthless since the moment he dragged me screaming from the car.

Knox hollers, the pain in his voice ripping through me. It gets me to shove my hand to the floor and shakily get back to my knees. Blood soaks the front of my shirt, and I ball my good hand into a fist. I'm exhausted. I'm in so much pain. The only thing that keeps me from giving up is the fact that if I do, I know that Alexander will kill Knox. I know Lawrence will let him.

Lawrence claps his hands, his laughter echoing through the gym. "Look at her go. You should see what she's like when her dhampir nature truly kicks on."

"And how the fuck am I supposed to get her to give in?" Alexander chomps his fangs, threatening me. He rushes toward me at vampire speed and snatches me by the front of my shirt.

Lifting me from the floor, he leers. "What is it going to take, Hayley? How much pain does your little blood source need to be in before you try to murder me? Do I have to kill him?"

I shudder, trying my best to push through the pain. The agony. I think I might be dying. It's as if I stare at myself from the outside.

"If you kill him, she'll never do as you say. Look how much she has taken already. This is not how you get a dhampir to obey." Cooper risks speaking out, rattling the chains stretching his arms high above his head.

Alexander drops me, and I scream in agony as my weight slams on my ankle, sending me to my face. Blurring through the room, Alexander appears in front of Cooper and jabs a knife into his stomach. It's the tenth time he's done so, and Cooper manages to only grunt instead of yell out this time.

"Then maybe I should kill you. If you know so much

about dhampirs and my baby doll, you pose a risk to me. We can't have that now." Alexander pulls out the knife and returns to me, holding it against my lips. "Or maybe I'll demand that she kills you instead."

My nostrils flare at the scent of Cooper's blood. It's not until this minute that I realize how hungry I am. I can't even remember the last time I properly ate. And this hunger...it's far worse than what I've experienced before. I never knew what it was like to be without blood. I feel like I'm on the verge of either exploding or shattering. If I shatter, that'll be it for me. But if I explode? I'm fucking taking down Alexander with me.

I can't control my body, and I flick my tongue between my lips and lick the middle of the bloody blade. I cut myself on the sharp edge, but I don't even care. Cooper's blood tastes incredible. It's exactly what I needed in this moment. Even the tiny taste is enough to send a burst of energy through me. I tense my muscles and jerk my attention to Cooper. His eyes flash silver. He sees what I feel. He knows me now on a different level that he can predict what to expect. And right now, I need to be the true monster. I need to show Alexander what I am capable of despite not wanting to obey him.

But it's not Alexander I'm going to go after. It's Cooper. If I can get within his reach for a second, I might be able to break the chains. I feel as if I could break bones and bricks and everything that rises in my path.

I lick the bloody knife again. "You're going to regret this," I snap, my voice sounding stronger than ever. I don't know how I manage to suppress the pain, but my adrenaline kicks on and my blood hunger suppresses my humanity.

"Prove it. Prove it, and perhaps I'll let your blood source go." Alexander grabs my hair and jerks my head to look at Knox bleeding on the floor. It's enough to kick me into action.

Jerking my hand out, I snatch the blade from Alexander's fingers and sink it into his stomach. My speed throws him off and startles him, and he throws me to the floor and smacks me with his hand, the force of the hit enough to knock the wind out of me.

"Lawrence, stab both those bastards five times each. Whatever Hayley does to me, they will experience the same but far worse." Alexander pins me down, and a moment later, my whole body stings and screams in pain as he slams his studded paddle across my ass.

"Don't do it! If you do it—" I scream again, my threat cutting off as Alexander hits me over and over with his vampire speed and strength. He hits me enough that my body shuts down. It wants to protect me from the pain.

He shatters me. I'm not sure I can continue fighting.

"Enough, Alex. That is pointless. You're hurting her out of anger and not for punishment. That is not how you train a dhampir to comply. If she believes you're just going to hurt her, then what's the point? She will not do anything." Lawrence stands tall over me, his shadow blocking out the bright lights from above.

Alexander snarls and abandons me, shoving Lawrence back. The two of them standoff and threaten each other like monsters, but then Alexander finally backs off.

"I want to see her in action now. I want to be able to control the leadership. They're growing weaker by the day, allowing more vampires coven union and power. They're proving not to be my allies. If they were my allies, they would stand beside me." Alexander's voice rips through the air as he yells the words.

I inhale and exhale slowly, my whole body just wishing this would end.

"Hayley." The soft whisper of my name draws my attention away from Lawrence and Alexander, and I manage to roll on my side to look at Knox. It's the first time I've been able to see him, and my heart sinks into my stomach at how beaten and bruised he is. Alexander took out his wrath on him first, beating him into submission.

My whole body quivers as I press my hands to the floor, trying to get to my feet. I don't know if I can. I don't know if my body will let me or if Alexander will just knock me back down again. I wish we would've put up more of a fight instead of believing Lawrence was still going to double cross Alexander. The only thing giving me hope is that Lawrence stopped him from beating the shit out of me. I know he's capable of doing the same. He did whip me before. I just hate this. I hate the fact that they're trying to turn me into a psycho at the same time as they try to lure the Bella Crew here.

I just hope they didn't believe Cooper. Because if they enter the building, it might be over for us.

"Hayley, get up and show him who you are. He won't expect it right now." Knox's words drift to me, his voice low, but I'm so focused on him that I'm able to shove away Alexander and Lawrence yelling over what to do next.

And he's absolutely right. I need to take the chance to get to him.

This could be the only thing that will save us.

I grab the discarded knife as I force my legs to cooperate. I stumble, but still, Lawrence and Alexander ignore me. They have so much confidence in themselves that they don't consider me a threat. I don't even consider myself a threat right now. The only thing I'm going to manage to do is probably get in one last blow before Alexander tears me apart.

But I have to try. I have to do something. I haven't been through everything I've been through already just to let him win in the end. He can't win. Lawrence can't win either. I need to summon everything in me to prove I'm worthy of the Bella Crew. I'm worthy of being more than a slave.

Gathering my nerves and focusing on the rage brewing inside me, I charge forward, my body kicking into action as I trigger my dhampir nature, focusing on the blood staining Alexander's clothes. I can smell him from here, and I imagine what it would be like to taste him as I drain him dry. I have drunk his blood before, but it will never be as sweet as it will be now. Because once I get my teeth into him, I'm not going to stop.

Lawrence darts his gaze to mine, but he doesn't even react. He doesn't warn Alexander either. I jump up and cling onto Alexander's back, locking my hands around his head as I bend it sideways. I sink my teeth into his flesh hard enough to break his skin. He hollers and spins around, trying to throw me off him, but I lock my feet at my ankles, tightening my hold on him the best I can. Blood fills my mouth, and I suck and suck, feeling the tingles blossoming through my body. Heat swells in my stomach, and I savor the sensation that comes with satisfying my dark need. Alexander spins and tries to shove me into the wall, smashing me into it as he crashes backwards. But still, I don't let go. It's as if I'm permanently adhered to him. He's going to know what it's like to be my donor.

"Get her off me now!" Alexander shouts, digging his nails into my arms, trying to hurt me.

"Prove your strength, Aris," Lawrence says, materializing in front of us. "You have to show her who is most powerful."

Alexander tries to grab the front of Lawrence's shirt, but he steps out of reach. Both of them are so focused on me that they don't see the door to the gym flying open. They don't hear the safeties clicking off on the guns.

I release Alexander for a split second only to bite him again, tearing into his flesh as hard as I can, hoping to make it hurt. Lawrence smiles at me, his fangs extending even more. They look like they're desperate for a kill bite, but he keeps himself in control.

"I'll give you a hotel if you show me your ways, Lawrence. I'll give you a fucking position on the La Vega leadership. Is that what you want?" Alexander growls and whips his body back-and-forth still trying to get me off of him.

"Like I said, I'm going to need you—" Lawrence hollers and spins around, jerking his body as loud pops ring through the air.

Monroe and Sawyer shoot their guns, the spray of bullets hitting everything in their paths. I shrink down behind Alexander, using him as a shield. He jerks as a couple of bullets penetrate his body, and I yelp as one splits through him and into me.

It's enough to make Monroe hesitate.

"Stand down," Lawrence shouts, holding his palms up. "I have it under control."

"This is a fucking trap!" Cooper shouts, rattling his chains in an attempt to break free.

Sawyer and Monroe glance at him, their bodies turning rigid.

"We know. We got word that this fucker wasn't in trouble." Sawyer unsheathes a long sword from a holster on his back, and he snarls, extending his fangs. "We have the fucking hotel surrounded. You need to give Hayley to us, and we will forget about it."

Alexander flies from the wall, heading right towards Sawyer. He prepares to fight the vampire, but he doesn't get a chance. The lights flash off, and an alarm blares through the air.

A dozen figures blur through the shadows, and more gunfire and yells create a cacophonous melody in the gym.

"I will not allow you to ruin our city!" a feminine voice says, shouting over the alarm.

I accidentally release Alexander, my ears hurting too

badly to ignore, and he snatches me from his back and throws me onto the floor in front of him. Stomping his boot down, he crushes my chest, and I cry in pain.

"Everyone drop your weapons or the leadership will have no choice but to execute you for treachery. We received word that you were planning something against us, Alexander. And now, this proves it." The lights flash back on with the silence of the alarm shutting off. A woman click-clacks forward in stilettos with a scowl crossing her face.

"You know nothing!" Alexander yells, stepping over me to face the female vampire. "Which traitor is trying to break the leadership apart? I was only working alongside Lawrence to get my donor back. We were also getting the Bella Crew in control. They plan to destroy our city. Not me."

The woman shifts on her heels and looks at the open door behind her. I stare in shock at Walcott and Govan standing in the doorway, crossing their arms over their chests.

"That's not what I've heard. The Bella Crew came to us first. They told us everything you've been doing." The woman rubs her lips together, a smug look crossing her face.

"Don't be foolish, Narcisa. What I'm doing here is far greater. We'll defeat the rebels and put new positions of power in the hotels. I can prove it." Alexander fists his hands. "I was planning on executing the leaders of the Bella Crew now."

Fear crashes through me, and I launch from the floor and at Alexander's back. I realize the true trigger of my dhampir nature lies in my need to protect those I care about. I will not let Alexander even pretend he's going to kill anyone.

I hiss and growl, the animalistic noises widening Narcisa's eyes. It's in this moment that I realize my mistake. I just revealed that I'm different to her.

"The donor! Did you transform her?" she accuses, unsheathing a dagger. "You know what kind of offense that is, Alexander."

Alexander spins and shoves me away from him. I land in Lawrence's outstretched arms, and he drops me to the ground but doesn't release me. He tightens his hands around my wrists and dangles me in front of him. The pain is enough to freeze my body.

"You're mistaken. She's a dhampir." Alexander whips his attention to me.

No. Fucking, oh no.

"She's going to change everything. She'll help us gain even more power. We can have more than La Vega, but you have to listen to me. You have to remember our alliance." Alexander offers out his hand to the woman.

She doesn't take it and instead places her hands on her hips. "And what of Lawrence? You know we can't allow him in with his despicable ways."

"Some ways are necessary," Alexander says. "I will prove it. Call upon the leadership and the top coven heads." Alexander straightens his bloody suit. "I have a presentation in store for you. If you will just hear me out, I think you'll be quite impressed and will change your mind."

The woman slowly nods her head. "If this turns into a fi—"

"I'll allow you to hold control over my hotel, Lawrence, Hayley, and the blasted Bella Crew until then to prove my loyalty." Alexander rolls his shoulders. "Trust me."

"This better be worth my time. If it's not, you will face execution." Without another word, the woman motions to her security team. They fly into the room and restrain everyone, not giving us a chance to speak or fight because they gag us.

The woman materializes in front of me and cocks her head to the side, staring deep into my eyes.

Grabbing a fabric bag, she pulls it over my head. She takes me away.

"WHERE ARE THEY?" Alexander hollers, getting into Sawyer's face. "Tell me where the fuck my Gemstones are!"

Scowling, Sawyer spits blood in Alexander's face. He hasn't said a single word despite Alexander's effort to break him.

"Enough. You promised the leadership a show, and it will not be as entertaining without Mr. Noble." This comes from the woman, Narcisa, who I think is the only female on the La Vega Leadership. I can't help wondering where she came from. I've never seen her except for maybe one time. I didn't know she was part of those ruling La Vega.

"I can still give you an incredible show of power even without him. He stole something precious to me, and I need them. They're my greatest, most profitable asset." Swinging his fist, Alexander punches Sawyer again.

"Stop it!" I scream, tugging against the chain around my neck. "It was Lawrence. He was the one who wanted to take the performers back to The Whiskey. He knows the value of a good show. You should fucking beat it out of him and not Sawyer. He even brought three other vampires with him."

Lawrence snarls and tries to fly at me, but his restraints keep them in place. We're backstage at the club, and I listen to a dozen people get the place ready for the fight. At least, that's what I think it is. I know Alexander wants to prove to Narcisa that I'm more than just a donor.

I swear. The second I'm free, they're going to regret it.

"You bitch!" Lawrence manages to break the chain, and it takes both Alexander and Narcisa to grab and restrain him before he murders me.

"Save it for the ring, Lawrence. You'll have plenty of time to prove how truly powerful you are. You'll be fighting against my baby doll." Alexander grins wider, his fangs protruding with his desire for blood and death.

Holy fuck. He's putting me in the ring against Lawrence? Is he fucking kidding me?

"How is that fair? Put me in instead." Sawyer stands as tall as he can, the chains forcing him to hunch down because they're intended for those of average height.

"Oh, you will be. All of you will be put to the test. The last one standing gets to live as my servant." Alexander wags his finger. "Except for Hayley. I haven't decided what to do with her yet. I might leave it up to the leadership to prove my loyalty."

"You could save everyone the trouble and just figure it out now instead of forcing her to fight. You know she could be killed. How is that useful?" Knox sits on the ground in defeat. It's only because he's been severely beaten already. I hate seeing him like this. I have the urge to rip open my own throat in hope that I can fling enough blood his way to help him heal.

But I can't. They have me restrained the tightest. My ankles, wrists, and neck are all bound. It's as if they think that I'm some monstrous, powerful opponent. Maybe sometimes. But right now? I feel weak and hopeless.

"He has a rather good point, Alex." Narcisa flies across the room to me and touches my chin. She moves my head from side to side, staring into my gaze. Her eyes spark silver, and a dozen questions flit through her expression. She's far more curious than she lets on, and I know she'd prefer to just kidnap me herself. But her leadership role stops her. Unlike Alexander, she seems like the type to lead by example instead of telling everybody to do as they say and not as they do.

"This is the best way. Because if she's weak, then she's useless. You'll see. Lawrence has assured me she can and will defeat quite a few powerful vampires. She's not going to have a choice. It'll be her human instincts and need to survive that will unleash her dhampir nature." Alexander materializes next to Narcisa and touches her on her lower back, forcing her away from me by encouraging her to walk with him.

"Then let's get on with it. The leadership is waiting, and they're growing impatient. You can find your donors later. What's important is we handle the situation before it gets out of control. Word on the Strip says some of the crews are planning an attack. It's not in our best interest to stay gathered here, especially when I don't trust your unreliable security." Narcisa flips her hair over her shoulder, strutting ahead of Alexander so he can't touch her any longer. "The members of the Bella Crew will try to take us down, considering their attempt to pit us against each other failed...at least for now."

I turn my gaze to Sawyer, and the expression he gives me speaks volumes. He smirks despite everything, and I realize I thought wrong. Walcott and Govan wouldn't turn against Sawyer, Knox, and Monroe. Of course, they wouldn't. They have a strategy in place. It's why no one gave a huge fight. The Bella Crew is strategic and smart...

Alexander spins around and claps his hands. "Forever. This ends here." Stopping to glower at my guys, he adds, "I have a few surprises in store for all of you traitors. This is going to be fantastic. Let the blood wrestling begin!"

The curtain parts away, revealing the crowded club. It's as if the leadership brought all of their personal security along with every member of their covens. I even think some of the other ruling covens that were invited brought a couple of people. This is absolute bullshit. They can't make us fight. If I can just survive Lawrence, they will see.

"Good evening, La Vega!" Alexander puts on his emcee smile and swivels around until one of the spotlights lands on him. The rest of the stage lights aglow, and I gawk at the fighting ring. In the middle is one of the swinging performance poles. It's as if he wants to encourage me to do some of my acrobatic moves. I don't know if he's trying to give me an advantage because he wants Lawrence dead or what, but I'm not even sure what I should do. This is so twisted.

"You're one of my greatest regrets, Hayley," Lawrence mutters as one of the stagehands jabs him with an electric pole. I think it might have once been used for animals, but they keep shocking him until he finally shuffles toward the ring.

"Welcome to this special event. We have an extravagant performance for you tonight. Have you ever wanted to see one of the back-world's most powerful vampires fight a donor?" Alexander motions to Lawrence. "And not just any donor, but my own baby doll. But let me tell you. She's not ordinary. I created her myself, and she'll be what helps us rise as a city. Along with the festivities tonight, I'll be giving you all a chance to claim a brand-new position on the leadership council. How does that sound?"

Murmurs break out from the crowd, and I squint through the lights, seeing the confused expressions crossing the faces of the vampires in the front row. They must make up the leadership.

"There is no position available," one of the men says.

Alexander tips his head back and laughs before zooming in his direction. No one even gets a chance to do anything as Alexander swings a short sword and decapitates the guy, sending his head rolling.

"I think he was wrong about that," Alexander says, smirking at Narcisa.

She nods her head in approval, and I realize they might have an agreement. I don't think all members of the leadership are on the same side, and the man he killed might've been one of their opposition.

"I will be taking it!" Lawrence says, swinging his fist and punching one of the security personnel away, giving him an opening to rush Alexander.

He doesn't make it far. The collar on his neck shocks him, sending him to his knees.

There's something satisfying about seeing him drop so quickly, especially because he's used a similar collar on me. If only I didn't also wear one now.

"Not from me, my poor dead sister's brother. None of this would be possible without you, though. So, I'll allow you to pick an opponent as a warm-up. We must save Hayley for the main event. Now, who shall it be?" Alexander waves his hand, motioning to my guys against the back wall.

My heart sinks into my stomach. No. He can't be suggesting that they fight Lawrence before me. They already said they didn't want Sawyer to take my place. What the fuck? I hate how he keeps making things up as he goes along. This is not how shows are supposed to go. But this isn't a show. This is a power struggle and strategic move to keep control.

I hold my breath in anticipation.

"I pick you," Lawrence says, snarling. "Or are you afraid that I will defeat you in front of everyone?"

Alexander barks a laugh, acting as if Lawrence said the funniest thing in the world. But I think Lawrence is right. Alexander hides behind the leadership and the show as a way to protect himself. He's weaker than ever. His alliances are shaken. And I'm pretty fucking certain he regrets ever creating me.

"Hardly," Alexander says, smiling. "But you need to warm up, and I don't want to kill you before others have a chance."

Lawrence only responds with a growl.

"Pick someone, or I will do it for you." Alexander taps his foot on the stage. "Or maybe we should have the audience decide."

The audience finally reacts and claps their hands, cheering at his suggestion. The stage lights sparkle, blinding me, and I hold my breath once more, trying to get my heartbeat under control. I hate this. I can't let this happen.

"So, who will it be? Shall we go with the Bella Crew's leader? Mr. Noble has already asked to fight this asshole. A part of me doesn't want to give him what he wants, though. What about you guys?" Alexander wiggles his fingers at the crowd.

One of the men in the front row boos, yelling that he

wants to see Monroe's head roll.

That gets another reaction from the crowd, and they all yell and cheer their agreement.

I guess being the Bella Crew's brawn and enforcer makes Monroe a target. He probably has a lot of enemies from the many assholes that he's killed and mutilated.

Monroe grins like the cute psycho bastard he is. He loves his notoriety. He enjoys being hated by those in power.

"You fuckers really love me, don't you? Don't you guys worry your ugly-ass faces and small dicks. I'll cut out the heart of this asshole and then go after you." Monroe snaps his teeth, his eyes lighting silver.

His confidence is the only thing keeping me from freaking out.

"Now that's what I'm talking about! Let's give it up for Lawrence and his first opponent, the vile, hideous, monstrous Monroe of the Bella!" Alexander signals to the security personnel to grab Monroe, releasing him from the chains.

I shift and yank at my own restraints, trying to see if there's anything I can do to snap them. If I can just free myself, I can go after Alexander. Now is the perfect time. He and the rest of the leadership will be distracted by the fight.

But I can't seem to gather enough strength. My mind and body are at war. My heart and soul want to fight, but every limb and inch of me aches in pain. The hunger in my stomach only seems to weaken me.

Pyrotechnic sparks light the stage, and music blasts in the air as Monroe strides toward the stage as if he's been waiting for this moment his entire life. And maybe he has. Not necessarily for Lawrence, but to prove to all of La Vega that his reputation is true. He is ruthless. He is monstrous. And he is one of the most psychotic, protective bastards in the universe.

But he's my bastard. He's one of the men I love, and I don't want to see him facing the man I hate most apart from Alexander.

"There are no rules to this fight. You'll each have one weapon. The winner will be who survives. I wish you both a place in hell." Alexander exits the ring and stands off to the side, bouncing on the balls of his dress shoes in excitement.

Whistling, Alexander calls on two stagehands, who bring the most pathetic knives I've ever seen. They look like something they found in the donor kitchen. It's not like they need them though. I've seen both of them fight bare-handed.

"I've been fucking waiting for this, you cock-sucker." Monroe flips the knife, catching the hilt. Flicking his arm, he throws it, sending it at Lawrence, sinking it into his shoulder.

I rattle my chains as the two of them blur across the stage. My eyes refuse to follow them, and I scream out, fighting my restraints.

I hate my inability to keep up. I want to see Monroe clearly, but if he was to slow down, Lawrence would overpower him. I know he is trying to wear him out because of it.

The fight is unfair, but it's purposefully that way. They want to see Monroe dead.

"Hayley! Close your eyes! Please, just close your eyes!" Knox yells, his voice loud enough to cut over the cheering crowd. Blood sprays across me, and I automatically glide my tongue over my lips, the indescribable taste sending fear striking my very soul. It's Monroe's.

Why would Knox beg me to close my eyes?

"Please, grant me one mercy. Don't let her see." Monroe's voice hitches, and the fighting comes to a halt.

I feel as if my world crashes down around me.

Pain and agony steal my breath. It's not physical, it's purely inside me yet it feels worse than anything I've ever experienced. I would rather be whipped a thousand times or beaten until I could no longer walk than see what unfolds in front of me.

"Mercy! We don't grant mercy! Finish him!" Alexander's voice rings to the air, and three spotlights drag across the stage and light the center of the ring.

Monroe blinks and squints, the brightness obscuring his vision. Cuts and bruises mar him already, and blood stains every inch of him.

I fight harder, yanking at my chains, trying everything I can to break free.

I need to go to him. Monroe needs my blood. If he can just get even an ounce, he'll have the strength to continue on. I could heal him.

"Hayley, I love you, little bird. Don't let these assholes get away with this. Fucking cut them apart." Monroe roars and thrashes in Lawrence's hold.

The fight only last for a minute but it feels as if it's an eternity.

"I'll have that seat on the leadership. No one can defeat me." Lawrence smiles as if he savors this moment.

Blood squirts from Monroe, and he drops to his knees before falling flat on his face.

Lawrence crushes something in his hand. It came from Monroe.

It feels as if he ripped my heart out.

Rage swells through me, and I screech, the whole world turning red around me.

I break my shackles.

This ends now.

"Whoever catches my baby doll can keep her for the night! If you get her to submit, you can have five percent of my donors. If you take out Lawrence, you'll get a seat on the leadership and the chance to execute the Bella Crew members." Alexander's words blast through the speakers in a rush.

His voice cracks.

I can sense his fear from here, and it pushes me forward.

"Hey, Ruby Vixen! Be a good girl, and I'll treat you like a queen," a man says, materializing in my way.

I catapult from the floor and crash into him. Jerking my face down, I bite him in the shoulder, filling my mouth with blood.

The crowd falls silent.

No one moves, not even the man beneath me. He likes the way I handle him.

I whip my head up, meeting Lawrence's gaze in the ring as Alexander stands behind him, knife drawn. My blood cools. Monroe remains unmoving in a pool of blood.

No. No. No.

Smashing my hand down, I break through the vampire's sternum and crush his heart out of my own grief and desperation.

"Grab her!" Narcisa shouts.

I fly from my spot, dodging around the security who tries to block me.

I will destroy this place.

This city will burn.

24

HAYLEY

REBEL

"YOU'RE DEAD!" I scream, rushing Lawrence. I flip over the ropes and grab the aerial pole, using it to swing around to disorient the vampire.

The crowd breaks out in the chaos, but I ignore the world around me. My eyes focus solely on the man who hurt Monroe. I can't even look at Monroe on the mat. My mind won't allow me to believe that he's not going to get up.

"Face me, my heir. Come here and let me remind you of your place!" Lawrence snaps, moving at vampire speed to circle me. But I climb higher out of his reach.

Wind gusts through my hair, and I use the strength of my thighs to keep the pole circling. If I can time it just right, I can drop down while I'm spinning and knock Lawrence off his feet with a powerful kick. The force of the move should be enough to give me a couple of seconds. A couple of seconds is all I need. It's all it will take to shove my hand into his chest to remove his heart. I will squish it like he did Monroe's.

"Come on, you assholes! Don't be afraid to enter the ring." Alexander's voice shouts commands at the crowd, and I notice a figure entering the ring.

Lawrence spins and manages to decapitate a vampire with the kitchen knife. He is far too powerful for any vampire to take alone.

I should feel discouraged. I should feel afraid. But all I feel in this moment is angry. Hungry. I feel like revenge.

The distraction is exactly what I need. Throwing my weight once more, I spin on the aerial pole as I release my grip and slide down until I manage to kick Lawrence in the back of the head, sending him sprawling. He trips over Monroe and crashes into the ropes. They send him tumbling back, and I jump from my spot and land on top of him.

"Kill him!" someone shouts.

It's the only thing I'm counting on.

Lawrence chomps his fangs and tries to bite me, but I shove my hand to the side of his head and jerk down and bite him.

I plan to keep biting him until I can rip his fucking head off with my teeth.

He needs to die in the most painful way. If I can bite a finger off, I know I can do this. His blood flooding my mouth sets me off, and I rip chunk after chunk, spitting his flesh out as he hollers and stabs me with the kitchen knife in my side. But I don't stop. I keep healing as I consume his blood.

An ear-piercing explosion quakes the building, and an alarm rings through the air. The stage lights flash out. A few of the security personnel shout. Growling into the microphone, Alexander calls demands. But I can't understand the words. It's as if he's speaking another language, but I know it's just because I can't get rid of the pounding in my head.

Gunfire showers through the club, and the strangest thing happens.

"Little bird, you gotta let him go. We only have seconds." Monroe's husky voice prods at me, and my heart splits open. I can't comprehend how this is possible. How am I hearing his voice?

"Just grab her. She's weakening me." Lawrence's voice shocks realization through me.

What the actual fuck?

Two hands lock around my waist and pull me up. The room shakes again. I don't know what's happening. It takes everything in me to release Lawrence.

"You obviously were too good of an actor. Remind her that we had a deal. I think only you will be able to talk some sense into her. She's too lost in her nature." Lawrence presses his palm against my chest, keeping space between us in case I jerk down to bite him again.

"Come on, little bird. Listen to my voice. You have to let him go. He only yanked out part of something useless. I'm sorry I scared you. We needed to buy time. The Bella Crew is attacking the city." Monroe slides his arm across my throat and gently eases me up until I pull my fingers from Lawrence's shoulders.

I hadn't realized I was gripping him so tightly that I sunk my fingertips into skin. How am I so strong? I have no fucking idea.

"You faked it?" My voice shakes with the words. I can't believe it. I was so scared. I was so angry.

"You can punish me later. We needed you to fight."

Monroe flips me around in his arms and presses his forehead to mine. "Forgive me."

"Save that for later. We have to go." Sawyer materializes beside me and reaches out to touch my cheek. "Our time is running out. Tatum says the leadership is calling upon all covens."

"The three fuckers can only corner Alexander for so long. They're too chickenshit to fight him to the death." Knox looks at me, shifting on his feet to bend down to inspect the rest of my body. His eyes focus on the healing stab marks, and he tenses.

"Remember, fucker. We're in charge. If you so much as try anything, you're a dead man." Cooper surprises me by stepping between us and Lawrence as if he could take on the vampire himself.

The air escapes my lungs. My whole body cools and I shiver. He didn't just say what I think he said. It sounds as if Lawrence plans to come with us. No.

No fucking way.

"Are you shitting me?" I ask, my body trembling.

"We made an arrangement. You have to trust us." Sawyer rubs his lips together, his face clearly showing how unhappy he is by the decision.

A part of me knows that I should just accept it. Sometimes, we have to choose between the two evils, and right now Alexander is the one we need to take down to save our home.

But when that's over...Lawrence will just fill his spot. There's no way I could ever trust this man. There is no way I could ever humor his ideals of a donor future.

I shake my head. "No."

Lawrence scowls at me. "Mind your place—"

I fly from Monroe's arms and use Cooper's shoulders to catapult and flip over him to land on my feet behind Lawrence. Rage steals my mind, and it's as if the world dims. All I can think about is ending this right here and now.

I can't stand by and let him live another moment longer. He's a monster. He's our enemy, and there's no fucking way I'm going to just accept that the Bella Crew keeps him alive because they think we need him. We don't need him. We have each other. Our strength is enough. I didn't know that until now.

I'll prove it to them. They'll see.

Fuck the consequences.

A burst of strength crashes through me, and I swing my fist into Lawrence's back, shattering through his spine, sending him sprawling into Cooper. It's as if I instinctually know exactly what to do to end his life.

My predatorial side wants nothing more than to finish

this here. We're not taking the chance. I will not risk my future. I've already been through so much. I'm not a donor, and I realize that now. I'm a fucking dhampir, and the vampire world should be afraid of me. I'm not an eternal blood source. I'm their worst nightmare, and I'll show them they can't control us any longer. The La Vega leadership will lose control. I'll help the Bella Crew win, and not because they've made some bullshit deal with a ruthless psycho.

"Wait! Wait, stop!" Lawrence hollers and thrashes, trying to knock me off of him.

I fall over, but don't let go of his heart, squishing the organ in my hand. I hit my back on the mat, and my hand thuds beside me, clutching his bloody heart. I stare at it in fascination. His life ends in my hand.

I had no idea something so gross could be so satisfying. My taste for blood grows by the second, and all I can think about is murdering another fucker.

"Shit. Grab her. We're out of time. Walcott needs to set off the bomb in the alley. It's the only way we're getting out of this." Sawyer decapitates a vampire who finally makes it through the fighting to us with more coming.

Monroe drags me from the ground, scooping me in his arms.

I stare at Lawrence's dead body on the mat of the

fighting ring. A part of me fears he'll wake up and tell me that he can't die. But in the end, he's only a vampire. He isn't invincible. He is just an overconfident bastard who now knows his place. And I'm so relieved that it was me who got to put him there.

"Get to the wall and hold on for a second. The blast is coming." Sawyer stabs another guy.

Knox, Sawyer, and Cooper surround me and Monroe, protectively shielding me as the whole world shakes, and a deafening crash stings my ears. I peek through their muscular bodies at the sight of the crowd. There are bodies everywhere, and people still fight.

I search around, hoping to find Alexander. But he's gone. So are the other recognizable leaders.

Fuck.

I don't get a chance to say anything. The rumbling stops and dust fills air. The world blurs around me as Monroe and the rest of the Bella Crew relocate me out of the building.

Sunshine engulfs us, and I panic at the sight of my guys risking getting burned to leave. But I think this is the plan. They're trying to keep vampires in the shadows.

Dozens of donors run across the Strip, and I stare in awe. It's the first time that I've seen anything like this.

I almost don't believe it.

It's as if the donors of La Vega are free.

"Suck it up and stay in the sun. I know it's fucking hot, but this is the fastest way. We're heading home." Knox leans in and touches my cheek, his knuckles red and burning, but he doesn't try to cover his hand. "You hear that, vixen? We're taking you home."

"To the Bella? Isn't that dangerous?" My nerves bunch in my stomach, and all I can think about is the leadership storming the hotel and destroying everything.

Monroe snuggles his face into my hair, inhaling a breath. "It's going to be the safest place in all of La Vega soon. We've been preparing for this moment for decades. We took the wall. We took out all the major vampire facilities. We're going to war, little bird. We're fighting back, and all of the donors are joining in. The city needs a change, and we're going to change it. For you. For us. For everyone."

"The rebels will rise again. This time, no one will stop us." Sawyer halts outside of the Bella and looks around at the gathering crowd of donors.

They're armed. They look dangerous as hell.

I can't believe it. This is the first time I've ever seen donors look so confident and ready to fight. They look ready to face anything. They will bring safety to the shadows again. I can feel it deep inside me. We're on the verge of another uprising, but this time, the leadership won't keep us down.

They will be ashes under our feet.

They will fall.

Voices hum through the air of the casino floor, and I pull myself away from Monroe long enough to peek around. I don't think I've ever seen a place so filled with people, not even the Aris. My heart swells, but a lingering fear clings to me. I feel as if all donors should go into hiding or some shit. Where would they would go? I have no fucking idea.

"Hayley! Fuck, Hayley!" Mya shouts and waves her hands from near one of the poker tables.

Tears burn my eyes. It's been a while since we've been together, and I wasn't sure if I would ever see her again. The other performers hug each other, hanging around her, looking more frightened than ever. I'm just so relieved to see them safe and away from the Aris hotel.

I don't even have to ask Monroe to take me to them, because he zooms the distance at vampire speed and Mya jumps into the air, wrapping the two of us in a full-body hug, sandwiching me in the middle. She snuggles her face to the crook of my neck and releases a whimpering cry. Her body shakes as her emotions break free, and it sets me off even more and I begin to sob.

"I thought you were dead. No one told me what was going on. Govan showed up for us and then...fuck. Are you okay? Where have you been?" Mya heaves a couple of deep breaths, trying to calm herself enough to strengthen her voice.

I open and close my mouth. I don't want to talk about it. I feel as if saying the words out loud will only bring me pain again. What I've been through was far more than I realized I could handle. I never want to go through it again, but fear lingers, because I know that this isn't the end of things despite it feeling as if we've reached a turning point in our existences.

"Mya, how about we give them some room and time to calm down and settle in. It's a fucking warzone out there. I'm sure Hayley wants to get cleaned up and eat something. Let me take you and your friends to the rooms. I bet you could use some attention as well." Govan rests his hands on her shoulders and carefully detaches her from me until she stands on her feet.

Monroe shifts me in his arms so I can look at her, and I watch as she smiles at Govan. I've never seen her look at anybody like that before, and she slowly nods her head, agreeing with his suggestion. And I'm so relieved. As much as I just want to hug Mya to feel her affection as my best friend, Govan is right. I need time to process. My mouth doesn't want to work anyways. I don't even know exactly what to say to her. So much has changed with me.

"Meet me for dinner?" I manage to say, licking my dry lips. I can taste the blood now turning sour on my face. It makes me more self-conscious as if I'm being paraded around after the blood rain. But this is far worse. I'm practically bathed in the blood of Lawrence. I just want to rinse it away with every thought of him. With every thought of the Fright Fights and The Whiskey.

"Yes, of course. Call me if you need anything. I'm here for you. I'm so happy that we're together again." Mya grins and reaches out her hand, squeezing my arm. "It's probably better if you showered anyway. You're looking a little bit too appetizing for these vampires, I'm sure." Her teasing words are far from true, considering that it's a vampire's blood coating my skin, but I humor her and laugh. It sounds forced and shaky, but it's the best I can do.

Knox motions to Monroe to hand me to him, and Govan snatches Mya up and takes her back to the other performers who watch us in silence. It's the strangest thing seeing them out of costume. None of them even wave at me or anything. I think they blame me for ruining their lives. I just hope they can forgive me one day.

"Why don't you guys help Tatum get the donors set-tled on their floor." Knox motions to where Tatum stands on one of the tables, giving instructions to the crowd.

"I'll go over security measures again. Take our girl to your suite and make sure she's healing properly." Sawyer stands tall and crosses his arms. He turns to Cooper. "I'll show you where you'll stay. It'll be on our floor. We keep it limited to just those in our inner circle."

"Are you good with that, little bird?" Monroe asks, rubbing his fingers through his beard. "We can make some time to—"

"Just come to us after you're done. This takes prece-dence." I motion to the craziness of the casino. I want so badly to beg them to stay with me, but I know they're need-ed elsewhere.

"We'll be fast." Monroe kisses me despite the blood on my face.

Sawyer hugs me and Cooper squeezes my hand, clearly unsure of what to do. I don't even know what to do. I feel something growing between us, but I don't want to think about it. I don't want to deal with it. Everything else is al-ready complicated enough.

Knox runs with me through the casino and to the ele-vators. The second the doors close, he searches my face and I lean into him, kissing him. I've been dying to do so since seeing the torture he'd been through. I'm more concerned about him than I am myself. Because I'm okay. I'm shaken and nervous, but I'm healed from my injuries already.

"Bite me. You need to drink. You have burns on you, and I'm not sure if your body is healing." I murmur the words against his mouth, loving how he doesn't even hesitate to return my affection.

He groans against my lips. "Hayley..."

"Do it. I demand it." I tighten my jaw with my words. I don't know where I get the nerve to speak to him like this, but it ignites silver sparkles in his eyes.

The elevator door dings open, and Knox spins without giving into my demand. I find myself standing in the bathroom of his room, and he kicks the door closed behind him. His body ripples as he flexes his muscles, his blood hunger turning into lust. I bet he's thinking about my command over and over again.

"Bite me. Let me take care of you." I strip my dirty shirt off and toss it to the floor, exposing my boobs to him. I shimmy out of my pants next, leaving them piled at my feet. "You know you want to. Bite me. Right now. You've been through enough, and it's my turn to see that you are okay."

His fangs extend from beneath his lip, but again, he doesn't obey me and just drinks in the sight of me standing before him.

I can't stand it another second. Striding toward him, I grab his shirt and yank it over his head before unbuckling his belt. He groans as I slide my hand into his pants and lace my fingers around his hard cock, stroking it as I pull him to the shower.

"Hayley, I—" His words cut off with another moan, and I grin as I lower myself to my knees.

"Stop talking. I want to make you cum. I want to make you feel good and reward you for being my hero. I'm going to get you to bite me. You can't resist me, Knox. I know you're trying to, and you need to know that I'm not a doll. You can't break someone who's already been shattered."

He braces on the wall as I lick his tip and suck him into my mouth, digging my fingers into his ass cheeks as I bob my head. All I can think about is pleasure and blood and everything we've been through to get to this moment. Who knows how long this will last? I'm tired of living each day as if my life is ending. I need to live each day as if it'll be one of infinity. I need to treat myself like a dhampir and not a donor. I need Knox to do the same.

His fingers tangle in my wet hair, and I lick and suck him, twirling my tongue and taking him as far as I can into my mouth. He moans and holds my head, guiding me into a motion he wants. And I let him. He can do whatever he wants with me. I'm here for him, and he is here for me. Being together is what makes this all worth it.

"You are so gorgeous. So sexy. So fierce." Knox leans back on the wall, enjoying my mouth as much as I enjoy the taste of him. "It's taking every ounce of me not to lose control, Hayley. I don't think you're ready for that."

I hum my disagreement. "You can't tell me when I'm ready for something, Knox."

He smiles at me as I stare at him, bobbing my head as I suck him off, rubbing my fingers over his ass cheeks, keeping him from trying to pull away to do something to me.

"I wasn't really telling you. I was warning you. You have no idea how badly I want to give in to your demands. But if I lose control..."

I pull away from his cock and grin at him, surprising him by tilting my head and biting his thigh. He grunts and twists his fingers in my hair, but he doesn't rip me away. He waits for me to release him and then drags me up and crashes my back into the wall.

"You naughty dhampir. You've asked for it." Knox guides my head to the side as he aligns our bodies.

"I'm begging." I wiggle my hips, trying to get him to push inside of me.

He flashes his fangs and sinks them into my throat at the same time he thrusts into me, the pressure making me moan as pleasure zings through me. I pant and squirm, scratching my nails into his shoulders as he drinks from me, giving me what I want. What I need. What we both crave.

Steam fills the air around us, and I clutch onto him as he swings his body into me hard and fast, fucking me with an intensity that leaves me moaning in scream-like bursts. My vision shadows as his hot aggression prods at my deep-seated nature. I grab his head and rip him from my neck. I want to sink my teeth into him again. Our mouths go to war with each other, and we bite and lick and kiss and suck, just turning to our natures to guide us through this passionate moment. It's not about who's in control. It's about our innate and feral desires.

Knox growls, the vibration humming over my skin and setting my heart racing. He lowers me to my feet and forces me to spin around, bending me forward. He grabs my hair as he thrusts into me again from behind, stopping me from biting him over and over again. I submit to him and let him have his way, enjoying the intensity of our fucking as if that's what I need to survive. He reaches around and strums my clit, playing with my body until my muscles tighten, and I tense. Leaning over, he holds me up with one hand as I hang in front of him with my feet off the floor. He bumps his hips to my ass, rocking into me and sending an explosion rolling through my body with my orgasm. I scream out and moan, my mind and body coming together and ripping apart and finally settling down as everything catches up with me. I feel so incredible in this moment. I feel so loved and desired. I feel so needed.

Knox bends over and sinks his teeth into my shoulder, drinking my blood as he bounces his hips against my ass cheeks until he cums. My whole body shakes, my energy wearing thin as the high of the moment starts to drift away and out of my reach.

It's as if things hit me like a building collapsing on me. I just want it to last longer. I want to experience it over and over again. I don't want to be done.

Knox scoops me up and kisses me tenderly, helping me wash my hair and whispering his words of thanks and love and appreciation. "What you're feeling might be scary, but it's only your endorphins and adrenaline leveling out. It'll pass. I'll cuddle and kiss and do whatever you need until it does."

Tears fill my eyes, and I choke out a sob, his words swelling through me as he bathes me and washes my hair.

"I don't know what's wrong with me. I'm sorry for crying." I sniffle and bury my face against the soft towel he uses to dry me off, still managing to hold me in his arms.

"Nothing is wrong with you. Just let yourself feel. I'm here for you, okay? You're everything to me. I love you,

Hayley. You need to know that. Everything that we do from now on is for us. It's for you." Knox takes me to his bed, and he grabs a couple of things from the fridge and wraps his arms around me, feeding me pieces of fruit as he continues to whisper his love for me until my body finally relaxes and my eyes dry.

I don't know how long we lay naked together, but it feels like hours yet it also doesn't feel long enough.

A knock sounds on the door, and I shift in Knox's arms and wait for him to tell me it's the others.

"You can come in," I say, remaining in my position with my leg over Knox's as I remain cradling his side. "Tell me that everything is fine."

The door cracks open, and I stare as Sawyer and Monroe enter. Cooper waits for me to motion to him, and the three of them stand near the bed looking at me. Nobody reacts to our state of undress. Their minds all look as if they wander elsewhere.

"We managed to take over the Palace. The leader of the Biddeford coven is dead. This is a great sign. They have as many donors as Alexander has." Sawyer takes a seat on the edge of the bed and rests his hand on my leg through the blankets. "We're going after the Grand next. We had to fall back as sunset hit, but we have everything in place. There's too much going on with the broken wall that the leadership has to focus on that for now. They have to focus on getting the Strip dwellers in control. It gives us time to continue to attack from within."

I blink my eyes a few times. For the first time in a long time, I feel hope. I feel as if we're more powerful than the leadership. I feel more powerful than Alexander.

"So, this is really happening? You're taking La Vega?" I lick my lips and look at each of my guys. My mind even includes Cooper, and he offers me a smile.

"La Vega is ours, little bird. The world will see its mistake. It's time to reclaim what was once lost. We will make it happen." Monroe grins, his eyes flashing silver with his excitement.

And I believe him.

The world is ours for the taking.

We will destroy anyone who gets in our way.

"WAKE UP, MY showgirl. Knox ordered that you eat some donor food before we meet Monroe in the gym. He wants us to join him for training." Cooper nudges me with the back of his hand.

I snap my eyes open and stare at Cooper's smiling face. "Monroe was supposed to wake me up. What time is it?"

"Eightish. He tried to wake you, but he said you got all cuddly, and he wasn't going to risk waking a sleeping dhampir. So, we switched places, though your cute ass started biting the damn pillow." He scoops up a handful of feathers and sprinkles them over me.

Heat burns my cheeks as I sit up and peer around. The bed is a mess of torn fabric, stuffing, and feathers. "Whoa."

"Right? I'd have let you devour me, but Monroe would've beat my ass for waking you." His grin widens. "It might've been worth it, though."

I rub the heels of my hands into my eyes. "Next time wake me, okay? It's taking everything in me not to attack you." My voice softens with my tease.

Cooper swallows, the hunger in his gaze sharpening his features. "Careful, Hayley. Playfulness can turn into a couple of things you might not want. It's been a while since you've had blood."

Just the mention of blood-drinking twists my stomach in starvation. I jerk my hand out and grab his arm, pulling it to my mouth. He intakes a soft breath, his whole body preparing for my bite. But I don't. I won't unless he offers.

I lick his arm, smiling at his reaction. He wants me to bite him. We both know it. The growing attraction between us is obvious, and Monroe has pointed it out a dozen times. Sawyer and Knox just shrug their shoulders, and I think they're waiting for Cooper to be brave enough. He doesn't think he's worthy of me yet.

His fangs peek from beneath his lips. "If you're that famished and can't wait..."

Someone taps their hand against the door, startling me, and Cooper vanishes from my side and looks through the peephole. He doesn't hesitate before he swings the door open, and Mya stands beside Pearl in the hallway. They both look from Cooper to me and back to him. No one has told them about me yet, but I know it's coming. I know that the Bella Crew is waiting for me to gather my nerve.

"Hey, Hayley, we were just heading down for breakfast. Do you want to join us? I'm sure that the cooks in the dining hall are a bit more capable than your boys. I know Govan can't cook for shit." Mya wags her eyebrows. "But that doesn't matter when there are so many other things he's quite talented at."

Pearl giggles from next to her, bumping her shoulder without saying anything.

I nod my head and slide from the bed despite Cooper's now pouty face. I know it's not his intention to make me feel bad, but now I do kind of wish I had denied my friends. But I miss them. I want to ensure that they're okay as much as I can.

I turn the Cooper. "Come join us. I'm sure you could

use some blood. I don't mind."

Mya claps her hands. "You should totally come. All the vampires around here stay far away from us as if we are contagious or some bullshit."

Cooper gets to his feet and shoves his hands into his pockets. "That's because you've been claimed, and these assholes know better than to interact with you without permission. It's for safety too."

Mya's mouth forms an O. "That's weird, but I'm perfectly fine with that. Some of these guys are a bit scary."

"Like Mr. Face Tat," Pearl murmurs, not realizing that I can hear her words.

I smirk and offer my hand to Cooper, tugging him along with me. "They are, aren't they? A lot of them are harmless to donors though. It's the vampires that should be afraid of them."

"Damn straight." Cooper widens the door and holds it open for me to exit into the hallway. Mya swings her arm over my shoulder and tugs me ahead. Pearl rushes to keep up, and she does her running split jump, showing off her moves as if she misses the stage. I realize that I miss it too.

I join her and Mya, and the three of us do an altered floor routine, flipping and doing cartwheels, creating more noise than we were ever allowed to do at the Aris hotel.

I don't see the vampire emerge from the room until it's

too late. Cooper hollers, and blood squirts from his neck as the vampire slices a blade across his throat and kicks him forward, sending him to his knees.

Mya and Pearl scream, and my body kicks into action. My hunger takes control of me and pushes me forward. I yell as I leap at the vampire, dying to bury my teeth into his neck to show him that he can't fuck around with us.

He snatches me by my hair and throws me against the wall, pinning me in place. Our eyes meet, and I realize my mistake immediately. I don't have blood in my system. It's been too long since I've drunk any.

My body slackens and fear devours me.

"Don't fight. Don't scream or make a sound. I will not hurt you. I've been sent by the renegades to bring you in for a meeting." The vampire searches my eyes with his mind manipulation.

Two donor men come from the hotel room, training their guns on Cooper. His injury has left him immobile, and it'll take him longer to heal because I'm nearly certain he was waiting for me to drink blood before consuming it himself.

"Grab those two donors. We need to alter their minds." The vampire motions at Mya and Pearl.

I can't do anything. I can't fight. I feel as helpless as I was in Alexander's care.

The vampire grins at me, leans forward, and plants his lips to mine, kissing me as I hang helplessly from his grip. His violation stabs me, shooting fear into my heart. I'm trapped in my own body and unable to do anything.

And then the world blurs.

"Is that her? Are you sure?" The masculine voice hums through the air. It takes me a moment to realize the vampire hasn't taken me far and he sets me down on one of the double beds of a room.

"Of fucking course I know it's her. Look at her eyes. She's perfect. But you must hurry. We won't have long." The vampire motions to the door. "Someone is bound to come for them soon. I didn't kill the bastard out there because we need him as her caretaker. Especially when we're successful."

Successful? Successful with what.

An older man comes to my side and looks down at me. He tightens his jaw and flicks his gaze down my body. Fear rises in my throat. If I could open my mouth, I would scream. I can read his expression. I recognize the darkness in his eyes. He might be a donor, but he's not a good person.

"Don't worry, sweetheart. We'll make sure you don't remember a thing. But you have to know that your gift will be what humanity needs. Your ability to create stronger, more powerful hunters will bless our cause. This will be quick." The man unfastens the buckle on his jeans and the other donor grabs at my pants.

Fuck.

Oh no. This can't be happening.

"Your offspring will be incredible." The man glances from the vampire and back to me. "Why don't you make her close her eyes."

My body and soul scream, and something wild and feral explodes through me. The vampire hovers over me, catching my gaze, and it's as if he unlocks the mind manipulation to instruct me to do something else. I feel my body tense, and I manage to snap from his hold. I screech, kicking my leg, hitting the donor right in the junk and sending him to his knees. The vampire grabs my throat and tries to get me to look at him again, but I jerk my head up and bash it into his face. He can't keep me down, and my vision reddens as I sink my teeth into him, filling my mouth with blood. A gun fires, but I realize it's not shooting at me. Someone else enters the room.

I don't stop though.

The weight of the vampire suddenly vanishes, and I realize his head hangs from my fingers. Whoever entered the room decapitated him, and now that his blood pours over me, my whole body awakens.

I jump from the bed and attack the donor man on the

ground next. He was going to fucking rape me, and he's going to pay for it. He doesn't even get the chance to move before I fist my hand and punch him over and over again until blood splashes over me and I shatter his pelvis in my attempt to prevent him from ever trying to hurt another woman again.

"You fools. You should've known better than to treat my baby doll this way. There are far more reliable and advanced technologies that can accomplish what I need." Alexander's familiar voice chimes through the air, but he doesn't sound nearby. He sounds as if he's coming from the speaker. "Be quick, doctor. If you are not in and out in a timely manner, you'll have no coven to return to. This is most crucial. It must be done now."

I jerk my head up to see another vampire. He materializes in front of me, and I realize that he placated Mya and Pearl. Touching my chin, he looks at my face, his curiosity pinching his brows.

"I apologize for those disgusting rebels. The insemination will be far less heinous in my care." Pulling out his com device, he shows Alexander's image before swiping it away and holding the device to me. "I need you to call one of the Bella Crew members and let them know you'll be hanging out with your friends for a while. You will meet them later."

I lick my lips, my whole body wanting to scream out.

"Do it, Hayley. If you don't, I'll instruct him to murder the bastard outside your door. He will murder my Gemstones as well. I'll not have him take you, but this must be done. You're worthless to me, and I need another chance with an heir of yours." Alexander's voice sounds from the device, but I can't see his face.

Still, I don't respond.

"Just make one of the other girls do it. Sedate her." Alexander growls with his words.

I inhale and exhale, trying to catch my breath.

He's going to do what? No. This can't be happening.

The vampire jabs a needle into the vein in my arm, and my skin stings before coolness rushes through my body.

My head spins.

My heart races.

The last thing I see is the man pinning Mya and trapping her in his gaze. This is so fucked up.

My life is over before it has even had a chance to begin.

"Easy now, dhampir. When you wake up, it'll be as if I were never here. Understand?" the vampire says.

I don't speak.

I lose myself to his sedation.

To be continued...

Thank you so much for reading Bloody Nights! Don't forget to check out Renegade Nights! As always, pre-order dates are never the actual release date. Many authors set them farther out to give themselves wiggle room, me included.

To stay up-to-date on new releases (dates get moved forward frequently), join Ginna's reading group Paranormal Center for Matches and Mates or join her at www.GinnaMoran.com.

THE VAMPIRE HEIRS WORLD

La Vega Vampire Showstoppers
Vampire Nights
Bloody Nights
Renegade Nights

The Divine Vampire Heirs
Blood Match
Blood Rebel
Blood Debt
Blood Feud
Blood Loss
Blood Vows
Blood Holiday

The Royale Vampire Heirs Series:
Rebel Vampires
Rebel Dhampir
Rebel Match
Rebel Heir
Rebel Fight

Academy of Vampire Heirs Series:
Dhampirs 101
Blood Sources 102
Coven Bonds 103
Personal Donors 104
Blood Wars 105

THE MATES OF MAGAELORUM WORLD

The Pack Mates of Lunar Crest:
The She-Wolf Games
The Wolf-Mate Trials
The Omega Hunt
The Witch Chase
Winter Wolf Games

Fated Mate of the Dragon Clans
Caged by Her Dragons
Freed by Her Dragons
Saved by Her Dragons

SEVEN SINNERS WORLD

The Seven Sinners of Hell's Kingdom
Her Personal Demons
Her Deadly Angels
Her Darkest Devils
Her Sinful Saints
Her Twisted Sinners

ABOUT GINNA MORAN

GINNA MORAN IS the author of over seventy novels including the popular La Vega Vampire Showstoppers, The Pack Mates of Lunar Crest, The Seven Sinners of Hell's Kingdom Academy of Vampire Heirs, The Divine Vampire Heirs, and The Royale Vampire Heirs WhyChoose novels.

She always carried a fascination for all things paranormal and wrote her first unpublished manuscript at age eighteen. Her love of the supernatural grew stronger through her adult life, and she now spends her days with different creatures of the night. Whether it's vampires, werewolves, dragons, fae, angels, demons, or mermaids, Ginna loves creating and living in worlds from her dreams.

Aside from Ginna's professional life, she enjoys binge watching TV, crafting and design, playing pretend with her daughter, and cuddling with her dogs. Some of her favorite things include chocolate, mermaids, anything that glitters, learning new things, cheesy jokes, and organizing her bookshelf.

Ginna is currently hard at work on her next novel and the one after, and the one after that.